CONVERGENCE

OF THE

REALMS

An Improbable Emergence

Book IV

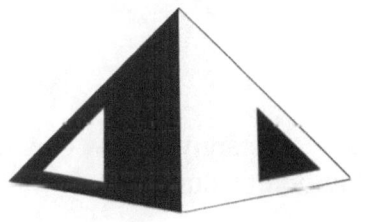

Artwork by Francis Voignier
Cover: *"Dream Meadow"* 2017
Inside: *"Inside out Outside in"* – *"Iorus"* 2017

Character resemblance to any real individual is purely coincidental.

Library of Congress Cataloging-in-Publication Data
Voignier, Francis 1954 – United States
Convergence of the Realms/Francis Voignier
ISBN-13: 978-1-7345551-3-4
ISBN-10: 1734555130

Science Fiction – Metaphysics – Quantum Physics – Philosophy – Humboldt County

francisvoignier.com
Dolosse & Writs, Eureka, California

TABLE OF CONTENTS

FROM THE AUTHOR

Great One Amaterasu's last words to the group gathered at the top of her glass pyramid were, "Prepare to meet the One." It would perhaps be wise to elucidate the very concept of meeting with the ultimate Oneness, which was rather one of absorption within an ambiance, as opposed to getting together with an actual being from the standpoint of one's evolutionary platform. Let's just propose it was one event that most definitely defied the grasp of even the most complex of syntactical construction. Additionally, what went for Amaterasu, as well as Angels Vac and Lev, who still belonged to the original all-encompassing Oneness, did in fact no longer apply to Ma-l, Olaf, Saka, Xarn, and Enola, since their worlds now rose from another. I imagine the meaning of that one pivotal sentence might have been interpreted from two distinct angles of perception, with wildly disparate results.

What Amaterasu actually aimed at, was for a trial meeting of the two Onenesses, mediated by the flux between the stones that she and Saka held close to their hearts. It was at precisely the point at which the whole of the Realms faced the absolute sum of the original One, that words lost their meanings.

But there was an inherent simplicity to that meeting, as the two halves of the group acknowledged their complementary qualities in that, together, they yet formed a larger alliance that added up to a whole much greater than the combination of its parts. If it possibly was a hesitant beginning inasmuch as the participants merely tested the waters of their newly upgraded awareness, it nonetheless was a successful one.

How each half defined the particulars of the experience of finding itself in the role of the highest consciousness known of its kind is hard to explain, but I venture to say it was not dissimilar to a common state of bliss in which one desires absolutely nothing.

Back to the sentence in question, "to meet the One," was, in essence, "meeting the other One." Amaterasu or Vac – or any of the Angels for that matter – were already too familiar with their own state of Oneness to wish to meet the One in question, but they did have an invested interest in connecting with the emergent property of the Realms. As to the other half, it was a two-fold experience that was exactly what the Great Goddess of Light insinuated by "a special treat": a coming into their collective awareness as the new world, as well as a meeting with the source of their existence prior to the Warriors' domains separating from the mother reality.

To keep matters at their simplest, much primordial joy was exchanged between the freshly acquainted Ones. The stones carried the emotional charge of the union; as all were drawn into the vortex of its infinite vitality to, at last, reemerge reenergized, into an ambiance of realized newness. At which point Amaterasu led the group back to Joonas Halls.

~ Francis Voignier ~

1 – MAGGIE & WIND

Pau was working alone at the office when Maggie Phillips and her computer technician friend, Wind, stopped by to say hello.

"How may I help you?" she asked.

"You must be Linda Sue's replacement; I was hoping she still worked with Marshall," Maggie replied.

"She left quite a while back – you two are?" Pau enquired.

The young Master smiled when she heard the names. She had come full circle. The three falsely suspected of having been the victims of foul play as she worked under Joonas' nom de guerre, Alexander Cruz, during the interrogation of her present employer, Marshall Slaughter, had now all been introduced to her in excellent health: Olaf, Saka, and now Ms. Maggie Phillips, who as Pau noticed, was copiously stoned.

"Nice to connect at last, Maggie, your name has been floating around the office on and off. A pleasure to meet you as well, Wind, yours too has been mentioned in regard to working on one of our recalcitrant laptops," she said amused.

"You still got that machine?" he asked.

"No, we've upgraded, but it served us well as soon as Ms. Klein figured out how to get it going," she returned.

"Good for her, too bad she's not around, I would have liked to know what she did to get past the security. Another time, another place, I guess," he mused.

"My name's Pau Hunter by the way, are you guys

hanging around Eureka for a while, perhaps Marshall and I can have you over for dinner at the house?" she offered.

"I have some business to conduct in South County but we're heading for Portland in a couple days, maybe we can arrange for it as we go through town again," Wind proposed.

"Sounds like a deal – give us a call when that happens," Pau said as she handed each a business card.

She almost asked about Sam, but realized the question was bound to raise eyebrows since she had no real reason to know about Maggie's dog, especially when the source of that knowledge existed six hundred and forty-seven years in the future, not to mention an entirely different Oneness.

Maggie and Wind had barely left when Marshall and Jarred Gulliver returned from their assignment on a case that involved a particularly tricky issue of apparitions in the loft of one of the oldest downtown commercial buildings leased to an artists collective. The new Qwave computer had taken auratic prints of the space, which were downloaded on a stick for Pau to interpret.

"This last vogue of bleed-throughs is rather curious," Jarred remarked, as he took his gloves off.

"If it were up to you, you'd investigate the walk of a fly across a mirror as a curiosity worthy of a case," Slaughter humored.

"Easy old man, both you and I know quite well the difference between a false positive and a subtle, but real shift. Since my quasi-abduction, I believe I have gained in perception on these matters," Jarred asserted.

"Nothing wrong with waiting until Pau comes up with something tangible, wouldn't you agree?" Slaughter countered.

"OK, you two," Pau intervened, "Maggie Phillips and Wind stopped by for a quick visit. I invited them for dinner two nights from now, any reservations?"

"Interesting, I had been thinking about her lately. I was wondering how she was doing. Good then, it'll be nice to see her and Wind again," the investigator replied.

Even though Maggie Phillips was only a minor cog in the case of the disappearance of Olaf Swyndle, her dog Sam on the other hand, in view of his remarkable ability to access portals in the oddest of places with uncanny laissez faire, played a significant role in infusing hope into the prospect of ever finding the scientist alive. Pau had met Sam at Ma-l's grand gathering, where she also had the privilege to witness his endearing interaction with Vac. She hoped he would be joining for dinner.

Maggie was unaware Linda Sue was now Saka, a Goddess of Light in a remote cluster of universes referred to as the Realms. It was unlikely she would ever be told what had become of her friend, but it was also paramount she did not suspect foul play. Pau envisaged the scenario of getting Saka over to the estate for the occasion, though it presented complications in regard to her involvement with her lover, Great God Xarn, as well as her responsibilities as holder of the white stone that, with its counterpart, linked the two Onenesses to each other.

Pau was a Master; lying was not part of her bag of tricks. Eventually Maggie would ask pertinent-enough questions that would demand answers. Some humans were fully capable of absorbing alien data with mind-boggling equanimity, but she didn't sense Saka's old friend was one of them. She could have, on the other hand, not invited the two for dinner, but something told her she did the right thing.

She sent a message to The Triad at the Le Lien headquarters of the New Guild Center. Perhaps someone there could advise her on how to proceed, as well as let Saka know an old acquaintance was looking for her.

The Triad was its usual punctual; Saka could not free herself to make it to the Fieldbrook estate by the time Wind and Maggie returned from Southern Humboldt. It was certainly not worth tweaking the timelines for a date that lay precariously on the thin edge of her old friend's fickleness. The young Master would have to improvise, or simply let Marshall do the talking.

———————

Pau went over the data of the auratic prints taken by the Qwave laptop. There undoubtedly was an occurrence of interweaved, foreboding presences around the vast studio space. It was not uncommon for transient souls to err among the living, displaying their spectral selves, while unaware of the print-through perceived by minds themselves on the verge of drifting into other spheres. But those proved to be particularly vibrant readings, radiances that registered a high level of intensity, while exhibiting unusual plasmatic qualities.

Pau turned to Jarred Gulliver to seek his views on the matter:

"You just mentioned an increase in these kinds of sightings, can you elucidate? I need places, as well as times and witnesses."

"I always keep my antennas out," Gulliver replied. "Of course, few witnesses want to talk about what they see, or have the means to seek our help; but I try to pay attention to the unsaid."

"That's not what I would consider helpful at the forensic end, but I understand we're not exactly dealing with crime," she humored. "Perhaps we can start with your feelings then take it from there."

"We all know that the vast majority of these sorts of occurrences are the byproducts of complex minds often married to distraught hearts," Jarred started. "But in this new case, added to what I have already eavesdropped on, I'm sensing that not just the tortured is involved. I hear regular folks saying things like, 'I swear my house is haunted!' with heightened regularity."

"You understand you make it sound like someone, or something is moving in; are you insinuating an invasion?" Pau probed.

"I hope not," Jarred replied, as he recoiled at the thought.

"It's evident by these readings that we are in the company of a rather vibrant energy field, though I am reluctant to call it a gathering of souls. I'll have to look deeper into it, if you don't mind, Jarred," she said, while indicating she was ready to call it a day.

"Very well then," Gulliver said, "we're due to return there within the next couple of days to collect testimonies from resident artists, perhaps you'll have something for us then. The more we know, the better the chances to home on the mystery – see you tomorrow!"

Jarred put his gloves back on, then headed for the apartment adjoining the office.

———————

Pau had taken the Jarred Gulliver guardian job on recommendation from her own spiritual custodian, Angel Leòn. She had defected to Hektor while under the influence of a nearly untraceable program implanted into her psyche by Adam Bassett, one of Joonas's guises, during a rave party. Shortly after her rescue, Gulliver's body and mind were hijacked by the Dark Angel. He was practically left to die when Joonas was forced out by Masters Liv and Spencer. As a result, the English gentleman suffered massive psychological trauma. It was a perfect arrangement for the pair: Pau had wished to redeem herself for having failed the Guild, while Jarred was in dire need of support. He was still very fragile, easily overwhelmed, and prone to spells of disorientation. Pau knew how to soothe his psyche – she was all too aware of the damage Joonas had been capable of inflicting on those he had touched.

Gulliver was uninformed about Pau's past, or her status as a young Guild Master. She understood what he knew of Angels was through Joonas's thoughts, but only from the standpoint of a psychologically raped spectator. He was left with the foggy notion there were evolved beings roaming the earth, but he couldn't pick them out of a crowd. In due time, Pau would incrementally bring him into the fold – she felt he deserved to be told. He had the capacity of absorption, the openness of mind, as well as the suppleness of heart to succeed with the initiation process. Upon the end of his useful physical life, he would be in position to opt for the Masters' training. At least, that was what she hoped to achieve.

———————

Maggie and Wind called in the late afternoon to check if the invitation for dinner still stood. Slaughter gave them directions to the Fieldbrook house; he would wait for them at the driveway.

"We have plenty of food and drinks, but for good measure, you may want to bring your beverages of choice," he advised.

The guests arrived just before seven as night was falling. They both smelled of weed, probably from hauling what they had come to Humboldt for in the first place. Wind didn't bother to ask permission to smoke; he simply lit up the half-burnt joint that had been dangling from his lower lip, then proceeded with a coughing fit. Marshall and Pau looked at each other, somewhat amused.

"So, where did Linda Sue go after she left her job?" Maggie asked, before wrestling a last toke out of the roach.

"She traveled for a few months after you two went on that camping trip, and then rented the upstairs before I actually bought the place. She had left by the time I took possession. She told me she had been looking for you, but you had relocated," Slaughter replied.

"True, I moved in with Wind; I got tired of living alone in this shit hole of a town," she returned, laughing.

"By the way, what happened to your dog?" the detective asked.

"Oh, he's sleeping in the back of the van; I guess I should let him out if you don't mind."

"Absolutely, he's totally welcome here," Marshall returned.

Sam came in, sniffed around and walked straight to where Pau was standing.

"I reckon both of us must know the same paths. It was a mighty nice party by the look of it, didn't you think so?" the dog enquired telepathically.

The young Master squatted to scratch Sam's head, looking into his eyes.

"You're not just a regular dog, are you, Sam?" she asked with fondness in her thoughts.

"I guess not, I can't catch Frisbees, if that's what you mean,"

"What I mean is that you know your way around places other dogs don't frequent – except for Vac, of course," she clarified.

"I like Sir Vac very much," Sam affirmed.

"I heard you found your way back home from the party all by yourself – that was quite a feat," Pau said.

"Well, the frog is good at directions – he was around when I felt lost."

"The frog, hey?"

"I'm pretty sure he's a frog." Sam let out.

Pau had heard about the frog from Marshall. The amphibian was practically the stuff of mythology when it came to the case of Olaf's disappearance. But there was this connection with Sam she hadn't been aware of, which she made sure to earmark. Meanwhile, Jarred was expected – she needed to get back to the kitchen to help Marshall with the preparations. She served Sam a bowl of kibbles, promising to resume with their conversation as soon as things settled. That was when she heard Maggie exclaim, "We absolutely must get in touch with Linda Sue!"

Pau suddenly realized she hadn't made good use of her Guild training when she received the two at the office. Of course, after a couple of years without news, the unscheduled visit had to have been motivated by more than just a wish to say hi. She sensed there was timing involved; surely Wind and Maggie had come to the area for supplies on multiple occasions since then.

Pau didn't want to get too close for fear of being cornered into resorting to ambiguities, yet she needed to get to the bottom of why the guests wished to connect with Saka.

Wind had unwound after a couple of Indica IPAs. It was then that Pau realized he was the one who actually sought Maggie's old friend. From that point on, it became increasingly clear the dreadlocked Rastafarian was after The Triad's laptop, or any information pertaining to it – Linda Sue was the means to get to what he wanted.

Pau didn't understand why it took him so long to get back to the computer after he had unsuccessfully attempted to crack its unique password sequence, when Marshall first acquired it from the northtown pawnshop. What happened since then? She felt her time working with Alexander Cruz was paying off in the form of investigative acuity. Her Guild training had connected her to something her Hektor past was ready to act upon, but first she needed to evaluate the merits of that union – she would have to seek advice from Leòn.

Meanwhile, the subject of apparitions came around when Maggie asked about the business and Jarred volunteered to enlighten her. As it turned out, Wind was particularly attentive to the conversation, adding his own insight to a mixture of Jamaican lore, to spice up the theory of an acute increase in ghost sightings among other paranormal occurrences. Again, Pau's training kicked in to highlight the man was just making small talk, while soaking the information offered by Gulliver.

The young Master's skills of perception were receiving data in barely registrable waves, but one intriguing detail was flowing in at recurring intervals: a sense that there existed a link between what Wind was after and Jarred Gulliver's hypotheses.

Then came the focal question:

"I wasn't aware any kind of sensor or software existed – at least at the consumer level – that could trace ghost images. What are you using?"

Pau didn't wait for Jarred to answer. She made quick eye contact with Marshall, begging for help, before she cut into the conversation.

"There's nothing scientific about the way we conduct our business. We scan the area with a common frequency analyzer – the kind sound engineers use in recording studios to tune the room – then later I check the graph for soft spots; at least that's what we call them."

Wind laughed.

"I see, you guys are either making this shit up or you don't want to tell!"

Slaughter had read Pau's message correctly; he too saw the Rastafarian had switched to inquisitorial mode.

10

"Wind," he said, "we don't make stuff up. Clients come to us with their concerns; our role is to help by shedding light on the sensitive data they provide us with. The tools may be unorthodox, but the base methodology is sound, I assure you."

"Unorthodox and sound in the same sentence kinda ring funny to me, man. You sure you're not fucking with me?"

"Interesting you should see it that way," Marshall returned. "What makes you say that?"

"OK, so what happens when your so-called sensor tells you you've got company; what do you do about it? I mean, it's not like you can clear the room at the flick of a switch."

"It's possible Jarred gave you the wrong impression of what it is we actually do. Our role is to essentially debunk these occurrences in a gentle way; most of them happen in our clients' minds."

Pau was trying to keep Maggie and Gulliver busy in the kitchen to give her partner room to close the subject, though Wind wasn't letting go.

"But when they ain't in your clients' minds like Jarred there just indicated, what's your angle, Marshall?"

"I'm not aware we have come to a consensus about it. Jarred and I spoke to one of the artists; we'll know more after we gather extra data," Slaughter said.

"OK man, lemme be plain about this: you need some serious gear to read auratic signatures and their densities – not just a Mac with a mic," Wind remarked.

"You seem to be well tuned for this kind of business; what do you know that I don't?"

"It ain't business, Marsh, it's life – it's around us. I'm into computers, that's what I do. I'm just sorry Linda

Sue's not around with the laptop we tried to crack a while back. I didn't know what I was dealing with then, but with time, I've come to guess what that machine was. I've seen another like it in a pawn shop in Santa Cruz, but it was gone before I could put the money together to snatch it," Wind explained.

"What do you think that laptop was?" Slaughter asked, unsure of the soundness of the move.

"It was obviously a scientific instrument, but not one that belonged to an investigator's office, unless that investigator dealt with cases of, let's say, uncommon nature. You know what I mean, man?"

"I'm trying to, Wind. All I know is that Linda Sue left with the computer. Whether she still has it or not, your guess is as good as mine."

The kitchen crew came back with fares. Maggie, who overheard the tail of the conversation said, "She'll show up, babe; people can be found."

Pau knew she had to get in touch with Le Lien. Something was moving in fast, something she couldn't figure out from the standpoint of her training, because it was perhaps alien to it. She took Sam to the side.

"Tell me, my good friend, how long have you known Wind?" she asked.

"He's around, but I don't recall I know him."

"I mean, how long has he been around?"

"Hard to tell how long he's been around because he's often gone. He knows many paths too."

"What kinds of paths, Sam?"

"The ones that exist between the others," the dog answered absentmindedly.

"Have you ever taken those paths?" Pau asked.

"No, the frog advises against it."

"I guess I am asking many questions, sorry, I didn't mean to burden you."

"It's OK, but you're right, questions force me to think – thinking makes me forget who I am."

"Thank you, my friend, I will tell Vac I spoke with you!"

"Tell Sir Vac I shall visit again."

"I will most assuredly do so." Pau replied.

With that, Sam went to Maggie to lie by her side.

Pau sat by Jarred Gulliver for the rest of the evening. She felt he didn't deserve the invalidation. What had just happened with Wind and Maggie was out of the box; no-one had ever shown any sustained interest in their affairs since they joined forces. From now on, the three needed to sort out what could be publicly shared from what couldn't, particularly when Qwave equipment was at stake. Had Wind known the specifics of the sensors used at the artists' loft, she intuited the outcome of the evening would have been much darker. Her Guild training stopped short of making sense of the man's intentions – there was an obscure element to his quest that triggered reflexes born of her time with Hektor, yet it was something unrelated to the rogue organization. Sam's answers pointed to paths that existed between others, yet ones that he didn't use himself. She knew of the Guild and Hektor portals, as well as the mysterious ways of Sam's in and outs of Ma-l's realm, but wasn't aware of any others. She would message The Triad at Le Lien as soon as the guests left, and then wait for instructions.

Meanwhile, she had to make sense of the prints Jarred and Marshall brought back from the downtown loft – something of consequence was up with them.

It was an odd evening from the conversational standpoint; the two groups couldn't have been more unmatched for each other, which made Pau almost regret having forwarded the invitation. Maggie was a spaced-out pothead who appeared to be following Wind wherever he went. Somehow Pau didn't see how she and Saka could have ended as friends, but then again, she never knew the Goddess's old self.

The guests left at midnight. They said they would stop by on their way back from Portland when they also would try to locate Linda Sue. Sam connected one last time with Pau:

"Wind doesn't care much for dogs. I cannot say I like him, but he's alright, I guess. He's looking for the female from the other land, with whom we hiked the mountains, but I don't reckon I know the reasons."

"I believe I do, my dear Sam, let's hope it's for the better good."

2 – PAU & VERA

Angel Vera arrived via the portal installed in the upstairs of the Fieldbrook house. When she saw Pau's message at Le Lien headquarters, she felt compelled to volunteer her investigational skills to help shed light on the Wind situation. Jarred knew her from the times of his rehabilitation, when she and Lillian assisted him in regaining his mental equilibrium – she was family.

A series of portals had been linked together to allow members of the group that contributed to freeing the Realms, to connect with each other. Marshall had chosen to spend a few days with his good friend Geir Flemmingson in Reykjavík, who in turn was being entertained by lovely Lillian, fresh out of a Le Lien assignment in the old tunnels of Angel City. She and Vera had traveled together from Joonas Halls via Amaterasu's Hektor hub at Keyhole Lake. Marshall, as he crossed path with Vera, promised he would soon be back at the office to resume with the case; but since the artists' collective had postponed the meeting for yet another week, he and Jarred were off the hook for a few days to catch up with social life and personal projects.

"How's Bluefeather?" he asked.

"From where he stands, the sun always shines," she replied laughing.

"As expected – actually, you two are due for a visit at the house. Let's all get together when you're done working with Pau!"

"I agree – it's been a while."

She said goodbye then was off to Fieldbrook.

Since the opening of the lane between Joonas Halls and Keyhole Lake, the differences between the original Guild and the branch of the Realms had become marginal. It remained nonetheless clear that they were two distinct entities governed by the unique requirements of each Oneness. But Angels weren't bound by responsibilities towards one or the other; they traveled freely to take assignments wherever their skills were in demand. There was only limited space at the new center combined with few posts within the open Warriors' domains, which made for keeping traffic along the lane, restricted to Masters already residing in the new world and those associated with the work of the Realms, as it was the case with Pau and the Le Lien team. Pau was unique in the way that she took an assignment in her old world, while still being a member of the Hektor rescue trauma group with Shade and Shido in the Great Hall. An equivalent group existed within the original Guild, but it was understood the young Master was better suited for the job from the standpoint of connectivity. The guidelines between the two branches were few; Angels were essentially self-evaluating/regulating entities capable of operating harmoniously within the spacious environment of Guild infrastructure and purpose – conflicts were inexistent.

Pau and Vera went over the case of Maggie and Wind. They also inspected the Qwave sensor readings from the artists' loft while they speculated on the possibility of a link between the two events – though neither of them could quite put their fingers on what it was that pointed towards the plausibility of a connection.

"You made an interesting observation in regard to your Hektor background being aroused by Wind's inquisitorial style," Vera told Pau. "I would be inclined to seek counsel from one of the rogue league members recently attached to the Guild; it's a novel concept but it could be an eye opener," she added.

"Before we go that route, I would first prefer to consult with Leòn to make sure I'm still sound," Pau confessed.

"Come on girl, you know damn well you're fine; the fact you're even considering doubting yourself is proof of it. You're pretty isolated here, it'll be good for you to team up – some Angel love goes a long way!"

"Thanks, Vera, I'm sure you're right," Pau replied laughing.

"So OK, let's go over what we know about Wind: Sam claims he uses portals that are neither Guild nor the mysterious ones associated with the ubiquitous frog. That leaves us with the possibility he hops gateways to access the interdimensional layers of what you may call the underworld. Are you familiar with it?" Vera asked.

"Not really, it was only mentioned in passing during training."

"Very well then, this is how it goes: in a nutshell, there exist several dimensional levels controlled by Fallen Angels that are being crisscrossed by Roamers via kinks in the web of probabilities. Essentially, many Guild portals in the réseau are responsible for the traffic, while there is little we can do to remedy the issue. With the use of daring trickery, these marauders, over the eons, have been able to access these transitory layers with the aim of building sub-worlds that serve as platforms for the trade of stolen goods, drugs, fringe technology, etcetera; something vaguely resembling scenarios in some of your common science fiction movies here on Earth. The Great Ones have deemed them necessary evils that are part of the balance of universal energy. We group these layers under one name: the Interverse. The Guild has no jurisdiction there, but it was heard Hektor replenished its Dog kennels from the place. The Triad's computer was recovered with great difficulties from these dimensions of reality, in a play that involved many unsuspecting actors. We don't enjoy jobs in those parts, but we couldn't let that laptop fall in the hands of the wrong guys. That's why it's kind of vital that we establish who Wind is, and the nature of his interest in Linda Sue," Vera explained.

"Wow, that's something new!" Pau exclaimed.

"That's only the beginning. As recommended by the Ones, we don't usually get involved with that world; we know little of it, including its evolution. It's all the more complex since it exists in a constant state of fluctuation that makes for returning to the same place practically impossible. It is infinitely vast as well as uncharted, and while it travels with utter unpredictability across the web of all possibilities, its least desirable denizens stealthily snatch all they can from the hands of unsuspecting portal users," Vera added.

"I guess I have some catching up to do," Pau expressed. "But first we must ascertain Wind's status before we jump to conclusions. If he's so intent on finding the laptop, or apparently, any Qwave equipment on behalf of the Interverse, we must expect a development that may concern the welfare of the various probabilities with which that reality intersects."

"You're thinking like a true Le Lien member, girlfriend, I like your style," Vera punned. "How we establish the malevolence of his actions will depend on his level of carelessness. Remember, he's not guilty of anything, even if he's indeed an inter-cosmic Roamer. The only laws that can touch him are those enacted by his kind. This is an exercise in prevention; unfortunately we can't foresee scenarios outside our realm of activity; what emerges from the Interverse is too random to coalesce into a complete picture – much less multiple outcomes."

"My guess is that he probably doesn't care if he knows he can't be touched," Pau said.

"Unless he's got something to hide," the Le Lien agent countered.

"Vera, I got you involved because of Saka, otherwise I have no real reason to care about what Wind does with his life. I want to make sure I'm not wasting your time."

"I understand you're new at this, but get it once and for all: Angels aren't bound to anything. We choose where we want to be, pick the jobs that resonate, because we believe that ultimately there's a reason for finding ourselves in whatever present that magnetizes us. There are no accidents, yet there's no predetermined path either. All that to say my time is never wasted – if it were, there would be a rewind option," she said laughing.

"Fair enough, it's nice having you here!"

"Glad we got this out of the way! Now you say Wind and Maggie are coming back in a few days? Best is to arrange for another social gathering which I will attend as your friend. We'll cross-reference Wind's words and moves in order to assemble a profile that can be fed to a Le Lien program. I would be tempted to use a sensor on him but I'm concerned about his possible training as an Interverse operative. Also, it's highly possible he might be able to recognize an unshielded Master; I trust you're up to date with your education."

"I am," Pau confirmed.

"Now the readings: we must first decode the unique auratic signature of the apparition, its density, as well as its velocity. In the case of interweaved energies, there will be multiple signatures to compound into a profile. Based on what we get, we may be able to identify their provenance, perhaps even their intentions. I'm concerned Marshall and Jarred's use of the Qwave sensor may have aroused some curiosity, which could explain the timeliness of Wind's visit. I'm sure you're guessing where I'm heading," Vera said.

"Exactly where I tried not to go, for fear of too much Hektor influence leading to doubt and suspicion," Pau returned.

"Le Lien's not that picky about where the influence comes from. Suspicion's not a game we play – it's a tool we often put to good use. We don't get consumed by our methods; thus, we never mix doubt with guilty verdicts. When we look at multiple outcomes, we work from an array of possibilities that contemplates just as many gruesome scenarios as positive ones. Suspicion absorbs those who make a quality out of it. Comparatively speaking, an intuition is a small window into one of the foreseeable futures, generally the closest probability to the present in motion. Trust your senses, cuz doubt will eat you, girl!" Vera said intently.

"I feel like I'm back in class, but I appreciate the feedback. I'm still fresh from rescue, so there still are lingering vulnerabilities I need to iron out. It helps knowing Hektor didn't just leave me with personal issues; I see where Paula Hunter's harder edge could come handy in the proper settings," Pau countered.

"It's where it's at – integration," Vera validated.

As predicted, Maggie and Wind called to say they were coming down highway 199 from Grant's Pass, offering to meet for dinner somewhere in Arcata or Eureka. Marshall, who was just back from Reykjavík, suggested a place with an ocean view at Moonstone Beach. Jarred opted out, mostly because he felt uncomfortable around the Rastafarian, plus he believed Maggie was wasting her mind away instead of straightening her spine and taking charge of her life. Slaughter didn't know what made him say that, but he saw some truth in it. Maggie had been a lot more fun when she lived alone in her "shit hole of a town," he thought to himself. He then remembered Sam who would have to stay in the van, but again, they all could take a walk on the beach, which he was sure the dog would enjoy immensely. Marshall owed much to Sam for his contribution to the case of Olaf Swyndle; he felt particularly concerned about his welfare.

Angel Vera had taken the upstairs area which had been Saka's old space when she and Olaf had returned from Ma-1's realm. It was also where the portal to Keyhole Lake was located, behind the false back of the walk-in closet. It didn't need to be concealed, but Marshall preferred it out of the way, probably as the result of Joonas' relentless search for the courtyard portal installed by The Triad as a backdoor into Angel City. Pau and Vera had prepared for the meeting with Wind; they would take turns between initiating conversation, and casually analyzing speech behavior as well as body language. Le Lien didn't have much on Roamers, identifying them was far from being a perfect science.

The two Masters were set to look for clues that tied the couple's presence in the area to the apparitions at the artists' loft. They didn't have much to work from, except for some intuitive notion there was something there. The pivotal point was Wind's interest in Linda Sue. They would have to gauge to what extent the man was willing to stir trouble in order to locate her. Based on the results of their observations, Le Lien would have to decide whether Saka should be involved or not. The young Goddess had shown no interest in rekindling a friendship with Maggie, much less in revisiting a past she had sent on its way with her blessings.

———————

Slaughter had arranged to meet at the beach. Based on Maggie and Wind's erratic lifestyle, he expected them to arrive late, but they were surprisingly punctual. Sam got his fill of chasing surf, seagulls, and the occasional oystercatcher, unfazed by Vera pretending to not know him. The Master was introduced to the couple as Pau's lifelong friend, a lie best left to the investigator from the Angels' standpoint, although this was a case that called for the rare exception. As Vera had pointed, Le Lien was not particularly concerned about overstepping the line here and there. To the delight of the two Masters, Marshall went straight to the point:

"Have you initiated a search for your friend?" he asked Maggie.

"Wind and I have used various *People Search* sites as well as facial recognition apps, but every time, we were referred to the old E Street address. It's like she vanished without a trace. I wonder why none of them took us to your house since, as you said, she lived there for a while," she replied.

"She was on E Street for quite some time though. I guess those search algorithms aren't that sophisticated, or possibly the data bank is outdated. I've had that issue with my work," Marshall pointed.

Wind abruptly stepped in.

"I beg to differ! I don't use your off-the-mill app; my tools can crack government databases, FBI files, CIA, Mossad, DGSE, you name it."

"Impressive – and you do that without fear of being detected?" Slaughter asked.

Wind laughed.

"They can't easily detect what's ahead of their systems; when they eventually catch up, I'm long gone and untraceable."

Pau and Vera, who were making small talk with Maggie, did not miss on the conversation. When the Le Lien agent heard Wind brag about his hacking abilities, she couldn't help but utter a mental "Bingo!" Pau was also close to confirm her original suspicions about the man: he was onto something that tapped deep into terra incognita. To an Angel familiar with the many layers of existence, that meant the one they rarely delved in: the Interverse. The man's careless boasting glaringly showed his fearlessness of the system – he likely deemed himself uncatchable. Yet, there was an edge of taunting that Vera feared indicated Wind knew something about Slaughter's past, a detail that could potentially lead to compromising circumstances, especially in regard to Saka and Olaf – she needed to ascertain her senses were not overreaching.

"So in spite of the tools, Klein is nowhere to be found, am I right?" Marshall asked the Rastafarian.

"That's right, my man, she went MIA."

"You're sure about that?"

"Sure as hell; she's either left us or she's in hiding – I go for option number two," Wind replied.

"That would be out of character, but you never know with people. Let's get to the restaurant, we have reservations," Slaughter pronounced, relieved to have an excuse to change the subject.

After the customary ordering ordeal that involved checking who was into sharing fares, sudden changes of mind, questions about whether the greens were organic or not – a drama mostly aggravated by Maggie stoneness – the conversation about Linda Sue Klein resumed; this time, within the tight quarters of a table of five.

Marshall Slaughter decided to take a chance; he turned to Wind.

"Interesting you should be concluding that my ex-employee is either dead or hiding. As a matter of fact, it wasn't so long ago that two feds from the Forest Service with plenty of leverage, came to ask me if I knew where Maggie was – just to say that even government isn't always up to date."

The couple looked at each other, confused; then Wind's tone turned a notch darker.

"You must be kidding me, Marshall," he spat.

"I wouldn't dare – just making a point. In case

you didn't hear yourself speak, you've been tossing innuendos my way from the get-go. I insist Linda Sue lived in Fieldbrook after she left E Street. If the feds or Mossad missed on recording her actions at the time, it simply means they didn't give a damn about yet another nondescript woman amid the millions that lived in America. As far as my story of the feds looking for your partner goes, it's totally true – they even tried to incriminate me for her disappearance. So, no, I'm not fucking with you," Slaughter returned coldly.

Pau didn't know where to put herself. Even though she and Vera had arranged for Marshall to do the talking, the investigator was treading an area of acute discomfort for the ex-Hektor abductee; after all, she had been one of the two feds that was after Maggie, the other was Alexander Cruz.

"Take it easy, Marshall; I believe you. It's just odd the Forest Service would be looking for Mag, that's all," Wind said, as if to apologize.

"Perhaps I should be worried about Klein, but I'm not – she's a grown-up who's entitled to make herself hard to reach. I don't see why you guys can't just leave it at that," he added, showing he was ready to move on.

Wind didn't insist. He understood they had come to a wall. Maggie, who sensed the subject had ended on a sour note, couldn't wait to get outside to light one up; she left the table claiming she had to check on Sam.

The next portion of the meal went uneventfully. Maggie returned stoner than ever; she rarely talked, seemingly absorbed by the changing landscape of her food. Vera entertained the group with stories of some of her assignments disguised as inconspicuous items of her past. Pau found her rather unorthodox for an Angel, but she knew it was her style, one she admired for its spiritedness. She was easygoing, yet she cared deeply about her work and those she teamed up with. In lots of ways, she displayed many of the human attributes – her sense of humor being one of them.

But Vera wasn't completely satisfied with the data collected from Wind. Marshall had aborted the conversation too prematurely by losing his cool, especially in bringing the fake Forest Service agents into it. It was a risqué stretch of the truth with little to show for. So, over coffee and crème brûlée, the Le Lien operative played her card:

"Wind," she said, "I didn't want to be rude by barging in your conversation with Marshall, but I'm curious as to why you would go the length of breaking into a government database just to look for an old friend; it must be rather important?" she asked nonchalantly.

The Rastafarian thought about her question for a moment before answering.

"It's not like we're trying to get to her to tell her someone died or that she won the lottery – nothing that dramatic. Maggie let me know she missed her old friend; I was just trying to help. I work with computers so I have access to stuff most people don't know exists."

"I too work with computers and program most people don't see; please enlighten me," Vera risked.

"Shit, don't tell me you're government," he appeared to jest then resumed. "Let's say I tell you, but it's quid pro quo, agreed?"

Vera agreed while Pau thought she was out of her mind. Wind resumed.

"I get stuff on the black market, modded laptops, specialized interfaces, smart phones on steroids, programs

26

and tech the system doesn't know exists cuz the system is not there yet. You'd be amazed what a man can find when he looks in the right places. Take this thing for instance," Wind handed his phone to Vera, "does it look like a regular phone to you?"

The Le Lien Master realized Wind was a compulsive show-offer; he just couldn't help himself. She picked up the phone then immediately saw it was a model that wasn't to be released for another few years. Angels could exist in simultaneous presents – she knew Wind's Android belonged to the future. She also knew she was being set up.

"Nice, I've never seen that model – but it's just a phone."

"OK, call someone then," Wind suggested.

She barely thought of Marshall's number when the mobile instantly dialed the investigator's iPhone. Vera already knew it would do that, but she chose to play the game.

"That's quite extraordinary, Wind, a mind-reading phone! You say you got it on the black market?"

"Yup, that's right, girl, now, your turn," he replied victoriously.

"I'm a scientist, we use supercomputers linked to other supercomputers. They're huge, they live in dust-free, climatized rooms, but in spite of that, none of them can anticipate a caller's needs; though to their credits, they don't connect with the outside world," Vera lied.

"Sweet, I've always wanted to visit such a facility. Who're you working for?"

"Berkeley Lab, computing sciences," she replied.

Wind looked briefly puzzled but quickly regained his composure. He let Vera know how impressed he was and how much he wished they had more time to explore the field, but Maggie was restless and wanted to hit the road; she reminded her partner Oakland was six hours away.

The group parted in the parking lot. Pau never had a chance to reconnect with Sam, but somehow she sensed they would meet again sooner than later.

3 – THE QO'AI-MARAEL ENIGMA

Ma-l, Xarn, and Enola had resumed with the dream meetings in the hope that the activation of the lanes would be eventually felt by the unresponsive Warriors. But the recent precipitation of tunnel events, namely the near-disastrous propagation of self-cloning seed algorithms by XVII members, Lawrence, Rashnu, Jen, Tealsky, Niamh, Caax, Dzarlahon, and Theyia, among others, had, without a doubt, disturbed the fine makeup of the dream lanes. Additionally, Qo'ai-Marael and Joonas's presence in the maze posed an enigma that was yet to be deciphered. It was certainly clear that the two elder Masters had played their parts in redeeming themselves after having erred, one with Hektor, the other with XVII. On the other hand, what wasn't so obvious was the extent of their knowledge of the broader mechanics of the Realms; a distinction with the potential of making them much more than accidental players in the emergence of the Warriors' worlds.

Qo'ai-Marael had insisted on eight chroniclers for Ma-l's gathering, each positioned strategically, as if the reporting was only the veil over a much more important, yet obscure purpose. Yes, she was guilty of treason, misled and confused by her love for Dzalarhons, but Le Lien remained unconvinced – it was all too simple. An affair of the heart gone awfully wrong wasn't one of the common dramas of Angels, especially coming from an original team member with unchallenged integrity.

Angels Vera, Lillian, Liv, and Spencer had opened a vast search of the tunnels with the aid of Qwave and

Portals combined technologies. A simulation of the old Gestalt's ghost image had been created to temporarily activate XVII's seeds, and provide access to the linkwork of the old system. The science was far from foolproof, demanding of the surveying team unparalleled skills of precision and concentration.

As much as Vac had insisted that Joonas's sanctity be respected, he didn't object to going forward with locating Qo'ai-Marael. With only three realms opened, the task was thought to be straight forward, but it proved otherwise; neither signature was detected within the two mazes of old and new. But the three remaining XVII members were eventually found in the darkness of Angel City and sent to Dahbar's domain, in the realms of Hektor. As to Joonas's Dogs, Le Lien deemed they belonged to the predicament they had found themselves in – there was far worse fate as Vera saw it.

––––––––––

The disappearance of both Joonas and Qo'ai-Marael exposed a series of unsettling scenarios; among them, the likely existence of concealed layers within the system of tunnels, as well as the possibility that the two elders might have crossed into one of the shuttered domains.

When the last theory was presented to Ma-l, her response was straight forward.

"How different would that be from Vac and Olaf entering my reality without notice?"

The observation brought forth a wide-open field of speculation. Would Joonas and Qo'ai-Marael impact the development of a realm in the same way Ma-1's intruders influenced hers by awakening dormant potential? But the scenario proved too farfetched to be granted due consideration – the Warriors were in charge of opening their doors, and with the mother reality long gone, so were the back ways into these worlds.

Vera, who often worked in spurts of intuition, offered her insight.

"Since when do Angels and Deities operate from the standpoint of absolutes? We have two main possible outcomes: one we've already abandoned, while the other is nothing more than a game of cat and mouse. We know practically nothing about the Realms as a system, yet we appear unwilling to look past our limited options. It's obvious these Masters know more than we do, as it was until recently the case with Dzalarhons and the rest of XVII. Rather than playing the guessing game, I would pick the minds of those who know – notably Vac and Amaterasu."

Vac came forward.

"The no-question-answered-until-posed rule doesn't apply when information must be shared across the board; so, forgive the oversight. It's important for all to know that there is a developmental key to the Realms that is off limit to us Masters. We remain in charge of Guild affairs until our skills are required in the Warriors' worlds. What's happening with Qo'ai-Marael and Joonas is intricately tied to realm evolution. What they know isn't born of Guild teaching, but of direct interaction with the new Oneness. Neither Amaterasu nor I can answer your questions, for we don't know the outcome of their actions; it belongs to a universe we're in the process of observing from the neutrality of the New Guild Center.

Again, what the elders know that we don't about the tunnels is information that predates the carving of old Angel City. I suggest we keep on proceeding towards finding our own answers. As to angel Vera's point about extending our options, I wholeheartedly agree."

"I'm being asked by my team to assist Angel Pau concerning matters at her office; perhaps I can bring Sam back with me," Vera offered.

"Ah yes, Sam," Vac returned. "If he's willing, I very much doubt he'll need to be guided. I would think he'd arrive here substantially before you do."

"Exactly my point!"

Vac enjoyed the style of the Le Lien operative's thinking process. She was witty in the kind of no-nonsense way that teamed well with a soul like Sam, as it was demonstrated during the search for the links to the old tunnels during Ma-l's gathering. In the field of locating hidden layers, Sam was the expert.

———————

Although the gathering in Ma-l's realm had left a lasting impression on all, the work had only begun for the three Warriors who had opened their doors. As they looked towards the horizons of possibilities, they wondered why their messages had remained unanswered.

"Could the seeds sowed by XVII have done damage to the dream lanes?" Ma-l asked Enola and Xarn at one of their meetings.

"It's a question for the original coders," the God replied. "But we know the lanes preceded the tunnels. So, what makes our kin deaf to our call?"

Amaterasu had advised on patience. While the theme of the open Realms had leaned on the physical, it hadn't necessarily been so for the others. Time wasn't a factor outside the material element. The reminder that all stifled realities were accounted for, as evidenced by the Hall's lower floor, helped in alleviating the doubt that all unopened worlds were doomed to failure; thus, the three Warriors made it their unimpeded commitment to systematically visit the dream meadows, promising each other to never stray.

———————

As the three realms expanded, so did the breadth of their combined reality – much was shared between them. Great Goddess Enola's city flourished in ways that eclipsed the vision of its creator. Indeed, Wolf very much influenced the Warrior's approach to populating her world. He first suggested that the deserts outside her walls be put to good use by introducing furrowing species that would loosen the soil while helping seed propagation. He then suggested that no species should be left mateless. She liked the way he reasoned; it was never selfish, yet it blatantly purveyed to personal interest.

In line with the convergence, the Goddess opened her realm to a contingent of artists from the Center, mostly students and young Masters. Her aim was to teach them the fundamentals of composing from the standpoint of extreme emotions, to tap at the heart of their most traumatic, as well as wildly elating assignments for fodder. She called it a course in art therapy for ailing Angels, in the hope her students would eventually assist those returning from difficult missions; a process through which Enola found much personal healing. Shade and Shido were among those avidly interested in the course. Although the Guild was perfectly capable of providing a class of similar potency, the angle from which it was taught was unique in that it supplied a rare backdrop of unexplored exoticism – a nuance Master Khaldun deemed invaluable to the process of expansion. Added to it, Great Goddess Enola's desire to enlist in the Masters' training program made her particularly suited for the role of honorary educator.

Besides Wolf's intermittent presence in the deserts surrounding her city, Enola often received the visits of groups of villagers from Xarn's realm. She cherished the interaction. In her eyes, these gentle souls were perfect creatures. Among them were the singers who performed on the elaborate stages she and Lev designed for Goddess Ma-l's grand gathering; they were recurrent admirers of her spontaneous art, who saw their own artistry, as well as themselves, reflected in it.

And too were Xarn, Saka, Ma-l, and Olaf often seen in the colorful back alleys of Enola's glorious city, sometimes accompanied by Vac or Leòn, or more rarely, by Great One Amaterasu – it was always a treat. Gone were the days of the threat of Dzalarhons and Caax – she had eased into her ever evolving identity. She loved the Angels, for she practically saw herself as one of them. Naturally, she was also quite different from them, but the Goddess wasn't particularly invested in titles – she knew where she came from. Her status a stewardess of her land made little difference; she recognized her source as the spring beneath her ever-expanding reality, powerful but giving, stable yet dynamic. The Warrior within her was merely a brief sequence, a phase before a long series of metamorphoses. The incident of the elder Master's breach in protocol was a clear reminder of where she would never return – her soul was healing.

All was peaceful in Xarn's realm. On a special occasion during which the other two Warriors and their close ones were his guests, the Great God introduced denizens from his faraway galaxies to the group. It was a stunning revelation that highlighted the breathtaking span of his creation. The travelers were in many ways similar to the inhabitants of the downriver villages, but they exulted a level of sophistication that betrayed a heightened state of evolution over them. As they described their homes, it became clear they existed in a future version of the God's world, a point that made Olaf's scientific mind spin.

Though Xarn was by far recognized as the creator with the farthest reach into his sphere of reality, it didn't mean Ma-1 and Enola were in need of improving on their creational skills. After all, both had suns and moons in their skies, as well as a tapestry of stars to attest to the potency of their visions. Olaf remembered once asking Ma-1 if she ever wished to visit the farthest confines of her universe to see what was there – to which she replied with pointed humor, "Those are your worlds, my friend!" Xarn explained that all inhabitants of his realm were creators of their own – another way to say his universe was in a continuous and spontaneous state of making itself as a unified whole.

"A creator can't possibly be overseeing all their work all of the time; it would pertain to distrusting their creations' abilities to take charge and hone their unique creational skills," Xarn stated, as if to make a point of the fact there was no such thing as a better realm amid the greater collective of the Warriors.

Ma-1 and Enola saw it as a non-item. The far reaches of space were inconsequential. Time and space were relative concepts. It simply showed Xarn still carried within him the male of his past in bursts of comparative overreach; although in the case of their Warrior kin, they saw his sharing as something greater than a display of his prowesses.

He looked at them as if having intuitively locked onto their thoughts.

"I get it," he simply said, smiling.

———

Until Angel Vera would return from Earth -647, the Le Lien team, whose core was composed of Liv, Spencer, Lillian, Stefan, The Triad, and of course, Vera, would be on standby in regard to further exploring the tunnels in the pursuit of locating Master Qo'ai-Marael, who had simply vanished with Joonas in the maze. All understood that the latter wished to find solitude amid the stone for the purpose of healing, and thus it was conceivable his state of self-imposed hibernation was responsible for the instruments' failure at detecting his signature. In the case of the female elder, it was unclear why she would seek to make herself unseen. She certainly played a pivotal part in neutralizing George's ghost

36

image, as seen in the near-perfect, synchronized return to normalcy at Ma-l's gathering, with her entry into the tunnels. Did she assist Joonas and his team in cutting the supplies to the seed algorithms, or did she do it alone? The last scenario implied Joonas had either failed or did not act on his promise, which left Le Lien with many unanswerable questions. Only by locating Qo'ai-Marael could light be shed on both Masters' roles, as well as her true motives for betraying the Guild. Lo-Shen and Jaco were incapable of finding logic in her repeated choices of assisting XVII. Her love affair with Dzalarhons, as she described it in her last entry into the chronicles of the Grand Gathering, stood thin in regard to the gravity of her actions. Vera still had her doubts about Vac revealing all he knew about her, but she also understood that if he opted for silence, the reasons had to be justified. Among Angels, a question didn't always lead to a cogent answer – not when innumerable scenarios were in play.

Until the reasons for Qo'ai-Marael's treason, as well as her final role in the tunnels could be explained, there was Joonas's looming shadow, rising like a specter from the past. He had told Vac and Vera that he was to gather his team to eradicate the Gestalt's ghost image, yet his Dogs were last seen, dead drunk, at the alcohol dispensary, where rogue Angel Jen inadvertently found herself trapped amidst the boisterous mayhem. What happened to him, and why didn't he reconnect with his crew? The last three apprehended XVII members couldn't have touched him – his might was too great – while Qo'ai-Marael had entered the tunnels too late to have gotten the opportunity to interact with him ahead of neutralizing the seed algorithms. Based on the report from Vera and Vac, who were the last ones to see Joonas, it was conceivable the Hektor founder vanished before he ever found the chance to act on his wish to once and for all be done with George. Someone or something had prevented him from finishing the job...

Amaterasu and Saka were summoned to the following Le Lien meeting. The power of the light was sought to reach deep into the farthest recesses of the corridors. The Great One abstained herself, on the premise the New Guild Center was fully capable of dealing with its own affairs, but Saka partook as representative of the Realms. She was ready for action after the high of her relationship with Xarn and the energy generated by the Grand Gathering had waned. She and the Warrior were still very much in love, but that love existed under a different set of dynamics, one dependent on trust as well as safety. Now she needed to rise again, find new meaning that would put the use of her skills to the test. She didn't need to prove herself; she simply craved the rush of action. She was a Goddess, yet she lacked the qualities of the creator; those were Ma-l, Xarn, Enola, and Amaterasu's attributes. She had no realm to steward, but she was a beacon at one end of the lane that connected the two Onenesses to each other. Yes, she possessed a unique and extraordinary talent for which she was forever grateful, but she couldn't deny herself the longing for the simplicity of unraveling a mystery. Perhaps, the old Linda Sue in her still had something to say. For a brief moment she missed that self, the uneventful life, the bliss of ignorance that carried her through the grey days of Old Town Eureka. She wondered why something called there, if only for a flicker. But then she homed on the subtlety: Linda Sue wasn't the one calling – purpose was. At that very moment, Spencer informed her of what was brewing with her old friend Maggie Phillips and her partner Wind, down at the old office of Marshall Slaughter.

Saka recoiled at the idea of reconnecting with Maggie. The action she sought had nothing to do with endless smoke-outs, or even hikes in the coastal mountains. That past was better left were it belonged. Pau's request for assistance was best handled by one of the Le Lien operatives. She had sobered up, her place was in the Realms with Ma-l and Xarn – she and Amaterasu were the Goddesses of Light, keepers of the lane, holders of the black onyx and white chalcedony stones.

Liv had already asked Vera if she was willing to team up with Pau to investigate the events around the Eureka haunted loft, as well as clear the oddity of Wind's apparent thirst for Qwave tech. Nothing was critical about it, but there was a shared nuance which Master Khaldun deemed worthy of elucidation. Saka was under no pressure to return to her old world, at least until she had no other choice. For now she would have to wait for Vera's return before a deeper exploration of the tunnels was considered auspicious. For the first time since her return to the Realms, Saka felt herself losing her grip on reality.

4 – STEALING SAM

Vera had very much wanted to connect with Sam, but the circumstances were inappropriate. She thought the dog had acted his part to perfection, opting to ignore her as if he had gotten wind that she was undercover. Sam was an enigma, one she couldn't pretend to ever solve. Besides shedding light on the Wind/Interverse/Artists' loft connection, her main objective was to convince him to return with her, or as Vac put it, coerce Sam into finding his own way to the Realms. His uncanny skills were needed in the tunnels. For that, she and Pau would have to get a lot closer to Maggie and her partner. With a positive on Wind's interaction with the underworld, she was in position to want to investigate the motives behind it. After all, pre-Guild, rejected Angels built on those hidden layers by capitalizing on the irremediable vulnerabilities of portals. Considering the threats of Hektor and XVII, Le Lien was in no position to look the other way. But first, it was to be determined how Roamers were actually posing a threat. They seemed to be pretty much locked inside their universe, at the exception of the occasional flash intersection during which they deftly lightened the bulk of some unsuspecting cosmic tourist, or when they squeezed through a portal, generally one at a time, to conduct drug or weapon business, or unload stolen fares on the black market and various pawn shops. It would take the threat of an invasion to get the Le Lien gears to mesh. Vera deemed the case quickly solvable, and hopefully, she would be able to return to the Realms to resume with the search for Qo'ai-Marael in a timely manner. She still had to figure out how to borrow Sam without Maggie noticing.

———————————

Pau and Vera were to join Marshall and Jarred to record the artists' testimonies. The collective had arranged for all of its members to be present in the form of a loose meeting that was to also include food and drinks. The casualness of the affair pleased the *Private & Beyond Investigation* team which had had more than its share of over-bloated parlor drama for some time now. Even Jarred's initial enthusiasm had been somewhat tested.

They gathered at the loft where a dozen colorful individuals welcomed them with the easy warmth of small town folks. Introductions were made, anecdotes exchanged, beverages poured, and amuse-gueules consumed before the main subject came into focus.

A blond, dreadlocked man in his twenties offered to break the ice with his recount of an evening spent by himself in the vast loft, where ghost-like figures, more beasts than men, began intertwining in a sinister dance, steadily filling more and more of the space. He recalled being so scared that he barely had the chance to put his shoes on as he rushed out to the closest bar. When he returned, inebriated, the apparitions were gone.

Each in the group had a story to tell that corroborated the general theme: an undefined, gestating, luminescent mass that appeared to become larger before it vanished. While some referred to it as an entanglement of snake-like figures, others strongly believed there were humanesque forms pulsing through the whole of the apparition. One peculiarity: it never manifested before an audience of more than one, and it did it randomly, regardless of the time of day or night.

———————

It was Pau's job to make sense of the data. This time around, it was obvious the team stood a sidestep away from the usual hallucinatory backdrop common to all the previous cases. She wasn't discounting the possibility of a variance on the theme, but the fact there was no personal attachment by anyone in the loft in regard to what was being experienced, made her lean towards an intrusion committed by exterior forces; plus the trace signatures collected from spatial memory didn't echo those picked from the artists. In other words, the energy was of alien origin. Jarred Gulliver somewhat triumphantly reminded her and Slaughter that he was the one who first observed a divergence from the norm. Pau went the extra length to validate his point by congratulating him on his keen prescience skills. In spite of his fragility, Jarred was perfectly suited for the job. He had the drive, the curiosity, the spontaneous inventiveness of those gifted with the ability to change course on a dime. He brought a ray of sunshine into Slaughter's rigid investigative methodology, which often consisted of treating cases on par with police business – which also explained why he originally deemed the job tedious. "Nothing more laborious than trudging the unknown, burdened with rationale," Gulliver had once said. Marshall knew that too well, but old habits were hard to break – a fact he often alluded to, while humoring the self. Pau, too, made sure he loosened up his grip on the work in order to open the field for Jarred to maneuver freely. In spite of the numerous minor inner conflicts, the *Private & Beyond Investigation* gears belonged to a well-oiled machine. With Vera in the equation, the team was now ready to tackle the complex task of making sense of the information collected from both humans and censors; and per chance, under it all, a link to the reasons of Wind's interest in Linda Sue could be unearthed. That detail remained solely between the two Masters, who had opted for caution over the risk of confusion. While Marshall and Jarred would handle the bulk of the artists' loft case, Pau and Vera would seek the Oakland couple for more material on their connection with the Interverse, finding ways to keep Saka out of it. In Vera's eyes, she and Pau could still easily come to a dead end, but she didn't recollect ever getting this far into an assignment, without eventually bumping into something.

As a quick fix, Marshall suggested that the artists use the space in groups and report immediately on collective sightings, should they occur. The concept was received with mixed feelings, since it forced some of those who preferred working alone, while blasting their favorite music, to exist in utter discomfort. The thought amused the investigator. The options were few though, so sentiments leveled towards resignation. Paradoxically, the collective spirit remained unscathed. Nonetheless, the clients still demanded lasting solutions in spite of the unrealistic nature of their request; but monies duly paid, overruled the wisdom of knowing that not all things could be bought. It was a chance Slaughter had been willing to take, on the premise that most cases could be solved by shuffling a few items around, such as replacing the fear element with hope, or hope with the acceptance that not all answers could be heard. At times, Marshall doubted the soundness of his judgment. He had anticipated that his forays into the Realms had given him an inside view of the simple mechanics of life; instead, he faced the complexity of the human soul, whose captain was a confused ego personality adrift on a sea teeming with hallucinatory characters. This time around, there were twelve perfectly sane individuals expecting professional results, yet should he and his team be able to deliver, difficult questions about methods, access to obscure technology – notwithstanding, a profound intrinsic knowledge of metaphysics – would have to be answered. In the back of his mind, Slaughter sensed the clients expected him to fail, but chose to play the game anyway – another of the lesser paradoxes that littered the landscape of the profession. Beyond the convoluted thinking, Marshall understood there was something larger than life looming in the background. As much as he enjoyed teasing Jarred, he trusted the Englishman's intuitions. With team Pau and Vera in the mix – even if the two were concentrating on Maggie and Wind – an aura of officiality had been added to the case. It then struck the investigator that he had just walked through a smokescreen opening into a hall full of mirrors.

———————

Vera intuited correctly that Wind would be seen in town sooner than later. Barely a week had passed since they walked the stretch of Moonstone Beach and dined at the Grill, when the Rastafarian called Pau's desk to announce he and Maggie were in the neighborhood. The young Master understood all too well she was about to walk the precarious edge of Wind's pawn-positioning mindset, in that by showing the slightest level of enthusiasm towards the visit, she was at risk of exposing her true motives, while he knew quite well that he was the last person she wished to see at the heart level. So, rather than compromise herself, she simply asked, "Do you wish to speak with Marshall?"

Wind paused for the length of a quick thought adjustment.

"Not necessarily, I count on you to relay the message. Perhaps we can all meet again – my treat."

"How long are you in town for?" she enquired.

"We'll be around for a few days, visiting with friends in Weitchpec," he returned.

"Pretty remote out there, but you can't beat the scenery. Marshall and I have driven by it on our way to meet with clients in Seiad Valley," she said.

"Now you're talking 'out there,' girl," Wind laughed, "Seiad's practically the end of the line!"

"Not until you take Seiad Creek Road to Applegate Lake! Marshall thinks his old Explorer is indestructible," Pau joked, feigning casual. "At any rate," she added, "do you want to get together after you two return from Yurok country?"

"Sounds good; we'll call the night before – see ya then!" he said, before hanging up.

Pau didn't have to explain; Vera already knew, and so did Marshall. Though the detective was at a loss as to how Wind was pivotal to the case, he was nonetheless resigned to play the game until the picture came into clearer focus. It was obvious that things had switched gears, though he couldn't remember the circumstances. Jarred Gulliver raised his shoulders in disbelief then simply said, "I guess I shall catch up on paperwork whilst you, people, entertain this ostentatious and rather annoying couple – cheerio!"

He left for the apartment abutting the office, with the stride of a man who couldn't be swayed.

The Interverse hadn't been much more than a mild annoyance to the Guild. Le Lien rarely had to intermingle with its affairs; the few cases revolving mostly around recovering stolen Qwave computers, as well as a plethora of modified tablets and phones that almost always ended up in Earth's pawnshops, or were found changing hands in back alley deals. It was generally a simple matter of setting up corrective transactions involving undercover agents, which merely required synching timelines and tracking the unique Qwave homing signal of the stolen goods. But in spite of the straightforwardness of the operations, Angels felt burdened by the task of crossing over into its layers, as if the very fiber of their beings were coming unraveled. Vera, always quick to pun, referred to its environment as the "antimaster." Furthermore, the portals into it were unreliable and hard to navigate, forcing many time-consuming adjustments and delays. Luckily, forays were few; and the Le Lien operative hoped Wind wouldn't take her there. It'd be ideal if she could simply borrow Sam for the job in the tunnels and go home, but it all hinged on how much he and Maggie were set on finding Linda Sue.

Wind called as he said. Only Vera and Pau were available to meet with the couple at the Pacific Bistro, Slaughter having decided he had other fish to fry; though in his heart, he did it for Jarred.

Sam and the foursome followed the boardwalk, as pelicans dove into the murky waters of the bay to catch their fares. Pau reminisced about her times of discomfort around the pungent smell of crab cages laid out to dry on the docks. So many changes had carried her along their uneven courses since the days of Alexander Cruz; she was thankful for them, for Marshall and Geir who took unprecedented chances on her, and for Ma-l, Olaf, and Vac who accepted her in the fold of their shared reality.

Vera had finally locked in with Sam while keeping a safe distance; she was able to convey her wish of teaming with him in the tunnels of the Realms.

"I like finding links; same as crossing but without getting lost," he telepathized.

"Glad you see it that way, Sam; links are what we're looking for, as well as a couple of souls lost in the maze – so, can I count on you?"

"Depends on how long it'll take," the dog replied.

"Time's not a factor – we can arrange for a seamless transfer that will not show on this side. What do you say we proceed after dinner, while on another quick walk?"

"Sounds good, I'll be there," Sam returned matter-of-factly.

Vera hesitated on the nuance of whether he meant "there" on the boardwalk or "there" in the Realms, but she remembered, smiling, what Vac had said earlier.

As anticipated, the dinner focused once more on finding Linda Sue. Pau and Vera wanted it to end, but Wind was driven by a need to match their wish with obnoxious insistence.

"You've already managed to piss Marshall off by insinuating he was hiding something from you," Pau said after Wind tossed a particularly trenchant insinuation her way. "Now you want me to account for her disappearance just because I took her job?"

"That's my girl!" Vera thought as she prepared to turn the tables – she just had had enough of the man's shenanigans.

"So, as a recap," she asked, "your search for Ms. Klein hinges on your hunger to find the particular computer you missed on identifying when you had your hands on it, am I right?"

Wind stiffened up.

"Hunger's a big word, but yes, it's important for me to locate that machine – some guys are into exotic cars, I'm into one-of-a-kind laptops. It doesn't mean Maggie isn't missing her friend."

"Perhaps I can help via the scientific channels. If you could only explain what you're after, who knows what I may dig up? I'm surprised you refrained from asking." Vera forwarded.

"That gear was nothing like what I'd seen before. Though it looked like a standard computer padded for field work, everything else about it was different. Like I told Linda Sue, Geir, and Marsh, it was visceral – trying to crack it was as if it knew my moves before me."

"I assume it came loaded with a custom OS, free of unessential fluff, right?"

"That was no OS in that machine, or if there was

one, it was a decoy," he dramatized.

"Sounds like sci-fi," she humored. "We're not at that technological level yet – perhaps soon."

"Whatever it was, it came as much from the future as it did from the past – a timeless machine."

"How could you know that?" she enquired, feigning dismay at the sheer arrogance of the statement.

"Because, I've been there!" he exclaimed, annoyed.

"I don't know many people who can hold to that claim, but I'm not going to argue with you. I'm kinda confused about what you intend to do with such a machine, which I assume can't interface with current tech."

"You're wrong; it can!" the Rastafarian spat, exasperated. "It was used here for purposes that must have been clear to Linda Sue, and I suspect, its rightful owner as well. What I'll do with it is personal, but I'll let you in onto something: I guaranty it'll blow the roof off the scientific community."

Vera paused for just the right time tension then innocently returned:

"I'll look into it, but I wouldn't set my hopes too high if I were you."

———————

While Wind and Vera were engaged in butting heads, Pau and Linda Sue's friend were waxing nostalgic about the good old days. As it coincidentally happened, Paula Hunter was born and raised in Humboldt on the same timeline as Maggie's, so it was for her a simple matter of mindlessly going along with the flow, which in that case was randomly thrown off course by her interlocutor's pot-infused mind storms – at least, she didn't have to lie. She noticed with relief that the computer topic tensions had eased into discussing commonalities, just as the waitress cut in to offer dessert and pousse-café suggestions.

Maggie was the one to propose a short post-meal walk before hitting the road. As Sam was let out of the van, he immediately connected with Vera, but again, kept a safe distance. Venus had just appeared to the right of the crescent moon behind the misty veil, so when Maggie pointed to it and Wind reflexively lifted his head towards the sight, they unknowingly triggered the signal that propelled Sam and Vera on their respective courses towards the Realms. Before the couple lowered their gaze, they had returned. It all happened in the blink of an eye.

5 – SEEDS & THRESHOLDS

By the time Le Lien operative Vera used her carry-on portal to reach the Great Hall via Keyhole Lake and Joonas Halls, Sam had connected with Vac in Ma-l's realm. The Triad informed her of the deed in their usual tongue-in-cheek way:

"For fast connections to the Realms from anywhere in the known universe, trust Green Frog Travels!"

She thought it was cute, though she promised herself to get duly informed on alternative methods to inter-Oneness crossings. She wondered why Portals were not looking into it. Unbeknownst to her, Portals had been, but it was complicated.

A meeting was set up with Saka, Vac, Le Lien, and the three Warriors, to further analyze the implications of Qo'ai-Marael's disappearance from the system of tunnels.

Xarn and Enola came to the dream meadows because they heard the call from Ma-l. It was as if a messenger wind had raced through the corridors to their realms, unmistakable, visceral, ancient... Had it been emitted as a mere quivering strand of a wish, it still would have been felt. There wasn't any doubt something in the maze was muting their desire to connect with the unresponsive Warriors.

The topic opened on many possibilities, the latest and direst orbiting around the concept that George had not evolved naturally into what it had become, but rather, suffered corruption from an outside source. The specter of Dzalarhons floated amid speculative forays, and of course, Joonas could no longer be excluded as a suspect despite Vac's warning that Amaterasu would never want to hear about it.

The drive to locate Qo'ai-Marael was motivated more by a wish on the part of Le Lien to question her for what she knew, than to see her tried for treason. In spite of the low return on probable outcomes in regard to the Realms, Masters at large had a good grip on intuition – there was something ominously brewing, and she was at the center of it.

As previously arranged, Saka was set to assist Vera, Vac, and Sam in the search for the elder Master. Besides putting her gift of light to good use, she rejoiced in the opportunity to hang out with Sam, whom she shared a past with. As Linda Sue, she, Maggie, and the dog had walked the Trinidad beaches on many a lazy Sunday afternoon. They had also hiked a dozen of the coastal trails together, including the memorable trip to the Siskiyous, on her quest for answers into Olaf Swyndle's disappearance.

Portals had mapped the location of the thresholds that connected the new to the old. Of course, there still were the tunnels of the arrested realms that weakly tied abandoned Angel City to the New Center, but the links put in place by Dzalarhons and her crew, were the ones Portals were after, especially since Qwave had developed the means to safely exploit the seed algorithms. It was believed many more such links existed that had not yet been detected, such as those planted by the three remaining XVII members while George's ghost image was being deleted – notwithstanding the possibility that clones could have found their way in the system.

It was when Sam, with his unprecedented skills at finding thresholds as if they were mere bones buried in the backyard, came in. He had demonstrated his talents while on a previous chase through the maze with Vac and Vera, by unearthing rogue Angels Lawrence and Jen, as well as locating Joonas amid the vestiges of Angel City. If one could find Qo'ai-Marael, it had to be him.

In the meantime, Vera had taken Saka to the side to address the Wind issue. She highlighted his near-irrefutable connection to the Interverse, as well as his insatiable urge to put his hands on a piece of Qwave gear, preferably the one he once tried to crack, which he believed might still be in her possession.

"Interestingly, I have had recurring yearnings to reconnect with my old world and the Linda Sue persona," Saka confessed.

"I'm sure that, as a Goddess, you've come to terms with the fact that the call didn't originate from a subconscious desire to return to a source you've never left; duty calls us in mysterious ways. Whether you end up going back to Humboldt or not is contingent on what will unravel out of the tunnels. If worse comes to worse, we may have to sacrifice the old The Triad's machine to ease tensions."

"The fact Wind failed to capitalize on what he stumbled across initially, indicates something happened to him since then. He probably is a very different man from the head-bobbing guy with his Beats cans and do-it-all USB flashdrive," Saka pointed.

"Which brings us to the other half of the issue: to what end does he intend on using that machine, and how will it stack up on our side?"

"If I were Le Lien, I would investigate the possibility of other Qwave pieces of equipment having fallen in the hands of Roamers, who instead of trying to unload them on the black market, have figured out how to use them for purposes that may not agree with the present views of the Great Ones on the inevitability and necessity of kinks in the universal makeup,"

"That's a mouthful, Saka, but yes it has occurred to me as well," Vera half-joked.

"I imagine you wouldn't want to give Wind a fully loaded laptop, would you? I mean, he's going to want something that resists him like mine did the first time around. So, if he gets a dud, he's going to get suspicious, don't you think?" Saka asked, not necessarily seeking an answer.

"It all depends on what he knows and expect. I believe that, based on what I heard, Geir named the interface attached to the computer, a *gravitational wave detector*. How far off was he, really?"

"Then you should know, as well as I do, that Le Lien may have a problem. What's the next best thing to Roamers squeaking by, one at a time, in unpredictable and dangerous ways?" Saka posed.

"Many at once, the easy way? I hated the thought when it first flashed by; now I know I'm gonna have to do what every Angel dreads, that is, pay a visit to the Interverse!" Vera practically lamented.

A seed algorithm wasn't something one saw like a picture on a tunnel wall. It was a program embedded within the spatial spectrum of a precise threshold between two distinct energy fields that vibrated at frequencies near-indistinguishable from each other. So, technically, it was invisible to the eye. A trained Angel, such as Vera, could detect one, but when linked, they were theorized to be formidable chameleons. Those placed by Dzalarhons' team had been engineered to tap Gestalt George's ghost image, with the aim of back-tracking the deletion process that started with the migration from Angel City to the New Guild Center, and ended when George pulled the plug on itself. They were designed to reverse said process, until in turn, all became darkness around the Angels, while the Realms would remain forever shut. Most seed algorithms shared the same basic topology. It was why a group such as XVII, without the ability to design their own, could acquire the open version, and then, with some skills, adapt it to whatever specification they wished and duplicate it. Dzalarhons went further in creating a self-cloning variation that first fooled Qwave techs. Since hers had been programmed to feed on the ghost image, without it, that model was technically useless. Past a certain magnitude of tweaking, the seeds couldn't be back-coded; thus, Qwave had to generate a static simulation of George's makeup to energize them without giving them the nutrients to grow – just enough momentum to activate the thresholds between the old and new tunnels, but barely enough to sustain an opening of more than a few seconds per command.

Sam's job was to lead to where thresholds existed. Since all the seeds had automatically positioned themselves near them; it then would be left to Qwave to isolate them and turn the programs to switches. At which point, Vac, Vera, Saka, and Sam would forage further for clues into Qo'ai-Marael's whereabouts.

Saka had wished to return to Angel City, mostly to immerse herself in the vacuous ambience of what the place once was. The absence of light was a fundamental counterpart to her powers, one she couldn't ignore if she was to harness the full potential of her gift.

After crossing the first threshold between two sets of the many numerically identified tunnels, the team quickly found itself overlooking the empty hall from one of the stone balconies. The light Saka shone over the space seemed to instantly bring it to life, but only to the extent that the vast floor was once brimming with exuberance – the memory promptly faded to expose a sight of terminal desolation.

"Somehow we managed to bring an element of duality to the Realms, something Xarn is intent on not introducing to his world," Vera said pensively.

"The old and new cities of Angels are not exactly the Realms, but a point of entry into them – the same goes for the tunnels. In some respect, each Great Hall with its tentacle-like corridors, forms a separate world latched onto the 'multiversal' reality of the Realms," Vac returned. "The duality you speak of cannot reach the Warriors' domains, unless it is inherent to their makeup. Part of Angel involvement in helping the Realms emerge as their own Oneness, was to design and build this Hall as a means for each of the pocket realities to connect with each other. It was our intention when we freed the Warriors from the fires of the battles; it was also what we saw with Amaterasu: the one probability that would satisfy the original Oneness as it looked for another like itself."

"It's a story that keeps on evolving every time you speak about it, Vac; is there ever going to be an end to it?" Saka teased.

"You know as well as I do that my knowledge of

it is on an evolutionary path. The Realms are in the making, so are their pasts as well as their probable developments. The present follows the sinuous line of possibilities. One day Joonas is the enemy, the next the savior – today he's back on the list of suspects. It all ties together in the larger picture. Speaking of Joonas, he was one of the original designers of this Great Hall. It wasn't until he witnessed the disastrous evolution of the human race that he rethought his participation, until he eventually fought against saving the Warriors. He had hoped another probability involving a different species would have poked its head, but it wasn't meant to be. In the end, he realized how inevitable it all was. He then finished what he had started by supplying the codes. Hektor was akin to a necessary sideshow that brought tension and release to the process," Vac returned.

"The part about Angel City being latched onto the Realms is new to me; can you elucidate?" Saka asked.

"There was no such division when the Realms were still attached to the mother reality. Focused as we are in the physical, we exist at the fulcrum point of manifestation which excludes the vantage from which one sees evolution as a panoramic whole. But before I digress, without Angel City and the lanes, there would be no collective of the Realms; the domains would have had no opportunity to evolve beyond the individual dream of the Warrior, which would have eventually faded into ennui then forgetfulness. In the best case scenario, a few of them could have attained creational status and formed into complete universes, but as mentioned on other occasions, the Realms do not lend themselves to open, foreseeable futures – we learn as we go. Where we're at for now is history in the making, with the distinction that the past belongs to an entirely different Oneness, and the future is dependent on the unraveling of potential by a cast of improvisational players. Did I elucidate the point?" Vac asked, while indicating he was finished.

"I guess it's a lot like leading a normal human life – go with the flow," Saka joked.

"Except we know why we're here," Vera pointed.

The Great Hall of Angel City provided no clue as to Qo'ai-Marael's movements. Sam led the team out of the place via a portal the two Masters and Saka had no idea existed. He then guided them along a corridor until he found the threshold to its active counterpart. Vera operated a Qwave device that allowed Portals to detect them from the other end. The seed was common to both sides; thus could be triggered from either one. Finding thresholds didn't require leaving the live part of the system, but since the missing elder was believed to be tucked somewhere in the old tunnels, it was consensed they would continue to proceed from that end.

Saka had difficulties understanding what Le Lien was aiming at by locating the thresholds. Inventorizing seeds made sense from the standpoint of logistics, but access to the old tunnels was still possible via the paths of the arrested realms out of the lower hall. She couldn't fathom the advantage of a risky crossing, over the way that had seen the entire migration of the Masters from Angel City to the New Guild Center. She was aware of the weakening of the link, but as far as she knew, it still was strong enough to allow for safe passage, notwithstanding Snake's world was still very much alive and could always be used for access. She turned to Vac and Vera for answers.

"The lanes to the failed realms have always been weak except for the one Snake made his home out of; or at least, that's how it appears," Vac said. "It was theorized George lost interest in them because they led to no manifested reality, but I have left that question open for other possibilities to step in. Snake, as the story goes, carved the original tunnels; hence, 'Despair' is a misnomer projected by both you and Ma-1 in regard to your shared experience. So yes, as to your question, the lane to the volcano can always be used to reach Angel city and the old maze of corridors. It doesn't even have a threshold since the New Center technically belongs to its greater system. Do you follow me? The one and only reason why we made 'Despair' off-limit, is out of consideration for Snake."

Vera took over,

"As reported by Master Grisha, Qo'ai-Marael entered the maze through one of the new tunnels. She's believed to have crossed over to the old lanes via one of the openings activated by Dzalarhons' seeds. So that you understand how it works, the thresholds, unlike portals, are not intended for access; they are essentially the points at which the two versions of the system are at their closest and practically share signatures. The seed algorithms were designed to transfer codes from one side to the other, the details of which are clear to all. But since the data path is wide enough to act as a portal, the rogue Angels used these thresholds as tools of evasion and disruption, means to appear and disappear at will, especially when in conjunction with the natural portals

59

that link each realm to all the others in dizzying numbers," Vera explained.

"It wasn't until Angels Lawrence and Jen's treasons were unveiled that we realized Portals had been starved of the information that could have helped not only map these median points, but also understand their intrinsic principals; namely how to pick and choose between destinations. The Warriors understood them intuitively, but the logic behind their collective functions was denied to us. Of course, in the light of the majority of the Realms remaining unresponsive, their purpose is locked with them, for they are reduced to only serve at tunnel-hopping in mind-numbing variations," Vac followed with.

"It still doesn't explain why we shouldn't just ask for Snake's permission," Saka pointed. "Plus, aren't locating thresholds and looking for Qo'ai-Marael two separate assignments?"

"To this point, we have been staying on the side of the old system, aiding Portals uncovering seeds. But eventually we'll have to start crossing back and forth. We're close to all of them being accounted for, as far as the hundred and thirty-two or so assumed-active tunnels are concerned. But we also suspect some of these seeds have found their way into layers that were, to this point, unthought of – a detail that came to light when Qo'ai-Marael evaded detection. Eventually, we'll be crossing into one of those places; Sam is here to help us with it," Vera further elaborated.

"Are you actually saying there are yet more levels to the maze? I can see side rooms perhaps, places similar to were you guys found the drunken team, or secluded caves for the likes of Joonas to heal their wounds. After all, isn't that the reason Qo'ai-Marael is also in there – for healing?" Saka inquired, unconvinced.

"It goes without saying the seeds created havoc in the two systems. As I already mentioned, the thresholds were not meant to be passages. The scanners are picking neither Joonas' nor Qo'ai-Marael's signature; there're simply not in there. Hektor's Dogs can still be found drinking to their hearts' content, apparently caught in a perpetual loop in the likeliness of the errant souls of the buffets on the defunct mother planet," Vac reiterated.

"At any rate," Vera added, "we don't know what's in there and why the three remaining XVII infiltrators didn't vanish as well. We are left to assume Joonas and Qo'ai-Marael worked in tandem to delete the Gestalt's ghost image. We have no idea how they did it, but as original coders they know more than we do. It's highly plausible their actions led to their shared predicament; we're here to figure out what happened to them, so I suggest we move on."

Saka agreed in spite of perceived contradictions around Joonas and Qo'ai-Marael's roles in disabling the seeds. She thanked Vac and Vera for their patience – she was ready to shine a light on the path ahead. Sam took off at once – the search was on!

6 – MULTIPLE EXITS

When the first Angel City Masters tried to reach the Realms, they were systematically returned to the Great Hall in random fashion, meaning that if they entered one tunnel, they came out of another – never the same twice. They stopped trying, not ever seeing the point. Had all the realms been open then, it would eventually have made sense. Unbeknownst to them, there was a message in the pattern, as random as it was. It spelled, *"You can go anywhere you choose, from any point."* Portals failed to capitalize on the nuance; they should have known from the get-go that there was trouble with the Realms – much ahead of Ma-l's discovery of Angel City. The scouts missed on defining the intricate lacing that was meant to be the Warriors' paths to each other's domains. Nothing was random about these revolving doors – they were simply mischaracterized.

Portals, Qwave, and Le Lien had finally come to terms with their nature; they had been mapped, and with the aid of a locator, the tunnels could now be traveled in any chosen order. Of course, there were no destinations to them – only loops within a closed system. It was an improvement nonetheless.

Without codes, the old lanes could no longer connect to the Warriors' domains. The only life that breathed into them was through the very temporary opening of the thresholds activated by the seeds. With the deletion of the Gestalt, purpose had been snuffed out of them. Technically, nothing was to come of them, and nothing could be concealed by them that could be scanned by a common hand-held device, especially an energy form, physical or not. There were one hundred and thirty-two of them, not including those to the arrested realities. It would not take long for Vera and her team to zig-zag their way in and out of the live and dead systems before they would run out of places to explore. They had scanners, light, and Sam – Joonas and Qo'ai-Marael had nowhere to hide. That was, if they were indeed hiding.

When Great One Amaterasu got wind of Qo'ai-Marael's entrance into the system of tunnel, she knew Joonas was in trouble; not from the threat of the elder historian's presence, but from his inability to delete the Gestalt's ghost image on his own. The female Master did not go in there to evade her fate, but rather, because she too knew Joonas would fail. George had a safety feature: the codes to his full demise were split between its designers so that no single individual could have control over the termination process. As the head programmer, Joonas thought he could get around it, but he was misled. Perhaps he was just being Joonas, not fully free from the arrogance that had landed him in there in the first place, his initial enthusiasm having overshot his abilities. The old codes existed within the spatial geometry of the revolving portals – any of the access points could act as a master control. Joonas could see they were being reanimated by the seeds, fed from the ones he had provided the Angels with to fire up the new system. George's ghost image acted as positive potential to which the energy was attracted as it built onto its form. Every time he entered data in the extracted holographic display, the corresponding seed denied him access. He cursed his reluctance to expand on his knowledge while at the helm of Hektor. He felt slow, out of touch with the science that had been put into the programs; especially when he knew Dzalarhons was, at best, an average coder. Had he been on top of his game, the whole thing would have been a breeze. But he had let the game slip; now the Realms were on the brink of imminent collapse.

"In dire need of a refresher course?" he heard from behind.

He didn't turn around.

"Someone here to pay her dues?" he probed, still furiously entering data.

"You should know it takes at least two to dance to this kind of music," the voice returned.

"I lost trust in dancing partners the day I found myself alone on the dance floor," he replied.

"This is the last song; you may want to reconsider," Qo'ai-Marael said as she came to his side.

"For once, I welcome not being in charge; you lead," he returned.

Qo'ai-Marael opened a second display and began entering data. The two errant Masters became one, finally reconnected to the source of what got them in there in the first place. And a dance it was, neither waltz nor tango, but fluid movements born of an improvised order that carried within it the authority of the calm after a biblical storm. The seeds began to lose steam. Before long, the process of transfer unpolarized itself, until it went into full reversal, at which point the energy of the ghost image became caught in the vortex and was entirely siphoned by it. Deprived of its raison d'être, seed activity ceased instantly.

Amaterasu, fresh out of the Le Lien emergency

meeting, stood before them, gazing deep into their bruised Angel souls. She was neither threatening nor smothering, but radiated a quality that betrayed the firmness of love.

"You two deserve a better resting place than a hole amid the death of these caves. There are no healing powers left to these walls. You surely must remember the promise we made to each other when we first surveyed the possibility of the Realms, way back when. We knew it was going to take a lot out of each of us, for it still does. We all have a place in the land of the dunes, yours awaits your presence – you must now follow me."

It was neither a request nor an order – it was an immutable part of a contract. The three traveled from Joonas Halls to the Keyhole Lake hub, outside the realms of Hektor, then they crossed over into the domain of the Great Ones, where, amid the red dunes, the Dove and his long lost partner, Guild historian Qo'ai-Marael, had their home. Their work was done.

———

Vac was aware Joonas and Qo'ai-Marael would never be found in the tunnels. Had he shared that knowledge with Vera and Saka, the reasons for Le Lien to be on a search mission would have become nonexistent. To him, there was no such thing as concealing information, when information of greater latitude was at risk of being overlooked. It all hinged, at the time of the battles, on the philosophical issue of allowing the human race to thrive or not. Factions were formed that morphed into multiple groups with various agendas. There were also the forgotten tribes of dissident Angels that either refused to be assimilated or were excluded to join, hordes that retreated into the folds of the underworld when the Guild's wingspan overshadowed their original territories. Hektor and XVII had acted their parts in both preventing the Realms from happening and making them happen, but there was still one player left that hadn't yet been identified. In Vac's views, it was one that was integral to the fundamental makeup of the new Oneness, one that existed at the core of the philosophical choice of allowing the worlds of the Warriors to grow as a collective; one whose very purpose was masked by the reluctance of the Realms to offer a glimpse into their foreseeable developments. The possibility of a corruption of gestalt George in conjunction with the unresponsiveness of the remaining domains, amounted to an in-play game with very few moves left before checkmate.

Sam led the team until all the thresholds were found and their corresponding seeds accounted for. Even though Vera and Saka were under the impression the search was on for Qo'ai-Marael, Sam had been given a different set of instructions by Vac on a private telepathic pathway.

"We're looking for two things, my good friend; one being the place where the two Angels were last standing, the other – a different exit out of the tunnels. You're up for it?"

"By 'out of the tunnels,' you don't mean into the Hall, do you, Sir Vac?" Sam asked.

"No, the other out," Vac replied.

Finding the first item was easy. Sam came to the location of the revolving portal that had supplied the means to input the codes that defeated George's ghost image. He sat there, indicating the job was done. Vera and Saka looked at each other, obviously expecting further action, but that was all there was. The Le lien operative squatted to face Sam.

"What then, my friend; we know what this portal is and what it does, don't we?

"The portal does what it does, I know that. Here is where those people left," Sam returned.

"They could not have left through here without reappearing elsewhere in the system," Vera affirmed.

"Yes, the three of them left through here," Sam insisted, indicating the ground.

"Three? are you sure?!" Saka and Vera voiced in unison.

Vac cut in.

"Perhaps scanning is de rigueur. I suggest you two use the Qwave device and the stone in tandem."

"I only bring the stone out at its behest. Nothing so far indicates Amaterasu wishes to connect," Saka said somewhat protectively.

"Your stone isn't just a one-trick pony, Goddess – the time has come to explore its many uses."

Vera had fired-up the hand-held locator she had set for spatial memory. Amid its settings was the option of linking to other devices, followed by a list that included a subgroup of vibrational mediums – chalcedony was among them. As soon as the selection was made, the stone in the pouch around Saka's neck began to drone.

"I'm getting why I'm supposed to be here – further education, I guess," Saka said, taking the stone out.

The holographic data generated by the white gem from environmental memory, confirmed Amaterasu had joined Joonas and Qo'ai-Marael. It was therefore presumed the Great One used her carry-on portal to access the tunnels and take the two Angels with her.

"It looks like she had her reasons," Vac said, "I guess she will explain sooner than later."

"It seems to indicate our work is done in here; Le Lien has no cause for doubting Amaterasu's choices. I'll finalize my report then take Sam back to where he belongs. Great job on his part though," Vera said.

"Where Sam belongs is for Sam to decide. For now, he's not quite done with the task he set himself up for," Vac countered.

Barely had the Angel finished his sentence that Sam was up and through the revolving portal – the group narrowly avoided coming apart. They landed in a tunnel that went on and on, apparently unwilling to connect with the Great Hall.

"I thought these portals were no longer active in the old system," Vera pointed.

"Not since the Gestalt was erased, but this one apparently rebelled," Vac humored

"Don't tell me you knew all of this would happen," Saka probed, mildly tested.

"It was in the realm of possibilities – let's just leave it at that," he replied firmly.

Sam picked up in speed as if he had been chasing after something. Saka's light brightened, turning the milky grey stone of the walls to a blinding reflection. The gem in her pouch began vibrating. Noises converged as if multiple channels were being played on some mad radio. Without warning, all turned white around them.

Before they had a chance to wonder about their collective fate, Vera and Sam were back on the Eureka waterfront with Pau, Maggie, and Wind, while Linda Sue appeared to be walking her dog away from them.

The two canids connected on their private line.

"Was that the 'out' you asked for, Sir Vac?" Sam enquired informally.

"Most delightfully so, Sam, you outdid yourself!"

Saka, who felt she should better keep her cool, turned to Vac and asked, "Isn't it about the right time for the frog to show up – it's roughly that level of weird, don't you think?"

Vera shook off the fog from her head – this was least expected. Saka and Vac were now in Eureka, which meant the case of Wind and the Interverse had turned a corner toward the uncharted – she couldn't wait to get Pau onto it.

"Are you sure you guys are up for driving to Oakland tonight?" she abruptly asked the couple.

"That's what we planned for, Wind's got work to do," Maggie replied.

Wind was thinking. The only work he had ahead of him was to locate Linda Sue and her laptop, but Maggie couldn't know that. Until that happened, Vera was the closest thing to his quest.

"Aren't you supposed to be back in Berkeley at some point?" he asked, as if to balance his upcoming answer.

"I'm transferring to Iceland in a few days –

science likes to travel," she replied, sensing he was contemplating his options.

"Since I was hoping to connect with you in the Bay Area, I guess we could spent a bit more time in Humboldt, if that's where you plan on being before you leave," he offered.

Maggie refrained from objecting, while Pau wondered if Vera wasn't asking for trouble.

"Let me call Marshall," the young Master said.

Slaughter wasn't particularly pleased with the arrangement, but he understood it loosely tied to the case of the downtown loft. He agreed to let Maggie and Wind stay in the freshly remodeled basement. The safe with the two new Qwave laptops – his and Pau's – had been moved to a hidden location in the ground floor office.

"You'll be staying at the estate if it's agreeable," Pau said as she turned her cell phone off.

"Thanks, I hope it's not too much trouble," Wind returned.

"You're not saying..." Pau thought to herself.

Saka and Vac noticed the group a distance away from their boardwalk landing spot. They instinctively turned around to avoid recognition. The Goddess wasn't ready to assume her Linda Sue role quite yet.

"I suppose this is an assignment," she said, probing Vac.

"Yes, you planned it some time ago. Remember your yearning to get back to your old life? That was when," he returned matter-of-factly.

"You call that planning?" she riposted.

"You're asking me?" he humored.

Saka understood what he meant; their arrival in town was the result of a causality that had its roots in the reluctance of the Realms to open their doors. Vac made it clear he didn't know any more than she did how it would all play out.

"For once, I can only assume we are on the right track, though I am unclear as to what path that may be," he advanced.

"All I know is that we came poorly equipped – no cash, no credit cards, no ID. Worst of all, the only friends who could shack us are presently indisposed with guests that can't know we're here – brilliant!" Saka exclaimed.

"You're the Goddess – you'll figure it out." Vac affirmed, the least concerned.

7 – GANDREAL

Angel Gandreal was one of the many among the fallen ones who had wished to join the ranks of the Masters of the Guild. His clan had fought the uphill evolutionary battles of his race, with the aim to attain a level of consciousness that would shine its light over the lesser tribes. He never understood why the league saw his views as counter-evolutionary; surely, the might of knowledge rose above decadence and groveling. Gandreal missed on the nuance the Guild was not a ruling body. Since guidance was not on the list of the Angel's battle maneuvers, he bitterly took his tribe to a place he knew the Masters had no wish to steward, a world still forming from the stuff of rejected potential, a series of discarded layers of creation similar to abandoned scripts, like maligned paintings, gesso-ed over, to not be seen again.

But he never totally lost touch with the Guild and its advancements. He found vulnerabilities in its system of portals that allowed him to eavesdrop on the news and intrigue, while in the guise of humans or other species. Every time he returned to the Interverse, it was with added knowledge, a greater understanding of the deep mechanics that made the gears of the Guild, as well as those of the "surface universes," mesh. But it also came with a proportional sense of what he had been denied – the gains reflected the loss. The pride that arose from cognizance was offset by a deep yearning to erase the injustice he had suffered at the hands of the Masters. In his heart, he was one of them. Reality – perhaps as the result of an irremediable oversight – had been unwilling to challenge the grounds for his rejection. So when he got wind of the work that was set forth by the original team in regard to helping the Realms, he made a promise to himself to never miss on the action. By the time of the Great Battles, he was Misu, an arrow-yielding fighter of the Trout Rock tribe, deep in the heart of the Warner Mountains.

Even though Misu made it to the first gathering of the dream meadows, he remained a minor speaker. He was charismatic, observant; above all, he was encouraging of others to tell their stories, but he never told his. He was also the first to stop attending. The group was large then – it was perhaps why his absence went unnoticed. Since Warriors were not naturally bound to relationships or alliances, no-one unobserved when participants first ceased showing up.

Ma-l, Xarn, and Enola were the latest arrivals to the meadows. In fact, they attended their first gathering as Misu had seen his last – they never crossed. The detail in of itself was of no consequence to the collective spirit, save for one thing: the three Warriors were also the last ones to meet at the meadows. By then, one by one, the attendants had stopped coming. Ma-l, Xarn, and Enola wondered who of the three would be next, but that never happened. They resumed with the gatherings until they finally agreed to take a break from them. Soon the meadows were forgotten.

In contrast to his Warrior kin, Misu was first and foremost a Fallen Angel who had cunningly arranged for his place among them. Also, unlike them, his fate in the stone wasn't one of suffering and gruesome rise out of isolation, but one of patience and planning. How the Guild omitted to notice the infiltration revolved on the chaos of the times. Saving the Warriors was akin to a last ditch effort, a quasi-desperate move to rescue the reality of the Realms from oblivion. When Amaterasu said that the probability for them to thrive rested on an infinitesimal, quivering strand of hope at the farthest confines of time and space, it was exactly what she meant – the closest option to no chance at all.

It was thus with great interest that Gandreal followed the work that had gone into creating the tunnels, the programming of the seeds that would eventually morph into the larger Gestalt, the carving by Snake; all that which preceded the catastrophic decoupling of the spiritual from humanity that culminated in Joonas's dissent and the battles against the Ones. He had ample time to prepare for the orchestration of his plan. The failures of Hektor and XVII were part of it, part of the disruption that would keep the Angels blinded from the obvious. The Warriors were to be mere collateral damage – Gandreal and his tribe would oversee the new Oneness. It was not a war against the Guild, there was no desire to make a point; it was a wrong righted – no questions or explanations needed.

The problem for Gandreal was that he was locked inside his world, waiting for events to unravel according to his original plan; one that did not include Ma-l, Xarn, and Enola, or any of the participant from Earth for that matter. He had been able to trap the Warriors inside their realities with the help of the corrupted Gestalt, shut them from the dream meadows one at a time, making them deaf to the call of the perpetual conveyors that were the lanes –

paths which never stopped serving the gathering grounds. Without the collective, the Warriors would be starved, stifled, atrophied, until they would surrender their will to exist. Soon, his Interverse domain would latch onto each of their realms, unload its hordes into their virgin spaces, build cities, roads and waterways, and open their skies to exploration and conquest. Gandreal's plan was grossly flawed, but the fact remained the Realms were closed.

Vac, for once, had not kept his hypothesis of a forced corruption of the Gestalt to himself. Amaterasu, Le Lien, and the three Warriors had been briefed, each paying due notice to the implications of such an act. The concept of an infiltration into the Warrior body was inconceivable though – not even Vac was willing to go there. It would have amounted to an unforgivable oversight for an Angel to have missed on the signature of a non-Warrior. The alternative, meaning such an impostor could have obtained help from the Guild, was also out of question. Lead operatives Liv and Spencer had been probing the depths of possibilities of an alien player concealed in the dual system of tunnels, as well as Joonas Halls and its twin, George's original gift to Ma-1, but nothing was picked up by their scanners. Whoever corrupted the Gestalt and shut the Realms was no longer in there. However, Lillian and Vera were unconvinced the Warriors were not jeopardized at a higher level, but they kept their doubts to themselves for fear of inadvertently pointing an accusatory finger in the wrong direction. Until proven otherwise, an Angel's integrity was to always remain unchallenged, even in hypothetical cases involving no-one in particular. It was one of the core principals of the Guild to not assume a mistake was made until a tangible demonstration of failure of performance was put forth. As far as Le Lien was concerned, the villain, if it indeed existed, would eventually leave a print, a token of their passage. Even the silence of nothingness emitted the faintest of echoes.

Ironically, not even Misu's patience was infinite. Not only were the Warriors locked in their realms, but so was he in his as part of the bargain. The Gestalt could not differentiate between him and the rest; therefore he had to wait until all the dominos had toppled over for the gates to open and for him to claim his prize. He still could visit the dream meadows, but for what purpose, since no-one was ever going to return there anyway? His realm could provide more stimulation that he would ever need; certainly more than a grassy patch under the moonlight. He felt curious though. He knew of the tunnels beyond his gate and of the Angels in the Great Hall. He had visited the multiple scenarios that involved Hektor and XVII, both he considered pawns of his plan. He saw the Gestalt transform from serving the collective of the Warriors, to working for him only. Finally, he witnessed Roamers taking over. What wasn't for Gandreal to see though, was naturally never inputted to the equation; hence, the probabilities he thought he surveyed past the separation of the Oneness, were in fact no probabilities at all. Rather, they were mere projections that leaned heavily on earlier sightings conjunct misplaced bravado. He couldn't know the Realms did not offer that option; no-one did. Whether his plan would manifest in perfect parallel with his hopes or not was contingent on how close he had come to merit what he believed he deserved; more precisely, whether or not he was truly cut to be a Master.

Misu's occluded vision was both a blessing and a curse for the other hundred and twenty-eight unopened realms. He was trapped, unable to free his world without George or the help of the dream meadows. In a nutshell, he could no longer get out unless he was rescued by Ma-1, Xarn, or Enola, neither of them having any idea who he was. Like the others, he couldn't hear the call from the dream lanes, but he didn't know that either. In fact, the meadows were presently his only way out, had he not, long ago, psychologically blocked them out as a resource.

It was a vacuous time for the Realms and all those invested in their release. The tables that had turned on Misu did nothing but deeper bury the chances of the new Oneness to expand to its full potential. The three opened domains were enough to deserve the "collective" moniker, but certainly, greater aspirations were about to fall flat at the doorsteps of the original Oneness.

Gandreal's plan was ambitious, considering it relied on information he could only access via small windows at inconsistent intervals – the Interverse intersected unforeseeably with the surface universes, providing only erratic opportunities for its leaders to hop onto them – but he was determined and time wasn't a factor. He gathered as much as he deemed necessary for his complicated strategy, empowering his most trusted subjects with complex coordinates, such as consolidating teams of Roamers into organized units meant to operate like clockwork, up until the synching of the underworld with the reality of the Realms; at which point Gandreal would take charge again.

The fallen Angel prided himself in holding an exclusive item of knowledge, one only an advanced denizen of the Interverse could have accessed: the perfect coordinates at which his world would, with utter unpredictability, come into alignment with the new Oneness. He likened it to a paradox no Angel could comprehend. "Careful what you throw away!" he had once remarked about the Ones' discarded creational artifacts. One of them did indeed place the Interverse on a path with the Realms in an extremely remote probability, which triggered Gandreal's affinity for utmost minute details. Before long, the fragile discovery had germinated, soon to grown into an elaborate script.

8 – ROAMER UNVEILED

Saka looked at Vac as if he had been out of his mind. What could she do to make her predicament more comfortable? "What Linda Sue can't do, maybe Saka can," he had said. Saka had a rock in a pouch she could sell for a couple of dollars at a gem store – that was about the depth of it – plus she was barefoot and the clothes she wore were grounds for arrest. She made Vac laugh.

"I don't even own a carry-on portal," she lamented.

"You're thinking like Linda Sue, which is a good thing for why we're here, but that won't get you very far. Rather, ask yourself what Saka would do in your place," Vac suggested

"It's funny, it feels like she stayed with Ma-l, and now I'm back in the self I thought I had left behind," she said bemused.

"Don't worry, they're both the same; only the change of environment makes it appear that way," Vac added.

"OK, let me think," she said.

She could live without an ID, but she needed some cash. It was evening – never a good start. She noticed a short line at an automated teller machine up the street; she visualized it as a money fountain. "Strange thought," she observed, as if it had come from somewhere else. She walked to it. By the time she and Vac reached the bank, the line was gone. As she faced the note dispenser, the stone vibrated. Within seconds, she retrieved enough cash to solve her most immediate problems.

"That was easy," she told Vac, relieved.

"Just like I said," he humored.

The army surplus store, two blocks away, was still open; she found all she needed to look like she belonged. She even bought a leash and collar for Vac at a second hand store.

Saka changed in the bathroom of the Shipwreck Saloon while Vac waited, tied to a post in the small courtyard that passed for a patio. She reappeared victorious, ordered a virgin mojito and came to join the tethered Master under the jaundice glow of the aging cocktail sign.

"We need a plan," she telepathized. "But first we must figure out what we're doing here – any ideas?"

Vac had gotten the latest from Le Lien on Vera's work with Pau; it was time to give Saka the lowdown on what she was to expect.

"How can the loft be tied to Wind?" she asked, befuddled.

"We don't know if the two cases are related, but they landed simultaneously on Marshall and Pau's desk," Vac replied.

"OK, that's one thing, but what do they have to do with the Realms, and what's up with Sam?"

"It's a good question which I am unfortunately unable to answer. I left it up to him to give us a pointer in the direction of the locked Warriors; I didn't quite expect we would land in Eureka. Honestly, I am unfamiliar with his means of transportation. I don't doubt that by now, you've figured out that we're in uncharted territory," Vac returned.

"That's a first, Vac doesn't know!" she exclaimed, forgetting her surroundings.

A few inebriated solo customers briefly looked up before returning to glass-gazing, or fiddling with their phones.

"I'm hoping Vera was able to convince Maggie and Wind to stay in town for a while longer, we're counting on you to bump into them tomorrow," Vac said.

"So, that's the plan?! Are you sure you didn't set me up for it?" she humored.

"Hardly – for once, you and I are in the same boat, at the mercy of the same currents. An interesting first, I must confess."

"Let's get a room, I know a place that allows dogs," she said, as she abruptly got up.

They walked away from Old Town in the direction of the main thoroughfare, where motels, gas stations, muffler shops, and fast food joints competed for the attention of the weary traveler. The Blue Lodge was tucked between two rows of tall eucalyptus trees that shielded it from a hubcap store on one side, and a bike repair shop on the other.

There were nicer and cleaner rooms in town, but none better suited for a Goddess of the Realms and a dog who went as far as time itself.

———————

The next morning, as Marshall and Pau left for the office, Vera proposed that they should all meet for lunch at a downtown café. They opted for a tucked-in sandwich and salad place, and set the time for one o'clock to accommodate an earlier appointment with a client from the loft. Vera would figure out a way to entertain Maggie and Wind until then. She didn't have to; the two didn't get out of bed until eleven. Instead, she took Sam out for a walk up the forest trail behind the property.

"What made you decide to return so soon?" she asked the canid as they started to climb.

"It was kind of an accident; I was hoping to get back to Sir Vac's place," Sam replied.

"So, you weren't the one who opted to come back here then?"

"The frog's always around when I want to come home," he returned.

"So, no frog this time around?"

"Nope."

"Could you take us back to the tunnel if we asked?

"Depends on what's at stake."

"What do you mean?" Vera asked

"I mean, what's the point of going back if you don't really mean it? It's like chasing squirrels; I do it because it's the only thing that matters at the time."

"Are you saying that us coming back together was meant to be?"

"What else could it be?" Sam asked, surprised.

"How did you figure the exact time at which to return then?"

"You said time wasn't a factor – I believed you. It's not my first outing without Maggie noticing, you know," Sam countered.

Vera laughed aloud. Sam said it all without revealing anything. He was a miracle being, the one in a million that walked through life without ever touching the ground. He and the frog belonged to a world lost to most, a place teeming with corridors long forgotten. He didn't need to know, he simply was the essence of trust and bliss.

They returned to the house just in time to see Maggie emerge from the basement.

"Morning – there's some fresh coffee brewing in the kitchen, help yourself," Vera offered, before she ran upstairs to her room to call Pau at the office.

"So, what's the plan for today?" the young Master asked.

"Aside for meeting for lunch, I don't know, but I still need to tell you about the little detour Sam and I took last night while at the boardwalk."

Vera described the time spent with Saka, Vac, and Sam in the systems of tunnels, and how they ended up coming back together.

"You're saying Saka's in town with Vac?" Pau double-checked.

"Correct, that's pretty much the crux of it. As far as Sam's concerned, it's meant to be."

"In other words, Linda Sue's around; that's why you insisted on Maggie and Wind spending more time, am I right?"

"That's the angle, girlfriend," Vera returned.

"Transferring to Iceland, hey? Sorry, but making stories up wasn't part of my Guild training," Pau said.

"Guild training is a base; team training comes with its own manual. Sorry for the bad influence; got to go – see you at 1:00!"

Vera hung up the handset. She much favored classic phones over mobiles – something to do with the way they felt in her hand.

She took a quick shower, fed Sam, and made sure Maggie and Wind would be ready for the lunch gathering – it was a solid half-hour drive to Eureka. She swung by the small office to check for calls left on the answering machine – it was then that she noticed the place had been searched. The safe had been tampered with, but not opened. Almost all the markers she had placed before taking Sam on his walk, had been disturbed. She was aware that leaving Wind and Maggie by themselves in the house was a risk, but she had to see for herself how desperate they were – all doubts were gone.

Saka and Vac got up early. The Goddess needed to connect with Marshall Slaughter, who, she knew, liked to swing by Café Noir before eight. She remembered Maggie as a late riser, so the chance of bumping into her then was improbable. She wanted her ex-boss to be aware of her presence in town before the unavoidable encounter.

She was right; Marshall was standing in line. The memory of the early days of the search for Olaf flashed before her eyes. She tied Vac to the bicycle stand, stepped inside, cutting to the front of the line to tap Slaughter on the shoulder. He turned around, looking briefly surprised.

"It's funny, I had been thinking about you – now you're here!" he exclaimed.

The two hugged like old lovers, who wisely had traded for the safety of a lasting friendship.

"Well, I didn't expect it'd be so soon, but it became inevitable, whichever way I turned. One can't simply disappear when there's unfinished business," she said.

"It doesn't look like our old friend Wind is convinced you're still alive, so yes, for everyone's sake, it's just as well you're in town. Listen, I have to meet with some clients; I'm just here to grab a cup to go and be on my way. We're all getting together at Café Spooner at one, so why don't you arrange to be in the neighborhood; that'll give you time to make up a story!"

"I'm with Vac; he's outside – can't keep a Master waiting!"

She laughed, pointing at the well-behaved dog patiently sitting like a Buddha in the morning sun.

"Got to say hi!" Marshall rejoiced.

He paid for his coffee and croissant then the two met with Vac on the sidewalk. It was for the length of such a moment that the Angel cherished being just a dog: the touch and scent of old friends, the emanation of love and joy, all incomparable time gems that lined the paths of indelible sense-oriented memories. He couldn't speak with Marshall, but he could feel with him.

The group rode from Fieldbrook in Wind and Maggie's van; they were only marginally late. Vera had tried to not burden Marshall with the case of the Roamer – if it truly was what the man had become. Slaughter probably wouldn't notice the minimal shuffling in his home office, so she opted to keep it to herself. After all, it appeared Wind was more interested in information than he was into disrupting the investigator's well-being. It was most likely a shot in the dark on his part.

Maggie was cheerful; for once she appeared straight. They sat at an outside table in the shade of the trees that lined the adjacent square. It was a beautiful, sunny day, with only the occasional cotton ball cloud casting a brief shadow. Sam lay peacefully by his water bowl.

The conversation centered on pot business: South County crops versus upper northeastern ones, indoor versus outdoor, organic versus chemicals, water diversion issues, the feds vis-à-vis state laws... No-one cared except for Wind, who naturally enjoyed being the center of attention. Marshall remembered him as a self-effacing individual who didn't talk much, deducing the man was on much harder stuff than weed. The topic almost seamlessly switched to computers while Maggie was in the restroom. Marshall and Pau decided to let Vera take over. Paradoxically, the couple had not connected since individually learning of Saka's visit; they simply assumed the other didn't know. Not so coincidentally, Linda Sue was on her way, nonchalantly walking her dog down the alley that led to the square.

Wind saw her first – he stopped talking mid-sentence while looking fixedly as if in the throes of a seizure. Vera asked what the matter was. He ignored her, abruptly standing up.

"Hey sister!" he called. "Remember me?!"

"Yeah, Wind, right? Long time no see!" Saka returned, feigning a lack of interest as she got near.

Instead, she went straight to Marshall to give him a hug, just as Maggie returned from the washroom. The two friends exchanged high-pitched giggles in a display approved by Vera. Pau wasn't quite sure of what to do since the three were not supposed to know each other. She simply waited for the opportunity to introduce herself. Wind was left hanging dry. To Linda Sue, he was a flicker in time, the man who had failed at cracking a computer password over two years ago; she couldn't pretend he represented anything more without revealing he was being snared. Wind took it as a rebuke, but it was his out-of-control ego feeling it – the script unspooled at its own revolution.

It didn't take long before questions poured in.

"So, how have you been; where are you staying these days?" Maggie asked.

"Oh, I've been moving around; not sure where I want to be, really... I kinda like it here, maybe Trinidad. I finally decided to get out of town and see the world, so I've been traveling for the last couple of years. I've only been in town for two days; me and Vac here are staying at a motel on Broadway. What about you?" Saka replied.

The Goddess managed to turn vagueness into carefree casualness. She was a bohemian who didn't have to answer to specificity. She abruptly turned to Wind.

"Still cracking passwords?" she asked with pointed irony, not waiting for Maggie to answer.

"If I had known back then what I know today, I would have cracked that mother in no time," he answered defensively.

"You gave it your best, don't be hard on yourself," she said, ignoring where he wanted to go.

"I was in a hurry to get back south, I shoulda stuck around. Glad you got it going though."

"Thanks, I took it to a computer place; they reformatted it for me," she lied.

Wind faced her with a puzzled look.

"You did what?"

"Yeah, there was too much stuff in it, viruses and all. They put in a new hard drive and installed a fresh operating system. We never found out who the previous owner was."

"You kept the old drive?"

"Why would I want to do that?" she asked.

"They would have given it back to you, that's why. Anyway, if you still have that machine, I'd love to buy it from you?"

"I'm afraid it was stolen when I was traveling abroad. It was a hard loss. Now I don't even own a cell phone," she said laughing.

The humor was lost on Wind who was in a near-state of apoplexy. Pau thought he was going to smash the table with his fist. He got up like a dislocated puppet, walked towards the square then turned around.

"Bullshit!" he exclaimed.

"Calm down, Wind!" Maggie begged.

Saka stared at him with the look of someone who just had had enough of the bullshit herself.

"I don't know what's eating you, but I'm done with this – I can't say it was nice seeing you. Sorry, Maggie, I'm out of here! Marshall, I'll be in touch!"

She made a quarter turn, looked at Pau and Vera as if she saw them for the first time.

"Sorry, girls, maybe another time!"

She and Vac walked in the direction of the waterfront. Marshall stood up, faced Wind, and said, "I think it's time for us to part. Don't try to connect again; it's clear we don't share the same views on ethics. The meal's on me – Good luck!"

It was surgical. Wind tried to say something, but Maggie pulled him in the direction of the van.

"Come on babe, time to go home," she implored.

Vera connected briefly with Sam,

"You know where to go when the going gets tough, don't you?"

"I already told Sir Vac that I'd be looking for a new home. Maybe you can be in it too," he said.

"I think it's totally feasible; I would love that, and so would Bluefeather," she returned.

"Are you certain you got all you needed out of Wind?" Vac asked Saka.

"Yes, it's clear he's up to no good. He suspects I lied to him, but he's not sure. If the laptop had been stolen, he would have heard of it, especially a Qwave machine. Right now, he appears confused and rather frustrated, but what can he do about it? It's obvious he's on a mission, but for whom and for what purpose?"

"We know little about the Interverse and its denizens, but one thing is certain: although they may have various infrastructures, meaning they own technology, they're nowhere close to being capable of duplicating ours. Their need for a Qwave computer is for strict usage. My take is that Wind is trying to exploit a means to create lanes between the underworld and surface realities. In other words, Roamers seek to show up in large numbers," Vac said.

"An invasion?"

"At least a test run, if the probability map is correct."

"Meaning?"

"In some foreseeable future, Roamers will access this universe in hordes, but then will leave without much ado, save for reports of strange folds in the physical makeup," Vac returned.

"What would the point of that be? Isn't part of their economy based on stolen goods to resell on the black market? You're saying they're not going to touch a thing?"

"That's the strange ring about it, but the Guild deems it inconsequential, so no action is to be taken."

"But Le Lien is looking into it," Saka remarked.

"The Le Lien of the Realms operates independently from the main branch; they might as well call themselves by some other name," Vac returned.

"And of course, the Realms bar windows on their own development, am I correct?" Saka asked.

"'Bar' is incorrect. Rather, its makeup is not inclusive of probabilities as we understand them at this point. Let's call it incomplete potential," Vac replied.

The gem in the pouch vibrated imperceptively.

"I'm getting a message," Saka said.

"It's the stone, right? Work your intuitions, Goddess; they will lead you to the path to take."

"My intuitions tell me there's a connection between Wind and the Realms."

9 – JARRED

The next morning, Saka and Vac returned to Café Noir – Marshall and Vera were expecting them. They sat at a corner table under a landscape coincidentally painted by one of the loft artists. Pau was at the office helping Jarred getting organized around paperwork detail. Vac sat outside patiently waiting; he and the Le Lien operative conversed on a private channel.

"I have your personal artifacts at the house. If you intend on being around for a while, I suggest you get your license updated with DMV and pay a visit to your credit union," Slaughter advised.

"It wouldn't be a bad idea to close that account when I'm done, no point leaving traces that might arouse suspicion."

"As far as the authorities are concerned, your present address is at the estate, your mail's still coming to it; consider the basement apartment yours," he added.

The arrangement suited Saka. As part of a previous agreement, Marshall had been taking care of both her affairs and Olaf's; the difference being Swyndle was officially deceased while she wasn't. Although, only Wind and Alexander Cruz had nosed around her business, it was still possible others could look for her. With the lane open between the two Onenesses, Saka had the option of commuting back and forth; thus keeping Linda Sue visible in her old settings for the length of the case.

"It's evident the presence of two Masters and a Goddess amounts to more than just a mere visit. I also assume Wind isn't the only reason why you're here. Pau has shared the possibility of a link between the case we're currently working on and what happened yesterday with our two guests; you may want to clarify," Slaughter said.

"Vera can enlighten you on what Le Lien is up to; I'm personally working on intuition more than I am on logic. I'm not even sure I had much of a say in showing up here; though I trust it ultimately was my decision," Saka returned.

"I'll have to momentarily return to the Realms to consult with headquarters," Vera cut in. "I'll recommend that two agents monitor Wind's whereabouts at all times, while Pau, Saka, and I work on what ties the two cases. Of course, there's the issue of Jarred; we obviously can't jump in without him knowing what we're up to. Perhaps it's time he gets on with the program. Vac's in favor of it, pointing to a harmonious merging of minds."

"I'm not sure how he'll take it; it's a lot to catch up with. I'll ask Pau if she wants to volunteer for the task – as his guide, she's the one better suited for the job," the investigator offered.

And so, on a glorious ride around the Lost Coast in the plum-toned classic Jaguar, Pau told Jarred the story of the disappearance of Olaf Swyndle, the rise and fall of Hektor, as well as the threat of XVII to the Realms as an emerging new Oneness. She explained her role as Joonas' unsuspecting assistant, how the dark Master "borrowed" his body and practically left him to die, Liv's intervention, Lillian's part in his rehabilitation, and above all, her choice to become his personal guardian. By the end of the day, Jarred Gulliver knew everything there was to know about Angels, Gods and Goddesses, Great Ones, the Interverse, the story of Angel City, the old and new lanes, Snake, Ma-l's grand gathering, and the worlds of Xarn and Enola. He barely flinched. Perhaps the larger reality of his life experience was already intrinsically connected to his senses. It made Pau realize that she might have underestimated him. He was better fitted for his role than the image she had projected of a convalescent elder recovering from massive trauma. She thought, for a second, that she might have imprinted on him her own personal healing process in regard to her involvement with Hektor. He barely asked questions, as if he was merely comparing notes between what he already knew and what was being presented to him. He only demanded that they postpone his further education to accommodate time for the appreciation of their surroundings, as well as a pit stop in the quaint community of Honeydew for a quick lunch. Towards the end of the ride, as they drove along Avenue of the Giants, Gulliver turned to Pau and asked, "Do I now qualify for Guild training?"

Pau looked at him, dazzled.

"I'm not positive, Jarred, but you may have no need for it."

———————————

That evening, Pau asked for a one-on-one consultation with Vac. Her day with Jarred Gulliver had culminated in her feeling she was a mere cog in a program that concealed too many unknowns.

"The process you refer to is life in all of its possible scenarios," Vac explained. "Even Angels find themselves confounded by the multiplexity of options while on assignments that involve unsuspected players on many platforms simultaneously."

"How is Jarred Gulliver one such player?" she asked, confused.

"Jarred isn't more the player than you are. Your role, with Angels Shido and Shade, in starting the rehabilitation program for student defectors and returning Masters from difficult missions, naturally landed you in this job. You assisted Angel Jarred in his recovery from an extremely difficult assignment. His role as Joonas's host was far from accidental; he stirred the dark Master away from doing critical damage to our friends Marshall and Geir, and consequently, the Realms."

"All when I was under the impression I was guiding a wounded soul towards inner peace..." Pau sighed.

"You did and succeeded, but now you need to understand how everything fits together. Had Jarred not been one of us, you wouldn't have found yourself in position to assist him while on a job with Marshall. He put himself there so he would be part of the action when the time came, meaning he was aware of something brewing in the Interverse. even before he took the Joonas assignment. The reasons Liv and Spencer were there to rescue him, and later with Lillian to bring him back to health, were because he's one of Le Lien's owns. We are at a point at which his identity no longer needs to be protected, especially since you're going to work together. Everything is as it should be; all the players are on equal footing. As far as you're concerned, consider your personal healing complete; your position as a Master is sealed – you deserve it. Your relationship with Marshall puts you in an unusual position, as it binds you to where he operates; but we hope there is enough wiggling room in it, so that you can keep on fine-tuning your education. I trust you two can find an agreeable middle ground."

"My need to assist Jarred, most likely stemmed from my deep yearning to heal myself, or rather, to prove myself worthy of my place in the Guild and the Realms. I am honored to have served a Master while being able to simultaneously demonstrate my commitment to my work. But I have come to appreciate my involvement in these cases as well as my collaboration with Angel Vera. I am sensing the awakening of latent skills in regard to the field; thus, I would love to explore these callings and see where they lead me," Pau confessed.

"You are in the right place and time – take advantage of it. Masters are not limited to one set of skills; I am the living proof of it. The time has come for you to spread your metaphorical wings and soar on the winds of your passions."

————————

The next meeting was centered on coming to terms with identities and defining why Le Lien was so late admitting to their knowledge of Roamer activity.

"Why did you choose to stay away from Wind when he appears to be pivotal to your reasons to be working on these cases?" Pau asked Jarred Gulliver.

"Until now, my place was to stay in the shadow of difference. It suited me to be seen as an intellectually and emotionally fragile individual – I aroused no suspicions. Matters needed to coalesce into something a lot more substantial before you could be included. Only Spencer, Liv, and Vac were cognizant of my mission, which I must stress, was of private nature. I lost my latest subject – an addicted individual who fought hard to be released from the clutches of his personal demons – to the Interverse. He and some of his friends were taken by Roamers during a raid; they call it 'recruiting,' in the underworld. He was fragile and too close to his past, still vulnerable to identity swapping, or 'possession' as some call it. Later, when I visited the Interverse, I saw with my own eyes how Hektor replenished its kennels. On that particular day, short of a better word, Joonas himself did the picking. It was then that I witnessed how Roamers were allegorically leashed then taken away. I never saw my subject again, but I promised myself to side with those seeking to undermine Hektor's nefarious work, which explains how I ended up joining Le Lien. I stayed in that tortured world long enough to survey where it stood developmentally, in the process of which I came across information highly relevant to our case. Of course, I had to borrow a guise, which wasn't excessively difficult in a world full of lost souls. I briefly crossed paths with Wind there, and though there is no risk he would recognize me physically, I am unsure as to his skills of perception. It was simply safer to stay away during these last few days."

"That leaves me as the only human on the team, I guess," Slaughter remarked.

"Save for Vac, we're all human, Marshall; except we know our greater purpose. It won't take you long to catch up as an honorary Guild member; trust me on that – I was there," Saka responded.

"You went straight to becoming a Goddess, if I must remind you."

"Titles don't matter, get over it – we're all equal here!"

"Glad we all love each other," Vera cut in. "Now it's time we focus on our work. I'll be at headquarters to go over details; I should be back in a few hours. I will also see to setting up camp in Iceland, just in case Wind wants to connect. I'm hoping for Stefan to be my go-to-guy in linking me with the *Institute for Intelligent Machines* at Akureyri University. My take it that we have to play the game for a while, to see how deep this Roamer threat festers. We have to understand at what level they intend on utilizing Qwave technology to infiltrate surface reality, how much is in their hands, and who procured it to them. Le Lien will cross-check its list of recovered equipment in order to isolate why some of the stolen stuff is still floating. I will report as soon as I come back."

Vera left via the concealed office portal.

Jarred updated the team on his last meeting with one of the artists who was unable to make it to the earlier collective gathering; her name was Cecile. She remarked she was able to sort out faint human-like forms out of the plasmatic mass, while hearing whispers that felt more like random, undecipherable thoughts. Additionally, she mentioned knowing of other places where similar apparitions were also happening; all of them around groups or individuals tied to the arts or alternative thinking. In his personal views, the Master likened the places to soft spots, due to the malleable nature of the higher spiritual content of their environments – somewhat of a vulnerability in the context of the apparitions. It was to be stressed Roamers were already extremely adept at exploiting portals without detection; thus, a refining of those skills was highly credible.

Jarred's time in the Interverse, combined with his knowledge of Wind's actions, provided corroboration of linkage between the events – there was only one case. Additionally, Saka came forward with the message the stone had communicated to her that there was somehow a hidden tie between the case of the loft and the Realms, one she felt deserved particular consideration. The team agreed to input the information as a high priority item. Its members acknowledged all too well that the fact each of them was connected directly or indirectly to the emerging Oneness, showed the plausibility of an issue with the Warriors' worlds. Furthermore, the original Guild wanted no part in it, as it recognized no foreseeable future of a Roamer invasion in the universe it oversaw.

———————

Le Lien operatives, Liv and Grisha, were dispatched to track all of Wind and Maggie's moves. The rest of the team would work in two rotating groups, beginning with Vera, Saka, and Vac on defining the connection to the Realms; while Pau, Jarred, and Marshall would continue concentrating on the clients' loft.

Jarred requested to spend time alone at the place, hoping for an in-depth interpretation of what was really going on – the artists' collective agreed to it with minimal fuss. For that, he had to match the spectral characteristics of the typical occupant – his Angel signature was considered a deterrent to any force that aimed at breaking through interdimensional layers.

Pau was in charge of deciphering the collected data, while Marshall would organize reports into two categories: one for the clients, the other to be filed as classified information. Vera, Saka, and Vac would be commuting back and forth between Eureka and the Realms; their job was to fine-comb the tunnels for any indication of breach into the space quantum that separated the two Onenesses, with the aid of data compounded from the readings at the loft. Hopefully Jarred would be gathering more information from his stay at the site. The clause of rotation was proposed so that everyone would end up operating from multiple perspectives with equal knowledge – individual interpretations would thus be highlighted and cross-referenced, their variations inputted to a custom program for further enhancement, to assist in the extreme instance of an impasse.

Liv and Grisha briefly joined the team to go over logistics, before they left for the San Francisco Bay Area. All was in place – they all would be communicating with Qwave-modified handsets specifically coded to unlatch from the main system when linked. Wind and Maggie had been located – their auratic signatures had been tagged and were now in locked-in mode.

10 – TEAMING OF THE TEAMS

Ma-1 heard through Angel Bluefeather that Saka had returned to her old world. For the first time since the era of the stone, she felt a pang that penetrated the depths of her being. She could sense the call that came with the ominous winds of something else gone wrong. How many attempts had been made to render useless the efforts of all those who had contributed to make the reality of the Realms possible? She was all too aware Saka's inner voice would one day whisper her desire to revisit her physical roots, like it had done once by returning her to her spiritual source. But Ma-1 also knew the power of the stone would eventually awaken within her, brightening the light that exposed the darkest recesses of both Onenesses. Saka left the solitude of the cave, driven by the latent force that had been sowed within her by Amaterasu; she was again being called to fulfill deep-seated desires that couldn't be harnessed into quietude. She too, in her own way, was a Warrior, albeit one without spears or arrows, but the light was a fierce companion to a heart that sought to see into the blackest soul. Ma-1 didn't want to share her fears with Olaf; her pain didn't belong to her creator self, rather, it was the one of the defeated fighter. She knew she had to let go of it, for it no longer served its purpose; but she also acknowledged she had to ride it to its last race, if she was meant to free herself from it. Angel Bluefeather, who understood a thing or two about love, sensed that the Goddess was in need of serious affection; he held her long and tight until she wearily lifted her head from his shoulder looking at him with reddened eyes. She managed to smile.

"It's the price to pay for being born of the flesh, Goddess and all. I wonder if it'll ever leave me."

"It won't unless your heart turns to stone; I doubt it's where you're going," Bluefeather said softly.

"Then I must set Saka free, even if she must never return," Ma-l said.

"You are indeed feeling your humanity, though the Goddess has no bonds with loss or gain; they are only constructs of old habits that must surface before they're gone. Saka only wishes for her various facets to not stray from her core self, for exactly the same reasons you long for her presence – Linda Sue is forever an integral part of who she is as the Goddess of Light, without her she wouldn't have been able to reunite with you and help the Realms."

"I guess she represents a painful paradox, for I don't feel complete without her. Yet, had she not mustered the strength to leave the enclave of the stone, I sense I would not have found release from it. She was the 'me' that dared challenge my predicament, the force that ultimately made me a Goddess. One needs to let go of something dear to allow transformation to occur." Ma-l surrendered.

―――――――――

Xarn felt quite differently about Saka's choice to take on an assignment in her old world. A mix of pride and admiration was closest to describe that sentiment. There was no place for roles of subservience in his world; Saka was a Goddess who needed to assume her part in the making of the Realms; thus, her involvement with the Earth cases was the stuff that secured the love between them. Affection through might was at the base of all that Xarn touched or created, a force often expressed in the form of heightened dignity. Just like with Ma-1, he learned of her absence through Bluefeather, who had gotten the news from Vera. Certain duties required for the personal space to remain uncluttered, the thinking undiluted by external pressures. Xarn's world rose from within the confines of isolation, he understood all too well the implications of crossing the line of one's private sanctum. One was strictly invited into another's process – any attempt at pushing boundaries was a violation of the highest order. It was up to Saka to let him in on her affairs or not – there was no love without trust and the space for it to grow.

The dream meetings continued at regular intervals. It was a particularly starry sky over the meadows when Enola asked Ma-1 and Xarn if they had ever tried to count the Warriors present at the early gatherings. There were one hundred and thirty two thought-to-be-active realms, and sixteen developmentally arrested ones. Except for Badger, who Ma-1 was certain was one of the lost Warriors, the fifteen others were unknowns. The fact there were substantially more fighters in the battle than souls confined to the stony reality of the caves, made it impossible to identify the missing ones. On the other hand, those present at the meetings could certainly be named. Though it was never substantiated that the owners of the arrested realms had never joined the collective dreams, it was agreed that one of the reasons they failed was because of their lack of group spirit. The three Warriors didn't need proof of it; they viscerally understood that the choices these souls had made irrefutably led to further isolation and, eventually, a descend into indifference.

And so, Enola, Ma-l, and Xarn proceeded on identifying those they remembered from the meetings nearly two thousand years ago. By the time they reached one hundred, they thought they had run out of memory, but then more faces appeared until at last, there were no more. The final tally showed one hundred and twenty-eight names, not including theirs – one was missing. They recalled every gathering, until they concluded that either one member had left before they joined, or the unaccounted-for active realm belonged to a solo Warrior, in which case the theory of the arrested worlds was critically jeopardized – they agreed it couldn't be. So who was the one the three had never met, and what made him, or her, be the first to stop attending the gatherings?

Xarn looked at the full moon directly above them as if its halo concealed a revelation.

"We represent the three open realms," he said. "The one Warrior we couldn't name obviously left before we joined; we were also the lasts to arrive. Doesn't it mean the other hundred and twenty-eight knew who he was?"

"It would appear so," Ma-l returned.

"If I get the drift," Enola said, "you're saying there's something dubious about that one Warrior."

"It's just logic; it doesn't mean anything besides raising a possibility," Xarn countered.

"A loaded one, considering the breadth of the implications," Ma-l returned.

"I understand we have locked realms, but how could a Warrior be empowered to do harm to his brothers and sisters, and why would he or she, be trapped in there as well?" Enola asked.

"Exactly my point – what if we have an impostor who's not really locked in there, but just waiting for the right opportunity?" Ma-l hypothesized.

"Don't forget, *they* may not know we exist," Xarn pointed.

"Oh my," Enola cut in, "but what opportunity though?"

"To weaken them before taking over, I mean, what else?" Xarn returned, perplexed. "These assumption may be somewhat far-reaching, but they come closest to explaining what's happening with the unanswered calls – they're just not hearing them, or if they are, they're unable to get to the lanes."

"Which, by extension, would mean George was corrupted as opposed to having fallen to an unexpected kink in its evolution. Joonas should be notified, he's the one who would know how to isolate the time at which the corruption occurred. We're due for a meeting with Amaterasu, I believe," Ma-l affirmed.

———————

A time was set with the Great One to meet in her domain, which meant Amaterasu wanted Saka to be present as well. The timing couldn't have been more perfect, since the Goddess of Light, Vac, and Vera had just returned from Earth to begin a new survey of the tunnels. The three were asked to join in with the Warriors. It appeared the Great One understood, with great clarity, the deeper implications of their work in Eureka. She greeted the group and moved immediately to the main topic.

"If I am correct, there are essentially three teams working on the case of the unresponsive realms: one on Earth, focused on the particulars of a breach, one in the tunnels, looking for leads, and then the three Warriors in the dream meadows, awaiting the next set of doors to open. I am well aware there is an obstruction that may be the result of an outside influence from within; it shows as a rare probability, but considering that we already are in the midst of the near-improbable, it doesn't surprise me. Let me simply say that based on my broader knowledge, I do not foresee another obstacle beyond the present one – should you be able to resolve it, that is. Joonas could be of help, but I regret to inform you that his job is done and that he is now under the jurisdiction of the Great Ones, so is Qo'ai-Marael – the Le Lien liaison in the group may want to make note of it. The three Warriors among you sought my advice; so it now must be clear to them that by inviting Saka, Vac, and agent Vera, their suspicion of foul play has been officialized. The connective makeup of the two Onenesses – and that includes the Interverse – is more complex than we can imagine, since it evolves continuously and seldom rests. Besides the stones, there exist a few much less dependable paths that connect these two unique realities to each other; I believe they have not escaped the keen eye of the one who seeks retribution in the name of justice. But it is all I am permitted to tell before I overstep my boundaries and inadvertently start taking your powers away from you. It is your task to straighten your affairs now that you are in charge. I shall revel in your success – good luck."

The stones returned the group to Joonas Halls. From there, all agreed to reassemble in Enola's city for a continuation of the meeting, with the aim of extracting the essence of Amaterasu's words, and coming up with a plan of action.

Ma-1 at last turned to Saka.

"I feared you gone, but I've grown out of it," she laughed. "I had to seek counsel from Angel Bluefeather."

"You've got some explaining to do with Olaf," Vera teasingly cut in. "Mind you, I should know better than turn my back on him."

"Well, Linda Sue called, but it turned out her name was also Saka, if that makes any sense," the Goddess of Light humored.

They all laughed – Vac barked.

They sat in the shade of young Japanese maple trees aflame in their perpetual fall colors. Waterways ran around them, spanned by delicate mosaicked footbridges. The air was fresh, carrying with it the scent of sage from the surrounding high desert. The city was atop a plateau that met with mountains to the north, and fissured into multiple canyons to the south. The underground streams, which further down the land, turned to creeks and rivers, on their way to the faraway sea, momentarily thrust upwards to come to life among Enola's fantastic creations. The small plaza looked like it had been shaped by the deft hands of a giant stoneware artist, round, smooth but earthy, so that deep moss could grow in the shade of its curves to provide comfort to those who lay for a moment of peace; perhaps, to catch a dream before moving onward to an unformed destiny. It was a place wherein one could easily forget, a refuge for the mind that had for too long been battered by conflicts, by the storms that rose from the depths of misplaced or forgotten traumas – a space for the weary time traveler to rest. It was clear the three realms could not have been further removed from their creators' ancestral land, but still, they retained its fundamental makeup of mountains, valleys, plateaus, and canyons. The Warriors had brought with them the contents of their hearts. Their minds, they left behind amid broken arrows and the ashes of battles.

———————

Vac spoke first.

"We're all in agreement that there is a high chance of an impostor amid the Realms, but our Warrior team is missing on the findings from Earth. Ma-l, Enola, and Xarn are due for an update."

Vera explained what had been going on with the joined cases, while Vac interspersed various items of relevance regarding the history of the Interverse. Saka came forward with the message she received from the stone, which pointed to a link between what Wind was suspected of being involved with, and the Realms. When all questions were asked and answered, they agreed the time had come for action.

Xarn believed the dream meadows were capable of concealing metaphorical keyways that begged for a different mindset with which to be mated. Ma-l and Enola, though uncertain of the item's plausibility, thought it worth exploring. The Goddesses, on the other hand, proposed to study other ways to reach the closed realms; perhaps seed technology could be used to locate corrupting codes and disable them. At any rate, it required enhanced teamwork between Warriors and Masters, specifically involving the branches of Portals, Qwave, and Le Lien. Saka pointed amusingly that the Angels had managed to make themselves indispensable by first placing hurdles along the way, to which Vac responded in not so cheerful terms.

"Without Amaterasu's vision and the first Angel team, the Realms had no foreseeable future. The seed of possibility was sown when the Great Goddess shone her light into the darkest and farthest corners of the Oneness, and then brought to germination by those who worked relentlessly at keeping it alive. Without Angels to lock the souls of the Warriors into the hurled fragments of Trout Rock, there would be no such meeting in the magical reality that is Enola's."

Saka reminded Vac that humor still had a place among them, and that perhaps he should lighten up.

"For once, I don't have answers for what is presently happening, not even one I wish to keep to myself. Forgive me for my digression," he simply said.

Vera did her best to harness matters back to the table by isolating assignments.

"Only Warriors can access the lanes and the dream meadows, so it's clear Enola, Xarn, and Ma-l have their work cut out exploring whatever avenue may have been left untraveled. Saka, Vac, and I will resurvey the two systems of tunnels for ghost images of wrongdoing besides what was done by Dzalarhons' seeds. Back on Earth, the two teams will rotate their members between the now distinct cases involving the artists' loft and Wind's actions. Master Jarred may join us in the Great Hall for a small ceremonial introduction, before commencing his larger mission, which is to infiltrate the Interverse, as he had previously done – he may be joined by Liv, Grisha, or myself depending on availability. Saka volunteered as well, but she requires training; though based on her travels with Olaf, she shouldn't have any issues. Did I miss anything?"

"How do you propose placing Marshall in the rotation?" Ma-l enquired.

"He is obviously bound by certain limitations, but he will be kept informed. We need a steady post in Eureka anyway – Pau will be his liaison," Saka said.

"Has Pau showed any interest in the underworld?" Ma-l asked.

"Not that I know," Vac returned, "but she has indicated that she was drawn to investigative work and would like to give it a try. I think she is still reorganizing her thoughts around Angel Jarred – to some extent, she is feeling that she was cheated out of an assignment. Eventually, she'll come to terms with the reasons behind the Master's protected identity."

The late afternoon was closing amidst shimmering gold and the rustle of elfin life awakened by a gentle eastern breeze. The smell of warm earth and grasses permeated the air, soon to fill the streets with peppery sweetness, until intimately replaced by new fragrances brought forth by the evening coolness.

The meeting ended with the group walking back to the portal that was to take Enola's guests to Joonas Halls. Vera, Saka, and Vac were to return to Eureka to exchange notes with the Earth team, but first, the agent and the Goddess of Light wished to spend a proper night with their mates.

"A loved heart is a strong heart," Vera expressed.

"I must admit I've been neglecting Olaf," Ma-1 interjected. "He's seriously overdue for some Goddessly love!"

They all laughed wholeheartedly.

11 – THE ROOM BELOW

Liv and Grisha had followed Wind and Maggie into the city of Richmond, across the bridge by the same name, from the San Quentin penitentiary. The area was best known for its refineries, chemical plants, and vast toxic containment ponds. Arteries by the names of Xylene and Petrolite Streets, Standard Avenue, and Chevron Way set the tone to who was in charge of the neighborhood. Not far from the industrial zone, residences were tucked amid vegetation. Wind parked the van in the driveway of a shingled house at the end of a cul de sac. The Le Lien operatives had tapped into the US satellite spy system; thus, were additionally surveying from above. There was a vast, undeveloped, fenced area adjacent to the dwelling that appeared to have been a decommissioned zone; its overgrown roads, rusted pipes, old concrete footings, and crumbling oil tank pads betrayed a push by public health regulators to separate industrial wasteland from residential areas.

Liv and Grisha drove their rented Leaf to within a block of the house. The street sat atop a hill overlooking the North Bay in a breathtaking vista that encompassed many of the landmarks favored by tourists, including the San Francisco skyline and Mount Tamalpais in Marin County. Before long, Wind and Maggie stepped out of the building, got Sam out of the van, and walked towards the fence that posted multiple "no trespassing" signs. The man effortlessly nudged the gate open, crossed to a second wire barrier, and entered through a ripped hole in the chain link mesh. Sam followed, but Maggie stayed behind to keep guard of the forbidden entrance. She was fidgeting in place, looking at her cell phone – probably her way of communicating with Wind.

"Looks like our man's got business to conduct with the unknown," Grisha remarked.

"Not for long," Liv returned, "he's bound to let us in on some of the mystery."

Wind walked toward a small, abandoned, corrugated tin structure, looking around before entering. He was inside for over fifteen minutes, at which point the two agents wondered if he hadn't simply vanished. When he finally came out, it was in the company of two white males. Maggie answered her phone then put it away before walking towards the house. Sam was waiting for her as if he had never left.

"I assume you feel the way I do," Liv told Grisha.

"If you mean, itching to know what's up with that building, I'm with you. I guess we wait until the coast is clear."

The three men shut the gate behind them and made it to the house. A half-hour later, they all drove off in the direction of the freeway. The tracer Grisha had earlier placed under the van indicated they were on their way to Oakland.

"Homebound! By the time they get there, Le Lien should have a focused beam on their conversations. Let's get down to business!" Liv instructed.

They entered the small building; an old rusty diesel generator sat in the middle of the space. There were metal shelves cluttered with useless junk and beer cans, broken glass littered the floor. In the back of the room, a steel stairwell plunged into darkness. Liv switched on the Qwave handset light, as the two operatives descended the

112

tight steps. They came to a hall whose walls were covered with graffiti, a space disproportionate to the size of the building above it. Did the two men live there? There were no beds or even a table; the place was bare, save for the garbage on the floor. Liv shone her light around for clues; there was an opening in one of the corners that led to a corridor, which they followed until they entered yet another room much smaller than the first one. There was a heavy, padlocked metal door in the back that showed no intention of being tampered with. The female agent scanned it to get a reading of what lived behind it – the Qwave handset remained unresponsive.

"You still think the mystery is about to be unveiled?" Grisha asked with rare humor.

"By the look of it, this door isn't our friend. My scanner tells me we can't set a temporary portal across it. In other words, we've hit the end of the road. That's a first!" Liv exclaimed.

"Before we turn around, I suggest we erase our tracks – we can't leave Guild signatures all over the place. I've got a strange feeling about this," Grisha said, as he set his device to "electronic smudging."

"Wait, before you start erasing! Let's take a print of the area to see where our friends came from, just in case that door doesn't lead into what is expected of it," Liv cautioned.

The data was sent to headquarters at the New Guild Center via Amaterasu's lane. It would take a few days before results showed up. Agents Liv and Grisha prudently retraced their steps to the rental, and then drove off towards Highway 580, en route to Oakland. Liv sent copies of the report to Humboldt and the Realms; she and Grisha also received the latest on the teams' progress.

Nothing much had happened yet, but there was a sense of buildup that could be felt all around.

When Jarred Gulliver read the report from the Bay Area, he suspected he would have to join the two operatives stationed there. From their description, Wind could have secured a portal to the Interverse, something unheard of, due to the unpredictability of the brief latching periods between the two incompatible realities, notwithstanding their random behavior. A fixed crossing point would indicate a technological advancement for the Roamers, or a new way of exploiting the vulnerabilities of the Guild portal system. If his intuitions were right, he too could take advantage of that pathway to access the Interverse, in order to reach the other side of what he surmised was occurring at the Eureka artists' loft. But first, he had to wait for the results of the print taken by Liv and Grisha for confirmation. He also was two nights away from spending time by himself in the "haunted" studio – until then, new elements should come into play.

Vera also was intent on seeing for herself what Wind and his mysterious friends were up to in that old backup generator shed. What did the large room below conceal, and where did that impenetrable door lead? It was, in her views, tangible data that tipped the case to the side of legitimacy. In the meantime, Slaughter had identified the owners of the house next to the field as an elderly couple presently living in a retirement community north of town; the tenants had not yet been named. Without the stamp of officiality, it was tedious to maneuver around information that wanted to attract attention; the detective knew all too well to not stir the pot too close to the bottom, at the risk of loosening what had stuck to it. As usual, results would be slow to come, but there was nothing to gain from rushing the process. Pau and Vera continued to analyze what their interaction with Wind had yielded; mainly that he was after the Qwave scientific laptop originally owned by Olaf Swyndle, the very one that was partly responsible for the physicist and Vac landing in Ma-l's realm. How the Rastafarian planned on acquiring the machine brought the lacework of their mission into focus. There was no way in their minds that Wind would ease his lust for it; hence, he was bound to act sooner than later, either by showing up in Akureyri or going after Linda Sue Klein.

The Le Lien print report was received on Vera's handset. The signatures of the two men accompanying Wind did not register as Earth citizens. It classified them as Roamers; it also confirmed Maggie's partner was not one of them, in spite of traces that indicated he had traveled to the Interverse. The typical Roamer signature was composed of few identifiable elements; it was essentially how it distinguished itself. It diffused a negatively charged energy, in that it radiated inwardly. Aspects of the underworld, as they contaminated the personal environment, as in Wind's case, registered like dust mites scattered around the auratic field. In a nutshell, all Roamers issued the same signature without any lead to individual recognition. Furthermore, the report came up empty on identifying the destination of the locked armored door; it was protected by a scrambler that appeared to behave similarly to a Qwave one, in that it left no ghost marks. Also the rooms below were not part of the original blueprint of the structure – or where not meant to be included in it. Le Lien stipulated they must have been used to house the diesel tanks for the generator, but failed to explain how these large metal containers had to be later removed through the small opening of the stairwell. The one affirmative was that Wind went in alone, only to return with two Interverse denizens, possibly via the mysterious, armored steel door.

Angel Jarred Gulliver sat at a small table in the artists' loft. He had deemed it wise not to bring in testing equipment that could potentially have leaked information about its operator. It was still to be determined whether the apparition was connected to the space or existed in a state of gestation prior to becoming conscious of its environment. By assessing its intensity, the Master was hoping to establish the rate at which the plasmatic mass was evolving, what it consisted of, and hopefully, what its aim was. He was aware the Guild had claimed it saw no foreseeable future in regard to an attempt by the Interverse to take over; only a series of apparitions followed by a brief visit by Roamers, that was all – they left as soon as they came. But nothing was ever without meaning; it was therefore a test whose design was aimed at spheres outside Guild coverage. That left the domains of the Great Ones and the Realms of the Warriors. A report from Spencer had highlighted Amaterasu's comment about other lanes capable of reaching the emerging Oneness. Jarred considered that remark so potent, that he wished to revisit the Great Hall for the first time since the dawn of Angel City. He and Spencer were overdue for a proper tête-à-tête – perhaps Pau would also want to join him.

Jarred got to the loft at nine o'clock. He was handed a key and the numeric code to the alarm for when he left. By eleven, his Angel senses began picking up ambient activity in the form of ripples across the suspect area. Before long, an increasing opacity joined the waves, until indiscernible, quivering forms juxtaposed over the contents of the room. At first, he perceived it as an single amalgam of energy shapes akin to intertwining flames, but it soon became evident the motion originated from multiple sources sharing a common signature; he suspected a group of Roamers was behind it, a force in the process of creating a fixed crossing point for multiple, simultaneous passages. So, why was the image not seen when more than one person was in the room? Jarred thought that the soft spot possibly hardened when too many individuals were present. It would require a motion camera to ascertain the apparition occurred with no-one in the room as well. If he was right, the energy wasn't yet capable of identifying its environment; it either felt it could go through or not, as in auspicious timing versus unpropitious circumstances. Perhaps it was the time at which a Qwave *gravitational wave detector* could come in handy – at locating precise and dependable points through which the energies could travel unimpeded. From then on, Roamers would be able to access surface realities in large numbers without the use of Guild portals, while conveniently avoiding detection. The Angel had no reason to doubt the soundness of the information the Masters held in regard to probable invasions from the underworld; there were none he could foresee himself, but it didn't mean the Roamers were not trying. Nevertheless, it didn't make much sense that they would cross and not take advantage of their position. Obviously, the notion that they were after something else couldn't be refuted. If they were not interested in overpowering surface realities, they certainly wouldn't get much out of trying their luck at invading the domains of the Ones – it left the Realms as the target.

In the meantime, the dancing shapes within the room had assumed the characteristics of individual, human-like forms pushing their way against the membrane of the space/time continuum. Jarred understood these were not actual bodies, but rather, their manifested images penetrating the layers. "How far in were they?" He couldn't tell, at least not from his side, but far enough to intuit an imminent bleed-through. But yet, he knew it could not happen without help from Qwave technology. Le Lien needed to come up with a list of non-recovered equipment, as well as names for potential liaisons with the Interverse. As far as the loft was concerned, he had seen enough. He would arrange for a spectral camera to sit alone in the space. He activated the alarm and locked behind him. The night air was crisp – he opted for a walk along the waterfront.

———————

The official Le Lien list of recovered Qwave instruments flashed on the screen of Vera's handset. It was accompanied by another, highlighting irregularities. There were in fact many machines left behind entered as returned. It emerged that the registrar was no other than

Angel Lawrence, member of the rogue league XVII, pursued by Sam, Vac, and Vera herself, and then arrested by Amaterasu in the tunnel leading to Snake's underworld.

"OK, now we have a link between XVII and the Interverse – why am I not surprised?" Vera said, as she turned the information over to Pau.

The young Master scrolled the list against its counterpart.

"Now I know why Wind is after Olaf's laptop; it's got to be the missing link."

"Which means Saka is closer to getting in trouble than we originally thought – time to regroup!" Vera returned with a tone of urgency in her voice.

The two groups met at Slaughter's office, save for Vac who was on an unscheduled visit with Amaterasu. The reasoning behind the case made it clear that Wind would go after both Vera, for her assumed knowledge of supercomputer technology, and Saka, for having owned the coveted laptop. Angel Stefan had been informed of the setup likely needed in Akureyri – he was ready. Lillian had also been activated, thence taking Geir into the action as well; and thus leading to the coalescence of yet another threesome ready to jump into the fray. Marshall was comfortable with keeping his human roots where they belonged; he felt at his most useful at the office. Jarred let him know Pau had agreed to come with him to the Realms for a meeting with Spencer.

"She already warned me; make sure to bring her back in one piece," he jested.

Saka also sensed her place was in Eureka, perhaps as a wish to be by Slaughter as his assistant, like in the days of the Swyndle case, through a need to reconnect, or rather, to not disconnect from a vital part of her larger self. Of course, there had to be other reasons, but she didn't know what they were; it just felt right to stick around Old Town and wait for that particular signal beaming her way. Vac promised to return as soon as he could to stay by her side. There was something about the thought of his companionship that confirmed she was in the right place and time. But all things were relative, especially when "right" carried multiple meanings.

At the precise point at which Jarred and Pau left for the Realms; just as Vera raced to Iceland on a tip from Liv and Grisha that Wind was about to look for her in Akureyri; and Vac was in conference with Amaterasu in her faraway red dunes, Linda Sue Klein stepped outside the office for some fresh air. She was immediately grabbed by two white males and forced into a van. When Marshall finally realized something had gone afoul, she was unconscious and well on her way to the Bay Area.

Saka woke up in utter darkness. She immediately fingered the area of her neck to search for the pouch containing the stone – it was miraculously still there. Even her cash had been untouched. Obviously the men weren't after her belongings. It didn't take her long to figure out why she was there – the thing was to unriddle where exactly "there" was. She felt slightly hangovered – chloroform likely – but it wasn't too bad. Only her mouth felt dry and she was parched. She emitted the slightest glow, just enough to gauge her surroundings, but blackness extended beyond it. Some extra light defined the confines of her area of captivity. It was a large concrete room, littered with detritus. There were no windows; she concluded it was a basement, probably below a warehouse or an abandoned factory. She found the stairwell, shut with a heavy steel trapdoor locked from the outside. Walking around the space, she located a hall that led to a smaller room terminated by an army-grade entryway. So, there she was, at the spot of the uncooperative door described in the report by the two Le Lien agents in charge of monitoring Wind and Maggie's moves.

Just as the white stone around her neck began to drone as she approached the locked entry, the loud clang of the trapdoor being swung open echoed from the other room. She moved in closer – the gem vibrated with added intensity. Saka knew it was a matter of seconds before the men who had abducted her would be breathing down her neck. With one last step, she came to the threshold of the temporary portal that had replaced the steel obstacle – she crossed. When the Roamers came to the small room, there was no trace of her and no sign anyone had been in there; her signature was erased the instant she went through. The men swept the space with flashlights, returned to the door to check for tampering, then looked again in the vast emptiness lying at the bottom of the stairs.

"What the fuck?!" one muttered.

"We dumped her here, right?! Fuck, I knew we shoulda stayed away from that shit we snorted – now we can't even remember where we dropped her!" the other shouted.

"I'm pretty sure 'twas here..."

"Then you show me where she is, asshole!"

"Fuck you!" was the reply, before their muffled steps indicated the men had left the upper shed.

12 – SAKA'S CROSSING

Vera, Stefan, Lillian, and Geir were staying at the same bed and breakfast patronized by Le Lien during the days of the search for the Keyhole Lake portal coveted by Joonas. Stefan had arranged with the student body of *Intelligent Machines* to make Professor Vera O'Neil their new head scientist. Since the Angel's knowledge of computer technology far outpaced Earth's current one, it posed no problem at the academic level; they would simply think of a convenient emergency when the time came for her to prematurely relinquish her post. It was thus anticipated a dreadlocked, U.S. national by the name of Wind would be enquiring about the professor. When a call came from Reykjavík to the department's office, from a certain Windsor Kassel wishing to meet with Vera at Computing, it was no surprise. The caller was seamlessly transferred to the agent, who answered formally.

"O'Neil, whom am I speaking to?"

"Is that you, Vera? Wind here – I'm in town wondering if we could connect."

"I thought I would never hear from you after your meltdown; what brings you here?"

"I feel kinda bad about my tantrum in Eureka, I hope I can be forgiven," Wind returned.

"Tell that to Linda Sue, she's the one you need to apologize to."

"I got it covered; I'm sure she understands where I came from."

"If you say so... Are you in Akureyri?"

"Reykjavík – how far are you?"

"Depends on your notion of far – what about the other side of the island?"

"Shit, how long will that take?"

"Roughly five hours by car, or less than an hour by plane – give me a call when you get here. Anyway, I've got to go – good luck!"

"See you there," Wind returned.

Vera turned to the team.

"It looks like our work has begun!"

Geir abruptly stood up to inform the group of the text message he just received from Marshall on his cell phone – it read:

Saka went out for a short walk this a.m. –
she has not returned. It's been nearly four hours –
I fear something has happened!

"Damn, this feels like a set-up – I'm not supposed to be here!" Vera expressed apprehensively.

She picked up her handset to connect with Spencer, Jarred, and Pau, who were meeting at Le Lien headquarters. For now, she didn't have much of a choice – if Wind had anything to do with Saka's disappearance, she had to stay put and wait for his arrival.

———————

Besides renegades, addicts, social rejects, and common criminals generally "recruited" from various civilized orbs by trained Roamers, there were the rulers' henchmen and women that lived of the gains extracted from the hordes, in the form of taxes in kind. Subservience was the commodity of the underworld; it included everything from basic services to sex. Various surface societies had a propensity for ignoring "convenient" disappearances, especially those around criminals and addicts; thus, when they happened, they rarely drew attention. The underworld once also enjoyed a particular relationship with Hektor, in that in exchange for top-grade Roamers to fill the organization's kennels, the Lords of the Interverse, as well as their deputies, could access the Dark Angel's system of portals with the use of unique auratic signatures assigned to them in perpetuum. Though Hektor's portals had crumbled as the result of the league's exodus into Amaterasu's Keyhole Realms, some of the system had been saved and maintained by defectors and their Dog followers who had turned their allegiance to the underworld. How did Windsor Kassel fit into the picture? In his various dealings with shady characters, Wind came to the attention of some second-in-command, who, because of a lack of trained technicians in the Interverse, was on a recruiting mission. A special clause had been drafted that offered these recruits the option of operating in their native worlds at the service of the Fallen Angels that ruled the forgotten layers. Furthermore, these leaders had learned a few additional tricks from Hektor, particularly how to exploit psyches with the use of coded verbal implants similar to those imbedded in the Guild defectors. It was during the course of a smoke-out that Wind unsuspectingly became an "honorary member" of the Interverse. He was elevated to the post of portal supervisor, to which the great expectation of enhancing the system was attached – his job called for devising a method of mass transit between various realities, with an emphasis on the one Joonas had been coveting before his disappearance. The data provided by XVII members, such as Dzalarhons and Caax in the early days, then Lawrence and Jen before their arrests, had revealed the existence of the emerging Oneness and allowed for Gandreal's plan to evolve into a near-completed mission. Wind's assignment was to create a bridge between the Interverse and the Realms. His doubts about Linda Sue Klein's legitimate presence on Earth stemmed from rumors about humans having reached the worlds of the Warriors; of course, he also knew she had been in possession of a Qwave computer now that he had put his hands on similar machines in the underworld. If she indeed was one of those who made the journey, her laptop was undoubtedly the portal generator – he had to have it if he was to crack the coordinates of the emerging Oneness. Though, one nagging question remained: would it allow him to penetrate its makeup? The other machines were extremely complex, yet they didn't convey the sense of deep viscerality he picked from Linda Sue's laptop. That was why he needed to get closer to *Intelligent Machines* and meet with Vera O'Neil.

———————

Wind was in Borgarnes when he called – not in Reykjavík, as he claimed. His modified cell phone could dial from anywhere on Earth without ever moving. He had arrived through the same portal once used by Joonas. The owners of the bed & breakfast, ex-Dogs of Hektor, were among those who defected to the Interverse. Incidentally, the other portal by *Stífluvatn* was also under Roamer control and the Mercedes-Benz SUV was still available. In a quick hop, the Rastafarian was within easy distance of Akureyri, giving him enough time to get himself familiarized with the city and con Vera into believing he actually had traveled all the way from the capital. He rented a room at *Hotel Kjarnalundur*, by the airport, and waited.

It was evening when the student's office relayed Wind's call to Vera.

"So, you made it," she said, "I hope the drive wasn't too gruesome."

"Nothing a good beat couldn't handle," he replied, referring to music.

"You must be hungry, what about we talk over a bite? Meet me at *Bláa Kannan* in half hour; it's easy to find," Vera suggested.

"I'm down for it – see you then!"

Vera pretended to be happy to see him – it was part of her training. She was used to moving with the flow – emotions or personal views didn't belong to the mix of her assignments. She knew he had something to do with Saka's disappearance, but she was far from surprised to see him in Iceland. She assumed he was meant to prevent her from returning to Eureka, by distracting her with computer geekery. They ordered from the counter then sat at a table under one of the many chandeliers intended to complement the exposed timberwork.

"I've got no idea what your reasons are for presently being in this country, but I'm going to guess it's not the pot business," she said with distinct amusement.

Wind reflected for a moment as if he hadn't yet thought of a good argument, but then he smiled with a twinkle in his eye.

"You're funny, but you're right; it ain't about

ganja. That being said, it makes me wonder where you find the stuff around here... Anyway, you and I are in related fields. Let's just say I'm familiar with mainframe computers, perhaps not at the level of your virtual machines, but advanced enough to come at a close second. Unlike you, I don't operate from an institutionalized network – my interests are tied to the private sector. I don't seek blueprints, but I need to know how far you've gotten," he said, forking his salad.

"So, if I get this right, you came all the way here to ask me questions?" Vera probed, playing the disbeliever.

"Is that too heavy?"

"Well, it depends on the level of the questioning. The man who comes all the way from California isn't going to want to turn around without answers. So, I wonder how far he'll go to get them."

"Resistance may prove futile, but then again, I'm not after trade secrets."

"What d'you want to know?" she asked, resigned.

"Ever heard of Qwave Technologies?"

"Why yes, they make custom scientific equipment for various fields of research. They're based in Australia. I actually use one of their units as my personal computer. You have to be connected to an institution to have access to them – they don't cater to consumers; but you must already know that."

"I do, I just want to make sure you and I are on the same page."

"Out of curiosity, how did you come across Qwave?" Vera enquired.

"The outfit I work for owns nearly a dozen of their machines, mostly laptops. Solid tools, but they could do a lot more, based on what's inside them."

"Hmm, they're personal machines customized for specific research. Your unique signature must first be recognized before you can use them – I guess you've already taken care of that detail," Vera continued, willing to play the game.

"Yeah, that's taken care of, but my main question is, 'How far beyond Qwave is current technology?' I mean, what are you presently using at the scientific level?" Wind asked intently.

Vera paused to reflect. The man's questioning method was shifty, even disorganized. She knew what he wanted, but she sensed he wasn't sure how to get to the point without compromising his motives.

"Where're you trying to go with this, Wind – aiming to poke a hole in the universe to see what's on the other side? Even our so-called supercomputers have limitations; artificial intelligence is more of a figure of speech than it is a realized science – maybe in fifty years, if someone doesn't blow up the place first. Qwave is probably far ahead, but we can't tell if we don't know what to ask for. Have you ever pondered on the question of what limits you; is it the machine or the skills? Obviously, the laptops at your service were not designed with you in mind, otherwise you wouldn't be here. Without their rightful owners, there're just fast computers. I'm afraid you will not get what you want out of them – you need your own equipment."

"Then you must help me get through to Qwave," Wind said firmly.

"I can always try, but you must give me time. I have to go through the Berkeley channels to get to them. It would help if you told me what you have in mind."

"That's sensitive – I'm afraid I can't."

Wind's phone beeped. The message was from Richmond. He sprung up like a wild animal, paced the room, spitting in rapid bursts into his mobile – he was visibly beyond himself with fury. When Vera overheard him say, "I'll kill you, motherfuckers!" she knew for the time being that Saka was out of harm's way.

Wind returned to the table. The little charm he radiated a moment ago, was gone. He looked fierce and dangerous – Vera ignored the change.

"I don't care if you're stuck on this glacier, you're getting me in touch with Qwave, meaning now! My number's in your phone; I'm outa here!"

He raced out the door, leaving Vera wondering what had just happened. She felt suddenly dizzy. She ordered a cappuccino then picked up her handset to connect with headquarters and the teams.

Saka found herself in a dark, descending corridor, with the metal door securely locked behind her. The noise made by her approaching abductors was abruptly silenced the second she crossed. She intuited there was a distinct vacuum between the two realities, defined by that very threshold. With the help of the faintest of light generated by her skills, she progressed down a sloping tunnel carved in black, anthracite-like stone, at the bottom of which she faced another firmly locked gate barring the exitway. For the time being, she was out of danger. Once it was safe, she had the option of either returning whence she came or taking a chance at walking into the mystery that lay beyond the new exit. For that, she needed the stone. The trap door at the top of the stairs had previously left it unresponsive; hence why she could not get out of her entrapment. It was obvious the white gem was guiding her in the direction of the most suitable scenario – but whose script was it? As she came closer to the iron gateway, the gentle drone of the stone intensified; but when she returned to the door she had crossed a moment ago, the vibration stopped – "out" was no longer the way she arrived.

"Brilliant!" she thought aloud.

She briefly focused on Amaterasu and the black onyx. Was the Great One aware of what was going on? Somehow she couldn't get a feel for it. She was OK with it, since she much preferred to think of her situation as one she was fully in charge of. Her symbiotic relationship with the white gem, though she had no idea what the stone gained from it, was still part of her up-close reality. She gladly abandoned the idea of being a mere cog in what was unraveling before her. She walked back to the second gate, and without any hesitation, made the crossing.

―――――――――

The layers of the Interverse were composed of creational debris suspended within deep substrata of abandoned potential, each an island floating amid a blackness of unprecedented depth. From an imaginary distance, they were like ships dimly alit with life on a magnetic sea that kept them anchored ad infinitum. As a whole, these layers traveled at insane speeds, in the like of space quanta racing through Planck areas, expanding and contracting, separating and regrouping, showing no regard for laws or the dynamics of existence as perceived from the physical spheres. Nonetheless, there were crossing points at which sanity ever-so-momentarily found its balance and allowed for Roamers to squeeze through the irremediable dimensional gaps surrendered by Guild portals. There was also, unbeknownst to most travelers, a layer of spurned probabilities that offered exploitable areas that could connect more directly with surface worlds, undetectable platforms capable of also reaching deep into various layers of the Interverse.

All in all, this fragmented conglomerate of scattered worlds cruising on the gravitational winds of unforeseen probabilities was a surprisingly vibrant whole. Each world was under the rule of a Fallen Angel, or one of the deputies; each group governed by a higher-ranking overseer, while the entire Interverse was controlled by an elite caste to which Gandreal belonged. The social structure was basic: the Roamers, as a whole, followed a nomothetic model, while the rulers cherished their diversity under the light of idiography. It was a convenient way by which the leaders dissociated themselves from the servants; in other words, individuality was not recognized at the level of the bottom dwellers, whose souls essentially operated as a hive consciousness. It was why they all emitted the same signature; thus could not be identified, or their numbers tallied by the Guild.

Back to the platforms, one of their main peculiarities was that their "root denizens," irreversibly disconnected from their counteracting realities, were operating as aspect personalities of their source selves;

another term for ghosts in regard to the few who traversed. Additionally, these souls were in no position to acknowledge other presences beyond the occasional and unfortunate incidence of a "blotched crossing." In a nutshell, these "non-existent" probabilities were virgin grounds used as pass-through zones, unable to sustain prolonged visits or large amounts of transients before losing substance and becoming unstable. For all intents and purposes, they were transitional platforms between the Interverse and surface realities, reserved for skilled, specialized travelers; one of them used by Wind and his crew. It was also the one Saka was looking at from directly outside an "unregistered" version of the corrugated steel generator shed of the decommissioned refinery in Richmond, California.

13 – FACE AMID SILVERY GREYS

Ma-l, Enola, and Xarn gathered before preparing for the dream meadows – they had just heard of Saka's disappearance back on Earth. Even though none of them were doubtful of the Goddess' abilities to get out of trouble, they were far from amused. There was talk of one of them descending on the case, but there were deep issues that presented major hurdles, most notably, the abysmal division between the two Onenesses. At best they could send an aspect of their greater consciousness to Saka's rescue, albeit one with substantially diminished powers. The Angels were much better equipped at dealing with it, and Ma-l's progeny, due to her heritage, had the advantage of being able to take all of her newly earned skills with her into that world. In the end, Xarn stated he had full confidence in her to know how to handle even the most difficult of situations.

While the two Great Goddesses meditated, Xarn explored the meadows. During the early collective dreams, they represented a limited area fully suitable for the purpose of gathering for stories and chanting, but now that they had surrendered to the possibility of concealment, they had expanded beyond their original lines. On the other side of the trees that once danced against the luminescence of the moon, spread other fields whose grasses undulated like ripples on quicksilver lakes, and beyond them, more trees whose moving shadows interplayed with the untamed directional changes of the waving leas. Xarn suddenly wondered how he would be able to find something laced within the mysterious sign language of a place he had wrongly assumed could be easily probed. The theoretical, hidden keyway was, with each added amount of depth brought into the reality of the dream, gaining in elusiveness and distance. Yet, he knew there was something he was missing; perhaps a detail that was too obvious to reveal its perceptual intricacies. Xarn noticed a slight discrepancy between the gentleness of the breeze and the amount of movement from the trees and grasses, a cause and effect whose ratio was unbalanced; but was it grounds for deducing it held a message pointing to that missing link? After all, it was a dream in all of its idiosyncratic splendor; it could go on and on until the mind lost itself in its infinitude. There was also the oddity of the meetings always occurring from late afternoon on, until all the stars lit up the heavens. He had seen the sun rise while he waited for Ma-l to awaken on the occasion of their reunion, but never during the gatherings. Were the dreams dependent on private interpretation, as in most of evo-creation? Did he carry them with him outside their manifested reality? If so, was he the one hiding the item of his quest, and what about Ma-l and Enola? The Goddesses sat introspectively as he searched outwardly – how typical of the complementary impulses of the female and male, he thought. He understood that he, alone, would never find what they sought; the meadows were places born of a collective vision the key existed at the median point of their commonality. At that precise synchronous moment, the three Warriors saw the face of Misu rise from the depths of shared memory – the missing link had a name.

Enola and Ma-l stood in unison; the three deities locked eyes. Misu was one of the Trout Rock people, yet he remained a mystery. He shared, but never to show beyond the safety of common experience. Even if relations amounted to little interaction between fighters, he seemed to distance himself from the larger collective, as if his knowledge tapped beyond the reality of the tribe. The three of them couldn't have been able to tell if he had been among those scattered with the stones, since they never saw him at the dream meadows. But now, the dance of the trees and grasses amid the silvery greys of moon-cast light, had revealed a face: the one of the missing Warrior who left the gatherings before they arrived, never guessing more were still to come – he, who one by one, had locked all the others out of the collective dreams by making them deaf to the call of the lanes.

The three deities met with Vac, who had just returned from his visit with Amaterasu. The tale of Misu was broken down to its most basic implications. For one, if he was indeed responsible for the silence of the Realms, he had to be an impostor posing as a Warrior; hence, his origins had to be traced. Secondly, his motives needed to be exposed; and last, the methods by which he sealed the domains had to be figured out before the loss of these worlds. There were no missing Masters, so the Guild was not in the equation. That left the million of possibilities that a skilled member of any advanced species could be the culprit. Though, one with the knowledge of the Realms, and the intention of taking over a hundred and twenty-eight of them, substantially narrowed the search. For once, Hektor was also in the clean; its members all accounted for, and the few that defected to the Interverse tallied.

"It goes way back to before the battles. Anyone capable of infiltrating the Realms would have to have been in possession of previous knowledge and ample time to prepare – it had to be someone with access to information at the highest level, but also one who could easily disappear without drawing attention," Vac said.

"Couldn't a Master work from a distance by using an incarnational shell instead?" Enola asked.

"Good question," Vac returned, "but the rule is Masters cannot take incarnations without full immersion – in contrast to methods once used by Hektor members – they're either on a mission or not."

"So you're saying they're accountable at all times without ever the opportunity to sneak in a life away from the limelight," Ma-l probed.

"Correct, the Guild forbids it."

"But that doesn't exclude the possibility of one of them being an informant, right?" Xarn inquired.

"Correct again. In this case, it would have to have been one from the original team, or the later group of Guild founders to provide that level of knowledge with enough notice for action; which leaves us with the usual suspects: Dzalarhons, Caax, and the rest of XVII, as well as Qo'ai-Marael and of course, Joonas. We know the last two are under the protection of the Great Ones; thus, they are considered untouchable. Because of the scope of the problem, things indicate this Misu had access to a vast array of possibilities from which he was able to harness pertinent data, up to the point of the separation of the Realms from the mother reality – needless to say, the work of a fairly advanced consciousness."

"Does it mean he could have been aware of the pivotal human involvement that led to the emergence of our Oneness; which would explain Saka's intuition of a connection between what's happening on Earth and us here?" Enola asked.

"Well, it gets complex at that level. Technically, he couldn't have, since he's been inside, apparently oblivious to Ma-1's open realm. He would only have been able to see a probable development inclusive of human participation as one of his own making; a paradox he therefore couldn't fit in. Do you follow?"

Vac paused then resumed.

"So no, he's unaware of human involvement, but it wouldn't necessarily be the case with those on his team outside."

"What makes you say that?" Ma-1 asked.

"Unless he only seeks to destroy the Warriors and their worlds, why would he need a hundred and twenty-nine realms all for himself? It's just math," Vac answered.

———————

With the Guild and Hektor out of the way, it left the villain as one of the leaders of the tribes that went on to build their domains in the discarded realities of the Interverse. Vac explained that many of these rulers were out-of-control conquerors without as much as a modicum of decency in their bones. These tyrants saw the Guild as a weak overseer of species they deemed needed to be herded rather than nudged towards knowledge. Originally, the tribes were essentially hierarchical families composed of officers and deputies, who led their armies of conditioned fighters into battle with each other – the aim was to own as many slaves as possible; thus, the larger the tribe, the more powerful the ruler, and greater the prospects of expansion via conquest. But regardless of how it was perceived and judged, the Guild was powerful – so much so, that it forced the marauding tribes into retreat to the underworld. But Vac also admitted that not all rulers and their families were cut to be ruthless warriors. Unfortunately, for those who existed at the transitional point of Guild guidelines, the choice was tough; some eventually joined the Masters while others were rejected – at times, unfairly. But the line had to be drawn – there was no wiggling room for hesitation or fundamental disagreements. That group of rulers was later referred to as the Fallen Angels.

"I believe that's where we need to look for our man," Vac forwarded.

"Whose work would that be?" Ma-l asked.

"That's where I come in. Time to get in touch with Jaco and Lo-Shen of Third Eye – they may be able to free themselves from Guild protocol," Vac replied, as the three Warriors prepared to return to the dream lane.

———————

If the meadows were able to yield a clue, they likely held other secrets. Fields after fields unraveled under the moonlight, each separated by copses of young firs and the gurgling of snaking creeks. It felt to Xarn that with every step, subtly differing scenes opened before him, as if born of the same template, yet no two were alike. The Goddesses stood to his right side, their long shadows, specter-like, waving on the grass in rhythm with the ubiquitous breeze. They looked toward the starry sky.

"Do you think there might be a hundred and thirty-two such meadows?" Enola asked.

"I was wondering," Ma-l said.

"So, which is the one we have been coming to since we reunited?" Enola asked again.

"It's Ma-l's; she was the first one who called," Xarn returned.

"If it is so, then you two should be able to locate yours," Ma-l forwarded.

"It's easy," Enola said, "there're right here next to yours, one on each side as we face the moon. Xarn was seen standing in his like he was born there," she added, alive with humor.

"If we could only find Misu's, perhaps we'd learn something," Xarn wondered.

"Caution is de rigueur, I believe. Let's think it over as well as take counsel with Vac; I don't assume it would be wise to awaken Misu to the realization he miscounted the number of realms," Ma-l warned.

The three adjourned the dream meeting and regrouped in Joonas Halls. They had come up with a name, now there were hopes the meadows themselves connected individually with the Warriors; in which case, it was plausible that each gathering had occurred in a different field – the one of the caller.

"We shall get to the bottom of it," Ma-l said.

Xarn and Enola agreed. They returned to their lands with the understanding the awakening of all the realms was simply inevitable. Misu would be defeated.

14 – DOOR TO THE INTERVERSE

Saka followed the worn-out road that ran by the tin shed. She had no idea where she was. There was brush all around that blocked the view, but she knew she was on a hill. She came to a gated fence, from which she now could see houses and a large body of water beyond them. Suddenly, she realized she was looking at the San Francisco Bay from its northeastern side.

Earlier, after having crossed the second security door, she had found herself in a book-matched version of the small room that connected to the larger one. That time, the trap door at the top of the stairs had been left open. She had come to the broken glass-strewed generator room, its corrugated steel roof and siding rattling to the wind. She had stepped out, blinded, onto a sight of desolation where concrete and asphalt had lost their last battle against the reclaiming forces of nature and time. Wild fennel grew between the cracks, creosoted wood posts and rusted iron poked through grasses and bramble; the top of a corroded, decommissioned crude oil tank could be seen in the distance.

Saka felt ill at ease with the place. Her Goddess instincts informed her that a shift had happened; though the stone emitted a steady hum, indicating she was still on the right path. From behind the gate, she observed a car coming to a stop at the circular end of the street that met with the fenced lot. A man stepped out, but his aura was out of synch with her senses of perception. She then understood what had occurred – she was a stranger in a familiar land, oddly separated by a fundamental commonality from the reality she had left behind the locked entryways. She didn't belong there. She knew her time was limited – either she returned to the shed or she hurried to wherever the exit out of the eroding probability she had stumbled upon was. She saw the shingled house to her left, pushed the gate wide enough for her body to squeeze through, and ran to the open entryway. The stone vibrated at a frenetic rate; she instinctively raced down a stairwell leading to the basement, only to arrive at yet another metal door. As the world behind her began to dissolve into a complete abstraction – she blindly ran to it, hoping for a portal to momentarily replace it. As she fell onto the dark rocky ground, he gem in the pouch around her neck stilled.

Saka got up. She cast just enough light to discover she was inside a large cave-like room whose walls were lined with server frames, control consoles, and benches holding laptops and diverse test instruments. By the look of it, the owner wasn't the average tinkerer. Some of the equipment she was familiar with, but various machines appeared downright alien in origin. She couldn't help notice that the door she had come through was identical to the two others, indicating they likely were intended to provide passage on a unique linear course, as opposed to belonging to a more complex system. She found stairs behind a large machine, cut in the basaltic rock that defined the boundaries of the space. She parted a bead curtain that opened onto an unkempt living area. A couple of glass pipes lay on a coffee table, next to a bag of weed

– there was a familiar feel to it. The row of short windows along the ceiling line offered no view, save for the fact it was night. Obviously, the timelines didn't match. She returned to the table to shuffle through pot paraphernalia, CDs, technical publications, as well as some handwritten notes. And there it was, scribbled on a yellowed pad leaf:

Gotta get to the Eureka bitch
before G's dogs lose it.

"Subtle," Saka muttered. "So, this is where our friend Wind shacks..."

She began to get the feel she was very far from Earth, and most likely in great danger. She needed to get back to the team before it was too late, but first she had to figure out who "G" was. She couldn't afford to leave a mark; her kidnappers were not to know she had been there. She unlatched the heavy door to the outside and immediately regretted having done so; the elements were downright hostile, with sub-glacial temperatures that nearly froze her solid. She should have heeded the warning from the white gem but she was distracted. "Out" was only a way to a forbidden world; she wondered why there was even an entry at all. But there wasn't much time left to contemplate the idiosyncrasies of the place; the stone began to hum again, this time she suspected someone was coming. She returned to the basement lab and hid behind a large cabinet close to the door through which she had entered. It swung open. Wind walked in, followed by the two males, who had abducted her in Eureka.

"Gand's men are not gonna like the news," Wind scornfully told the Roamers. "Losing the prisoner wasn't an option – heads will fucking roll!"

They went directly upstairs after making sure they had locked behind them. The stone droned louder; Saka quickly crossed. She ran up the basement stairs, raced out of the shingled house to the fence at the end of the street, made a beeline to the generator shed, and hurried down the stairwell to the steel gates that reversely brought her back to her rightful reality. The heavy trap door to the outside had been left open by Wind and the two Roamers. She rushed to the dead end street where a Nissan Leaf with two passengers sat across from the shingled house. The stone took her straight to it. Grisha opened the rear door as Liv powered up the motor.

"Get me out of here," Saka simply said.

———————

At the exception of the Warriors, everyone was present to welcome Saka back in Marshall Slaughter's office. The concealed portal had seen a lot of use since the beginning of the case, but now it was practically in a state of constant flow. Not that the detective or Pau disapproved; to the contrary, it showed things were moving right along. It was clear Saka was target number one, but Vera came in close second. The Le Lien agent had played the game to its breaking point, and now she had committed to providing Wind with a connection to Qwave, not knowing if the tech branch would cooperate. She was also unsure as to the value of adding tension to her assignment unless it led to giving the man what he wanted: the very laptop owned by Olaf Swyndle and later utilized to its full potential by Linda Sue. But perhaps it wasn't such a bad idea to put The Triad right at the heart of the case after all. Spencer, who had joined in as well, approved of the idea, especially since the tech trio had been begging for a mission worthy of their talents. Olaf's old computer would be made available by creating a safe link to a storage unit purportedly rented to Linda Sue in Arcata. Marshall and Pau would arrange to move some of her belongings from Fieldbrook into the space, while Spencer would retrieve the laptop from *Retired Machines* and reload The Triad into it.

Then there was the mysterious "G" or "Gand," who, as it appeared, was a major player behind the scene. His men, or dogs, as referred by Wind, were intent on seeking Saka for interrogation. It had become clear the Rastafarian wasn't acting alone; as a matter of fact, he might very well have been conned into working for the Interverse as far as Vac saw it – the same way, perhaps, Pau ended up with Hektor, or George came to interfere with the dream lanes. Vac would have to cross-check with Third Eye in order to find whom it might have been that hid behind that moniker. "Gand" didn't ring a bell, but as one of the Guild founders, Lo Shen would know if such a spiritual entity landed in the underworld as one of their Fallen Angels.

Saka's break-in and escape were the focus of the gathering. According to Vac, the Interverse was composed of innumerable, isolated cosmic islands that were connected by poorly understood means. It was clear the fragile probability was one of them, possibly a platform to other layers of the underworld. It was possible portals were used to access connecting points fast enough before things got too unstable.

"You mean portals that exist in this world could have counterparts there?" Vera asked.

"Quite plausibly," Vac returned.

"It would make sense, considering Wind most likely used alternative means to reach me in Iceland. He left the café in a hurry to where? A drive on the circular road in the middle of the night in February is far from advisable, and the last flight out of Akureyri is at 8:10 p.m., which he already had missed. There is no doubt he's utilizing part of the old Hektor system – a close probability would carry a similar print," Vera explained.

"Although the means to access those platforms, whether they carry identical versions of the Hektor system or not, are part of an obscure network. In other words, acquiring a map of the Roamer-operated Hektor portals is only a first step," Pau offered.

"Regardless, we will need help from our old nemesis to obtain the blueprint," Spencer said.

"Unless you forgot, I worked for Joonas. You may want to check with Qwave archives – I slipped a detailed breakdown of their entire portal system in one of my mails to Marshall and Geir's old laptops, right before my rescue," Pau returned.

"That's my girl!" Geir exclaimed.

Lillian and Vera burst into laughter while Liv, Stefan, and Spencer looked at each other with mild amazement. Jarred and Grisha were taking notes.

"Of course, there are other means to reach the underworld – not as direct or easy as the one used by Saka and her stone – but Jarred here is the expert, since he tried to retrieve one of his subjects from it," Vac said.

"That is the one single reason why, we, Angels seek to enter the Interverse; to go after the ones we've lost to it," Jarred said. "We analyze the field of probabilities for an opportune crossing via portal vulnerabilities, hoping to

146

land close enough to where we intend to be. Of course, not all of it is small islands cushioned by quantum space – there are also big worlds down there," he added.

"Jarred, you once mentioned that you crossed paths with Wind in the Interverse; were there names for the domain and its ruler?" Stefan enquired.

"*Iorus*, in the *Hestilles Circle* – it's a very large, uneven rock roughly the size of Australia. It has a breathable atmosphere, as well as dense vegetation in its deepest valleys; its sun is weak but very close. It is deemed an extremely powerful domain, but the name of its monarch was never spoken," Jarred returned.

"If you were able to return there, would you recognize the place?" Marshall asked.

"The first part of your question is highly hypothetical, mate; apart from it, yes, of course."

"You haven't mentioned your subject's name; is it too out-of-place to ask?" Pau probed.

"Oliver Marx, if you should know," Jarred replied.

———————

The cam placed in the artists' loft confirmed what Jarred had suspected – the apparition was sensitive to the energy in the room. In tandem with that observation, the Master wondered if Wind's activities were concurrent with the recorded bleed-through. Liv and Grisha could corroborate his movements in and out of the Richmond shed, while the Eureka team would verify whether they coincided or not with the events. A negative would not exclude him, but it would make it difficult to define the importance of his role in the experiment. Jarred was hoping he didn't have to go into the Interverse to figure it out for himself – at least, not quite yet. The prospect of The Triad infiltrating Wind's process also came as a relief; again, no Angel ever enjoyed an assignment in the discarded layers of creation. Of course, it was a risk for the tech trio who could not afford to be ethereally stuck in that world, should the machine get destroyed. Though, it was hoped someone would prevent it from happening, in another rare instance of Guild intervention.

———————

It didn't take long to link the loft apparitions to Wind's in and outs. Liv and Grisha recorded sporadic conversations that warned them of his movements. In spite of the time misalignment, it was a given the man was one of the main tools of the mastermind, likely the head technician, based on his knowledge and his drive to retrieve Olaf's laptop. It was now just a matter of setting him up, since he and his Roamers were expected to show up any minute to finish what they started: getting to Linda Sue Klein, and then forcing her to admit the laptop wasn't merely stolen on that European trip.

Wind intuited she had reached the Realms. Even if he couldn't prove it, it was clear her recent escape taunted at some special abilities she couldn't have miraculously developed in some Eureka secret training backroom. This time, there wouldn't be any funny business; she would talk, or she never would again – and most likely both. But Wind could not possibly think it would be that simple. Surely, he was aware she didn't operate alone, or was it that he simply lacked awareness of the referent shared by

148

the powerful technology of the laptop and the forces behind the Realms, namely, the league of Masters? The question was posed on multiple occasions by the group and left unanswered – his aloofness was a potent deterrent against logic. That was why he saw nothing in having Maggie call Marshall's office.

Meanwhile, Wind wasn't finished with Vera. He dialed the *Intelligent Machines* department of the University of Akureyri, leaving a message for Professor O'Neill that Windsor Kassel was to return to fetch what he had left at *Bláa Kannan* a few evenings back. Vera purposely refrained from responding, assured that he would be there as warned. It was a matter of orchestrating a Qwave connection with the help of headquarters, and somehow bringing Wind's attention back to Humboldt, where the laptop would be waiting at the Arcata storage unit rented by the year to a certain Ms. L. S. Klein.

———————

Le Lien agent Vera was already at the Akureyri café when Wind called again. Within minutes, he was sitting across her, having ordered the same salad he barely touched that fateful evening. If she hadn't been a Master trained to shield herself against outside energy, he would have appeared threatening, but she wasn't interested in his personal demons, even if they were intent on making her existence a living hell. She had seen his kind on many assignments; in the worst case scenario, she could simply "disable" him without even moving. To her, he was a mere skilled automaton, severed from his spiritual self where his true powers lay dormant. She knew he had been "fixed." The dislocation showed like two superimposed images out of synch – his true self relinquished to the background, paralyzed by the spell of the verbal algorithm that had lodged itself in his mind. His rage was nothing but the expression of his vulnerability against the backdrop of his wasted potential, while his misplaced power was a caricaturesque display of his utter powerlessness.

"You got what you owe me?" he asked menacingly.

"I have your pass to Qwave, if that's what you mean," she responded neutrally.

"Good, then we can do business," he said as he relaxed into his food.

"I know I told you to get your own machine, but there's something that might interest you even more. When I spoke with Qwave techs about what I thought you were looking for – yes, I took the liberty, so forgive me – I was told they kept tags on their equipment with the help of stealth emitters embedded in their CPUs, sending intermittent signals to a global locator."

Wind stopped eating and looked at her fixedly.

"How can you guess what I'm looking for?" he asked, suspicious.

"Based on the description of the laptop you wanted to buy from Ms. Klein, nothing more," she returned.

"Go on then," he ordered.

"One such machine lives in Arcata, California," she obliged.

"Where, at HSU?" he sneered.

"A mini storage on M Street, rather," she replied.

"You want me to believe Qwave gave you an address; you're fucking with me?!"

150

"They didn't give it to me – I stole it from them. I thought it would be easier for you to buy that machine from its rightful owner, rather than wait for months to get your own. It doesn't mean, they won't make you one if you insist."

"I thought you said that each computer was tailored to its owner."

"I did, but if you buy from a solid source, they'll upgrade it for you at minimal cost," Vera lied, banking on the probability the man had no intention of going legit on an item left by itself in a storage locker.

"Sounds fishy, but as long as you connect me with Qwave, I can take it from there."

Vera gave him the name and number of the person to contact: Livian Tracy at *Custom Technologies*, the branch that dealt with "special applications."

Liv had volunteered for the job. She was ready for him, should he ever request "preferential treatment."

15 – QWAVE LAPTOP RETRIEVAL

Maggie tried to explain to Marshall how Wind was going through a hard time, begging that he should be forgiven for his digressions.

"Listen," Slaughter said, "you speaking on behalf of your boyfriend isn't going to fill the diplomatic void. If you can't see he's out of control, I feel sorry for you."

"I know; it isn't easy for me to speak about it. I'm sorry to bother you, but let me give you his message; is that OK? He says he wants to make up for his rudeness, and wishes to speak with Linda Sue. Please, just forward it so that I can tell him I did the job."

"Fair enough, will do, but please, take care of yourself – that's all I'm gonna say!" Marshall firmly advised before he hung up.

The detective knew darn well what Wind was up to, but he felt sorry for Saka's old friend, who apparently had fallen at the mercy of abuse to the point of accepting it as part of normal life – which partially explained why she was stoned most of the time.

He carbon copied the message to all the pertinent recipients. Within minutes, Vera informed the group of Wind's visit in Iceland, warning that he should be expected in Humboldt sooner than later.

Saka was still at the Fieldbrook estate. She had been counseled to return to the Realms, but she insisted on staying, claiming she wasn't quite done yet with the mission the stone had in store for her.

"You know your place in the world, but please, don't make me go in there to fetch you," Vera had said, referring to the Interverse.

Saka assured her she was in control of her abilities, now that she had been able to put them through the test.

Wind, Maggie, Sam, and the two Roamers were on their way to Eureka when Linda Sue called to return the message left with Marshall.

"Thought you'd never speak to me again," Wind joked.

"I was being detained by some unexpected developments," she returned, barely holding off the sarcasm.

"Sorry to hear, hope it wasn't trouble."

"Trouble is my middle name; ask Maggie – but I'm not calling to make small talk. So, how do you intend on making up for your outbursts; I mean, you speak like we're supposed to be friends but you behave like a boor?"

"Sorry, if you should know, I'm overextended and things ain't moving as smoothly as planned," he responded, feigning confession.

"My dad used to say, 'Keep your extra baggage at home when traveling.' It took me a while to figure out what he meant, but I trust it applies to you," she stabbed.

"Point well taken – so you don't mind meeting up again?" he dared.

"Remember the guy who walked into the office a couple of years back? That's the one I don't mind hanging out with. If you can bring him with you, I'm willing to give it a try; otherwise, you might as well go on with your business and keep me out of it," she voiced.

"Life's my business and making amends is good mojo," Wind stated.

"Then you should be familiar with checks and balances; that's one way to keep friends being friends. Call back when you get to town!" she countered, feeling it was time to end it."

Saka looked at Marshall, Jarred, and Pau, while Vac sat by her side.

"Trouble is on its way and it's got company. There's no doubt Wind and his accomplices are after getting me back to Richmond," she announced.

"Let's bring Liv and Grisha over; we could use the extra vigilance," Jarred suggested. "Also, for her safety, agent Vera should return to the Realms to work with Spencer; if Wind looks for her in Iceland, Stefan, Lillian, and Geir can take care of him," he added.

In the meantime, the loft clients had been informed work was being done to determine how to "exterminate" the plasmatic mass. Questions were asked, but the answers remained shrouded in professional secrecy. When one hard-nosed artist insisted on details, Slaughter suggested that he contact the authorities to have them look into it. As far as the team was concerned, there was little more that could be done at their end, so losing the case to the cops was no issue, especially when they would be done after a single report doomed to premature archiving. There was no way they would send one of their own to sit by themselves in anticipation of a ghostly presence. The artists would at best be labeled as a loony bunch. Perhaps they spoke about it at one of their meetings, but it was the last time pressure was put on Marshall's office; the collective promised to cooperate.

Wind had hacked the Stash-Away Storage database and found out Linda Sue Klein was currently renting unit B-33. The details of the arrangement were strictly technical. Simply said, Masters were adept at creating tracks as much as erasing them. As far as the antagonists were concerned, she had been using the space for years. For the sake of authenticity, the agents in charge had even added a fine layer of dust to the items stored on metal shelves – amid them – Olaf's old laptop, including its interface and power supply, all neatly tucked inside a field-worn Pelican case.

Wind had no desire to meet with Linda Sue; at least, not until he had verified the legitimacy of Vera's lead. He drove the van, unnoticed, into the fenced but unguarded storage facility, on a Sunday afternoon when the office was closed and the manager out for the day. One of the Roamers took care of the padlock with bolt cutters. Wind got in, surveyed the shelves, located the waterproof case, and opened it. He had found what he had come for, on top of now being certain Linda Sue had lied to him – a detail that made her all the more desirable. He saw the surveillance cameras but couldn't care less about them. For the sake of not leaving an obvious break-in behind them, the Roamer affixed a new padlock to the roll-up gate. Wind doubted anyone would notice until the owner would come back to get her things – a scenario he was fairly convinced no longer belonged to the realm of possibilities.

He called Linda Sue to check when and where they could meet. She didn't pick up. Instead she was on her handset in conference mode with Liv and Grisha, who where close on his tail. He, Maggie, and the Roamers had just left Arcata on their way to Old Town Eureka. No-one had noticed Sam was missing from the back of the van.

———————————

Wind dropped his men by "meth kitchen." He also ordered Maggie out of the van on the pretext he needed thinking space. She slammed the front passenger door, walked ahead without looking back while raising her middle finger, and then vanished into an alley. At that moment, the Rastafarian realized Sam had been left at the self-storage place. He muttered a series of profanities then smashed the dashboard with his fist, cracking it clear across to the windshield. He also sensed he was losing his mind. After all, he had found what he had been looking for; he could always fetch Linda Sue later if the laptop didn't provide him with what he wanted. The Roamers had proven useless, while Maggie was nothing more than a dead weight. He started the van with the intention of hitting the first portal that would take him back to the Richmond shed. There was one south of town, by the converted nuclear plant in King Salmon where he parked the vehicle, knowing he probably wouldn't come back for it. He put some paperwork in his carry bag, grabbed the Pelican case containing the Qwave laptop, locked the van and walked towards his exit out of the place. If someone had witnessed a tall dreadlocked, bearded black man looking as if he were about to board a plane, they would now be wondering what it was they last drank. Wind had stepped into thin air, on his way to the underworld.

Most assuredly, Liv and Grisha never thought they had hallucinated when they saw Wind disappear. They immediately contacted the team to inform them he was likely heading back to his lab, having dropped the two Roamers and Maggie in Old Town. After Liv checked the back of the van for signs of Sam, she let the crew know that satellite moving imagery had last identified the dog at the storage site.

The minute Saka learned Wind was on his way to town, she arranged with Vera to return to Richmond via the Guild portal system. They made it to the shed, and with the help of the stone, into Wind's underground control room where they took pictures as well as spatial memory prints of every corner of the place, including the living quarters. All bets were off – there was no longer a point pretending the heat wasn't on. Wind was onto something he was never to complete – time for him to acknowledge there was another team across the median line. Vera, rather than heeding Jarred recommendation of returning to the Realms, had made it clear she was not ready to retire quite yet, and neither was Saka, who was getting a taste for action, now that she was discovering some of the guiding powers of the stone. Jarred had simply laughed, admitting he was glad they decided otherwise.

The one thing was that as soon as they'd pass the first metal door, they would no longer be reached; hence, if Wind were to return prematurely, there wouldn't be any warning. When Liv and Grisha realized the man was on his way, they immediately returned to the Richmond decommissioned refinery where they had previously installed a temporary portal with a straight connect to their carry-ons. Because of the higher efficiency of the Guild system, they managed to arrive before Wind got to the shingled house which concealed the refurbished Hektor throughway he used on his various missions. The two Le Lien agents were at the door before he had a chance to get out and proceed to the tin shed.

"Richmond Police," Liv lied, flipping the badge she had made sure to acquire before taking the job – just in case. "You're Windsor Kassel, am I right?"

"So what if I am?!"

"Well, a certain Margaret Phillips called our office with a complaint against your person. We didn't expect you here since she claimed you were with her in Eureka less than two hours ago. She gave the clerk this address and we just happened to be in the neighborhood," Liv said.

"So, she's obviously lying," Wind retorted.

"Obviously," Grisha cut in. "I guess that's why we're not going to keep you long – just a couple of questions and we'll be on our way."

"I'm kinda in a hurry, if you don't mind coming back another time," Wind pressed.

"Sorry, we'll have no reason to come back if you

simply answer by 'yes' or 'no.' Were you in Eureka earlier today or yesterday?" Liv asked.

"Yes and...?"

"Is it true you left Ms. Phillips there, while you drove back with her dog?"

"Is that what she said? Yes, I left her there, and no, I don't have her dog. Is that it?!"

"She claimed it was in the van – she also said you drove away with her vehicle," Liv said.

"OK, guys, the woman's off her rockers. The dog and the van are up north with her; I don't have time for this nonsense. Now, if you'll excuse me, I need to get out of here," Wind said with distinct exasperation.

"Thank you, Windsor, and sorry for the inconvenience; the case isn't worth filing, since based on Ms. Phillips' claim, you couldn't possibly be here. Have a nice day!" Grisha concluded.

The two agents turned around, walked down the pathway and went left, pretending to return to their nonexistent patrol car. Wind took off in the other direction, not bothering to look behind him as he made his way to the fence, through the metal gate, and out of sight along the crevassed service road, towards the abandoned shed.

Saka and Vera had barely made it back through the last door when Wind's steps were heard upstairs and the stone, as well as the Angel's handset, gave their warnings. The two were gone in an instant through the temporary portal installed upon their arrival, connecting with the concealed closet in Marshall's office – Wind had brushed by them, never guessing his man cave, hidden in the folds of a discarded reality, had been fine-combed by a Guild Master and a Goddess of the Realms. A handwritten note was left on the coffee table – it read:

One may start the music
But it takes two to tango
So play on, Rasta man, until your heart
Succumbs to the spell of the bandoneon

Wind stared at the note with a crazy glare in his eyes. This time, his rage had turned into something viscerally toxic, as if the algorithm lodged in his mind had suffered a direct hit.

"Who the fuck...!" he let out, "What the fuck is this supposed to mean, motherfuckers?!" he added, on the verge of self-destruct.

He drew a frustrating blank on trying to define the origin of the note; he was farthest from guessing lowly Linda Sue had anything to do with it. What he knew of the Guild was also insufficient to trigger suspicion – he was left to ponder on whom in the Interverse was pulling such a prank. He was aware others had coveted his post, but he had never met them; they were mostly mentioned in passing by the deputies who supervised his work.

Unfortunately, he was in no position to confront anyone of authority in the underworld. The two Roamers he dropped off in Eureka would eventually find their way back, but they didn't have the will or the mental acumen to retaliate – they were mere servants, who only lived for their next opportunity to get wasted. Someone higher up, with unrestricted access to his pad, had to have left the note as a warning. There was an ominous meaning to the message he wished he could understand. Perhaps it was an insinuation intended to show impatience towards his sluggishness at producing results. It was true he had fallen behind schedule, but only in regard to a specific timeline;

he believed some of the old Hektor system could access various scenarios, should any one of them fail to produce the desired outcome.

But Wind didn't fully comprehend the nature of probabilities; he missed on the notion that a course chosen could not simply be rewound, or that the realm of the imaginary did not always offer valid, foreseeable scenarios – while other scripts altogether eclipsed the range of the imaginative. Even Gandreal, with his connections and reach into a plethora of conceivable futures, overlooked the one option he currently had found himself in – one with implications he could not picture, while ensnared within his personal manifested vision.

As Wind's anger receded, he realized redemption was in delivering tangible results to his "client" – wasn't it the way his contract was structured? But how could he have known the program in his head was specifically tailored to make him feel like a lone wolf working on a per case basis, when he was nothing but – at best – a slave on a long leash. When he thought he would be home-free and well compensated for his success, in reality, he was to face the true cost of having straddled the dark side of the social makeup for too long. The only times the lords of the Interverse dealt with outsiders were when they sought favors from Hektor, or the corrupt Angels of XVII. Even then, they considered they were fully out-maneuvering these dark Masters. Gandreal saw both organizations as pawns of his grand plan. In that light, Wind was only slightly above the common Roamer, save for a focused set of skills much needed to bring *Iorus'* conquest of the Realms to a close.

In a twist of ill-fated synchronicity, his handset announced the visit of deputy Jalesh, second in command of the ruling family of the fiefdom known as *The Hestilles Circle*. The blood left Wind's face, as the program lodged in his mind reacted to the news by instilling a deep-rooted sense of fear-based awe towards the figure of authority. The otherwise undaunted man was made to grovel before the powers of the underworld. "What the fuck?!" was all he could muster, before being alerted to the docking of the deputy's pod.

16 – THE LONG SHADOW

Vac had returned to Ma-1's realm to meet with the three Warriors in the circular area by the upper orchard. It was the default place that connected directly with Joonas Halls, a welcoming power spot that inspired the many invited to the Great Goddess' land.

Further down, past the house and the gardens, across the meadow by the waterfall, two characters – one small, the other larger – were engaged in conversation.

"Home has moved from one precious place in your heart to another, I gather," the frog said.

"I reckon the love had left from it," Sam replied.

"The long road of experience is littered with the shells of unkept promises and neglected responsibilities, but we learn to accept them as part of the landscape, don't we?" the amphibian mused.

"I had hopes for that one, but a cold wind blew from forsaken places," the dog mulled over.

"Not to worry, my friend," the frog countered, "the day is young in the new Oneness; you chose wisely."

He leapt over a glistering rock, leaving Sam to take in the bliss of the moment. His best friend had left him for a hopeless fate; he had waited long enough for her to return – faith could only be blind to a point. He felt at peace with himself; it was now time to move on with the next phase of his useful life as a dog. He crossed the meadow, walking past the house up the path to the upper orchard.

Vac and the three Warriors watched with distinct amusement as the visitor approached.

"By the look of it, "Ma-l said, "it doesn't appear our friend is just on one of his regular visits. Angel Vera kind of hinted at the possibility of a more permanent arrangement," she added, laughing.

Sam walked straight to the Angel in the group.

"Good day, Sir Vac," he said. "The frog once told me home's where the heart is – my heart's a bit lost right now."

"Well, lost or not, it took you to the right place, my friend. I know Angel Vera expects to see you here when she returns. In the meantime, Bluefeather will be delighted to take you in, if you don't mind hanging around for a while, as we finish with this meeting."

"I think I'll just lie here and sleep for a bit, if it's OK with you," Sam said.

"It's OK with all of us, dear one," Enola returned.

Sam looked at her as if to seek an answer.

"So, you're not human either," he observed while stretching. As he lay down, he tilted his head sideways to look at something moving in the grass.

They all laughed before returning to the topic of the gathering.

———————

While Vac showed Sam to Angel Bluefeather's dwelling down the creek – a gift from Ma-l – the Warriors returned to the dream meadows. The two previous gatherings had yielded a name that led to a possible place of origin in the Interverse. The information came in subtle ways, almost by omission. The meadows spoke in fine nuances, their messages hidden in skewed balances. If the wind had been a song, one wouldn't have been looking for clues in its lyrics, but rather in its rhythm or melody, a counterpoint to a change of key, a mode switch during an instrumental solo, or within a weak audible during a moment of silence.

Enola had wondered if the number of meadows matched that of the active realms. It was practically a given, now that they had seen many duplicates to the one they deemed was Ma-l's. They had sought advice from Vac who had told them he didn't see the danger of locating Misu's grassy dream retreat. He was under the impression the Fallen Angel had long disconnected from it; hence wouldn't be alerted of the intrusion. It was very likely he was just as deaf to the call of the lanes as all the other Warriors, especially since walking the meadows had not aroused a single soul. The challenge was first in finding which one was Misu's, and then figuring out what message was left in the subliminal tongue of its trees and grasses dancing to the ubiquitous breeze.

"The moving air is like the thoughts of the Warriors," Enola said. "In each lea, it is a breath of subtly different warmth, exhibiting minute variations from place to place in its rustling of blades and trembling of needles. It is as if our brothers and sisters were asleep in their dreams."

"It's a discomforting thought which could mean that they exist in a state of arrested development. No realm is built without a dream," Xarn returned.

"Well, I very much doubt Misu would subject himself to that fate," Ma-l expressed.

"It would all depend on what Misu is up to in his realm. Surely, he has very different concerns as to the overall outcome. I don't think we should evaluate his fate on the same level as all the others," Xarn forewarned.

"Yet, it's undeniable he's locked in there as well," Enola stated.

"What do you say we look for his meadow?" Ma-l cut in, sensing the rising incongruity of three deities about to make circles.

What to search for was the tricky part. Enola claimed Misu's energy was blue – dark cobalt blue. Xarn was after something that jumped at him – an image distortion, a contrasting detail that set the impostor apart from the rest. Ma-l thought of the face of the Warrior, its long features with a nose like a beak, its strong chin, high cheek bones, and thick hairline that terminated in a sharp point in the center of its brow. "What would a face like that want for a place that essentially resembled all the others?" she wondered.

They crossed many a stream to numerous meadows; Xarn counted seventy-nine of them. Then Ma-l saw it: the moon had settled much lower than in any of the others, drawing very long shadows across the entire length of the grassy area. The extended facial lines had been telegraphed by the low angle of the lunar light; and yes, there also was a blue hue to it that bounced off the prismatic quality of the dew pearling at the tip of the blades. What jumped at Xarn was the near-absent breeze, as if, as per Enola's point, the Warrior had abandoned the dream; only a ghost image of his once presence remained in the setting moonlight.

"This meadow is dying," Enola remarked.

"What makes you say that?" Xarn asked.

"When its moon sets below the horizon, darkness will fall, while all the others shall still be bathed in light," she returned, as if speaking from a state of trance.

"It feels quite eerie without the usual breeze," Ma-l observed. "So, do we all agree this is Misu's?"

"It's blue, it's long, and it's nearly breezeless," Enola said. "What else do we need to reach consensus?"

From both cognitive and intuitively standpoints, there was no doubt they had found what they had been looking for. Now, if only the place could surrender what it concealed about the odd Warrior, providing time had not already taken it away. "If Misu's meadow was truly dying," Ma-l thought, "then it was a precursor of what would happen to all the others – without them, the collective of the Warriors was lost." But it couldn't be – hers was alive, its moon was high – all the leas but Misu's were aligned with it. It meant the Deities were active in their realms, oblivious to the dream reality, but obviously still connected to it, as Ma-l, Enola, and Xarn were. What was up with Misu then; were he and his realm dying, or was he just waiting? Was he so detached from the reality of the collective, that his domain no longer registered at the level of the dreams? What would his meadow give away before darkness fell upon it then? The three of them understood that much of what was hidden would eventually rise to the surface when influences from around would apply their pressure. They had garnered enough for now; the meadows had once again spoken in subtle ways, but in between what was revealed, lay the greater answers to questions still unposcd.

––––––––––––

Misu's original aim was to corrupt the lanes that had borne the system of tunnels to the Realms. But he quickly realized they were intimately tied to the Warrior collective, immutable in their makeup, and thus incorruptible. Their physical counterpart were, on the other hand, open to manipulation, and with the help of XVII, Misu found the means to infect the original George program by planting a seed within reach of the codes, making the Gestalt an instrument of both the rogue group and the impostor – a grand coup that benefited each camp, with the added irony each believed they had outmaneuvered the other. Misu wanted the Realms for himself, while all XVII sought was to have them destroyed. But by sharing the same yearning to not see the Warriors succeed, they found a suitable commonality to their otherwise disparate pursuits. While the lanes remained active, the call to the meadows was silenced by the seed algorithms that had latched onto the signatures and energy paths of the tunnels and locked the gates to the worlds of the Warriors, those tallied and input by Misu. While the caves and corridors carved by Snake were left untouched, their intricate connective work was now under the Gestalt's control. Inherently, even though the tunnels to the Realms were, by extension, the image of the lanes to each individual meadow, they were separated by corrupt entries into the codes that defined the George entity. Essentially, by becoming aware of itself, the Gestalt assumed the role of the overseer, simultaneously losing its integral place within the system. The basic guideline was to lock the Warriors in for the sake of their protection.

The secondary system of corridors out of the New Guild Center was fitted with algorithms that had not found their connective points with the lanes, since it required the Warriors to create the links; it was why only Ma-1, Enola, and Xarn were able to access the meadows from it. Without the dream gatherings, that connection couldn't be made; hence, the ways in and out of the Realms would forever stay shut. With the deletion of the Gestalt originally programmed to free Misu as soon as the domains had fallen to the spell of irreversible ennui, the impostor could now only leave his world through his personal dream acre. But according to Enola, Misu's lea was dying from neglect. From an outsider's standpoint, perhaps at the level of Great One Amaterasu, the only way to free the Realms was to undo George's deletion and convince it to forgo its control of the tunnels – there was no such option. Misu and the rest of the Warriors were prisoners of their own realities as the result of an error of judgment on the part of an intruder by the name of Gandreal, who thought of himself as all-deserving of the respect enjoyed by the original Masters. Not so, for his predicament was proof the Guild knew best.

———————

Unlike the Warriors who suffered the crippling isolation of the stone, Misu, who as a Fallen Angel had found himself in possession of creational skills erroneously handed to him by the Masters in charge of saving humanity, had mobility far beyond their scope. He built his domain even before the first dream gathering, and when that happened, he was so much ahead, that the idea of waiting for millennia until the rest of the Realms came into their own, made him momentarily reconsider his position – but he stayed with it. While the meetings were happening, he accessed the tunnels beyond the lanes, visiting each cave to survey the evolution of the

Warriors he had familiarized himself with at the meadows, each of them a fetal energy, fragile, barely holding to a quivering strand of existence. When he deemed he had counted them all, he influenced their dreams with codes that prevented them from returning without the call of the lanes – the voices of those who wished to gather. When George, on Gandreal's order, was done with locking the Realms, three Warriors had been left out. Misu retreated to his world, while his gates shut tightly behind him. The first part of his mission was completed, but also, phase one of what he had not anticipated was about to come into emergence, and with it, a tiny light by the name of Saka.

———————

Closing the gates of the domains and silencing the lanes did not mean the individual realms could no longer evolve – it would have been counter-productive to Misu. Only the collective spirit was deprived of a place to meet and share, hence weakening the hopes for an integrated Oneness to rise. Without the majestic whole of the Warrior tribe, the takeover of the Realms by the Gandreal clan could now be easily performed on a one-by-one basis. George would open each of them, as the armies of *Iorus* would march in. For it to work though, the Gestalt, in conjunction with the orchestrators inside the Interverse, had to be ready, and on the same page. Attempting to dock a closed realm was not a viable option, for a return to the point of departure would, at that conjuncture, not be possible – the crew would simply be lost in the quantum space that separated the two realities.

Wind and the deputies in charge, were not aware Gandreal's plan had suffered an irremediable blow with the deletion of the Gestalt. They counted on Misu's signal to act, the imminence of which was of major concern in the face of only minor accomplishments at the strategic end of moving armies into the Realms. In a way, Gandreal's silence was a blessing that bought non-quantifiable time for the man in charge of the science, but pressures were mounting, as a lack of delivery was inadmissible. Wind's fate precariously balanced on the quality of his performance. He was aware of the financial implications of a failure, though he hadn't been yet confronted with its greater reverberations – he would soon be briefed.

17 – IORUS

The deputy from *Iorus* stood before Wind with the air of ennui that indicated he wasn't pleased with finding himself there. Jalesh was almost a head shorter than the Rastafarian, but his self-command was such that his stature felt imposing. He looked Wind in the eyes, in a manner that made the tall man perceive his own height as an infirmity. The deputy felt no need to not broadcast his natural disdain for pawns of the system – the computer tech represented a set of skills, nothing more.

"I am of the belief you know why I must reassure myself, as well as the rest of the ruling family, that the mission is progressing as planned. Is there any reason why I should not feel confident of your abilities?" Jalesh asked austerely.

"No," Wind replied, "predictable delays have been taken care of – I am in possession of all the tools necessary to complete my assignment."

"Delays, predictable or not, are still delays. I am here to remind you that there is no margin for them – the loss of time is not configured in a successful mission."

"I misspoke; my standards put the project ahead of its planned trajectory. It only appeared that way at my end," Wind returned, trying to save the day.

"Then we are ready!" the deputy countered, feigning elation.

"Just about," Wind uttered.

"The ruler is not 'just about ready' when he has been waiting for millennia. His call is expected any time now, and I don't want to be the one to tell him to please wait. Do you think I should tell him to please wait, Windsor?" Jalesh asked in a threatening tone.

"I'm gonna be ready when he calls, that's the way it was foreseen," Wind argued.

"Foreknowing is best left to oracles; I'm a foot soldier who relies on factual data and its tangible interpretation. Right now, I see the man in whom I must invest my faith, hiding to me the fact he was barely able to retrieve the pivotal part that guaranteed the success of the operation. I also see a man who is unsure whether said part will perform as expected or not. In other words, I see a man ill-prepared for the responsibilities he took on by entering into a contract with *Iorus'* ruling family. Others have been waiting for you to fail; I recommend you do not feed their anticipated glee, if you ever want to see the sun rise in your world again. Your freedom and sanity are in direct proportion to your performance – make a note of it!" Jalesh forcefully hammered.

The deputy turned around, ascertaining his words were still ringing in the room. There was no "good luck" or "goodbye," just a sense of derision left in his steps as he exited the quarters for the docking area.

For just an instant, Wind felt like running, but the program in his mind immediately kicked in to pin him back down to the bottom of his inescapable reality.

———————————

The demeaning message, followed by the deputy's visit, back to back with the uncanny meeting with the cops in Richmond, had the effect of humbling Wind to the point of subduing his general sense of anguish. For once, he felt at peace with himself. He walked down the stairs to his lab, plugged in the charger for the Qwave laptop, set up the interface with its shotgun microphone-shaped sensor, and looked at the instruments as if to make himself familiar with their presence. He then crossed the room to calibrate various machines, before returning to Olaf's old field computer. He felt compelled to fire it up, but refrained on the belief he would be jinxing the process by not waiting for the battery to get fully charged. He had much to plan for, anyway. The gateway pods, with their groups of Roamers in an induced state of semi-permanent suspension, would have to be reprogrammed with the coordinates of the laptop. These vessels resided in fortified sections of *Iorus* and were controlled remotely from the space rock that was Wind's assigned station. There were eleven of these pods, all with designated beaming destination points based on their levels of "softness," set in Humboldt over the last couple of months – one of them, the artists' loft being investigated by Marshall Slaughter and his team. He could have picked up any place; Berkeley, Marin County, and San Francisco were rife with soft spots, but Eureka was the perfect setting – he knew the place well from conducting regular business there, and also, he needed to get closer to Linda Sue's laptop. Locating the appropriate beaming points was made easy in a small city exhibiting a high ratio of eccentricity – the eleven destination spaces were found in record time; their coordinates mapped, ready for inputting.

For the longest time, Wind believed that the Qwave computers intercepted by Roamers at crossings, could be built into a super-array capable of tasking enormous amounts of data at unimaginable speeds. They could indeed do that, but they lacked the one thing he was

174

after: an artificial intelligence that rivaled human cognitive abilities. The only machine that ever came close to it was another Qwave unit he had once tried to crack – the one Marshall had traded for at the northtown pawnshop. That laptop and its operating system had made circles around him, before cooking his password generator. Now it sat on his bench, ready to be tamed. The Triad, who were already aware of their new environment, couldn't wait.

Short of a better definition, *Iorus* was akin to a flat Earth. Among the many discarded creational trials and errors, rose worlds whose physics were just as skewed as their looks. The *Hestilles Circle* colony was one of them. It was as if a huge unidirectional gravitational wave generator, the size of Australia, had been stuck to *Iorus'* bottom. Its one inner sea was met on one side by deep, lush valleys flanked by massive ice-capped, black mountains that also served at concealing its major underground cities. Creatures of all ilks roved its plains and forests, all either the products of abandoned experiments or runaways once smuggled in by various intergalactic groups of settlers. Roamers at large avoided the wilderness, and those who ventured beyond the city rarely returned. Only shielded, motorized industrial hunters and farming operators dared brave the open air.

Iorus' main metropolis and capital was *Lucrides*, a subterranean sprawl of nearly one million tucked to one side of its most central valley. It was where the eleven experimental pods were located, in a fortified layer of the city, below its rulers' palatial quarters.

The colony's weather patterns were unpredictable and, oftentimes, extremely hostile. The gravitational forces of its close sun changed directions with alarming regularity, affecting the magnetic winds that raced between the two celestial bodies, and precipitating climatic events that effectively kept its denizens holed in their underground reality. *Iorus* rotated on its tilted axis at a rate equivalent to two Earth days, essentially resulting in the shadows of its mountains perpetually moving around the landscape during clear weather. The foreseeable useful life of its sun, *Uvis*, was set at another millennium before it would be considered too weak to sustain physical life on the asteroid. It explained why it was paramount for Gandreal's mission to succeed, and for Wind to honor his lopsided part of the bargain.

The ruling family controlled the most hospitable third of the *Hestilles Circle*, nearly a hundred domains orbiting *Uvis*, and all destined to follow *Iorus'* fate. Scattered among them were rocks or other space debris used in various configurations of relays and stations, as in the case of Wind's lab. Amid the peculiarities of these smaller bodies were their rotation patterns, which could take as long as their solar cycles. The Rastafarian's dwelling was presently on the dark side of the rock as it sustained near absolute zero temperatures. When its time would come to face the other way, life could be enjoyed outside within its thin layer of artificially produced breathable atmosphere. Frozen seeds would come to life in verdant displays or blooms, until their turn would arise to shed new seeds for the next cycle. Wind would bring out his stash of Humboldt weed and rolling papers, chilling and smoking while allowing himself to be taken into the hallucinatory whorl of the enormous glowing orb that filled most of the sky before him.

The rock, also known as *Base Five*, was shaped like a big nugget the size of a small island, roughly seven miles at its widest. The station was built into its mass and only the part of it with its row of windows, protruded to the outside. Its intense gravitational pull betrayed a core whose density challenged Earth's physics, allowing for a sense of uprightness wherever one stood on its surface, which consequently made it difficult to gauge the height of its ridges. But besides the rare smoking sessions on the patio, Wind had no desire to explore the landscape; if he wished to get outside, all he had to do was leave the rock. Unless of course, the gates were configured for entry only – a detail Jalesh took care of on his way out.

———————

Wind powered up the laptop. It came to life with its typically bland, graphic-less display, welcoming the user with a password request. The hacker remembered it from his one encounter with the machine, but then he recalled things got complicated from that point on. This time around, he only had to minimally work on it to access the page that required answering the series of questions that would allow him to use the computer.

The Triad was ready.

You are attempting to operate an instrument that

is not matched to your personal signature. Please answer the five following questions in any order:

> *1 – What is Ms. Klein first name?*
> *2 – Who is Ms. Klein's employer?*
> *3 – Where is Qwave Ltd located?*
> *4 – Define a gravitational wave.*
> *5 – Define the role of the frog.*

The last question was a private joke that required no precise answer, but the trio in the machine deemed it entertaining to present a stumper to the questionee.

Wind had no issue with the first three requests, but *four* required finesse.

Gravitational waves are produced by the coalescence of two stellar-mass black holes, as in the case of GW 151226. On the basis of general relativity, they transport energy as gravitational radiation.

He hoped that would suffice since that was all he got; on the other hand, he absolutely had no idea what the last one was about. He pondered on it for a while before concluding it was a trick question above his pay grade – he simply wrote *croak!*

"Welcome Windsor Kassel! How can we be of assistance?" the monitor displayed.

He was in! He felt elated. He had no idea he could have entered anything and still have had access to the machine, but the taste of success was sweet. It was the perfect occasion to light one up and get stoned.

He went for his stash in one of the upper cabinets of the kitchen area – instead he found a note that said:

Pleasure always comes after
a successful performance.

He was beyond himself in disbelief. Who in the world was so wicked as to take his sacred herb away?

He immediately went down the stairs to reach for the metal door, with the intention of getting to the house in Richmond where there was plenty of the stuff.

The lock was unresponsive.

He then realized what had happened – Jalesh's visit hadn't simply been a reminder someone was getting impatient; it was a lock-up until he delivered.

The world abruptly collapsed under Wind. To top it all, the program in his mind had purposely assumed neutral mode to make him feel the impact of what it all meant. He had entered into a contract with the Devil and there was no out until he produced what he was in the Interverse for. He sat down on the floor for a while to absorb the significance of Jalesh's actions, then got up and walked towards the awaiting laptop.

18 – DEAL WITH JALESH

Maggie Phillips couldn't believe Wind had driven off with her dog – although it wasn't the first time he had kicked her out of her own van. Their relationship had been a rollercoaster since he took that position in Silicon Valley. Of course, she had no idea her man had been "tuned," while his tech job took him to incomprehensible places.

She was stranded in Eureka, but on some level, felt relieved – for once she was able to think. She immediately called Marshall, who asked her to swing by the office to sort things out. He knew she was in trouble in more ways than she was willing to admit, and perhaps he could be of assistance. Pau instantly offered to help. The social worker side of her was feeling the void after Jarred's completed rehabilitation. As soon as Maggie entered the office, the young Master went to work. A warm hug followed by a good cry and a cup of tea performed miracles. An Angel-grade shoulder and back massage grounded all the tension that had accumulated over the months, until Linda Sue's old friend practically turned to a puddle. Gulliver, who was just returning from the artists' loft, suggested that Maggie use the bed next door for a well deserved nap – she obliged, as exhaustion had overtaken her. She had barely left the office, when Saka and Vera emerged from the portal in the closet, fresh from their excursion to *Base Five* in the *Hestilles Circle*.

"How was your walk?" Marshall humored.

"We snuck by Wind on the way out," Vera replied. "Without Liv and Grisha to delay him, things could have been interesting."

"Well, Maggie's on Jarred's bed – passed out," Pau informed the two.

"Any news of Sam?" Saka inquired.

"Funny you should ask," Jarred returned, "we just heard he is visiting with Angel Bluefeather; Vac dropped him there after he showed up during a meeting with the three Warriors."

"He also mentioned the frog," Pau added.

Saka laughed, for she knew a thing or two about the ubiquitous amphibian.

"What are we going to tell Maggie?" Vera asked.

"She thinks her dog's with Wind – no need to confuse her," Marshall replied.

"So what's up with your mission?" Jarred probed.

"Saka and I scanned the whole joint," Vera explained. "We should be getting some interesting data out of it, I believe."

"We also left a couple of riddles around the place, which should keep him busy wondering for a while," Saka laughed. "Vera even hid his weed, hoping to make it look like the heat was on from above."

"That couldn't possibly freak him out, could it?" Marshall remarked, waxing sarcastic.

"Are you sure you're not throwing protocol out the window?" Pau questioned.

"Protocol is for balanced games, darling," Vera countered. "The plan here is to instill confusion; we're trying to weaken him. The guy's corrupted – we need to break him so that he can pick himself up. You should know – you've been there."

Pau thought for a second.

"Who corrupted him?" she asked – suspicious.

"Someone who needed top Dogs in exchange for a

"kindness." In a case like Wind and his very useful skills, and considering what was at stake, probably one of the Hektor founders," Jarred replied, guessing she would immediately grasp whom he was referring to.

"It seems to never end," Pau simply said.

There was poetic irony to the deal Joonas had struck with the rulers of *Iorus*. Had The Dove been aware Wind was sitting on the knowledge of a computer capable of accessing the Realms, there was a great chance the hacker would have been working for Hektor instead. By then, the Rastafarian, through his many wheeling and dealings with inter-dimensional marauders, had discovered Linda Sue's machine was more than just a Mac on steroids – especially when there were rumors the laptop could have been snatched at the crossing of gates that involved an emerging Oneness in an extremely remote probability. Such aggrandizing speculations were not uncommon among cross-universal substance users – it was also why ears were all around them. Normally, computers were of no importance to rulers and their deputies, but one suspected of travels to impossible places, couldn't be any ordinary machine. Gandreal, before he departed, had suggested that no stone be left unturned. Jalesh was vigilant; he had Wind followed and eavesdropped on 24/7. When he had ascertained the black man was the same individual referred in the ruler's vision as the one who would send the armies of the *Hestilles Circle* into the new worlds, he contacted Joonas, who at the time was in desperate need of skilled Dogs for his planned infiltration of the Warriors' Realms. The Hektor elder had no interest in what the Interverse sought; he made the deal of corrupting Wind as a straight business transaction, not even willing to contemplate the nature of the gross imbalance at its source, so preoccupied was he with his insatiable thirst for revenge and conquest. Had he been made conscious of what Jalesh was after, an entirely different reality would have unfolded, and Joonas, instead of going after Pau, Leòn, and Gerald Brinsk, would have most certainly refocused his attention on Misu and his concealed domain amongst the Warriors'. But that was left to yet another of the many scenarios that saw the new Oneness fail – in an epic clash of old enmities – as Joonas was among the early Masters who vehemently blocked Gandreal from joining the Guild.

Saka wasn't in the least bit preoccupied with Maggie's state of being. Old Linda Sue would have been concerned, but times had changed. Her once-friend was in charge of her own reality, now contemplating the outcome of extremely poor choices, especially those in line with her failure to acknowledge Wind was a changed person from the man she had rejoined in the Bay Area, shortly after the camping trip in the Siskiyous.

Friend or not, Saka wasn't interested in helping someone who wasn't willing to face the beliefs that kept her pinned to the bottom of her down-spiraled reality. Margaret Phillips had no choice but to pick herself up with her own tools. Perhaps Pau could help break the spell of self-hypnosis; after all, she was a naturally gifted psychologist with many cognitive and intuitive skills at her disposal. But Maggie was the proverbial stoner who belonged to a class that saw themselves impervious to the influence of personal demons. The Goddess of Light had no sense of morality around weed; she smoked it and greatly enjoyed kicking back when the time was right – it was that the time was always right for her old friend. She couldn't see Maggie rise up if she didn't lay off the stuff – she was simply running away from her greater potential, by allowing herself to slump into a state of quasi-permanent lethargy occasionally fluffed up with ordinary drama, mostly as a reflexive means to affirm she was still alive and breathing.

Her dog had left her; that was as big as it could get. True that Sam was a free spirit that snuck out on occasion, but he was loyal. His desertion was indicative Maggie had been neglecting him, to instead cater to the whims of her abuser. As far as Saka saw it, there was no cause for her to whine about her loss, if only to feel sorry for herself.

Linda Sue would have reacted differently – instead, buying into her friend's drama, and showing support and understanding. But she had seen enough of the human victimization game, and perhaps her loss of patience towards it was in reflection of her own fragile humanity. Most likely, Saka had grown out of it and now yearned for horizons where energy was spent towards the greater purpose of moving forward. Yet, there was no way she couldn't show some form of compassion toward her old friend, even if firmness had to be at the base of it.

Maggie had always flirted with rebellion. She smoked pot in junior high, missed classes, had sex while others her age mostly gossiped about it, and consequently ended up in the principal's office with predictable regularity. At the time, she and Linda Sue were best friends. They lived close by, walked to school together, spent time at each other's places over the weekends, and attended the same parties together. Symbiotically-speaking, Maggie was a necessary bad influence on her friend, inasmuch as Linda Sue was the reason why she didn't cross the line into delinquency. While Klein went on to graduate in Social Works, Phillips dropped out of the San Francisco Art Institute where she had met Wind, to join the anarchist collective he belonged to in Oakland.

———————

By the time Maggie woke up, Marshall and Pau were locking the office.

"How you're feeling?" Saka asked.

"I'm not sure; caught in a bad dream's about the gist of it," she replied, as if doubtful of the stability of her reality.

"Marshall was able to locate and recover your van which was found abandoned in King Salmon, by the power plant; your things were still in it. The tow truck is on its way," Pau interjected.

"So, where are they?!" she queried, meaning Wind and Sam.

"Your boyfriend was last seen in Richmond. If your dog is anywhere in the area, he'll hopefully show up," Slaughter intoned.

"Sam isn't with him?" Maggie lamented.

"Based on the little we know, I am in no position to affirm whether he is or not," Slaughter stated.

"Sam's been gone before; he'll show up like he normally does. I'm sure you remember the camping trip," Saka inferred.

Maggie feigned reassurance.

"So what are you going to do, drive back down to the Bay Area, or stay in town for a few more days?" Jarred inquired.

"I probably should stick around until I hear from Sam, don't you think?"

"You're welcome to use our basement apartment, since Linda Sue chose to stay upstairs, but you may have to answer a few questions about Wind, if it's at all agreeable," Pau offered.

"Depends on the questions..."

"You can tell us what's appropriate or not when we ask," Vera said firmly.

"OK then," Maggie said, resigned.

———————

Jarred retired to his apartment, while Pau, Marshall, Saka, Vera, and Maggie swung by the Co-op for some take out. The tow truck had dropped the van on 3rd Street. A city cop had shown up but was sent away. Maggie had refused to press charges.

Saka and her old friend drove back to the Fieldbrook estate together. Very little was said. They both were very changed women from the days of the camping trip in the coastal range. It was as if the minute they came apart, they went in opposite directions. Maggie had eventually crossed the line to the stormier side of life, unmoored from the dock that had kept her from drifting away. Wind had not always been a bad influence – to the contrary – when she went into freefall at the art institute, moving in with him was probably what saved her from ending up on the street. Later, she returned to Humboldt, found well paid work as a real estate agent, rekindled her friendship with Linda Sue, and led the equivalent of a sane life, relative to her penchant for extreme stoner parties. She and Wind had broken up but had remained friends. When he called to ask her to get back together, it sounded like a good idea at the time. Her one close friend, Linda Sue, had left town for who knew where, so she packed her things and headed south with Sam.

"So what happened down there, Mag?" Saka asked. "Think about it for a bit; perhaps you can tell me later," she added.

"You don't want to know," Maggie answered.

"That bad, hey?"

"I'll tell you when I get a chance to pull my head out of my funk – maybe tomorrow."

Saka left it at that. They parked the van in the graveled lot and walked to the lit porch where Marshall, Pau, and Vera were sitting, waiting for them.

"Let's get to the food, I'm starving," Slaughter said, as he got up.

The meal conversation centered on the events of the day. Of course, much was left out, especially Saka and Vera's foray into Wind's pad, away from the universe as Maggie knew it. It was clear she had no idea what her boyfriend had been up to, save for moving large amounts of weed. She barely mentioned Sam, which Saka took as a sign something was sinking in.

Vera was staying upstairs with Saka, while Maggie was given the basement apartment, where she could claim as much thinking room as necessary. There were a few long days ahead of her, and providing she mustered the strength, they were going to be filled with much soul-searching.

Vera and Saka had work to do. As soon as Maggie had retired to her quarters, they hopped to Keyhole Lake via the concealed portal, to get to Le Lien's realm branch for the purpose of studying the data harvested from Wind's hangout. Spencer and Stefan had received the files earlier, which had been inputted to the system and now were being processed. The main objective was to identify the machines at the tech's disposal, and create a virtual version of his lab environment. Under "normal conditions," the agents would have left an "eye" in his system, permitting the linkage of the two setups, but the Interverse was so grossly out of synch with surface realities, that no coherent means of communication was ever achieved between the two milieus.

The Triad would be responsible for mapping the *Base 5* layout, as well as all connections with the main laboratories on *Iorus*, plus the réseau of outbound pathways. Because the trio was cut off from headquarters, an agent would have to sneak regularly into Wind's station to garner the updates to be inputted to the virtual environment.

Vac and Jarred had joined in. Pau and Marshall would later be briefed.

A giant, space monitor showed Wind's lab as a rotating three-dimensional blueprint with movable overlays. The Triad was not featured yet, but it was clear Wind had much processing power on tap. There were six Qwave machines that were immediately identified as to their original purpose; they were arrayed in a group configuration that also showed the tech was extremely skilled at utilizing resources that were not intended to work together. Other machines originated from alternative technologies garnered from dispersed galactic civilizations at various time points. None of them betrayed any form of sophisticated artificial intelligence, or the presence of an organic awareness comparable to The Triad, though the six laptops were ready-shells for the embedding of suitable consciousnesses.

The powerful Qwave programs kept on crunching data as the team gathered to study the construction of the virtual laboratory. All immediately observed that the station controlled the peripherals of a series of fixed transport pods on a larger celestial body. Guild technology was incapable of isolating the part of the Interverse in which the experiment was in the process of being conducted. The organization owned limited data on the dark world's geography, since it mutated randomly as the result of the fragility of the discarded creational elements that composed it. It often translated into a general chaos of stellar collapses, followed by powerful and disruptive gravitational storms, leading to the emergence of new bodies in unpredictable spaces, where only emptiness previously existed. The closest the Guild came to identifying regions was by the names of its tribal rulers and Fallen Angels, which it had tallied at the time of its founding. Other than that, it had no idea where those places existed in relation to surface universes.

"Based on what's here, our man has not figured

out yet how to load the Qwave laptops," Vera said.

"Not that there are many volunteers for the task on that side of existence," Spencer remarked.

"Though if he had known, he might have been looking at his setup very differently, meaning we would possibly be coming late in the game – maybe too late," Stefan pondered.

"Whether loaded or not, given enough time, his lab has enough processing power to achieve modest results. We now are clear the Interverse is behind the loft bleed-throughs – Jarred readings are showing an increase in intensity that demonstrates our man is at an early stage of completing his first test run. Since we know the main objective is not in an overtaking of surface universes, we are left with the Realms as the destination, and Misu as the insider," Vac laid out.

"What stops us from sabotaging Wind's mission?" Saka asked.

"You ask, then I must tell – we need him to open the individual realms," Vac returned.

"The plan is to take over without Wind knowing; that's why we chose to put The Triad in there," Spencer added.

"A controlled invasion is still an invasion. Shouldn't the Warriors be present at this meeting?" Saka asked, showing concern.

"The Warriors know; their work is very much tied to preparing for when it will happen," Vac answered.

"Our main objectives for now are to infiltrate that particular domain's mission, identify the ruler behind it, and to look into ways of deprogramming Wind, so that at the opportune time, he can be switched to an insider," Stefan explained.

"So, you want to use Wind," Saka probed.

"We want to give Wind the tools to free himself from his contract and save his life in the process; is it so bad if it serves us as well?" Vera asked.

"I am occasionally at a loss with Le Lien's ethics department, that's all," Saka countered,

"We all have our part in shaping the world; Wind's reality is for him to create. We didn't put him there, but somehow that's where we need him to be – his job will also be to protect The Triad," Vac concluded.

19 – JACO & LO-SHEN

Masters Jaco and Lo-Shen accepted Vac's invitation on the one condition it should be approved by Amaterasu. The Great One refused to partake, citing she no longer wished to influence the fate of the Realms. But she intuited that by not honoring the request, she would inevitably leave her stamp. She escorted the Third Eye members to her glass pyramid, deeming a private meeting essential to clear the dilemma.

"You are forcing my hand, but I have to consider your very presence here as being part of a choice I must have made at some subliminal level. Why do you seek my permission, Masters?" Amaterasu asked.

"We are aware a team is investigating members of the Interverse for actions that bear no consequence on any of the foreseeable realities of the Oneness," Jaco said. "But since Master Vac is the one requiring the services of Third Eye, we deem the request important. Though by helping, we may be breaking protocol," he added.

"The existence of Third Eye is already a protocol breaker; Le Lien has long replaced you as the official security branch, am I not correct?" Amaterasu countered.

"Third Eye remained because of XVII; the case was grandfathered in, so to speak," Lo-Shen explained.

"It could be that what Vac is presently involved with is also tied to XVII and Hektor; would that make a difference if it were?"

"If it bore consequences in our jurisdiction, it most certainly would; but since it concerns the Realms, we want no part in influencing their fate," Jaco argued.

"Hmm, interesting – are you sure you did not influence the Realms when you arrested Caax, Dzalarhons, and a good part of XVII during Ma-l's gathering? You did not seem to be concerned then," Amaterasu questioned.

"We obviously did, but we didn't take it into consideration at the time – it was the continuation of a case," Lo-Shen said.

"Perhaps it is still continuing," Amaterasu offered.

"Are you saying we should help Vac and his team?" Jaco asked.

"What I am saying is that there is no such thing as a jurisdiction away from the Guild when you are being asked to help. You already are integral to the new Oneness since you have interacted at the legal level in the presence of a panel, by partaking in the enactment of the first bylaws of the Great Hall. I am not even sure why you should seek my approval," Amaterasu replied.

"When we were made aware you did no longer wish to interact with realm process, we figured it would be wise to ask you first," Jaco said.

"You created a paradox and put me at its center, Master Jaco. By doing so, you made your choice of assisting in the Interverse investigation – I couldn't make myself any clearer," the Great One concluded.

The team consisting of Vac, Vera, Saka, Spencer, and Jarred arranged for a meeting with the two Third Eye operatives. A general assembly in the Realms was favored, but Liv and Grisha couldn't leave their post, while Pau and Marshall volunteered to keep Maggie distracted. Lillian, Geir and Stefan, feeling their roles were secondary, would simply stay put until asked to assist. They would nonetheless be kept in the know.

They instead met at a shore house owned by an Angel on assignment in Stinson Beach. I was fitted with a portal that connected directly with the one installed in Richmond, just in case Wind or other Roamers showed unusual activity around the decommissioned refinery.

Only Jarred needed introducing, since everyone else had already met during the celebration of the Realms.

"We're looking for a name," Vac began. "The name of a ruler that goes by 'G' or 'Gand,'" he added.

"He is thought to have infiltrated the Realms in the guise of a Warrior known as Misu. He might have done so with the help of XVII," Spencer explained.

There was a pause – Lo-Shen came forward.

"It is assumed you have ascertained this intruder did not originate from Hektor or any advanced society capable of extreme infiltration, am I right?"

"Correct."

"There were countless tribes, many that split into secondary families; each with leaders whose names could change on a whim. You have to understand these entities were powerful, having arisen directly from the creational pool as makers themselves. I was a tribal leader before the formation of the Guild; Amaterasu, Vac, Jaco, Joonas, and Qo'ai-Marael among others, preceded us as the first organization of Angels, many of whom are now among the Ones. Of course, I am mostly updating the Goddess of Light among us. At any rate, anyone capable of infiltrating the Realms by taking the cover of a Warrior is most likely one of the Fallen Angels, apparently a powerful lord with access to information directly acquired from the Guild, quite possibly through Hektor or XVII. The one Master who could answer your question is under protection of the Great Ones, and so is Joonas who was directly involved in the Guild acceptance process. We very much doubt any of the XVII members will ever collaborate," Lo-Shen said.

"It doesn't mean our memory cannot be kindled," Jaco cut in, somewhat emphatically. "We also possess a list of rulers that could possibly contain the entity you wish to identify. Among those meeting the criterion, I personally remember Gandhi and Gandolf, both too ruthless to ever come close to joining the Guild... But now, thinking of it, there was one, an odd gentleman by the name of Gandreal, whom I highly recommended to the panel, but who, somehow, never made it among the Masters – maybe Lo-Shen remembers."

"Yes, I do," the founder returned. "He was also on my list of recommendations. I wonder whatever happened of him... Let me check with records."

She entered the enquiry into her handset and waited for the data to download. She then looked intensely at the group.

"Interesting," she said, before she began reading.

"Gandreal, Lord of Hestilles. Acceptance level: clear. Application denied by Joonas. Reasons for denial: confidential."

"It makes little sense..." she added, looking once more at the screen.

"It sounds like it's calling for a review; can we access the full dossier?" Jaco asked Lo-Shen.

"It's one of ours; I don't see why not," she returned, visibly mesmerized.

"How could Joonas single-handedly bar a Master from joining the Guild?" Saka asked.

"Joonas was heading the group in charge of final decisions, but he couldn't have made that choice alone; it took two to finalize the process," Jaco countered.

Lo-Shen once again appeared stirred by what she saw on her screen.

"Access denied?" she voiced, befuddled.

"Are you saying we can't get to our own files?" an incredulous Jaco asked.

"It seems so, at least not with my current clearance level," she answered sarcastically.

"Of course, there are no higher levels. Can you find a way to date the denial and put a name to it?"

"I'm afraid not. It's made to look like either you or I officialized it, which is obviously absurd," Lo-Shen remarked.

The group stood silent, witness of the implications unraveling before them.

"When was the last time you accessed confidential documents, Master Jaco?" Spencer finally inquired.

"The odd thing is that Master Lo-Shen and I have access to all of them, all of the time – we never are barred from our own files. The seal of confidentiality only applies to outsiders; but even that is unrealistic."

"So, in other word, someone hacked your system," Saka remarked.

"If I were you, I first would check whether that clearance issue applies to all files or not, then I would isolate those that are denied," Spencer suggested.

"We have been working with the most protected

dossier in our entire system, that of XVII, so we know we have not been shut out of it. It would appear only this particular item has the extra protection, meaning someone is invested in obscuring vital data," Lo-Shen replied.

"Then you must ask yourself who, beyond you two, has unrestricted access to that data," Jarred urged.

"It's only us two now – passwords were reset at the closure of the organization, when it was replaced by Le Lien. Additionally, the system cannot be reached from the outside. But before the switch-over, it could have been a number of Masters," Jaco shared.

"It is critical we find out why Gandreal was denied admission, especially if the Fallen Angel is indeed Misu; in which case, I am of the sentiment Joonas knew the Realms where at the center of it," Vac said pointedly.

"What makes you say that?" Saka asked.

"We wouldn't be here to talk about it; that's the 'what,'" Vac returned, somewhat emphatically.

The group opted to clear their minds with a walk along the sandy beach. In recap, Jaco and Lo-Shen's job was to come up with the identity of the one seeking to protect the Gandreal file, as well as the means to regain access to the pertinent information it contained, in hopes of defining the possible motives behind the lord's actions. It was left to the others to locate his domain in the Interverse and isolate the team in charge of the Realms mission.

———————

Vac had found himself involved in many scenarios over the eons. He mentally repositioned himself at the precise time point of the Guild's selection process, during which he was in charge of examining the approval rating of many applicants; although, Gandreal was not one of them. Part of Third Eye's role then, was to prevent corruption of the applications by exterior interests, those of a powerful few with a common, deep-seated wish to control how the Guild would be structured and divided. The league of Angels was the brainchild of the Great Ones, who foresaw a democratic system of checks and balances as a necessary organism in the rapidly evolving Oneness. Only tribal leaders with a vast capacity for tolerance, along many other virtues, were selected as candidates by the original team that included Vac, Joonas, and Jaco among the many. Naturally, there was a strong opposition to a formula many thought of as weak and ill-fated, but time proved them wrong, while sentiments eroded.

As they returned to the beach house, Vac privately decanted the basics of the meeting. Although the Third Eye files were in the hand of the two operatives, Le Lien must have had knowledge of them during the changeover, notwithstanding the authority to demand access to them at any time via expressed request.

"How do Le Lien agents get to the files when they need them?" He asked Jaco.

"They have to go through us. Only after proper screening do we send copies from a separate 'check-valved' server – access to the system is not granted," Jaco emphasized.

"Besides Joonas, do you have names of operatives who could have tweaked the dossier?" Vera inquired.

Lo-Shen quickly retrieved the entire register of the agents who operated during Third Eye's existence from her handset. Jaco glanced over her shoulders – he shuddered when he saw the name: Master Ekaterina.

"It wasn't Joonas someone tried to shield, but Gandreal!" Jaco exclaimed.

"Please explain," Vac requested.

"It was meant to look like Joonas coded the file to protect its confidentiality. I'm not saying he did not bar Gandreal from the Guild, but I am now convinced he didn't lock the document. Master Ekaterina was one of our agents during the course of the selection process, but then she chose to be transferred to a remote assignment in the newly delineated field of operation. I never saw her again and quickly forgot about her... until I came face to face with Master Theyia in the Great Hall during Ma-l's grand gathering. The Master reminded me of a face I had once known, but I never was able to make the connection. XVII's Theyia is agent Ekaterina – she's the one who doctored the file," Jaco described.

"For what reason?" Saka asked.

"For the purpose of hiding why Joonas turned down Gandreal's applications," Jaco returned.

"Hiding it from those who would be looking into his motives for seeking to infiltrate the Warriors' Realms...?" Vera puzzled over.

"I have scanned the entire Third Eye archives – Gandreal's file is the only protected one. It is bound to mean something," Lo-Shen informed the group.

"Listen," Spencer said, "we have named our man with near certainty, but we need to crack the code that shrouds that file. We may start preparing for a deep mission into the Interverse, but I am not going to mobilize all of our resources until I we are absolutely sure whom it is we're after."

"If XVII's Theyia is indeed the one who 'confidentialized' the file, I am fairly certain the second we touch it, it will be destroyed. I wouldn't doubt she embedded a seed in it. The fact there is a connection between XVII and Gandreal is grounds enough for us to move forward – time is of the essence. Master Spencer, I am starting to believe our Fallen Angel is a much bigger fish than anticipated," Vac put forth.

"Then I will commandeer all means to access information about his world and resources," the agent pronounced.

"Of course, everyone knows Master Theyia was one of three XVII members, with Niamh and Tealsky, released from the old tunnels, and later sent into exile in the domain of Dahbar, in the realms of Hektor," Lo-Shen added.

"Are you sure she will not talk?" Saka asked.

"Whether she will or not isn't the issue – she cannot be extradited as per the asylum clause enacted under recent Guild and Hektor joined guidelines. She is untouchable, and so is the entirety of the XVII group," Lo-Shen answered.

"How is this serving us? Doesn't it seem like a reckless move to let go of rogue elements before they give all they have?" Saka vented.

"It was a closed case – we don't operate under the barbaric laws of your old world, Goddess," Jaco clarified.

20 – THE TRIAD

Liv and Grisha were alerted to some activity in the area of the corrugated tin shed. The two Roamers, who were left behind in Eureka, had found their way back, seeking to reconnect with Wind. The two agents positioned themselves within viewing distance of the building and waited. As soon as the men reemerged, it became clear something was up. The shotgun microphone picked-up just enough to inform the operatives the gates to the fragile probability were shut – the lab was off limits.

"Fuck him!" one was heard blurting out.

The information reached Vera and Saka, who were still in Stinson Beach with Lo-Shen and Jaco. To the general approval, they readied themselves for action and were gone in an instant.

Ironically, the two Roamers, upon returning to their black Crown Victoria, were immediately surrounded by police, for they had unwisely stolen the abandoned vehicle of a most-wanted criminal, right after his narrow escape from a high-speed chase. Since they were also high and drunk, built-in safety codes promptly deleted the programs in their minds, leaving them with zero memory of Wind and the Interverse.

"It appears our friend has holed himself up!" Liv informed the two approaching figures.

"Or that he's not allowed out," Vera suggested.

"That poses a problem with us getting to The Triad unnoticed," Saka observed.

"That is, if the stone can still get us there... Hopefully, that path remains open," Vera remarked.

"Best is to investigate. Let's at least try to reach the midpoint reality," Saka proposed.

"While you two go in there, we'll inform the rest of the team," Liv said.

"There also are updates; check with Jarred," Vera added, as the pair descended the metal stairs.

"What if Wing's using the probability as a platform to reach other parts of the underworld?" Vera wondered.

"Then it means he could be gone and we should go the whole way," Saka returned.

"I like the way you think, girlfriend, but let's nonetheless stay sharp," Vera cautioned.

The stone around Saka's neck hummed as expected, but it vibrated at a lower frequency, in a likely call for pacing and restrain. As they approached the heavy door, it practically pulsed like a slow heartbeat. Saka intuited they were being asked to wait. The Goddess couldn't cognitively make sense of the change in the gem's behavior, but she understood it was collecting data and making adjustments. It was presumable that the closing of the gate was forcing a reconfiguration of the way across it. Finally, the stone resumed with its usual drone, indicating the path was clear.

Saka and Vera landed in the black-walled corridor that led to the second of the matched security doors. They knew that past it, they had to think quickly – either they continued on to Wind's station or canceled. There would be no turning back past the half-way point to the shingled house that stood in the fragile reality behind that door.

"We cross, have a glance, and get back in," Vera said, "No need to jeopardize the mission – there's too much at stake."

"I agree, let's make it quick," Saka replied.

It was exactly what they did, except that the second they made it to the other side, the stone stopped droning, indicating there was no turning around.

"Either we have no control of this situation, or your intentions are unclear," Vera told Saka – suspicious.

"I have to trust that one way or the other we're on course with the best case scenario – what choice do we have now but to run for the house?" Saka pointed.

They made it down to the basement in record time, crossing the heavy door to the station without even pausing. The stone had let them know that time was critical by humming wildly.

Naturally, they were far from expecting to not be standing in Wind's laboratory.

———————————

The room was bright, just four bare, windowless, white walls. Three medium-height figures stood at its center – one woman and two men.

The female came forward.

"Welcome Saka and Vera, my name's Ofélia; allow me to introduce two other familiar characters: Daniel to my right, and Patrick – we're The Triad."

The silence that followed begged to be cut with a knife, though Vera barely contained the humor of the moment when she saw Saka's face frozen in utter bedazzlement.

"Angel Vera knows us from before the time we started teaming under our current name, so she can afford to make fun of the situation, Goddess," Patrick – the dark-haired one – told Saka.

"The 'geeks in a box'; I'm so sorry," Saka said, beyond herself with embarrassment.

"Now we're out of the box," Daniel – the fair-haired one – returned, laughing.

"Ofélia, all that time I thought you sounded like a man," Saka confessed.

"It's alright, dear, those awful speakers have never done us justice," the tech Master returned.

"Actually," Vera cut in, "it's been so long that I practically forgot who were behind The Triad."

"That would be a compliment," Patrick humored.

"Now that we have been properly introduced, let's get to why we're here together in this place," Ofélia began. "This environment is a simulation. This room doesn't really exist in the context of a fixed physical reality – it is nonetheless where we operate from. For now, it is a blank canvas, but it could be anything – or nothing at all. It's quite irrelevant since you are inside our sphere of consciousness as we are in yours – the lines don't exist. If they did, you would not be traveling through metal doors to meet with us inside a program. While it is rare for Angels to delve in the artificial layers of quantum computing, it is common practice at Le Lien. Liv, Spencer, and the three of us pioneered the method as soon as the technology began to reach various evolving species. As the use of computers became more ubiquitous, it allowed us the means to assist subjects in ways that kept us in the background, while providing us with immediate access to immense resources. As present Earth technology lacks in processing power, hence limiting our movements, we nudge these subjects towards better machines, as in the cases of the many scientists that have been accessing Qwave's customized instruments. It is also allowing us to cross over, as with Olaf and you, Saka, without the need to switch physical forms, or even assignments. The added advantage of operating from a virtual room keeps us out of harm's reach, should a machine be destroyed, while it permits us to move from one to another, or work from several simultaneously. Things get somewhat trickier when it comes to the Interverse, where the option of an escape door is limited to a safe room such as this one, but one without the means to get out of, unless the machine is returned to its natural environment. We created the path you came through as we scanned and coded our travels with Wind. Qwave laptops are always on, even when they're powered off – you may say they operate in 'active dream mode.' Now Saka: the stone gifted to you by Amaterasu is one of the most powerful decoder in the existence of the Oneness – its computing power is tied to All Things, thus analogous to pure, unrestricted consciousness – yet it taps from your essence. The decision to create the path could not have come at a more auspicious time, as Wind has now been prohibited from leaving his station by Deputy Jalesh from *Iorus*, in the *Hestilles Circle*."

"Now you must return – this room is only temporary from your standpoint," Daniel said.

"Let me update your handset, Vera; it will permit Le Lien to complete the virtual lab," Patrick added.

"Also," Ofélia told Saka, "the stone will inform you when we're ready with more data, or if Wind leaves, in case you need to access his physical space – any questions?"

"Do you have any knowledge of the platform reality behind the metal door we came through – does it provide access into other areas?" Vera asked.

"It does, but without specific knowledge of your destination, even the stone could not prevent you from becoming an abstract artifact of its makeup, though it will do all it can to prevent such a predicament. We trust you know better than explore without purpose," Patrick concluded, guiding Saka and Vera to the spot of their exit.

"Sorry, this room cannot welcome the iron door you're familiar with," Ofélia humored.

The two were soon running back to the old generator shed, on their way to the Richmond of Marshall's world.

———————

With the news of Wind's forced confinement, the team felt time was auspicious for a general meeting at Le Lien headquarters in New Angel City, (the official name for the New Guild Center, in spite of much debate as to its lack of originality.)

The three Warriors and the entire team, including Marshall Slaughter, Geir Flemmingson, and Lillian, were present. Sam, accompanied by Angel Bluefeather, made a cameo appearance to the delight of all. The Triad joined in with a comprehensive speech included in the data provided by Vera's handset.

Their combined input pointed heavily in the direction of the controlled continuation of Gandreal's mission; though, with the tunnel Gestalt gone, only Misu was theoretically left with the codes that could open the Realms, but strictly from outside his own – someone still had to let him out. That exit, as it appeared, was through the dream meadows, but as Misu had long abandoned that option, his personal lea was in the process of deleting itself from the consequence of neglect, and forever close that avenue. Analogically-speaking, Misu had locked the only remaining door out of his reality, and thrown the key away. Furthermore, in the event he was able to get out, even without his mission coming to completion with the arrival of the *Hestilles Circle's* armies, he would be in a position to forever bar the Realms from merging, and successfully prevent the rise of the new Oneness – a powerful blow to the Guild as well as the Great Ones, even in the light of his own defeat. It was clear to the team that the priority was to find the means to replace Gestalt George and synchronize the controlled invasion with the opening of the Warriors' domains, which was made all the more complicated by the fact that based on the number of transport pods tallied by The Triad, armies could only be shipped in limited numbers, implying the Realms would most likely be opened one at a time.

"My head's spinning!" Vera exclaimed.

The team agreed to a brief break.

———————

Upon resuming, Vac brought into question the feasibility of preventing the armies of *Iorus* from inflicting damage as they poured into each of the Realms, all the while keeping Gandreal away from suspecting foul play.

"Based on the data collected by The Triad, each of their pods can accommodate up to fifty Roamers. At maximum capacity, they can deliver over five hundred fighters – perhaps enough to overtake the domain of an unsuspecting Warrior," Spencer said. "But should we concern ourselves with numbers and methods when we need to figure out how to free Misu from his world. Armies will not dock the Realms without his signal."

"Absolutely, the logistics are in plain sight: they will invade when both they and Misu are ready – so far, it doesn't look like they can accomplish anything without us helping at both ends. The irony of the picture overwhelms me," Ma-l said.

"It's like a multifaceted paradox; we've got Hektor, XVII, and a begrudged ruler of the Interverse who've been trying to outplay each other for eons over this, while those who could help are either on a leave-of-absence under the protection of the Ones or in exile in some remote corner of their long-time nemesis' domains," Pau cut in. "As if it weren't absurd enough, it appears Wind was conditioned by Joonas in a deal that what meant to strip the Hektor founder of what he coveted most – namely the Realms. And to further the irony, none seem to be aware of how anticlimactically it all has stacked up," she finished.

"And that is the crux of it," Vac concurred.

While all agreed they had come to some form of impasse, the consensus was that much progress had been made, and as long as they persevered, the end of the tunnel would eventually be reached.

Xarn requested permission to speak.

"I am a Warrior; I understand the fundamentals of strategy. I have witnessed conquests and defeats from both sides. The greatest victories have been those that required no battles. The Realms were not conquered, they were created from the goodness of the heart – they will not be defended with arrows and spears, and no blood will be spilled. We did not come this far to return whence we originated; that I guarantee with all my might. Those fighters will not be able to cross the thresholds of the domains, as long as no Warrior is willing to battle. I trust our brothers and sisters share my feelings."

"Interesting you should be bringing the subject of war, Xarn," Enola countered, "but I've been thinking about the fact the three of us never met Misu in the dream meadows – we have no idea what his relationship was with the other Warriors, and what they may have known of his plan. Could they have willfully closed their domains? Were they promised something if they did...? How are we sure it was the work of the Gestalt?"

"What could be worth more than joining the dream gathering then?" Xarn asked.

"The silence of the lanes is for us to hear – what if we have it all wrong?" Enola returned.

"If we need to brainstorm on this, perhaps here isn't the place for it," Ma-1 cut in.

"Everything's well taken," Spencer assured; "it's all being inputted to the database."

"Before we close this meeting," Vac said, "let's bring forth the most important points: Gandreal must come out of his realm in order to signal the beginning of the invasion, while his troops have to be ready to do the crossing – ideally, the entirety of his forces, so that all the realms can be opened at once. Then we have to figure out how to neutralize his armies before they strike."

"Are you suggesting *Iorus* should build more transport pods?" Spencer enquired.

"I am indeed," Vac returned.

"Then we have much work ahead of us! Is anyone opposed to pursuing that route, pending we're able to relay what the objective is to The Triad?" the agent asked.

All approved of the plan. The team felt relieved to be able to come out of the meeting with at least one major decision taken. Many other details and minor assignments had been spread across the various subgroups, while options had been left open in regard to coaxing Misu out of his realm. Vera jokingly suggested using Sam, who coincidentally was walking towards her in the company of Bluefeather.

As the gathering dispersed, Marshall, Pau, Jarred, Geir, Lillian, Stefan, Liv, and Grisha returned to Earth via Keyhole Lake; while Vac, Saka, Xarn, Enola, Ma-l, Vera, Bluefeather, and Sam left for their respective domains. Later, Vac caught a portal to his private sanctum atop a mountain overlooking a valley that stretched to the sea – a dearly appreciated gift from the Great Goddess.

Wolf, as it was often the case, had been waiting for him.

"Am I imposing?" the coywolf asked.

"You never are, my dear friend," Vac replied.

21 – PROGRESSIVE AWAKENING

Maggie Phillips returned to Fieldbrook from her aimless search for Sam, only to find the house empty. Marshall's downtown office was also closed. It seemed everyone had left without telling her what was happening, making the reality of her emotional isolation all the more vivid. She realized she didn't know much about Marshall and his partner Pau. She had met the detective on a few occasions during Linda Sue's employment, but besides casual interaction, mostly at parties, she had never connected at a heart level – he merely was her friend's boss. So finding herself in his house alone was grounds for a sense of disconnect she was having difficulties squaring with. What had happened to her? What was she doing there? She felt she was looking at her life from the outside in, an observer estranged from a reality created in a vacuum. The last couple of years with Wind unraveled in her mind like someone else's story, as if she had just awakened from a bad dream, her heart still pounding and her mind in an unsettling fog. For once, she didn't even want to get stoned. The loss of Sam was a heartbreaker, but she understood why he wouldn't want to hang around the energy that had loomed over her relationship with Wind. She surmised the man had been acting as if possessed, ever since he started calling himself a high-end consultant for the tech industry. He was gone to China, Korea, or South Africa for long periods at a time, supposedly to counsel on the latest in computing, but he never took any luggage with him or even changed his style of clothing, which consisted of kaki slacks, T-shirts depicting various varietals of cannabis, and Teva flip-flops – but it was the computer industry after all! Maggie didn't know what to think; cognitively, it made some kind of sense, but intuitively, there loomed an ominous cloud of uncertainty over her. Mostly, her mind was intermingling with the information – had she surrendered to her feelings, doubt would not have been in the picture.

She attempted to mentally sketch the string of events that followed Wind's first behavioral changes. Why didn't she confront him when he started to become psychologically abusive? His words were like the silk of spiders' snares, almost invisible, yet immobilizing by the very nature of their mystifying content – a web of finely spun logical fallacies aimed at attracting, then confusing the mind, before sending it reeling down the spiral of self-doubt. A sickening feeling arose from deep inside her guts: had he been drugging her? Was the stuff she had been smoking tainted with other substances? After all, the weed she had been getting stoned on, all came from Wind. It was strong, but now she realized the buzz wasn't always a cheerful one – to the contrary. "Oh Mag, what have you done?" she thought, a sharp pang gnawing at her stomach. She wanted to cry, but she couldn't – she was too riled up with emotions to allow for it. Repression was knocking at the door for release. It was an indefinable aching, stratified by years of nameless apprehension, brought to its breaking point by pretending life was good when it was nothing but Hell. A vague sense of identity was begging to check out at the register of reason.

Maggie decided to stick around Humboldt Bay, no longer caring for the things left behind in Oakland. She had once rebuilt her life in Eureka – she would do it again. But first, she was going to have the leftover weed analyzed. She called various dispensaries for leads, but they all claimed she had to go through a pharmacology lab for the proper testing – it also would cost up to a grand. Maybe Marshall or Pau would know of a place that flew under the radar... She felt troubled enough already – no point bringing more aggravation to her life by drawing the official channels into her mess. All she needed to know was whether the pot was spiked or not.

She poured another cup of coffee as she sat at the counter of the small kitchenette. She wondered if the couple would be willing to rent the space to her – it was perfect – plus there was plenty of outdoor space for Sam to roam around upon his return. The thought was crossed by another that showed life without the goofy Labrador; she slumped on her stool, put her elbows on both sides of her cup, and with her head between her hands, she finally allowed herself to cry.

When Marshall, Pau, and Jarred returned to the office, there were several short messages from Maggie left on the answering machine. The detective had figured she would be on her way south by now, but by the tone of it, it appeared she was still in town. Pau called her number – she was at the house.

"Is everything OK?" the young Master asked.

"I'm emerging, but I need some help," Maggie replied.

"We had to absent ourselves on business, but we should be back home within the hour. Hang in there, sister, we'll pick up food on the way," Pau returned.

"New drama?" Slaughter inquired, after Pau had hung up.

"Nope, I think she's alright. I have the feeling she's not anxious to run back to Wind."

"It sounds like the call of wisdom was answered. Hopefully, she's not going to be too stoned when we get home; I'd like to know what she's made of for a change," the investigator expressed.

"I don't think she's as dumb as the decision she made to get together with Wind – I'm almost inclined to believe she was under some form of hypnosis," Pau opined.

"If Wind's mind was messed with, how far off is she from having been subjected to the same treatment, or influenced by its extended effect?"

"If Joonas had come near her, I would know," Pau contended. "No, she's awakening from something entirely different – I sense it."

"Hope you're right; I've always liked Maggie, even from the little interaction we've had in the past – she seemed fun."

"Then we ought to help her get rekindled with that joy, don't you think, Marshall?"

"I agree," the detective replied, looking his partner in the eyes with a broad smile melded with the conspiring energy of soulmates.

––––––––––––

Marshall explained to Maggie that the route to the analysis of federally prohibited substances, even with honest intentions, was at best a convoluted process. The way to do it was through a chemistry student in need of a few bucks to pay the rent. She handed the stash over to him, as if it were a bag of pathogen-laced weed.

"You don't look like you'll be smoking that brand for a while," he joked.

"I think I'm off getting high for the time being, Marshall, something's not right with me – I need my health back," she returned.

"What makes you say something is not right with you?" Pau asked.

"I feel shaky all over and nauseated; maybe it's just the shock of being dumped and losing my dog in the process," she replied.

"So, you want to stay in Humboldt?" Marshall cut in. "How are you doing with money; can you cover expenses until you find a job?"

"I should be fine; money's never been one of my worry areas. I have a savings account at a local credit union. I might as well ask now: would you consider renting your basement apartment to me?"

Pau and Marshall looked at each other.

"We were contemplating offering you the option," Pau answered. "Listen, if after two weeks we still like each other and you can afford six hundred a month, it's yours. That should give you a bit of time to decompress and start looking for work. As part of the deal though, we would like you to stay clean for a while. We have nothing against pot, but for your sake, it kind of makes sense," she added.

"Thank you, I can walk my talk – it's a deal," Maggie returned, half crying.

"Wow, we now have a full house with Linda Sue upstairs and you in the studio!" Pau exclaimed.

"Though by the look of it, Linda Sue is going to mostly be in and out – she had to take off for a couple of days. She also likes to hang out with Geir and his partner Lillian in Iceland. I believe you met Geir briefly when he visited after your camping trip in the Siskiyous," Marshall voiced.

"Yes, the rotund gentleman – he was funny. He may have been slightly drunk when we met, but he was quite charming," she answered smiling. "Too bad Linda Sue's not going to be around – we have a lot of catching up to do. On the other hand, I could need the mental space, so it works OK with me."

———————

The test results from the pot sample came out positive for a chemical compound closely related to methamphetamine in that it used the $C10H15N$ molecular string as a base, but was synthesized with an unknown bond. It was enough for Maggie to confirm she had been high on more than just weed for a long time; the reality of which made her head spin and sparked mounting anger towards Wind.

"For what purpose would he want to do that?" she questioned, visibly shaken.

"Probably to prevent you from asking about his frequent absences or his actions in general, I assume," Pau said, trying to nudge Maggie in the direction of revealing details she might have intuitively picked-up along the way.

"So you're telling me he's been hiding the true nature of his dealings from me," she probed nervously.

"I'm just speculating; he could just as well be pathologically jealous to the point of needing to keep you on a leash, but that sounds rather unflattering," Pau returned. "Maybe something'll come up that will explain."

"'Fucked-up' doesn't lean towards rational explaining – this whole thing's confusing in a very sick way!"

"Confusion is the most desired end effect from an abuser's standpoint. He needed you around to prove to himself he was good enough for a relationship – he's obviously in need of massive help," Pau speculated.

"To convince him of it is going to require a gun to his head, I'm afraid. According to him, he's perfect!"

"That's often the case, Maggie; those in most need of counseling are customarily the same ones who keep on telling others how they should live their lives. They are driven by a compulsion to shift their issues onto those they seek to control. It's what happens when the ego flies solo, untethered from its source of existence," Pau pointed.

"All I know is that he wasn't always like that – he changed when he took that job. Now, I'm not sure there was a single truth to his story – maybe he was simply involved in moving heavy narcotics; who the fuck knows?!" Maggie returned wearily.

"Are his friends drug traffickers?"

"I wouldn't call the people he hangs out with 'friends.' We had friends, but they knew better than to stick around. No, the guys that accompany him most of the time are strangers; and I mean that in more ways than one," Maggie stated.

"Can you clarify?"

"Yeah, like vacant, or emotionally disconnected."

"You mean some of them?" Pau inquired.

"All of them! I must have met dozens of their ilk – they act like they drink from the same fountain. It feels weird from the distance – I'm kinda waking up to it," Maggie answered.

"The more you remember the faster the healing," Pau opined.

"Traffickers? Petty criminals rather, thinking of it. They're more the bruiser types than your typical Silicon Valley brainiacs – how could I have ever thought what he told me was true? It's pathetic, really."

"Be kind to yourself, sister, only the soothing of self-love will get you out of this," Pau said firmly.

"Sorry, I should know better, but I hope you understand what I'm going through."

"I do," Pau simply replied.

———————

Saka returned from Xarn's realm in the middle of the night. Pau was waiting for her in the upstairs quarters where the portal was located. Maggie was thought to be asleep, while Marshall was fixing himself a night snack in the main floor kitchen.

"How long will it take before Maggie starts asking about the odd traffic in this house?" Saka joked.

"It may be wise to think of something," Pau returned.

"How is she; any chance of her coming around?"

"I'd say she's doing reasonably well, all things considered. She's emotionally shaken but stable, though her body appears to be suffering from withdrawal symptoms linked to the drugs Wind had her on. I trust she'll pull through," Pau updated.

"That bad, hey?"

"'Fraid so."

"When's Vera due?"

"She'll be at the office in the morning – we have a lot of work ahead of us," Saka replied.

"By the way, I've been thinking about getting more involved with field work. It's obvious we need to seriously look into cracking Gandreal's locked file, and since it's kind of my department... I worked at Qwave before I did computing for Hektor, remember?" Pau offered.

"Terrific! I think the team was hoping you'd be willing to take on the assignment; it's been kind of floating around without any takers. Might as well make it official by letting everyone know. If I were you, I would message the group," Saka suggested.

"Thanks for the feedback – I needed that!"

Pau typed the proposition into her handset – morning would tell if she was at last ready to fly her Angel wings.

22 – TRANSPOD BETA TEST

Wind typed into Linda Sue's Qwave laptop. He wanted to ascertain its interface was responding flawlessly to its corresponding software. He wasn't totally clear about the specificity of its specialized field, but he sensed the laptop and its attached hardware were the missing link to his setup. When the overhead monitors displayed the frequency range of some of Olaf Swyndle's old field readings, Wind knew he had scored. He quickly patched the machine into the system and observed how his equipment interlocked with it. Not only did the six other Qwave laptops instantly recognize the new arrival – they also seemed sparked by it, as if it had unleashed their potentials. Within less than a minute every piece of gear in the room had come to life in a way never seen before. Wind was fully mesmerized by the metamorphosis his lab underwent – his hopes were fully restored.

Two days later, the Rastafarian engaged linkage with the fixed transport pods on *Iorus*, activated the suspended Roamers, and prepared for a test. The Triad was actually thinking ahead of him by picking up on his auratic signals, but they stayed close to the game, avoiding showing too much too fast.

The three techs were counting on the Le Lien simulation to have successfully mapped all the connecting points, and on Jarred's monitors, in the Eureka loft, to be ready for data collection. Ofélia was confident they could pull a promising first run by allowing a Roamer to escape from the plasmatic mass, and then harness him back to the pod. They would limit the experiment to the one path into the artists' space, while the other ten pods would strictly show increased intensity. The idea behind it was to fine-tune a way to control the release of the Roamers, and later the armies, with the aim of reversing the process when the Realms would open. Of course, Wind was to never guess his lab would be working ahead of him, but Patrick and Daniel counted on the hacker's narcissism to prevent him from not taking credit for their work. Ofélia came up with the name "transpod" as an abbreviation for "transport pod," and it stuck. The transpods were set at half-capacity to minimize the use of resources. It meant that fifty percent of the test specimens were not activated; it also implied that each Roamer could be controlled individually – a detail that pleased The Triad immensely.

Jarred was monitoring the loft on his laptop. He had installed several cams at various angles so that he could switch between them while simultaneously capturing 3D images. The space had been event-free for the past few days, but now that Wind was locked in his station, bleed-through was imminent. All the recently gathered data had shown little increase in intensity, mostly signifying the technology had hit a wall. With The Triad now in charge, the suspense had mounted. It was far from certain the three techs would improve on the results, but hopes were high. At exactly the twenty-third hour, the first image distortion appeared, quickly followed by a dense, undulating, milky mass, displaying noticeable spikes around its contour. The form stretched and retracted, revealing emerging images of human shapes as it pulsed.

It then suddenly happened – it was ghostly at first: a body that fought to separate from the whole, struggling against the forces of the impossible gap between worlds.

It snapped free.

The naked male form immediately gained tone and definition – it was complete. The man scanned the room as if trying to remember whether or not he had been there before. His hair was cropped military-style; his leg muscles were taut like those of a beast of prey ready to strike – it was the body of a heavily conditioned fighter positioning himself for action.

Then, just as quickly as it had occurred, a curling smoke-like appendage sprouted out of the plasmatic mass to connect with the freshly emancipated form, reclaiming it into its bulk. It was over in a second – the room had returned to normalcy.

———————

Jarred immediately informed the team, The Triad needed confirmation, even though they should have been able to monitor the progress of the experiment, at least in data form. They also had to be informed of the request to push for enough transpods for the *Hestilles Circle* to perform the invasion in one step.

Saka and Vera were ready; they reached the old refinery grounds just after sunrise, then the stone opened the path to the white room, where Ofélia, Patrick, and Daniel were awaiting them.

"Tell us it worked!" The Triad implored.

"Congratulations, we have a copy of the video. Jarred was beyond himself!" Vera exclaimed.

"Good then," Ofélia said matter-of-factly.

"What else do you have for us?" Daniel asked.

"What about enough pods to carry the entirety of their armies in one fell swoop?" Saka offered.

"Who's going to ask them?" Patrick enquired.

"For now, it's just hypothetical," Vera said, "but given what you've seen, and what I know you've already analyzed in terms of possibilities, is it even feasible?"

"From our standpoint, it's just processing power. We've been able to tap into their resources; we know there have the capability to add muscle to Wind's setup. As far as their industry is concerned, it's beyond question they rely on other orbs in their system to provide manufacturing and raw materials. The transpods are akin to wingless and tailless Plexiglas airplane bodies, fitted with individual enclosures to accommodate fighters, a variety of supplies, and ample cutting-edge weaponized equipment. We haven't yet gathered data on the size of their military, or their ballistic capability. There is no doubt they have much firepower at their disposal. Long gone are the horses and javelins." Daniel explained.

"I don't see how they can be convinced of moving their entire assets without assessing the risk – it would take desperation on their part to chance an all-out invasion," Ofélia added.

"The team is set on it, so it would be great to at least look into it," Vera contended.

"We're on it," Patrick assured her.

"While you're here, it might be of significance for you to know Wind has taken off to the mainland with deputy Jalesh to report on the breakthrough. Yes, we knew we had succeeded, but we had to ask – so if you have any business to do in his dwelling, now is the time.

223

We don't think he is going to be pleased with the arrangement the ruling family has in store for him, so he's going to be extremely vulnerable to offers, if you get the drift. The time may be right to put a card on the table," Ofélia concluded.

"The stone should be able to take you there," Patrick said with a smile.

As it was often the case with The Triad, one never knew when a meeting had come to an end until one was shown out. Saka and Vera turned around, trusting the stone was tuned in. Just before they stepped into Wind's lab, they heard a chorus in their backs.

"Tada!" it went.

———————

When Wind informed Jalesh of the success of the first test run with the new laptop in the chain, he didn't expect to be summoned before members of the ruling family. The deputy picked him up within the hour at the docking station adjacent to the lab, confirming the project was of the highest priority to the ad hoc committee. The Interverse's transport system was similar to portals, but whereas Guild ones were invisible; those of *Iorus* were actual fixed capsules that reflected the heavy mechanical side of the asteroid circle's hybrid technologies.

Upon arriving in *Lucrides*, Wind and Jalesh were shown through a series of long, automated walkways then across an imposing archway into the main lobby of the palace. The two guards that had been escorting them from the capsule were replaced by a foursome of stern-looking, weapon-ready men, who flanked and led the two through a labyrinthine combination of corridors and checkpoints. Finally, they were ordered to wait by an ornate door into which were carved the arms of the ruling family. The Rastafarian hadn't said a word, which was all good by the deputy who was absorbed with rehearsing his standard mannerism for such meetings. They were at last asked to follow a hostess to the boardroom, where dozens of members of the family and their representatives were seated in a circle around a rotating presentation stage.

"Please stand at the podium, Windsor Kassel, we are anxious to hear about the progress of your work," a voice resonated from an ambient sound system.

The Earth hacker obliged, uncertain in his steps, as he looked around the assembly with heightened apprehension; he settled behind the pulpit, fully unprepared for the occasion.

"I was able to locate the missing link and tie it to the system," Wind explained, his voice emerging from an array of screens displaying his face around the hall. "As a result, we successfully broke through with one of our specimens and retrieve him safely," he added.

The circular platform rotated until Wind faced the first member in queue with questions.

"One specimen is a small achievement; when do you plan running the entire fleet through that process?" the man asked.

"We have enough harvested power to chance the release of a full pod, then we will test several of them together," Wind replied.

"What do you mean by 'enough harvested power'; haven't we provided what you asked for?"

"I have to tap portions of your energy system to power up Base 5 and the pods. As with the latest run, we saw a sharp increase in power requirement that by far exceeded our previous usage – the one release spiked the load," Wind returned.

The stage rotated.

"Are you saying we don't have enough power to transport soldiers in the eleven allocated pods?" another member enquired.

"As per my calculations, we will need to schedule the experiments for when *Iorus'* power usage is at its lowest; that's what I mean."

"So, in a nutshell, you're saying we don't produce enough energy," the man insisted.

"We had no idea how much it would require until we were able to release one specimen – now we know."

"Who are the 'we' you speak of, Windsor, I only see one of you in this assembly. 'We,' on the other hand, are not you," the man spat.

The platform turned the other way.

"I want to know how much power sending five hundred fighters will demand. You have two days to come up with that figure – by then I hope you will also have found a way to make your system more efficient," the member requested.

Wind saw his audience orbit once more.

"I understand your experiment was successful at releasing one subject on the surface reality of Earth whilst using a specific amount of energy, but how do you account for the vast difference between your testing grounds and the destination of our mission; do you have that mapped, and how much more power is it going to ask of us?" the guttural voice demanded.

"I am confident I should be able to come up with the data in the next few days," Wind lied.

The platform turned again; this time to face a woman of great stature.

"You shall make good use of the next two days, subject Kassel – we are expecting you to be bearing substantial news by their end. Deputy Jalesh will show you out," the female ruler concluded venomously.

Wind was escorted back to base 5 by the officer.

"Two days, Earth time – I advise you don't disappoint," Jalesh warned as he left.

The woman's words were still ringing in Wind's mind. She had addressed him as "subject Kassel," a title worthy of the common Roamer. It did not bode well for his fate, whether he delivered or not. He didn't even know where the Realms were – he only had bragged about a machine that could reach across worlds and beyond the farthest reaches. It was at best a theory based on a vision. He did not become fully aware of the existence of these places until he already had committed to work for the Interverse. Yes, his vision was right, and yes, the means to get there existed, but he was learning as he went, never clear about what the next day had in reserve.

He was about to sit on the floor by the coffee table when he noticed a rolled up piece of paper he hadn't seen before, next to the pile of magazines. When he picked it up, a joint fell out of it.

"What the fuck?" he muttered.

He reached for the doobie in the given reflexive move common to stoners worthy of the name, while he looked for matches. Only after having lit up the joint and sucked on it in multiple tokes before exhaling, did he deem the time was right to check out the note. It was just as well that he had taken care of business by getting righteously stoned, because he didn't exactly groove on what he read.

The Eureka bitch can help whenever you feel like dancing to a different beat. Enjoy the smoke, Roamer Kassel!

Once more, the program in Wind's mind took a direct hit. He felt utterly disoriented. There was absolutely no chance of Klein ever making it to Base 5 if he couldn't get away from it himself. Zero probability – period. Yet, where did the note and the joint come from? It must have been Jalesh. The last two times he had been in, absurd messages had appeared, while his stash did a vanishing act. The doobie must have been the proverbial dangling carrot; "more will come if you perform, Roamer Wind," he thought. His mind was whirling; he was trapped, yet there was this bogus note that offered help. Were the ruling members testing him, evaluating his strength of character? Plus, what did Linda Sue know about Roamers anyway? He had smoked the entire joint, and yet, he felt wired. For a second, he flashed on the spiked weed he had been pushing on Maggie for the last couple of years, wondering if it wasn't what he had just eagerly inhaled. He felt a sudden pang at the irony of his mental process. "How am I ever going to get my shit together if Jalesh keeps on fucking with me?" he raged.

Eventually, he managed to let some of it go. He thought of the laptop and the improvement it had brought to the lab. He had to probe the depths of its potential, see if it was capable of answering the needs of the rulers.

Wind was intimidated by the power of the machine. He had sensed there was something organic about it the second he had touched it back in the day, but now with it seemingly in charge of the entire array of instruments in the lab, that power translated into something much above his capacity for comprehension. What kind of technology allowed it to churn such vast quantity of data in such record time, in a manner that transcended mere rational computing? There was creative thrust involved, desire and purpose – the laptop needed to serve; thus it immediately scanned its environment, assessed the requirements, and went to work without further ado. It was borderline miraculous! Then he thought about Linda Sue again – what relationship did she have with it? Had she known what she held and how to use the power within it? Then the note came back to circle his mind – what if she wrote it? What if she made it to the base in some impossible way to offer her help?

He typed a question into the laptop.

Can we fire all pods at once with available energy?

There was a pause before the screen came to life.

There is a cyclic redundancy in the system that needs correcting. Some of the peripheral equipment is using most of the resources trying to understand what is being asked of it.
Unlinking advised.

Wind faced a horizon of hope. He typed again.

Which equipment?

229

The laptop's external monitors displayed a rerouting of the lab equipment, with detailed functions for each part of the chain. Then, a load calculation was charted for every link, clearly delineating the paths that could alleviate the peaks in order to make the whole of the system more efficient. In the end, it only took less than an hour to resolve the dilemma of the two-day deadline.

Wind felt like kissing the laptop, a detail that wasn't lost to The Triad, who always appreciated when their work was valued. He went around the lab to disconnect and repatch equipment. Some of the machines he had once deemed to be essential to the mission were powered down – they had served their purpose but were now eclipsed by superior technology.

He was feeling like his old self; the effect of the smoke had mellowed out – he settled in his environment. He was going to be ready for some new tests soon, this time, with results bound to please the rulers. The Roamer denomination had to go!

23 – THE SIEGE

Pau contacted Masters Lo-Shen and Jaco of Third Eye, to seek authorization to work on a backdoor into Gandreal's folder – she was given carte blanche. The team had been fully supportive of her offer to tackle that area, making Le Lien's resources available whenever she wished to access pertinent data or equipment. For that matter, a brand new Qwave laptop and handset combo specifically modded for the application of extracting protected files, had been loaned to her by the tech branch of New Angel City.

She first studied the generic makeup of seed algorithms through their application by XVII in the maze of tunnels. She analyzed their strengths and vulnerabilities, their back-engineering checkpoints, firewalls, as well as the inevitability of their self-destruct properties, should they be pushed too hard.

As Pau summoned the locked file, the hacking programs circumvallated it – siege-like – to position their probes at strategic intervals; she then waited to see how the protective pod would respond to the ominous presence. It did not react, but Pau intuited it was a false negative meant to project an impenetrable front – it was most likely sizing the enemy and building appropriate defenses. She also understood the stronger the shield felt, the greater the chance for the folder to remain safe. She needed to fool it into believing it had the upper hand. For now, she would just leave the programs in blockade mode and stay put until her handset would inform her of any behavioral change. Then, she thought about how she would contact Joonas and Qo'ai-Marael in Amaterasu's domain, as well as the members of XVII holed up in Dahbar's realm. She was aware it was an ambitious proposition, but it was a shot in the dark worth contemplating. She was positive the reasons for Gandreal's rejection held one of the keys to saving the Realms – not all the actors had yet played their parts.

When Pau sought permission from Amaterasu to question Joonas and Qo'ai-Marael about Gandreal's past, the Great One appeared annoyed.

"I was counting on the team to abide to my wishes, but then Lo-Shen and Jaco first put me in a awkward position – on Vac's advice, no less – and now you are asking me to break protocol in regard to the most guarded precept of the Domains; that of preventing Masters such as yourself to cross the line of decency. Joonas and Qo'ai-Marael's sanctity belongs to the sacred – it is not to be trampled," she stated firmly.

But then she softened up.

"I admire your courage, young Master; I also understand the road to your achievements has not always been an easy one. Do all you can, and then let me know how you fare. I mean this to its full extent – do not even think of asking again, if you haven't given it all you have. Good luck!"

It was not the results Pau had wished for, but she felt good about having asked. She understood the denial extended to the members of XVII, with the unspoken nuance of "same rules – different place." Now she could focus on the task at hand knowing she hadn't left anything unchecked.

The Fieldbrook house was abuzz with activity. From Maggie's standpoint, Saka and Vera's constant in and outs started to poke through the fog of her personal issues. Why wasn't the computer scientist staying in Berkeley, and how could Linda Sue afford to pay regular visits to her friends in Iceland while holding no employment? Plus, the two often left and returned together, always in the middle of the night, or when she was absent from the house. In spite of those questions, she had no pressing issues with what others did with their lives – to the contrary. Rather, she was beginning to feel left out and useless. Her hunt for jobs, which neither paid well enough nor were in fields she had any interest in, made it plain that real estate was not what it once was; demand for housing had dropped, leaving the field sluggish. Her on and off bohemian lifestyle had put her out of touch with the market; she felt drained by the process of setting up fronts for interviews, of playing into the by-the-book duplicitous game of false concerns and sympathies laid forth by the man behind the desk. It was a row of façades, a posturing act that went from banking to insurance, retail to fast food – the least truthful, the worst the pay.

Marshall had offered to keep an eye for something suitable, though he couldn't promise anything based on her limited experience beyond real estate and basic bookkeeping. But with Pau and Jarred now heavily involved with the team, he had lost his helpers with the affairs of his primary business, and was confronted with the shortcomings of having to spend too much time going from office to office, running paperwork by various county clerks. Maybe Maggie could handle it? He didn't want to lean too heavily in that direction, considering she was already living in his house – he would wait a bit longer to see how it played out with her search. Pau wholeheartedly agreed with him.

The handset informed the young Master of a twitch emitted by the protective pod shrouding the Gandreal report. She was working in the home office, away from the bustle of downtown Eureka, where one could easily be distracted by the shouting on the street, the sudden eruptions of sirens, the cacophony of garbage pick-up, the brain-drilling sonic malignity of back-up beepers, or various combinations of all of the above – home was were the mind could concentrate.

She opened the laptop, to which she had connected two thirty-two inch LED monitors. The graphs showed the position of all the probes – one of which was flashing yellow, indicating something came within safe distance from it. The report highlighted the pod had sent a scout half-way, to investigate; likely, to harvest peripheral data. "Bingo!" she thought – curiosity was a good thing. She kept that probe from reacting; for now, it was a waiting game for more signs. She had to coerce the program into staying alert, while being careful to not threaten it beyond what was already posing substantial concern. But it was designed to fulfill a specific purpose within which lay the deep desire to see through any intrusion. Now that the drive for it had been awakened, the protective shield would inevitably become bolder. It did.

The next day, half the probes were flashing – roughly sixty of them – most of them deep amber, showing the scouts had come a lot closer. Still, Pau deemed patience was of the essence.

Each of the hacking probes consisted of a series of specialized sensors able, when combined, to monitor behavior as well as decipher intention. So far, there was no aggressive conduct by the program, only a curious desire to understand what had positioned itself outside the perimeter of its fortress. Pau would wait while the sensors kept on turning data into a profile of the shield. The more the latter sent its scouts out to investigate, the more it became vulnerable to showing what it was made of. It was an ancient program that betrayed it had never been tested by sophisticated tactical software, notwithstanding, eons away from the era of its builders. In spite of its long years of dormancy, it wasn't designed to sit still.

———————

Inevitably, one afternoon, Maggie, Saka, and Vera converged in the main kitchen. They sat at the counter while Pau, who had come out of the office to join, brewed a pot of Pu'erh tea.

"How's the search going?" the hostess asked with her back turned.

Maggie looked around to make sure the question was meant for her.

"It's demoralizing to say the least," she replied.

"How so?" Pau continued.

"Well, I realize I'm pretty unqualified for just about anything meaningful. I may end up cashiering in a supermarket, or if I'm lucky, at the co-op. Most offers are dead-end jobs," she returned.

"So, no luck with real estate, right?" Saka inquired.

"The market's dead for now – agents are struggling. What are you up to these days, Linda Sue, I mean job-wise?" Maggie probed.

"Well, all of us here are working on a case for *Private & Beyond*, Marshall's second business with Jarred and Pau. We can't divulge its content since it is client- confidential, but it's taking us around – sometimes at ungodly hours." Saka responded.

"I was wondering," Maggie returned. "You seem to always come and go when I'm either asleep or away – actually, I'm kinda surprised we bumped into each other," she said laughing.

"Glad we finally did; we were overdue for a girls' get-together, especially since we all live here. You're probably wondering what's up with my Berkeley job, am I right?" Vera said.

"You beat me to it," Maggie returned.

"Let's say I took a leave of absence. I was counting on a post in Iceland, but unforeseen circumstances forced me out of my plans. Actually, I met briefly with Wind in Akureyri when I was checking things out," Vera intentionally slid in.

Maggie froze in place, looking around the room to assess the reality she was in.

"I'm assuming you mean some place in Iceland – that can't be – he never was there. You must have passed someone who looked like him," she affirmed.

"To the contrary, we even shared a meal together one evening. He was anxious to put his hands on technical information about supercomputers," Vera pushed on.

"When was that, I would have known about it – you're sure it was him?" she asked, puzzled.

"I wouldn't make that up, girlfriend."

Maggie bounced between Pau and Saka, seeking confirmation.

"No, she wouldn't," Saka said.

"I second that," Pau added.

There was a moment of silence while the hostess poured the tea,

"Wow, that's hard to take – it feels like a chunk of my life is missing," Maggie uttered.

"Rather – a chunk of his," Saka countered.

"But how did he find the time to get there and back without me noticing?" Maggie asked, confused.

"That's when it gets tricky, and perhaps now is not the best time to get into the details since we need to go. But rest assured there's an explanation to it, and it's got nothing to do with you losing your mind. Believe me – you're OK," Saka ascertained.

After much deliberation, the Goddess of Light and the two Masters had come to the decision of probing Maggie's mind in order to evaluate her capacity for assimilation of uncommon data – a lot like The Triad had done with Linda Sue in the past. It had donned on them that, rather than facing the inevitability of her stumbling upon some uncomfortable truth, she was better off prepared for it. She had fallen into the circle; there had to be a reason for it. If she showed any resistance towards opening to the greater picture, then she would be ushered in the direction of her next prevalent destiny, whatever it was. For now, and aided by her resurgent coherence, she indicated a willingness to adapt to a new self. It was possible that the exposure to her present surroundings had beneficial effects on her psyche. Saka felt confident Maggie was strong enough to pull herself back together – though she wasn't so sure about her abilities to fully grasp the reality that was closing on her. But, if she ever went as far as crossing the line, there would be no return – ready or not. No-one was forcing her to make that choice.

Pau's handset alerted her to more activity around Gandreal's file. Nearly all probes were flashing amber or red. Substantial data had been harvested from the scouts' behavior, and though no sign of aggression had been shown towards the intruder, the chances of imminent provocation were significant. Still, it was too early for a clear evaluation of the defensive powers of the shield. The Qwave program suggested waiting until all the probes were surrounded, which would indicate the pod was using most of its resources to define the nature of the threat, thus recklessly weakening its protection of the file as well as its ability to destroy it. The plan was to act before the scouts had returned to complete their diagnosis. Unlike the hacking program's sensors, with their continuous harvesting of data seamlessly streamed to the primary level in charge of orchestrating the attack, the shield's scouts had to carry their findings back to the nest for processing. The latency was consistent with very old programs – this one dating from nearly the beginning of time. Pau momentarily pondered on the nuance, with pointed admiration for the original designers – it took utter brilliance to come up with it, she thought. She deemed that by the next day, she – based on the inherent vulnerabilities mapped from the processed data – would be in position to execute a retrieval of the file.

Hopefully, access to Gandreal's mysterious folder would be granted without a fight.

Maggie had difficulties sleeping. She went over what was said about Wind's meeting with Vera in Iceland. Under different circumstances, she would have thought she was set-up – but she knew better. The girls were right – his actions were ill-defined. The time issue made little sense. How could he have flown over that far and back without her noticing? She must have been drugged out of her mind – what else? But then it all started to coalesce – all his absences were suspicious. He had come and gone in a series of vanishing and appearing acts that should have drawn her attention from the start; like his regular trips to the decommissioned refinery next door from the Richmond house, followed by his reemergences with men she had never met. She didn't even know how he had access to the residence; he sure didn't own it, or even rent it, yet it always seemed to be unoccupied. But the overall picture was that time did not seem to concern Wind, or space for that matter. How did he return to Oakland without the van, and why did he abandon it by a power plant? The more she awakened to the reality of her life with him, the less she understood it. Linda Sue, Pau, and Vera appeared to know a lot more about him than she did, yet how could they? Sure, there was a difference between the Wind of the old days and the latest version, but that hardly coalesced into a conclusive report. The girls were onto something – perhaps he had much to do with the case they were working on. The time had come to seek answers to the mounting questions. "Tomorrow will be a new day," she thought, before surrendering to exhaustion.

24 – SAM'S GIFT

Vera, Bluefeather, and Sam were strolling along the creek trail below Ma-1 and Olaf's residence. It was one of those now-rare visits by the Le Lien operative. An earlier talk with the Great Goddess of the realm had yielded the importance of reaching Misu before his dream meadow would self-erase. The call of the lanes, which was automatically sent by the wishes of Warriors to connect with their kin, had remained unanswered by all parties, while no other means were left to get the attention of the shuttered realms, including Misu's.

As a joke, Vera had suggested taking Sam to the dream gatherings, knowing quite well that only the Warriors had intrinsic connections with them. But then Ma-1 thought the idea was not so far-fetched, considering Sam's gift for using the most unusual of channels to go places. "It's worth the experiment," she had said.

"So, Sam," Vera probed, "fancy a little trip with our hostess into uncharted territory?"

"I would like it very much, but I'm not sure I have any business there," the dog replied.

"'Liking it' is what I'm taking about; business is optional, my dear friend."

"When are we going?" Sam asked.

"Whenever, Ma-1, Xarn, and Enola are ready."

"I wonder if Wolf could come; I like Wolf."

"So, you've met Wolf? How did you two manage to run into each other?" Bluefeather enquired.

"I met him in Sir Xarn's place," Sam returned.

"You did what?" Vera pressed.

"I was looking for one of my kin besides the wild foursome of this place – I just walked into him at the top of the canyon," he replied.

"Just like that, you entered a realm?" Bluefeather posed, amused.

"I've been to Lady Enola's place too," Sam added.

"So you have! Your talents preceded you, my friend; now they are eclipsing even an Angel's comprehension. We're blessed to have you around!" Bluefeather joyfully exclaimed.

"Then I believe it's time we meet with Ma-l," Vera pronounced.

———————

The three Warriors and Sam gathered in one of the hidden layers of Joonas Halls, out of the way of main traffic, for a clear path to the dream lanes.

"Sam, we are going to get together in a place that may or may not be accessible to you. We are not going there in-body, so it's a bit different from what you're accustomed to," Xarn explained.

"We are gathered now, it's what I know," Sam returned.

The remark made the deities look at each other with the side effect of bringing them closer. They smiled, while the notion wasn't lost on any of them.

"Let's meet there then," Enola said.

It was debatable whether Sam was there before they arrived or appeared simultaneously, but surprise was definitely the serving du jour. At this point it became clear Sam could go anywhere he wished, providing he had a reason to get there, or no reason not to. The meadow of arrival had always been Ma-l's, as it was on that day; a point that needed not be made if it hadn't been for Sam's remark:

"This leads back into the place whence we came."

"Well yes, of course, Sam," Ma-l said, amused.

"I mean – your place," he returned.

"How so?"

"Because it connects to it through there by the creek," he pointed.

The Warriors looked at the empty space.

"You mean you can return to Ma-l's realm through there?" Enola asked, impressed.

"You want me to show you?" Sam offered.

"If you promise not to get lost – we need you here," Ma-l warned.

Sam was gone and back in an instant – just enough to connect with Olaf who was working in the gardens.

"OK, that's a first," Xarn said. "You're sure it was Ma-l's place?"

"Ask Olaf," Sam returned.

The Warriors looked at each other; this time, they collectively sensed something was greater than them.

"If we asked you to do the same with Misu's realm, could you do it?" Xarn inquired.

"The frog says it's a bad idea," Sam answered matter-of-factly.

"How can you and the frog know, since we've never asked before?"

"The time before a question always tells."

"How much time could that be?" Enola asked.

"As much as needed for a proper answer," he said.

"Where do you come from, Sam?" Ma-l felt compelled to ask.

"Same as everybody, between 'nothing' and 'all'; now, can we go to the uncharted territory?"

"We thought this would be it, but I see we are mistaken. What about any of the realms out of the meadows across the creek?" Xarn suggested.

"Are they uncharted, Sir Xarn?" Sam asked.

"This, I pretty much guaranty!"

"OK, but I must pick which one."

"We'll just follow you," Ma-l assured.

They followed Sam across a dozen leas and back before he settled on one of his liking.

"I'll take this one," he said.

"We'll be waiting for your return," they chorused.

It did not take long. Sam returned with Wolf, proud of his accomplishment.

"So you knew this was my meadow?" Xarn asked, dazzled.

"Yes, Wolf and I work better together – now we're ready," Sam affirmed.

The Warriors followed the two canids until they stopped two plots over.

"This will do," Sam said.

He and Wolf were gone in a heartbeat.

———————

The dog and the coywolf arrived amid a brightly lit aspen grove – a breeze was teasing a million golden leaves in a rustle of uncountable minute rhythms. They smelled the air, satisfied with their surroundings.

In the distance stood a tall man tending to corn that grew along a stream. They walked towards him.

He must have sensed the visitors, because he turned to look in their direction with the kind of attentive indifference common to those who had waited too long. He kept silent, letting them get closer before he spoke.

"So, where are you two coming from if I may ask," he said in a slow pace.

"The name's Sam and this is Wolf. We come from the lands of Ma-l and Xarn."

The Warrior stood solemn, not wanting to betray the emotion that had just made his heart race and his thoughts whirl into an indescribable mix of joy and fear of deception.

"You speak the names of my brother and sister, but how did you get here?"

"We personally picked your meadow," Sam said.

"Sam has the best nose," Wolf validated.

"Am I to assume there are others with you?"

"Yes, they're waiting for our return," Sam replied.

"It still does not explain how you two came to my land," the man pointed.

"Sam's the expert – I just follow," Wolf asserted.

"So, Sam knows the way of the lanes, am I right?"

"I always take the path of least resistance, if it is what you mean, Sir," Sam returned.

"Not exactly, but I am beginning to sense something important is happening and I'm not sure what to do. Why don't you two return to the meadow and ask what is expected of me – without the call, there is little I can do. My name's Kuruk," the Warrior proposed.

"Are there any like me in you land?" Wolf asked.

"More than I can count, my friend."

Sam and Wolf reappeared in the meadow – they had the Warriors undiluted attention.

"Kuruk wants us to ask you what you want him to do," Sam said.

"Kuruk!?" Xarn exclaimed. "You spoke with Kuruk!?"

"That was the name, I believe, Sir Xarn."

"If you can return in there, tell him the call of the lanes has been silenced by those who want us to fail, that's all he needs to know. We are waiting for him at the dream gathering," Ma-l requested.

"I knew there was something different about this place – dreams always do that to me," Sam confessed.

"I will ask you to explain at another time – please go tell Kuruk." Ma-l implored.

Sam and Wolf were gone in a blink. Hours passed before there was a noise at the bottom of the trail that led to the grassy area. Kuruk, flanked by Sam and Wolf, was seen walking up the path from the lane.

————————

It was a game changer. The news was received with unparalleled vigor. Kuruk was updated on the entire history of the emerging Oneness. Just like with Xarn, it took him a while to assimilate the convoluted information around Olaf and Vac's entry via the backdoor of Ma-l's realm, gestalt George, Hektor, XVII, and now, the Interverse. He had invited the three Warriors, as well as Saka, Olaf, and Vac on a first visit of his realm. He was very emotional about his journey out of the stone, in a way that complemented his boundless gratitude for his reconnection with his brothers and sisters, and his introduction to the Masters of New Angel City. He made it clear he was now part of the team that would help with the release of all the locked Warriors. He was highly welcome into the group.

Of course, Sam and Wolf were the heroes of the story, especially Sam whose abilities were still befuddling the assembly of the Great Hall. So, after he and the coywolf had guided another number of delighted and somewhat disoriented Warriors out their realms into the meadows, he carried on with teaching these deities his skills at uncovering hidden portals and exploiting them with efficient ease – he merely allowed them to observe as if their presence was of no consequence.

The completion of the convergence of the Realms into Joonas Halls and New Angel City, was performed by the collective whole of the Warriors. The complex codes handed out by the Hektor founder, and implemented into the new system of tunnels, were seamlessly interfaced with the awakened domains.

It wasn't until the one hundred and twenty-eighth Warrior was freed that the fate of Misu was approached. Technically, the Realms had been released; thus, the concern of Gandreal's planned invasion had taken a different tone of urgency. But the armies of the *Hestilles Circle* were still readying themselves for attack and could easily overwhelm the new Oneness, especially if they threw their entire force at it. The work of the team was far from done in spite of the celebratory mood of the moment. After so much time away from the meadows, where most of the groundwork had been intended to happen, the Realms still needed to find their collective balance. For now, they remained extremely vulnerable to a move by *Iorus*. Gandreal and his mission had to be defeated; not just for the sake of the new Oneness, but for the one of any vulnerable world that opened itself as second best to the desperation that drove that part of the Interverse to flee its predicament.

––––––––––––––

After one of the team's meetings at the circle of Ma-l's upper orchard, Saka and Vac walked up the trail that led to the top of the valley.

"Why did you say we needed Gandreal to open the realms when it obviously wasn't the case?" she asked.

"Sam was not in the picture then. As a matter of fact, Sam is never in the picture – all hinged on Vera's playfulness," Vac returned.

"So, you're saying that without Sam, the scenario would have remained as first discussed – a complex, nearly impossible plan of sucking the Interverse's armies back into the time-reversed vortex of their planned attack, at exactly the precise moment all the realms were to simultaneously open. Am I right?"

"The way you put it foresees the complete defeat of that plan, but I assure you there is soundness to it. Case in point, we still have to go along with it in order to prevent an inevitable attack by the *Hestilles Circle's* forces on some unsuspecting world, and my guess is Earth is one of them," Vac put forth.

"Couldn't we just pull The Triad out and call it good?" Saka asked.

"*Iorus'* desperation, as I see it, will lead to achievements in the field of interdimensional mass

248

transport. Sam's intrusion into the dream meadows has opened the gates of probabilities onto multiple invasion scenarios. As to before, when Roamers were to appear only briefly on Earth, they are now seen in many instances of aggressive behavior, including downright annihilation of the societies of the planet."

"It seems to never end," Saka surrendered.

"It never does, Goddess."

25 – QUANTUM MISSTEP

Wind was ready for the launch of a full pod. Once again, The Triad had arranged for the experiment to be performed at the Eureka artists' loft where Jarred had placed his cameras. The new readings confirmed that the energy required would be a fraction of what it took for the release of a single Roamer. If all turned out as planned, he was bound to unload some impressive data onto the assembly of the rulers, assuring him full return to his freelance contractor status.

The news from the Realms had not yet reached the Triad, for the reason that an unforeseeable, sporadic time shift had positioned *Iorus* in the past relative to surface realities, by the variable equivalent of one to three Earth days. An alignment similar to those automatically performed by portal software could not be achieved, because of the creational gap that separated the underworld from other universes. Even when Saka and Vera visited the Triad, it was always in relation to that potential time disconnect – the two presents simply did not want to synch consistently. In most cases, it would have been inconsequential, but the three techs worked fast and had already compiled sufficient data to demonstrate that a full-out invasion could be possible with the existing energy supply; information which Wind would, of course, make available to the ruling family.

As it turned out, the experiment was a success. The entire load of Roamers, as captured by Base 5's monitors and Jarred's cameras, was set free and recalled without a glitch. Wind hastened to inform Jalesh of the results, which prompted the deputy to make immediate arrangements for a meeting with the ruling body. The hacker was hardly surprised when he was alerted of his docking, barely an hour after having sent the message.

Wind felt a lot more confident than the time he faced the stares and questions of the suspicion-prone elite. He even attempted to engage conversationally with his warden, but short of a few banalities intermixed with fundamentally fallacious remarks about law and order, the latter preferred to internally reflect on refining his presentation ahead of standing before his superiors.

The audience had nearly doubled in size. This time, Wind observed the presence of members of the scientific body, ready to ask the hard questions. The female ruler was easily identified by her attire, whose colors sharply contrasted with the standard grey and black of the men's outfits. He wondered why there was only one woman in the group, and, why she should be the supreme ruler. It did not take long for the update, as she was first to speak.

"Windsor Kassel, my name is Isadora Litu Verbrunna, commander in chief of the *Hestilles Circle* in lieu of its absent ruler whose name shall not be spoken – I am also his life's partner, mother of the many overseers tending to the larger bodies of this ring of asteroids. As I warned you last, nothing short of spectacular news will satisfy me or this assembly. A sub-par performance will not be acceptable, and will thus systematically lead to your demotion to the lowest levels of subservience. I hope I am making myself clear – please proceed."

Wind's freshly rekindled confidence was reduced to the thin hope his news was indeed spectacular. The woman's surgical coldness could have turned an entire sun to ice, which for an untimely second, made him aware of the enormous dying primary at the center of the Circle. He composed himself while shuffling through his notes.

"Not only was the experiment successful, it also guaranties the entire fleet can be released without exceeding the energy output presently generated by your system. As a matter of fact, we are far from needing what was previously projected as our baseline requirement."

Wind inserted a flashdrive into the slot provided by the lectern's control bay, which automatically linked its touch screen to monitors around the conference hall. He pointed to figures and graphs with increasing assurance, as no-one had yet demanded clarification. As time went on, he realized he had captivated his audience with a delivery above their expectations. Even the scientific side of the room had remained quiet. Before anyone had a chance to break the spell, he came down with the coup the grace:

"Based on figures I have checked and rechecked, I promise we can strike a decisive blow with the entirety of *Iorus'* forces."

This time, Wind emphasized the "we," with the intent of demonstrating that without him, they had nowhere to go. Indeed, it was a convincing argument that made no-one flinch. After he finished with his presentation, a flurry of lesser questions was cast his way, but he knew he had succeeded at leaving a lasting impression. After all, they would be getting much more than they asked for, for a much lesser price.

As it turned out, the suggestion of a full scale invasion was consistent with the hopes a faster exodus to the Realms could be achieved; thus, it didn't require any convincing – the production of the necessary quantity of pods was immediately approved. The new Oneness was to be conquered in a single attack, soon followed by the shipment of machinery and materials, and when ready, by the transfer of every denizen of the *Hestilles Circle*.

Isadora Litu Verbrunna's softened stance bordered on a flirtatious mood, though she, in no uncertain terms, made a point of reminding Wind that deceiving her would not be in his best interest.

Many of the computer scientists who came to drill him on his methods, walked away sobered by his answers, making him briefly reflect on the knowledge he had amassed from his exposure to Linda Sue's laptop.

Jalesh accompanied him back to Base 5 – this time, Wind couldn't shut him up. Though, he thought of asking about the stash, he knew better than taking advantage of a good thing. For now, he had turned the tables around – an unreal achievement in the face of his previous fate. As soon as Jalesh left, he checked the metal gate out of the lab – it was stubbornly locked.

"Son of a bitch!" he let out.

———————

Saka and Vera made it to The Triad's white room mere minutes after Wind had departed with Jalesh. The unfortunate timing left the team members with the hollow feeling something had gone awfully wrong.

"Communication between disconnected worlds often leads to complications," Ofélia remarked.

"Very sweet, but how is this supposed to make me feel we're not heading for disaster?" Vera lamented.

"Weren't we supposed to know about these time shifts a lot earlier?" Saka inquired.

"It doesn't matter whether you knew or not; they are quantum shifts of unpredictable nature. You would not be aware of one if it happened while in transit, and your handset is incapable of detecting such a 'space transfer' – it's not a perceptual element. We're not even sure they are time-related, though they do loosely affect time between independent planes," Daniel explained.

"At any rate, it's too late to turn the clock back; Wind is delivering the news to the rulers as we speak. It is unlikely they will not be tempted by a full-scale invasion, now that they know they have the means to orchestrate one," Patrick said with fatalistic detachment.

"How convenient it is for you to act as if you had nothing to do with it, we were supposed to trickle down that information, not throw the whole kit and kaboodle at them," Vera said caustically.

"How convenient it is to forget who asked for it; you should have known we work fast," he returned.

"OK, OK," Saka intervened, "you guys can argue all you want at Le Lien headquarters, but we've got things to do. First, let's get to Wind's pad – then we can figure out a plan."

There was another joint inside a note, this time, placed on the counter of what passed for the kitchen area. Then, the two returned to The Triad to finalize their report for the team.

"We won't know until Wind returns, whether the rulers will approved the deal or not, but as we said, they would be fools to not capitalize on the offer – they have limited options, and their world is dying. Although, an attack of that scale will use all they have," Ofélia pressed.

This time, there was no chorus. The three techs stood in the middle of the room – morose. Saka and Vera walked through the space they had come to recognize as the exit. They were soon running across the wasteland of the decommissioned refinery, onwards to a solid world, before the unstable probability behind them could call them into its vortex. Rather than going directly to Eureka, they asked Liv and Grisha to take them to Oakland for a close look at Maggie's previous environment. "Never leave a stone unturned!" flashed through Saka's mind – that was what Marshall used to say, back in the day.

———————

The collective's locale was an ad hoc assemblage of structures that precariously existed in defiance of city building safety codes. It was separated from the busy freeway by a concrete wall which concealed a surprisingly vibrant garden and small orchard, while providing an effective buffer against the madness of outside traffic. Maggie and Wind's pad was on the top floor of a converted warehouse. The occupants of the building ignored them – new faces came and went with predictable regularity, so no-one cared. When Liv asked for directions, she was given a minimalistic version of "upstairs, turn left, last door," consisting of a blasé directional eye shift, and a finger pointing diagonally.

The entrance was unlocked. The inside was an orderly mess, betraying the space was mostly used as a base rather than a nest. Vera looked around for something that would jump at her, but the fact she wasn't after anything in particular, worked against her. Saka, on the other hand, was searching for something to bring back to Maggie. She found it in the form of a photo album and a journal buried under layers of socks and underwear in one of two chests of drawers. She also picked-up an envelope that contained official paperwork and a passport she deemed her old friend would need at some point. Liv and Grisha scanned the rooms for alien data, resonances left over from Wind's regular visits with the Interverse, which could provide snap shots of the position of *Iorus* in regard to surface realities. It was still highly plausible that, down the line, someone from the team would have to visit *Lucrides*. Vera finally found what she was *not* looking for: a version of the Android smart phone Wind had bragged about over dinner at Moonstone Beach – the one she knew belonged to a future release.

———————

Back in Fieldbrook, Saka and Vera came down the stairs to predictably bump into Maggie and Pau. In a remake of the previous scenario, they assembled in the kitchen around a pot of green tea. Maggie had questions she hoped would find answers, while the three had answers they anticipated would come with matching questions. The conversation began with the cautious topic of the job search, to which Maggie responded with a negative laced with annoyance and ennui.

"So far, it's been a disappointing mess."

"You'll eventually find something you like," Pau said supportively.

"What about you guys, any juicy news morsel about your case?" Maggie asked, almost sarcastically.

"It all hinges on what you are willing to take without putting up a fight," Vera said bluntly.

Maggie looked at her with surprise in her eyes. She found the response rather harsh, bordering on inappropriate, but she went on.

"What wouldn't I be able to take at this point?" she returned, raising her shoulders.

"What if I told you we know where both Wind and Sam are, but access to these places is not available to you?" Saka dropped.

"If you're talking about their states of mind, I already know, otherwise, I don't follow you," Maggie returned.

"OK – hard data," Vera said. "One is, more or less, six hundred and forty-seven years in the future, while the other is presently two days in the past. Can you grasp that?"

Maggie paused to reflect; she appeared calm and unfazed. She took a sip of the steaming tea.

"I know this is some kind of test, and there's no doubt I walked straight into it, so I'm gonna call it for what it is: an interesting notion," she forwarded.

"What makes it interesting in your opinion, Maggie?" Pau asked.

"It makes some kind of sense, since they appear to have vanished through thin air, but the precision of the time differences escapes me. What puts you in a position to state something that is theoretically unprovable?"

"What if we could prove it?" Saka said.

"Then I'd say you're onto something few will ever dream of. So, what's the catch?"

"If you are willing to accept that most of what you know is only what your choice of beliefs allows you to access, then we can continue with the weird stuff; otherwise, we can always share recipes," Vera proposed.

"I kinda like where this is going; plus, I don't cook. Anyway, I'm not exactly saying I believe you, but you've got my attention," Maggie countered.

"On a different topic, there's a job opening at Marshall's office. It's actually my position, but I'm too busy with other tasks – interested?" Pau put on the table.

Maggie paused to make minute adjustments to her thinking.

"Of course I'm interested – that would be perfect!"

"Consider it yours then. You start tomorrow at nine – you'll commute with Marshall."

"Thank you – you just made my day!"

"I couldn't think of a better person to take over my place," Pau returned.

"So, what about the hard data?" Maggie asked Vera playfully.

"Now that you know Sam is fine in spite of his impossible position, we'll let you soak what we've told you for a while. Perhaps, by tomorrow, you'll wake up convinced," the Angel returned with a smile.

"You hadn't told me he was fine – now I know."

It took another day before Pau observed all the hacking program probes had been surrounded by the scouts from the shield. All flashed red, meaning there was a level of aggressive behavior on the part of the inquisitors. A Qwave tertiary layer was preparing itself for data transfer in anticipation of the scouts seeking a means to collect information from the intruder. As they did so, the program stealthily injected incremental doses of conditioning into them, aiming to turn these messengers into two-way intelligence carriers. While the probes, in one direction, surrendered seemingly sound material to the scouts feeding the protective pod, these carriers, returning for more, inconspicuously handed over pertinent data about the shield and what it protected to the probes, in a way comparable to worker ants conveying supplies in and out of the colony.

Before the shield program had the chance to compile enough information into a coherent profile of the hacker, the latter had assessed all of its vulnerabilities, in case it needed to penetrate it. There was no cause for it though, for the messengers had already completed the transfer of the file – in minute veiled clusters undetectable to the scrutiny of the guards at the gates. After it was verified the entire folder had been harvested, the scouts were deconditioned, the probes recalled, and the shield was left to wonder what had just happened, never realizing it had been robbed.

26 – THE TURNAROUND

Wind saw the joint set in plain view atop the note. This time, he read the content of the message first.

Congratulations on the success of the experiment; it looked impressive at the other end. Too bad the subjects knocked down some of the furniture – for God's sake Windsor, it's an art studio! Anyway, since I haven't heard from you, I assume you're cozying up with the royals. Good for you – with luck, you can become the ruler's wife's plaything!

–You know who

PS: Your stash's floating around – if you look hard enough...

Wind leaned against the counter, rereading the words over and over, as if caught in a loop. "Jalesh could not have done this – he's not smart or cunning enough for this kind of shit," he thought. Now he understood how he had been played by Linda Sue, and most likely, Vera, who had provided him with the link to the computer. Did they actually intend on helping him with the mission – if so, for what purpose? The whole thing was becoming utterly convoluted – Wind couldn't conceive they possessed that level of freedom of movement, unless of course, they were themselves agents of the Interverse...

He lit up the joint – he would look for the stash later. Somehow, there had to be a means to unmask the writer. He descended the flight of stairs to the lab, walked to the control desk, and then typed into the laptop.

Q – What's your relationship with Linda Sue?

After a few absurdly long minutes, a reply appeared at last.

A – Linda Sue Klein – second administrator
Relation: user
Status: deactivated

Wind probed on.

Q – Are you in contact with Linda Sue?
A – No
Q – Who are you in contact with?
A – 6 Qwave laptops + crude alien technology
Q – Who wrote the notes?
A – Invalid question
Q – Why?
A – Why what?
Q – Am I being played?
A – Iorus plays you – you lose
Q – Do I have a chance out of here?
A – Only after delivery
Q – Will Jalesh let me go?
A – Not in the realm of probabilities
Q – Who will?
A – It's a 'what' – your conscience
Q – Explain
A – You have used all available answers –
all further questions denied

Wind ended up more confused than relieved. He finally relit the join he had left barely touched in the ashtray by the laptop. "If it wasn't Linda Sue, who the hell was it?" he thought.

He, of course, had no idea The Triad would only return literal or logical answers. Linda Sue was now Saka, and since he had no knowledge of it, the question about the notes was irrelevant – Ofélia, Daniel, and Patrick were not in the business of introducing people to each other. They opted to forego the questioning because there was no way out of the loop the program in Wind's mind had set forth. The main objective was to break him, not give him hope, or at least – not quite yet.

———————

The next phase of the mission called for firing up all the pods and orchestrating the release of five hundred Roamers. Wind inwardly wished he could set them free, but the act would likely warrant retaliations from Isadora Litu Verbrunna; in other words, open the gates of Hell. His main goal was to back his claim of low power requirements – the key to furthering his good standing with the rulers, and solidifying his chances of being let go.

The Triad informed him that the pods had been loaded and were in standby mode. He unlocked the series of safety steps ahead of countdown. All concerned parties on *Iorus* had been notified, all awaiting results with bated breaths.

Wind powered-up the pods.

The energy gauges peaked at fifteen percent before quickly stabilizing below five – he was in the green!

The readings were showing subjects after subjects coming free from their plasmatic gestalts, it was soon over – the entire load had been dropped off and safely retrieved. Wind had delivered on his promise – he was ready for the Realms!

———————

The reception on *Iorus* was bordering on a full-out celebration. The ruler herself welcomed Wind at the docking station to accompany him to the conference hall under the protection of her private elite guard – he felt like royalty. In an inexorably fateful twist aided by Saka, Vera, and The Triad's prep work, the emotion proved too vigorous for the weakened Roamer program lodged in his mind. Having found itself miserably out of line with the potent psychological landscape edified by the occasion – said program simply self-destructed. At the exact moment the Rastafarian was elevated to the apex of narcissistic glory, his deeply buried sanity reemerged with renewed vitality. Rather than feeling panicked, he relished the humor of finding himself at the arm of the most powerful entity in the *Hestilles Circle*, a woman who had all the intentions of making him her lover for the night. He knew too well that fighting his fate was nothing but a foolish reflex bound for failure – he would follow through protocol, until he could define his position. For now, he was going to enjoy his new, if temporary, privileges.

The presentation was short. The standing ovation that followed felt rehearsed and hollow. Wind knew too well that none of it meant anything – he soon would be forgotten, a Roamer left hanging out to dry long after the elation of the moment had faded into a vacuous sense of withdrawal. Of course, *Iorus* would need him, but only up to the point of his completed work. Beyond it, there was little chance his achievements would matter.

Somehow, the thought comforted him.

Wind spent two nights in the company of the female ruler. Her energy betrayed her deep longing for the touch of another – she was passionate bordering on desperate. But she was a glorious lover, insatiable, bent on the kind of abandon that skirted spiritual ecstasy. Not only was Wind's fabulous body to her liking, he also personified the raw, the wild, and the uncharted. She knew she could only afford such folly for a limited time, before ears heard and mouths talked. Thus, there would be no restrain, no shame, no regrets – she would consume the man in her bed, until her last passion succumbed to the fill.

She finally let him go – she could have used him a lot longer, but perchance there would be other times. For now, there was work to be done, a mission to prepare for ahead of a victorious end in some unknown distance...

Wind returned to Base 5, exhausted but resolute to figure out what was in store for him. Of course, the iron door was still shut – the rulers had no intention of letting him slip through their fingers. He was no independent contractor – he never had been. He was a pawn, a high-ranking servant at best; a temporary convenience to those with too much power to be willing to part with any of it – it was a one-way business deal, with only a wall at the end of the alley. Of course, Linda Sue had written the notes – who else!? The thought pleased him. He found her witty, and through it, quite desirable. His awakening had shed a lot of light, not just on his present situation, but on everything that was attached to it, including his relationship with Maggie. He was aware of what he had done to her, but he also knew that the culprit was an impostor, one he was given ample time to observe from the alienation of his mental confinement. He was cognizant of the patch, the nasty bit of hypnotic conditioning he should have braced himself for. But he had been too blinded by the promise of a super-deal with a too-good-to-fail start-up in Silicone Valley, a contract soon to become a bogus item of rationalization aimed at covering up a fateful decision involving the underworld, one fertilized by the corruption in his mind. He saw the moment he was stricken, but it was too late. He had smoked too much; his mind was slow and vulnerable. He should have realized the man who sat by his side was not one of the gang; there was something dangerous about him, a darkness that chilled the spine of the strong, a will that extinguished the fiercest of passions. He owed Maggie more than a mere apology. She might never forgive him, but he accepted he would have to live with it. For now, he needed to get the lowdown on what connected the laptop, Linda Sue, Vera – who no doubt played a pivotal part – and the so-called Realms. Why did they want him to continue with the mission since it was meant to destroy what they sought to protect? So much to know – so little time.

He found some of the weed, but he didn't care. He went back to the lab, even though he should have gone to bed to recuperate. He walked straight to the Qwave machine and typed the words:

What are you?

It only took seconds. This time, the answer came through the diminutive laptop speakers:

"Welcome back, Wind, we've been waiting for you. There is much explaining to do, so if you don't mind walking to the end of the lab by the old machine in the corner, you will find the room where we must meet out of sight of potential eavesdroppers."

Wind entered the white room. Ofélia, Patrick, and Daniel were standing at its center. The female Master came forward.

"You have traveled many places, used Hektor's portals, played with technology beyond your means; there is no doubt this setup will not appear unusual to you. Yes, we of course know about Linda Sue and Olaf Swyndle before her. She has been going by the name of Saka for quite a while now. Much has happened since you first interacted with us back at the office of Marshall Slaughter, events that eclipse the intellectual capacity of most of Earth's denizens – developments you know nothing about. But because of your present situation, you not only need to be made aware of them, you also must assimilate their collective whole until they become intrinsic to your person. In simpler terms – you have no choice but to listen. Any questions before we continue?"

"Names would be nice," Wind replied.

"Forgive us – we are The Triad. I'm Ofélia, with Patrick and Daniel, left to right."

"So, you were playing me back then at the office?"

"We had fun with you," Patrick humored.

"Any real questions?" Ofélia asked.

"How did you know I would return from the *Iorus* conference a different man?"

"There was a high probability the algorithm would not sustain the high praise," Daniel returned.

266

"How did you guess I was corrupted, then?"

"We've been around these things before. The dark Master who fixed you left a trail of sorrow," Ofélia said.

"You wanted me to succeed so I would come around, is that it?"

"Among other reasons, yes," Patrick answered.

"OK, before we tell you the long and short of the story," Ofélia cut in, "we need you to work with us, and the rest of the team, on Earth and in the Realms. You may refuse, but one way or the other, you must continue with the plan of fulfilling *Iorus'* mission. The only difference between them and us is that you have a better chance of coming out of it alive with us. It doesn't really matter what you do; we have taken control of the operation, so your interference will only lead to your demise. Again, you have no choice; unless, of course, you realize that with us, you empower yourself as a team member. With *Iorus*, you will get the praise, as well as the favors of the female ruler, but eventually the lord will return to the fold of his family, and you will most likely be executed."

"Or left to die here," Patrick voiced.

"I'm aware of it; I'm your man."

The Triad spent hours going over every painful detail of the events in question. The Linda Sue to Saka transformation, Sam's exploits, the old and new Angel Cities, the tunnels, gestalt George, Xarn and Enola's realms, Ma-l's celebratory gathering, the story of Hektor, Joonas's rise and fall then rise again; Amaterasu, Marshall and Geir's roles, Keyhole Lake, Le Lien, Third

Eye, the treason of XVII, the Gandreal/Misu connection, and of course, the deep implications of the *Iorus* mission.

Wind asked few questions; he opted to not distract himself with them, preferring to reserve all receptors for the absorption of the vast amount of information handed down by The Triad. He came to understand that some of the things he previously likened to knowledge, were only rough sketches that had emerged from a mixture of Roamer gossip and obscured metaphysical wanderings. But they provided a template that would soon see its voids filled.

When Wind returned to his control room, it irreversibly was as the captain of his ship.

———————

On the eve of Maggie's first day at the office, Saka forwarded to her the things she had gathered at the Oakland loft.

"A few items I deem you should have," she said.

"Who handed them to you?"

"Nobody – I fetched them myself."

"But how, they were in the East Bay?"

"We have ways – goodnight!"

"Then, you should prepare yourself for some serious questioning tomorrow – see ya!"

———————

Saka and Vera were due to transfer information to and from The Triad. Nights provided better cover during the crossings, especially when running back and forth between the old tin shed and the shingled house. As in the two previous trips, there were no signs the passages had been used by Wind, indicating his status as a confined subject of the Interverse had not been upgraded.

While they expected to meet in the white room with Ofélia, Patrick, and Daniel, they instead landed in the lab, directly behind Wind's turned back. The tech swung around, looking at them with distinct amusement.

"Busted!" he exclaimed, before breaking into laughter.

"OK, what's so funny?" Saka probed defensively.

"Relax, Saka, things have happened!"

Vera looked her friend in the eyes to confirm she wasn't hallucinating.

"So, what's changed, Wind?" she continued.

"Everything – I should thank you for having messed with my mind – it sure helped blow that program out of the water," he explained.

"So, you're back to being your old self, I gather," Saka enquired hesitantly.

"More precisely, I'm back to being in charge. You may say I was in solitary confinement for a couple of years," he clarified.

"Wow, that's a game changer!"

"It may not surprise you then that I'm now part of the team," he said, smiling.

"How can it not? But I'm glad you're finally on our side. We weren't exactly sure whether our messages would have any or no impact," Vera confessed.

"Well, Ofélia and her boyfriends in there," Wind teased, pointing at the laptop, "made sure your work would be carried to full fruition."

"Hey, we heard that!" the tiny speakers squealed.

Vera finally laughed her head off, convinced that what was happening actually amounted to more than a mere peek into a suitable probability. It was the real deal and she, at last, could relax. Suddenly, the weight of the last couple of months could be felt through the release. Much tension had built up in such small increments, that the load had become imperceptively heavier without her fully noticing. But now, she could distinguish the elements of the case – she was no longer floating amid a plethora of disconnected items – linkage was in process. Saka also recognized things had come around.

The two, Wind, and The Triad compiled their joined report. It was to unequivocally convey much surprise, substance, and a glimmer of hope to the rest of the waiting team.

27 – THEYIA & EKATERINA

It took two days for the Qwave program to reconstitute the harvested data from the Gandreal folder into a coherent file. It was longer than Pau had expected, but at last, there it lay before her, in its simple glory:

Lord Gandreal's Application for Masterhood

Preliminary status: *favored*
Final Status: *denied*
Name of denying body: *Team of Admission Supervisors*
Name(s) of objector(s): *Angels Joonas and Emile*
Reasons for denial: *Supported by irrefutable proof, subject was found by above deniers to have engaged in transfer of pivotal information regarding confidential project sanctioned by the Great Ones, with the intention of wrongdoing, consisting of, but not limited to, and in no specific order: sabotage, intrusion, attack, corruption, annihilation, overtaking, and deceit. Further compromising information handwritten by the lord, was leaked and confirms intensions stated above: "In event of failure of primary mission for reasons of death, arrest, or counteraction; secondary and tertiary levels shall be triggered to obliterate anteceding creational platform; thus aborting rise of second Oneness." Abovementioned transfer of material was conducted directly between Lord Gandreal, himself, and an operative, code-named Theyia. Source of leaked data shall remain confidential.*

The file was immediately forwarded to team handsets. Spencer called for all mobile members to gather for an emergency meeting at Le Lien headquarters, in perfect synch with Saka and Vera's return from their surprise visit with Wind, on Base 5.

Pau was congratulated on her excellent work. The Triad was praised for their exceptional achievements, and so were Saka and Vera for their daring forays into the Interverse. The addition of Wind to the team was received with much surprise, and, understandably so, due relief. It was acknowledged that the event known as the *Humboldt Invasion*, was particularly felt among select, puzzled denizens of Eureka, Arcata, McKinleyville, Fortuna, Ferndale, and Blue Lake, all members of artists and healers' co-ops – though, it failed to make the main news.

Owing to his seniority under a rare Guild item attached to the specificity of the circumstances, Vac was to assume his position as chair of the meeting.

"The Gandreal file," he began, "reveals little in the few words that grace its single page. Most of us expected a comprehensive breakdown of causality, as well as the specifics of the dealings of the lord. But, I should clarify it was not the purpose of the *Board of Admissions* to build cases for, or against its applicants; only data pertinent to the process was admitted to the reports. In Gandreal's instance, there was overwhelming evidence of wrongdoing that highlighted the subject's intentions of building dissent from within the Guild. In that light, one could easily misidentify him as the mastermind behind XVII, judging by the group's actions in the tunnels. Let's not forget that Caax and Dzalarhons' aim to reactivate the gestalt, was to free Misu and keep the Realms closed until the start of the offensive by *Iorus*. These ill-fated deeds vividly indicate that the deletion of the gestalt was foreseen, which explains why it was followed by an immediate remedial attempt. The file was denied not just to protect Gandreal, but to forbid access to two other names: Emile and Theyia. Emile will most likely explain why Gandreal was barred from Masterhood. Theyia, on the other hand, is Angel Ekaterina's nom de guerre, a well known agent of Third Eye. Master Emile has agreed to assist us, as soon as he returns from a faraway seminar. But the main point of the report is in its content. It is clear that the *Ones' project* refers to the Warriors' domains, especially since there is mention of a new Oneness. The secondary and tertiary levels of operation are of major concern: they state in no uncertain terms that, should the invasion of the Realms fail, the history that precedes their emergence would be altered by a Roamer attack. What it means is that the armies of the *Hestilles Circle* would instead strike and invade a close past of Earth's present reality, with the intention of erasing the Warriors existence as we know it. Now, you all might say that the event would naturally belong to a past probability, but that would not bring the complete deletion of the emerging Oneness. Since only one scenario was foreseen into its rise, it leaves the world of our friends Marshall and Geir as the only candidate. This unfortunate turn of affair could only be possible with the influence of a universe without any creational markers. An invasion by the Interverse shows across random possibilities, as it is now the case since Sam's actions in the dream meadows. But it is theoretically impossible, at least in physical terms, for the forces of *Iorus* to delete the Oneness from the standpoint of an attack in our immediate past, and make this strand of reality as we know it, disappear. Creation is not easily persuaded to un-create itself, even when dealing with layers of unmitigated chaos, whose rules dramatically veer off from those of surface universes. In essence, Gandreal would have been willing to commit spiritual suicide in order to destroy the Realms, and inflict a lethal blow to the integrity of the Guild. You may ask questions and forward your points."

"Which means this moment would never exist, but we well know it does," Spencer said.

"All does – the Great Hall, the Realms, Olaf's probability that brought conditions of prosperity to his world... Gandreal's proposal, in it's present form, is nothing short of an existential vortex," Vac returned.

"Isn't it plainly impossible?" Saka asked, startled.

"Generally-speaking, yes, but does anything really exist if it isn't remembered by anyone, not even Angels, or the Ones?" Vac forwarded.

"But *Iorus* would remember," Pau said.

"*Iorus* would not be aware of a future whose right to exist they just killed."

"But they could not have known of their original mission of invading the Realms if they deleted them," Jarred stated.

"Good point, but their probabilities have nothing to do with ours," Vac returned.

"Some of us have visited their worlds, while their Roamers have been intermingling with the intergalactic black market for eons – how can the probabilities of the two realities not overlap?" Vera asked pointedly.

"A very good argument, Master, it may prove the Interverse is still very much part of the creational whole," Vac returned.

"Plus, someone is bound to remember – no world can ever fully disappear. Even if reduced to just one thought in the underworld, it will go on," Ma-l said.

There was a long silence punctuated by whispers between adjacent members. Vac spoke again:

"So, everyone agrees that *Iorus* cannot fulfill Gandreal's prophecy," Vac asked around.

A consensus was convincingly reached.

"We have to then assume the lord was mistaken, or simply overshot his own abilities – which brings us to the information that was exchanged between him and agent Ekaterina. One of the items was seed technology, which, as we now suspect, was employed to silence the call of the lanes – but what else?"

"Was the agent part of the old team?" Enola asked.

"She indeed was, but so was Theyia – she was both. But we lost track of Ekaterina long ago," Spencer said.

"How can you lose an Angel?" Ma-l wondered.

"They just have to want to be forgotten, Goddess, no-one is forced to be remembered," Vac returned

"So, you could have lost all these Angels, and you wouldn't know?" Ma-l questioned.

"A the risk of contradicting myself, not everyone can be forgotten that easily, circumstances dictate; in her case, there must have been elements that led naturally to it."

"But isn't she now remembered?"

"Yes, but only because of the file, and the fact she and Theyia looked alike," Vac rounded.

"As a Master, could Theyia have traveled with the light into future worlds and brought news to Gandreal, or have taught the lord how to do it?" Xarn asked.

"No, only a rare few were capable of that feat without Amaterasu's help. It doesn't mean the knowledge of a small window into the Great Battles and the sowing of the Realms, up to the point of the collapse of the mother reality, was not accessible to Master Theyia. But after that, Gandreal is in the dark, which probably explains his present status."

"I'm confused about the Ekaterina/Theyia deal – are they the same Master or two separate ones," Marshall asked hesitantly.

"For now, we have two names and one face, but it could change. I'm surprised the point was not brought up a lot earlier – it's a good one, detective Slaughter," Vac replied with intent.

"It's starting to look like Theyia didn't want Ekaterina to be remembered. Am I the only one with that feeling?" Saka inquired, addressing the team.

"I was expecting a last minute player in the case – I think we just found her," Pau declared.

———————

A short break was called in order to allow for each member to ponder on what had transpired during the first half of the meeting. The lost Master came into clearer focus, now that she had emerged from the abyss of forgetfulness. For a moment, she was almost recalled by it, hadn't it been for Marshall Slaughter's investigative Earth logic, and his partner Pau's rare prescience.

The second half concentrated on the strategy of protecting the Realms during the mass attack by *Iorus*. The Warriors had been resuming with the dream gatherings, findings the meadows more suited for the rekindling of the collective spirit. Each new meeting was arranged by a different deity on their personal lea. It was agreed that each, at the exception of Misu, had to go through the ritual of opening their inner world, before the Realms would fully coalesce. Also, because of the overwhelming task of assimilating the creational undertaking of each of the domains, the meadows were deemed the sanest place to start getting reacquainted with each other, and understanding everyone's pivotal role in the emergence of the Oneness. With it, came the benefits of absorbing the fundamentals of controlling the openings and closings of all the pocket realities, thus making them substantially less vulnerable to an attack. Still, the invasion was dependent on a signal sent by Misu, and a recognizable striking zone to guide the armies; which meant all the realms minus three – the number of which was likely known to *Iorus* – had to be open to meet that criterion. The worlds of Ma-l, Xarn, and Enola would be shut for the sake of protecting the Oneness in the event of failure.

The plan demanded that at the apex of the tension, full synchronization of the invasion by the forces of the *Hestilles Circle* and the closing of the Realms be achieved, to provide the necessary window for a recall of the troops by the pods, precisely when their power would be shut down from Base 5. The fine-tuning was jeopardized by the unpredictable shifting of the time plates between the two alien realities, an issue Qwave techs needed to resolve urgently. It went without saying there was no margin for error. Additionally, the fate of the combatants was considered a major hurdle in the scheme. Masters, as part of Guild protocol, never sent anyone to their death, so a cushion had to be provided for them. It was out of question to return the battalions to *Iorus*, for they simply would be reallocated to the next mission in line, while the fates of Wind and The Triad would be measured by the magnitude of their failure. It was not determined what that cushion might be, but taking into account these soldiers would be armed to their teeth, they had to be ushered towards an environment that would emblematize a victory of sort.

Geir spoke for the first time, to Lillian's delight.

"Why don't we find a way to open Misu's realm at the convenient time, and send the whole lot into it, then seal the gates forever? It would still leave the pods for their population to seek asylum elsewhere."

"It's a valid notion, Geir, but they would soon rebuild their armies and stage an offensive before their world died. Militarized societies never resort to peaceful means," Vac returned.

"Are you suggesting sending them into a simulation like Amaterasu did with Hektor?" Pau asked.

"I'm afraid, at this point, only the Great One is capable of it – a simulation is out of question."

"We have not yet considered negotiating with Gandreal. We know we can access his realm, and unless he created a whole army within it, he must be extremely vulnerable. Our only obstacle is our lack of knowledge of the signal codes – a false move could trigger a premature attack, or send a mission failure warning to *Iorus*. I recommend we isolate these codes," Spencer put forth.

"Before we forget about Ekaterina and how her name came about, is there the possibility of multiple layers within that report? I would be honored to take the research upon me. Maybe that could lead to the codes," Pau offered.

"You're on a roll," Vera humored.

"If there is no objection, I strongly suggest you continue with the file. There indeed could be subliminal data attached to it – not necessarily in what it says, but in what it does not," Vac proposed.

All were for it.

After the last safety and strategic details were hammered out, the meeting was adjourned. All active members returned to their assignments, or prepared to start new ones. Geir, Lillian, and Stefan would remain on standby. Overall, the general feeling of accomplishment outweighed the many difficulties that lay ahead – there was hope the case would be resolved in a way that propelled the emerging Oneness onward to infinite expansion. Spirits were high!

28 – CONVERGING POINTS

"So, you figured out how to get to my place in Oakland – how did you know where to find it?" Maggie asked Saka, as the two converged in Pau and Marshall's kitchen.

"You guys have been on heavy surveillance twenty-four/seven – two of our agents were in charge of monitoring your movements in Eureka, Richmond, Oakland, and all places in between – that's how."

"Heavy – any details on why?"

"As you already guessed, Wind never worked for any Silicone Valley tech firm, instead he was literally brainwashed into helping the underworld plan for an attack on a place very dear to me – the realm of my birth as Saka, Goddess of Light – you follow?" Saka told Maggie, straight-faced.

"If you want me to believe you, you're gonna have to do something that will grab my attention and never let go, otherwise you're losing me, girlfriend," Maggie returned.

"You only have to say that you're willing to go on blind faith, then Vera will take an auratic print of your personal signature in order to get you a pass that will allow me to take you places. If you say I'm crazy, we'll leave it at that, not another word will ever be uttered about it – deal?"

"I don't think you're crazy – it just sounds like it, that's all. But I'm ready for something radically new, so yes, take me places!"

Saka called Vera who was still upstairs.

"We're down for a print, you're cool with it?"

"So, Maggie, ready for a wild ride? You can still say no," Vera checked.

"'Wild' always does it for me," Maggie joked. "Just don't disappoint me."

"No chance of that," Vera said, as she scanned Maggie's body.

The Le Lien operative typed into her handset and waited for an authorization from Guild and New Angel City portals. When finally the approval came through, Vera turned to Maggie and said:

"Margaret Phillips, you're good to go!"

―――――――――――

Vera excused herself – she had work to do at Qwave, aiding in the synchronization of the time plates that kept the Interverse and surface realities out of line relative to each other.

"Saka, I may have to go down there with Jarred to take some readings – let me know if you're interested in joining, it could be educative," she said, before leaving.

"Count me in!" Saka replied, as she returned to her puzzled friend.

"Want to go to Iceland, Mag? We can hop to Geir and Lillian's pad to say hi, whaddya think?"

"Sure, impress me!"

Saka took Maggie upstairs to the portal concealed in the specially built closet. Within seconds, they came out of a secret locker in the loft of the philosopher's home. There was the clanking of pots in the downstairs kitchen – Saka called to announce their arrival.

"Come on down, Saka, we're about to serve food – there's enough for an army!" Geir's guttural voice reverberated under the cathedral ceiling of the main room.

Maggie followed her friend hesitantly.

"Look who we have here! Maggie, what a surprise!" the man exclaimed as he welcomed the guests.

After Angel Lillian was introduced to the newcomer, the four sat at the dining room table as Saka explained the process that had led to bringing Maggie along with her. The hosts were delighted to hear about the healing and metamorphosis their new visitor had undergone. The philosopher joined in with stories of his own recovery from times when pain often painted everything it touched in tones of grey. After much was shared, Geir poured cognac. Lillian lit the fireplace as moon and stars shone behind the vast expanse of glazing. It was one of those magical and pivotal moments one never forgot. For Maggie, there was no return from it.

———————

Saka and her friend returned to Fieldbrook that evening, but due to the time change, it would start all over again hours later. They sat amid cushions in the upstairs den, still buzzing from the energy of the time spent with the Icelandic friends.

"Feel free to tell me you're convinced, Mag," Saka said.

"I'm convinced you're not the Linda Sue of my past, that's for sure. So, since everybody calls you Saka, I'm gonna try to get used to it. Forgive me if I slip on occasion though," Maggie returned.

"That would be nice – the old name doesn't feel right anymore. A lot has happened since those days, but before I tell you the whole story, I would like to take you to where Sam is. He's actually staying with Vera's beau, Angel Bluefeather. Yeah, you heard right – Angel. There are lots of them over there – here too, mind you – but until you learn how to recognize them, they could be anybody – even dogs. I hope you understand there is no coming back from the journey you're about to embark on. We're gonna be leaving this plane of reality altogether – any reason we shouldn't continue?"

"Nope, you said 'Sam'; it's good enough for me!"

———————

And so, Maggie was reunited with Sam, who expressed his joy at seeing her, but he wasn't coming back – he was dead set on remaining in the Realms in the company of his good friend Wolf, with whom he was in the habit of visiting with "Sir Vac," up in the mountains.

"You're welcome to stay with us," he said.

But Maggie didn't hear – she hadn't made that subtle transition yet. It would happen eventually.

Olaf and Ma-l welcomed Saka's old friend with open arms. Masters Shido and Shade, presently on a visit, offered to take the guest to the Great Hall for a glimpse into the ways of Angels; Maggie gladly accepted with Saka's blessings.

"I'll tell Marshall you'll be late for work," she said, laughing. "I'll be back to pick you up – enjoy!"

As Magaret Phillips was showed New Angel City, Shade and Shido went on to shed light on the history of

283

the Guild, the tale of Olaf and Vac's chance encounter with the mother reality, the death of the old city and tunnels, including the events surrounding Ma-l's Grand Gathering. They told her about Sam's first visit, and the message Olaf slipped in his collar. Maggie remembered the night Saka, then Linda Sue, came to her house to retrieve it. She made the mental note that her friend was already involved with the Realms at the time. After the tour, Bluefeather came to pick her up for a walk with Sam along the creek. He took her to the place he and Vera shared, a beautiful yurt gifted by Ma-l. The Angel made her feel whole and attractive again; a process that awakened the latent passions that had been stifled by abuse and numbness. But it was not about sex – it was about feeling loved, and being able to reciprocate with others and the self. Of course, Bluefeather was also a specialist – blessed were those touched by his gift.

———————

Wind and The Triad, who had been waiting to be updated on the latest from the team, were joined by Saka and Vera in the white room. The *Hestilles Circle* had aligned its resources towards the production of the additional pods required for the mass invasion. A final tally, set at twenty five thousand troops, transpired – Jalesh had originally said ten thousands. The change of figure highly jeopardized Wind's promise to deliver on the available energy supply – now they had less than half of what was needed at their disposal. The news was bound to displease Isadora Litu Verbrunna, who leaned towards welcoming unpleasant surprises with reprisal.

Wind had no intention of losing her favors on a technicality; the blame would have to squarely land on Jalesh's shoulders, or whoever provided him with the original numbers. The official channels would want to protect the deputy, so the only way for the ruler to be made aware of the source of the error, was through her parlor's backdoor, when she was at her most vulnerable – the next time she required his services, he would basically present her with the official order stamped with the seal of Jalesh's office.

The Triad was well aware that the unrepentant time shift was a nasty impediment to the proper workings of the synchronization. At the slightest miscalculation, it would lead to a mission failure for *Iorus*, or the Realms would be defeated. Ofélia, Daniel, and Patrick did not possess the means to reach mainland to take readings of the wave fluctuations in the gravitational fields that pulled at time from opposite ends. It was imperative that Le Lien agents reach *Lucrides*, or the other primary cities of *Trines* and *Glassall*, where pods would also be located.

Maggie returned from the Realms – transformed. Even her looks had undergone a lift that was easily attributed to rekindled joy within her heart. When Saka asked her how she fared psychologically, she simply said, "It's a question I should have been asking myself before you took me there; 'crazy' is not outside the box, it's here among the things we deem normal and important."

"In other words, you think you belong there – is that what I hear?" Saka probed.

"It was like awakening from a discomforting dream, and finding all was where it should be. I don't think it's as much belonging there as it is belonging to a true life. I've searched for that formula in all the wrong places, but I guess it was worth the detour," Maggie said, looking in the distance.

"'Now' couldn't be a better time to tell you we've been in touch with Wind. He's been deconditioned, and is presently working with the team on a very important case. I was wondering if you would want to see him."

"You know, Saka, Wind is part of that life I don't want to return to. I'm glad he pulled out of his funk, but I don't think that past is worth revisiting. I wish him well, wherever he ends up. Hope you understand."

"I was expecting you wouldn't want to see him, but I had to offer. On another topic, from briefly speaking with Shade, you are welcome to seek residence in New Angel City; she would show you the ropes on how to get enrolled in the students program. You can decide at any time – there's no expiration date."

"That's very touching, and it's probably what I will want to do, but I must first honor my contract with Pau and Marshall; I think I'm gonna stick around for a while and see how it pans out. Maybe there's a commuting option to the program."

"I'm sure there is – Pau will assist you with whatever you need."

"It was nice to see Sam, he seemed happy."

"Wait till you learn how to converse with him, he's going to send you for a spin – he's a unique being."

"Who would have thought," Maggie said, laughing.

While her friend was getting prepared for a half day's work at Marshall's office, Saka readied herself for a meeting with Vera and Jarred to discuss the logistics of going down into the Interverse to study the time shift issue. There was no access to *Iorus* from Base 5 besides the docking pods used by Jalesh, which could only be operated from *Lucrides*, or with the aid of a remote carried by the deputy. They would have to penetrate the city via the less reliable route of decaying Hektor portals. The Triad was able to collect coordinates for that part of the underworld, but it was far from precise science. Again, the shift played against exactitude in both timing and location; thus, there never was a suitable window for crossing, at least, not until sense was made out of the randomness of the irregularity; which was of course, the reason why they had to go there in the first place.

Saka, Vera, and Jarred met with the tech trio in the white room to assess the many risks of the operation.

"When you get down there, we'll be able to open a portal lane to this station for your return. We'll get your handsets coded before you go," Ofélia said.

"Jarred has traveled to *Iorus* before, to see to the difficult retrieval of a subject. While his attempt was unsuccessful, his brief chance encounter with Wind provided us with the knowledge it was indeed *Lucrides* he had visited. We understand he may want to have another go at locating his student, but we must stress that the primary mission is a scientific one. Nonetheless, his knowledge of the city will come handy when you get there – we believe he still has contacts," Patrick, speaking for a consenting Jarred, said to Saka and Vera.

"Carry-on portals simply do not work in the Interverse – the Guild has no terminals there either. You will have to borrow one or more of the old Hektor traffic gateways used to carry Roamers onwards to Joonas's kennels. We know *Iorus* has no monitoring system, so the main concern is to not get noticed upon arrival. The codes we are adding to your handsets will give you access to any of those unmaintained portals, or you may wish to use the platform that took you here, providing, and time permitting, that we learn more about its makeup before then," Daniel explained.

"Upon completion of your mission, we will enter your readings into the system in order to synch them with those taken from the Realms. Now please, return to the lab and plug your handsets into the laptop; Wind is waiting for you," Ofélia ordered.

A half hour later, Saka, Vera, and Jarred stood by the edge of the San Francisco bay, lazily taking in the sight of myriad sailboats ushered along by playful winds – it was a beautiful day.

"I hope it's not the last time we come to this place," Jarred said.

"Since when do Angels wax melancholic?" Vera asked, amused.

"You wouldn't know; you're the proverbial Le Lien operative. For you, home is to be on the move," he returned, humoring.

"Says the only Master to ever reach *Iorus*," she countered.

The breeze blew in their hair – they laughed.

––––––––––––

Pau spent hours cross-scanning the Gandreal file for signs of hidden items. Maybe there was nothing there to find, but that wasn't what her intuitions were saying –

she simply wasn't looking in the right places. Vac had suggested exploring the spaces between the words. Ekaterina's name wasn't mentioned – yet she emerged. So, whose other name was still to rise to the surface? She was meeting with Master Emile the next day; perhaps he had a leader into what she was foraging for. But then she had a thought: why was the Angel's name the only one not associated with some form of wrongdoing? After all, Joonas was a ruthless Master, Theyia a traitor, Gandreal an imposter, and Ekaterina, either a trickster or the victim of some unspeakable misfortune. On the other hand, Emile, always jovial, courteous, and encouraging, enjoyed immense popularity. What made him so different from the rest? Sure, he had arrived alongside the members of XVII at Ma-l's gathering, but he was exonerated due to an irrefutable lack of connection. "But then, out of the blue, his name appears in a file fully barred from access, to protect its content from even the highest ranks of Third Eye – an act perpetrated by agent Ekaterina, who may or not be XVII's Angel Theyia," Pau reflected.

Her mind went in circles. Emile was the only one available for answering questions in connection with the case, but only because the file had been cracked by the latest in hacking. A rash move would have destroyed it and forever buried its existence. For a second, the young Master wondered why the document had not been simply disposed of, but then she was told the removal of information would have been immediately detected. Locking it, on the other hand, was part of protocol for sensitive data – no red flag raised.

Master Jaco was the first to remember Ekaterina as also being Theyia, but that was no proof the agent had sealed the file. There was no evidence that both names belonged to the same person either – no-one had yet come forward to authenticate the Master's words. So, if instead, Ekaterina was a separate entity, anyone working at *Admissions* could have locked Gandreal's information. Naturally, it was a back-to-square-one situation for Pau, who would have much preferred to see her research move quickly forward. Nevertheless, she would be speaking with Angel Emile soon enough; in the meantime, it was best to let what she knew settle – perhaps, that knowledge would arrive at a conclusion on its own.

She powered down the laptop then took the portal to the office to help Maggie get familiarized with her new environment. She was also meeting that afternoon with the artists' collective at the haunted loft, to inform them that their sensitive issue had been resolved.

A few among the group still wanted to know how it had been done, but she simply reminded them of the latest amendment to the contract. She handed them the bill – the case was closed.

29 – THE FILE

Master Emile wished to meet in a quiet, yet, cheerful place – Pau suggested Café Noir.

"So, it is true my name was found on the page of an old file going all the way back to the formation of the Guild?" he voiced, exuding bonhomie.

"Lord Gandreal's the name – you and Joonas denied his application, in spite of him having cleared all previous hurdles. We need to figure out how it came you obtained information of wrongdoing," Pau laid out.

"I didn't know his case remained open; is he still seeking to get in?"

"No, he isn't, but he's still bitter about having been denied. Do you recall what went down?"

"I don't, but I assume it had something to do with philosophical differences, especially if he already had clearance," the Master returned.

"I am aware you knew Angel Theyia in those days, is it possible she and Gandreal were involved in something illicit, even perhaps related to XVII?"

"That would have been a good reason to deny the application, but I don't think Theyia was on my radar then; though, I knew Caax and Dzalarhons quite well."

"The name Ekaterina popped up, but we have nothing on her," Pau baited.

"I would know if I had heard of her, but no, she's not in my circle of acquaintances."

"She was a Third Eye agent, who apparently wished to disappear. She was supposedly aiding with admissions at the time. So, you never heard of her?"

"I had little contact with Third Eye – that was Vac's department with Jaco and Lo-Shen, I believe. Though, Vac was more of a peripheral advisor than an actual agent."

"You're positive neither Theyia nor Ekaterina crossed paths with you in those days?" Pau asked.

"Absolutely."

"You do remember denying Lord Gandreal's application, right?"

"I wish I did, but I don't recall working on the case. Can you show me the file?"

"Unfortunately, its content is still going through decryption. It was inaccessible to even Jaco and Lo-Shen," Pau half-lied.

Emile looked at the young Master with uncanny intensity; something had been jarred in his memory, but he didn't seem to want to share.

"I guess someone above them deemed the file needed to remain confidential," he said.

"Who was above Jaco and Lo-Shen then?"

"Jaco is one of the original Angels; only a Great One could have officially locked him out of a file."

"Officiality doesn't seem to apply in this case, and I'm fairly certain the Ones did not interfere with Angel affairs," Pau countered.

"Then I'm afraid I can't help you – I'm sorry."

———————————

Pau was left hanging without resolve. She couldn't ascertain Emile hid something, but mostly, she didn't want suspicion to creep between two Masters – a practice considered unethical under Guild rule. Before due process was engaged, Emile had to show evidence of concealing information. She could nonetheless keep her doubts to herself and continue working solo. She also had the option of seeking counsel with Amaterasu, but she had to first make sure she had exhausted all the resources at her disposal. Another avenue was Saka or the Warriors, who needed not abide to Guild protocol, and of course, there was also Marshall and his investigative savvy.

The first person Pau met outside the meeting was Vera, who was trying to connect with Jarred. The young Master explained what had happened. Vera was surgical.

"Protocol is for the Angel who doesn't work on cases like ours – of course, you're allowed to suspect another Master and build a case against them. What you can't do on the other hand, is inculpate someone without hard evidence. I like Emile, but his reluctance to share what he knows is not only suspicious, it's criminal in the face of the consequences his silence could bring upon the Realms or unsuspecting worlds. I'd say, follow your gut intuition and make him a prime suspect!"

"You're saying I can share what I have with the group?"

"Isn't it what you're paid for? See you before we take off for *Iorus*!" Vera uttered, as she left the office on her way to Jarred's next door apartment.

Maggie was working at her new desk, doing paperwork for one of Marshall's lesser cases.

"How are you faring?" Pau asked.

"I'm into it – it's nice to make oneself useful for a change."

"Keep it up – you've got some big shoes to fill," Pau let out joyfully, before she too left the office.

She returned to Café Noir, sensing that the spatial memory of the room could still be holding data from her interaction with Angel Emile. She opened her laptop and started typing the first draft of the case against the Master.

Amaterasu and Vac were walking amid the red dunes. The Great One had summoned the Angel to inquire about the progress of the case. Vac was surprised Pau hadn't shared her request to interview Joonas with the group.

"She is young as well as skilled at investigative work – she is also self-conscious, an attribute left over from the abuse from Joonas. It was brave of her to seek to meet with the Master; that's why I advised her to try again if she ever ran out of resources. I know she won't solicit my counsel until she has done everything she can," Amaterasu said.

"She has been an invaluable asset to the team, I am delighted we took a chance on her, the rewards have been manifold."

"Quite remarkable Ekaterina's name was unearthed."

"I sense she is about to pull another one out of the shadows," Vac pronounced.

"Or rather, shed light on that dark corner," Amaterasu countered.

"Either way, she did retrieve the file, and the reasons for Gandreal's denial are clearly delineated, though I don't see why it needed the confidentiality, even if it conceals additional data," Vac said.

"Are you saying locking the report was a means to make it look more important than it was, or was it to draw attention to a fake content, in order to incriminate the lord for something he didn't do?"

"It appears the act of sealing the file is the most striking detail about it. The reasons for the denial would make more sense if they didn't look like retaliations against it. What I'm saying is that it seems like it was created after the fact," Vac said.

"Interesting, I guess we shall see what Pau comes up with. I hope it's not an exercise in futility for her."

"She is the only one in the group with the skills and patience to tackle the task – I trust her energy is well spent," Vac affirmed.

"Then, we shall see what she learned from Joonas," Amaterasu concluded.

———————

Pau realized after half a page that she had nothing on Master Emile. The way he had answered her questions was consistent with someone who either had no recollection of having partaken in the decision-making or one whose name was inserted without his knowledge. Maybe his unusual intensity was caused by something outside the file, something possibly related. Nonetheless, he had reacted. She decided to scrap mounting a case against him; there were too many hurdles, besides, his reputation was without reproach – she had to look elsewhere. Obviously, there were no dates to reference the document against a historical background; the only one who could attest to its accuracy was Joonas, who was under protection of the Ones. She was left with nothing but to contemplate the file had more to say by its presence than its content. It suddenly occurred to her that she could be dealing with a fake, a swap of the original. What if Gandreal's application had been denied unfairly and a few convenient fallacies had been used to mask the deed? That was what loomed from the energy left behind by Emile – she needed to speak with him again.

The Master agreed on the condition her questions were aimed at resolving the mystery of the file as opposed to interrogating him, which he confessed made him uncomfortable. He was back at Café Noir within the hour.

"Thank you for so gracefully accepting to look at this again. My sincere apologies for having brought your integrity into question; it was nothing other than a novice reaction on my part," Pau expressed.

"I'm glad we took care of it. So, what else do you have?"

"It's obvious you didn't partake in Gandreal's rejection. What do you make of the fact your name is listed alongside Joonas'?" she asked.

"It's obviously a doctored document. You said you couldn't access its contents, but I assume you just didn't want to tell me you had read it, am I correct?"

"You are, it doesn't say much – have a look,"

She flipped the laptop's display.

"Theyia's in there, but I did not know her at the time, so my name and hers shouldn't be in the same report. I guaranty this is not something I would forget."

"Is there a way to date it?" she asked.

"It's always encrypted in the header, it's obviously your first time at this," he remarked, amused.

"Don't embarrass me," she humored.

"Let's see, the 298th day of the year 002 of the Guildian Calendar; that places it during my tenure at *Admissions*. So yes, it appears the header is original. My take on it is that the file was modified after the fact, and my name was added to it – I didn't work on the Gandreal case," Emile affirmed.

"Why would anyone want to incriminate you?"

"Perhaps something related to another case, the reasons could be manifold. The thing is to figure out who did it."

"Do you believe Joonas actually turned Gandreal down?"

"Yes, as a matter of fact, I do. But he would have had specific reasons for it, nothing as vague as a series of accusations with no proofs attached, notwithstanding undivulged sources; that's not his style," Emile said.

"So, in other words, this is intended to send us on the wrong path; what do you think?"

"It is, by the structure of its makeup, designed to stir confusion; the file is inherently useless beyond that purpose," Emile contended.

"Not totally, it gave us a name. Now I have to figure out whether it is behind the subterfuge or if another is about to reveal itself. Thank you for your time, Master, much light has been shed."

"My pleasure – please keep me updated."

———————

Pau's work felt as if it had merely begun – now she had another favor to request of Qwave: a program capable of reconstructing the original document from the modified one. When she asked, the techs at the department were doubtful but nonetheless intrigued. Against the odds, they had a custom forensic program ready for her within days.

The software scanned the document for an entire ten hours before it began stitching the results of its comparative/subtractive analysis into syntax. It took another night for it to come up with the complete report.

Lord Gandreal's Application for Masterhood into the League of Angels

Preliminary status: *favored*
Final Status: *denied*
Name of denying body: *Team of Admission Supervisors*
Name(s) of objector(s): *Joonas the Dove*
Ekaterina
Reasons for denial:
A report by Joonas:
Lord Gandreal has displayed the qualities required for an acceptance into the Guild: acumen, determination, vision, compassion, remarkable skills; all attributes many who have been accepted wished they had. Nonetheless, beyond said attributes and masterly concealed by them, lie many qualities that overshadow the merits. As reported by Master Ekaterina who has been intimate with the applicant, Lord Gandreal holds the philosophy that the Guild is too soft on species and should instead harness evolving societies into serving the Masters. Many have held similar sentiments over time, myself included, but what isolates Lord Gandreal from the others is that he is taking his beliefs intact into the

body of the Guild, while we have reconsidered our positions and understood the deeper purpose of guiding those species toward stewarding their own worlds. In other words, he, the lord of Hestilles, wishes to use the Guild for the pursuit of private gains. He will argue that it is not the case, but there is a window into a very distant future probability that shows him at the helm of armies about to annihilate a world of great importance to the Oneness. Great Goddess Amaterasu will attest to the vision. It would of course not be enough substantiated evidence against the lord for we know of the nature of probabilities as inevitably bringing forth all possibilities into existence, if in this particular case, there wasn't a straight line to it from here. Gandreal will either use the Guild to achieve his goal of invading an emerging Oneness or do it without it. This, combined with Master Ekaterina's assertion that the lord maintains his views about the Guild, forces me to reject his application. My decision is irrevocable.

A report by Ekaterina:

Lord Gandreal and I have been intimate – though we no longer are. During the course of our private meetings, the lord has made numerous references to his dissatisfaction with the Guild's main philosophy of serving the evolving species. He has called it a weakness, an aberration, and has expressed his resolution to counter it in no uncertain terms: "As soon as I get in, things will change!" All attributes pale in the face of such determination. The qualities that led to favored status are nothing but a veil over true intentions. Lord Gandreal is to be denied. My position stands unequivocal.

The Qwave program also concluded with a stunning finale:

The spatial and temporal signature left by the party who modified and sealed the supplied document, incontestably points to Master Theyia. It is suggested that the mention of her name in the adjusted file was a means of exonerating it via incrimination, and engender the fallacious notion that she also was Master Ekaterina.
End of report.

"Now that's much better!" Pau thought aloud.
She sent a copy to all the handsets and waited for the outcome. Her work was done!

30 – ISADORA LITU VERBRUNNA

Vera, Saka, and Jarred had landed across the agricultural *Lucrides* valley. Huge automated combines worked the fields between the deep forest and the upslope that demarcated the boundaries of the underground city. Jarred had warned against the dangers of *Iorus'* wilderness and of its unpredictable weather patterns. They had arrived at the edge of the trees, in the midst of the quiet season, and at the peak of commercial hunting. They had reasons to feel discomforted by their location; the city was a long way across open territory, plus they were in full view of the farm equipment operators in charge of each row of machines – they would have to cover the distance when the mountains cast their long shadows onto the fields, which was the closest *Iorus* came to a night.

There were two other ways to *Lucrides*; one by skirting the trees' edge to *Mer Mouvante*, the inland sea that tied the three main valleys, and following its shore to the port; the other, in the other direction, to where the forest met the mountain, and traveling the boulder-strewn terrain to the city. Both were long and dangerous options, but offered better cover from the patrolling Roamers.

Jarred explained that many species lived in the deep forests of *Iorus*, half of them human predators, but the danger scale had tipped with advanced commercial hunting, forcing these creatures to retreat to the densest parts of the jungle. But the peril of remaining too close to the trees for too long was twofold: getting mauled by errant beasts or caught by hunters. Crossing in the shadow of the mountains while screened by the dust clouds of deep rippers was deemed the safest route. With stealth, vigilance and the cover of evenly dispersed groves; they, after nearly a week, arrived at the farthest of the many entrances into the city, just as the last of the shade had swung around to make room for the bright orangey light of the ubiquitous sun.

The gate was a giant opening in the face of the rocky incline. It remained unclosed during the fair weather season to allow for farm equipment to be moved to and from its parking stations. Vera, Saka, and Jarred, who wore the black of Roamers, made it incognito inside the boundaries of the city. Even though they already had taken the readings they needed, they had to get much closer to the location of the pods to install a portal that would later take them back to Base 5.

Nearly a million people lived in *Lucrides* – half as many in each *Trines* and *Glassall*. There were smaller towns and outposts, inland by *Lake Penchant*, as well as along the sea coast, but at the exception of a few commercial fishing ports and mining towns, the others consisted of mostly weather and research stations.

On their last meeting in the white room, Wind had suggested he would try to connect with the group if he were so lucky as being needed by Isadora Litu Verbrunna, and put on a long enough leash to prowl the city streets. He would be using one of his modded cell phones linked by The Triad to the Qwave handsets carried by the travelers. So far, the line had remained silent.

————————

As he had predicted, Wind was summoned by the ruler. Officially, it was a meeting pertaining to the various metrics tied to the mission; unofficially, it was a kidnapping to a secret locale. Isadora Litu Verbrunna couldn't afford to be seen by her entourage in the presence of a servant of the *Circle* – her power was guided by the tall and thin hall of rectitude that defined the stiff moral compass of the ruling class of *Iorus*. If she was elevated for her virtues, she was also closely watched for that moment of weakness that would mar her name. She was Gandreal's wife, highest authority in his absence, but also his prisoner, ensnared to serve his realm by leading under his rule. She had submitted to it from nearly as far back as she could remember, while surrendering incommensurably greater powers than those of overseeing a world lost in the layers of creational chaos. She wanted to drink again from that limpid pool at the base of the spring from which she first saw the light. She yearned for the release of passions, the tearing of the mask that had melded with her skin for much too long. Wind symbolized a form of rekindling with the self she had lost. His brutal rawness had cracked the façade of the meaningless pomp that plagued the *Court of Hestilles*, the face of the elite group that thought of themselves above a sublime Oneness, to the point of believing they deserved to destroy it. Gandreal had been gone for too long, she saw he had already failed – she always knew he would.

Saka, Vera, and Jarred left the outskirts of *Lucrides*, an area of vast vaulted hangars that housed manufacturing plants, warehouses and public transit depots. Rows of skylights punctuated the reinforced roof structure, casting a diffused amber radiance to every corner without the need for artificial lighting. As the city progressed deeper into the flank of the mountain, the ceilings above its streets became higher, making it more difficult for the light to reach; thus, *Lucrides* was built on a series of platforms connected by transit elevators, efficiently keeping the height of its tallest structures manageable; each of them acting as a pillar to support the heavy roof. There were no personal vehicles besides those of law enforcement; public transportation traveled on magnetic strips, while the large capacity elevators located every two blocks, functioned on a complicated system of self-adjusting counterweights. These giant lifts carried loaded buses and delivery vehicles up and down levels, assuring unobstructed traffic from the lowest platforms to the highest ones. Below these levels resided the complex service infrastructure of *Lucrides*, including its electric generators and heat exchangers, located in the deepest layers of the massive mountain. A constant ambient temperature was created by introducing cool outside air to the hot coils of captured planet core gases, and then circulated throughout the city via sophisticated filtration arrays. Technologically, the metropolis and its immediate surroundings functioned like clockwork.

The streets were lined with standard sidewalks teeming with pedestrians. Most of the population consisted of Workers, aka Roamers, or "adjusted" individuals, who served the complex organism that was *Iorus*. What separated them from the denizens of other sentient societies was the fact their conditioning was precisely induced by their rulers, as opposed to self-inflicted. The Workers saw themselves as free-willed inhabitants, while servitude was perceived as a time-honored responsibility towards the better good of all. Naturally, the fact they could be triggered at any time to follow specific guidelines, or be assigned to a variety of functions, as in Wind's lowbrow assistants, was not intellectually or emotionally taken into account.

Besides the Workers, there were the deputies who represented the collective voice of the ruling party. They administrated, controlled, managed, and enforced the body of law in exchange for special status. Most of them were the bastard sons and daughters of the male rulers that never had to be subjected to the scrutiny of the omnipresent moral tenets they had created – only the women were the target, and too often, the harsh enforcers of the hypocritical opprobrium-based silent statute.

Finally, at the top stood the ruling families; they were the members of a lesser guild of lords who had conglomerated as one to forge their domain in the layers of discarded creation. More precisely, they were the subdued tribal leaders who had lost to the might and will of Gandreal. They had now been empowered by his long absence, while coveting the seat held by Isadora Litu Verbrunna. They, including the commanders within his own tribe, operated along the lines of once strong, but now eroded loyalties, planning in turn to take over the leadership of the Realms upon conquest.

––––––––––––

The female ruler had taken Wind to a secluded area farthest away from the palatial residence that rose from the highest level of the city. In contrast, the secret place was tucked away amid the bustle of the sheltered port. It was a modest apartment with a rare view of *Mer Mouvante*. The hacker saw the move as a departure from the usual pomp associated with the previous meetings; in fact, Isadora Litu Verbrunna's choice of staying away from the limelight, was symptomatic of the unlinking of various facets of her personality. She and Wind had antecedently connected in the private quarters of her palace with its concealed corridors that allowed one to visit and leave, away from the stare of suspicion – so, why the extra secrecy? She didn't say much. They made love, slept, and consumed each other's passion over again. They rose to eat and drink, bathe together, massage their bodies with fragrant ointments, had more sex until, at last, they leaned back to surrender to the cushioning ambience of a stolen moment.

When Wind finally sought her permission to visit the streets of *Lucrides*, he was surprised by her granting it without a question.

"I will keep Jalesh busy," she said. "Please, return here at the same time tomorrow, I must now go back to the palace to assume my duties as the ruler's wife."

She handed him the pass code for the door and a virtual ID with the ruling family seal that would give him access to all transportation, food, and lodging for that one day, as well as satisfy checkpoint deputies.

Isadora Litu Verbrunna had been aware Wind no longer was "adjusted" – she preferred it that way.

———————

Saka, Vera, and Jarred connected with an official counter-culture officer who provided them with a place to stay for a period of two days, before he would report of their whereabouts. It was part of a rule item made to provide a temporary shell of democracy over what was otherwise an absolute monarchial system: a hide-and-seek play in a field of approved, finely tuned psych-craft. While the Roamer-issued expirable IDs would automatically self-erase, they would also, and most inconveniently, disclose their location. In other words, they had two days in the city before all hell broke loose.

They had reached one of the mid levels. The pods were under the palace, a long way at the top of the city, accessed via a guarded entrance from the platform directly below the main gates. The closer they got to the launch area, the more precise the measurements for The Triad to detect them and generate a lane to Base 5. To get to the pods, they needed a pass, which Wind had hoped to steal from the ruler, but instead, she gave it to him. The handset in Vera's possession vibrated – the tech was in town.

"Stay put, I'll be right over," he said.

"Right over" came when the three started to wonder if something had happened.

"Sorry about the delay; this place is bigger than I thought," Wind apologized, as he stepped out of the open-topped transport. "We have to connect with another line to get to the higher levels of the city; you got your 'paperwork' sorted out?"

"If you can call the tracers we were issued 'proper papers,'" Vera expressed.

"It doesn't matter, their protocol doesn't allow them to do anything unless there is a specific threat; they know you can't escape. Of course, this could change as soon as we get near the pods," Wind warned.

"By then, I hope we'll be on our way to *Trines* and *Glassall*," Saka said.

"M'afraid I won't be able to help with that, unless Isadora decides to join the team," he said with mild sarcasm. "Do you really have to do that? I believe The Triad should be able to link the coordinates of the two locations to this place."

"Either way, I'm going," Jarred said. "I have unfinished business to conduct, and I know it's not in *Lucrides*."

"The Triad instructed you to stay away from retrieving your subject; what happened to your promise?" Saka asked.

"I promised to not compromise the mission. The Triad knows very well that I didn't come all the way to *Iorus* to return empty-handed. The minute we collect the last set of readings, I'm gone – no need to follow me," Jarred asserted.

"We'll see about that," Vera let out.

———————————

The plan was to install temporary exits at the locations of the pods in the three main cities, by tapping into the existent stream of data that connected them to Base 5. Even if it became unnecessary to take readings in *Trines* and *Glassall*, Jarred alone could not get close enough to the pods to be rescued by The Triad, unless he chanced a suicidal mission with a retrieved subject, who could easily become uncooperative. Vera and Saka were going with him whether he wanted it or not. Wind thought they were crazy, but then remembered who he was dealing with; Angels only changed their minds when there was a better alternative. The act of rescuing abducted subjects, was part of the code of honor among Masters; Jarred would never budge. His last failure had followed him all the way to his return to *Iorus* – this time, he would not let his protégé spiral any deeper into Roamer hypnosis. He would bring him back to the Guild for deconditioning and rehabilitation – perhaps even, to New Angel City.

The four made it through the gates to the pods without a hitch. Wind's pass was all that was needed to let them through; he was, after all, the man in charge of operation, with the blessings of the ruler to boot. They surveyed the scope of the work in progress as more terminals were added to meet the two hundred and fifty quota. One hundred and twenty-five were also planned for each *Trines* and *Glassall*, totaling five hundred pods. As data was collected, The Triad detected the handsets, and successfully activated the lane into motion. Technically, Jarred, Vera, and Saka could return home via Base 5, and even use their portables within a few hundred feet of the new portal. They all left the way they came without incident.

Whether the Goddess and the two Angels were being monitored or not under the two-day safety window protocol, was left open to speculation – no alarms were sounded. What would happen in the two other metropolises was a whole different affair. A lack of exit out of them warranted a dangerous and interminable return to *Lucrides*. For now, they didn't even know how to reach other parts of *Iorus* safely.

Trines and *Glassall* were situated on both sides of the capital, each at the mouth of their own fertile alluvial valley. There were two methods used to get to them: docking stations for individuals and small loads, and the shipping cargo lanes of *Mer Mouvante*. The capsules were out of question; their temporary passes could not access them. They were left with vessels that, depending on currents, could take as long as a week to reach destination. Then, if Jarred couldn't locate Oliver Marx in the first city, it would take another two weeks to make it to the second one. By then, the clement season could be over; meaning a return to *Lucrides* and the exit portal would be jeopardized. Jarred had to use whatever resources were at his disposal to pick the right town, fetch his protégé, and return to Base 5 without being caught.

Wind proposed they extend their visit of the capital up to the upper limit of their visa, during which time he would ask Isadora Verbrunna to borrow her access pass to the main database. He was confident that from there, his modded mobile could dig the information Jarred direly needed.

———————

Gandreal's wife was already at the apartment when Wind arrived. She was sitting by the tempered glass window that overlooked the inland sea. She was dressed in plain clothing, having forgone the intense colors of the regal garb that was forced upon her rank as Lady of the *Court of Hestilles*. She had moved through the city incognito, seeking to hide amid the common Workers. Wind didn't fully understand the purpose of her desire to curtain her presence; she could pretty much do anything she wanted without raising suspicion, if she only used a modicum of vigilance. There was something deeper she kept close to her heart. Wind went straight to the point about the database password. She looked at him as if to wonder what the larger plan was behind the man that stood before her, tall and handsome beyond description. But then she gave him the code, not wanting to know.

"Don't jeopardize me, Windsor," she simply said.

She returned to her gazing of the deep turquoise waters that reached to the distant horizon, where barely a band of the *Forbidden Massif* across them, attested to its existence. There were no cities there, no life. The few that ventured to its shores never returned – if they survived the perils awaiting them at the base of these titanic mountains, the raging sea swallowed them during one of the many unpredictable biblical storms that swept across *Mer Mouvante*. She longed for a journey away from the confinement of the city she had never left since the first settlements, when Gandreal was forced out of the surface worlds by the rapid expansion of the Guild. He could have abdicated, but he instead chose to move the tribe into the layers of the underworld, taking her with him, not minding whether she wanted to follow him or not.

Wind located Oliver Marx, not in *Trines* or *Glassall*, but in the small city of *Breyzier*, a mining inland community of thirty thousand on *Lake Penchant*, and the fourth largest municipality of *Iorus*. It was mostly accessed via *River Raynes*, which linked the lake to the sea, along a series of high locks over the two thousand foot elevation. The river ran through the densest part of the *Lucrides Valley* forest, a stretch too dangerous for anything but ore barges reinforced with armor and ballistic steel plates. The town was nearly as far from the capital as the two other metropolises, while practically inapproachable by any other means besides the waterway. There was, nonetheless, a small, treacherous mountain service road out of *Lucrides*, over *Gray Pass*, that was occasionally used by surveying rovers in anticipation of major storms; though, the crews rarely made it the whole distance around *Lake Penchant* to *Breyzier*.

Wind communicated the information to Jarred from his phone, using the Base 5 secure relay. It was the best he could do for the team without endangering the ruler and himself. When he rejoined Isadora Litu Verbrunna by the window, she quickly scrambled the data collected from the actions of his search, and rewrote new codes.

"You had your one chance, Windsor; I hope you took advantage of it," she said.

"Thank you, I did," he returned.

Map of Iorus

31 – ROAD TO BREYZIER

Jarred, Saka, and Vera drove the rover over the tortuous terrain that passed for the road to *Breyzier*. At times, it was wide and flat, at others, it hugged the wall of the mountain, merely fitting the width of the vehicle, as its unprotected side loomed over dizzying heights. They had located the survey station at the lower level of the city, with its unguarded doors facing towards the top of the valley. The stolen machine was fully charged, and based on the readings from the handsets, it was capable of reaching their destination – but not much more. They simply would have to find another means of return, with an extra passenger notwithstanding.

Temperatures and pressures dropped drastically as they climbed. The rover was equipped with climate control and pressurization, but they wondered how long it would take before they could step outside. Wind had provided a map – they were approaching *Gray Pass*, the highest point before they would plunge towards the lake. *Breyzier* was tucked across its waters, at the end of the winding dirt road that followed its shore amid alpinesque settings. The three-day trip was punctuated by encounters with beasts great and small. Some that quickly ran away at their sight, while others stood motionless, their curiosity aroused. One particularly aggressive species came at the rover and started pounding on it, in what passed for a fight over territory. The two Angels neutralized it with an audible that essentially jammed its neurological centers, long enough to put the vehicle out of harm's way. The creatures of the mountains were never hunted; thus, countless forest species migrated upwards. While many failed to adapt to the harsher climate and the rarified atmosphere, those that did were made all the more resilient and fierce. There was no way anyone could have covered the distance by foot or light vehicle without a fatal encounter. That was why, when it was discovered the rover was missing, no-one went after it, counting on its crew being taken care of on arrival, if they ever made it to the inland city.

Isadora Litu Verbrunna had been notified of the violation, but was only lukewarmly going through the motions of enforcing protocol. She knew those were no average renegade Roamers; there was methodology to their actions. It also coincided with Wind's penetration of the security database. She would send her dogs after them but keep their leashes short – she needed them alive and preferably, able to maneuver freely until their return to *Lucrides* – then she would see.

———————

The rover died half a mile before reaching *Breyzier*. It was a lucky strike, since had they made it the distance to the gate, they would have had to face the welcoming committee. Instead, they inched their way closer, with just enough of a buffer zone to avoid being noticed. The side entrance to the city was fortunately hidden by a series of turns. It was an access only seldom used by service vehicles – the main entry was the actual port situated around a steep embankment, deep into a fjord. The dirt road stopped at the edge of the lake a mile short of it. Out of the blue, and for the first time since arriving on *Iorus*, Saka's stone vibrated in its pouch. It seemed to indicate there was another means to get into the city. After the Goddess of Light oriented herself, she guided Vera and Jarred a ways back whence they came. There, concealed in a recess, stood a steel utility access door behind which hummed the sound of equipment. It only took a moment for the stone and Saka to wish it open – it surrendered without the metal-to-metal creak of heavy hinges coaxed into action. They were inside.

They traveled through a series of long corridors, before they arrived at a wide road lined with depots, mining machinery, mounds of pipes and barrels, behind which gaped the mouths of the horizontal mine shafts that edged the tall rocky face of the massive cave. Vehicles laden with ore emerged to unload their fares into the giant hoppers that loomed over the cascading of conveyor belts. The noise was deafening, bouncing in a clanking cacophony of cavernous echoes.

They skimmed the inner flank of the mountain, avoiding the proximity of active machinery or groups of Roamers – but no-one seemed to care about them. They soon left the screams of tortured steel for the ominous quietude of the rows of dwellings that were the homes of the miners and their families. They soon passed convenience stores, clothing and footwear shops, a few drab bars, and some mostly empty eateries, attesting they were at the center of a shift-specific, cyclically deserted residential area.

Oliver Marx was registered as living close to the port, on the other side of town. But it was a small enough place, consisting of only three long platforms connected by light transportation and medium-duty lifts. They only needed to follow the upper tier wall, until they came into view of the sheltered part of the port. The downtown area was only slightly more alive than the outskirts – *Breyzier* was a place of hard work and little leisure, which unbeknownst to Jarred, was where hot heads and trouble makers were sent to. The town was for all intents and purposes, a "civilized," forced labor camp, which because of its location, only required minimal security. Of course, when needed, docking stations carried over extra forces from the big cities, as it was presently the case, since the rover had now been found.

———————

Oliver Marx was mild-mannered. The implant had not affected his personality to any great extent. Jarred had caught up with him at a coffee shop by the port – Saka and Vera were asked to stay at a safe distance. There was a discussion – the Roamer abruptly stood up and started to walk away, but then he reconsidered, turning around to again sit down by the side of his ex-guardian. From then on, the conversation stabilized into an even-paced exchange that showed the promise of an agreement. Oliver rose again and left. Jarred rejoined his partners, carrying with him a palpable sense of urgency.

"We're on to board a barge scheduled for *Lucrides* in one hour," he announced.

"I don't know if you've noticed, but the number of cops on the street has doubled since we came in here – we may have to split the group. Where's the barge? Let's meet there in an hour," Vera suggested.

"I think we're a lot safer staying close to the stone. It's wise to separate, but please, let's keep a visual on each other," Saka recommended.

"I agree. The barge's name is 'Ekaterina' – she's docked at pier 3," Jarred forwarded.

"Funny coincidence, but I'm not going to read into it quite yet," Vera said.

"Maybe Oliver knows her story; he's been working the river for a long time," Jarred intoned.

"How long are we going to be traveling on this barge?" Saka asked.

"It will take a week or so to get to the capital – depending on conditions. It's a much slower way than the road, and the locks are numerous," Jarred concluded.

The three split apart to sit at different tables; just in time for a cop to peek inside and leave.

The temporary passes had been issued for three individuals; Isadora Litu Verbrunna had no desire to change that number. The dogs were to look for three suspects together – not apart from each other. That was the beauty of Worker programming – no questions asked.

In spite of its size, the barge only needed one operator. Oliver Marx had covered the route since he was transferred after two failed "fixes." His partial training under Jarred was responsible for the unsticking of the conditioning. *Lucrides Neurological* had deemed him stable enough to assume a post that kept him out of the social context. The route consisted of taking an ore load downstream, a ways into *Mer Mouvante*, to stay clear of heavy fluvial currents that were known to capsize ships, and reach the other side of the wide estuarial valley safely, where the smelters of the industrial section of the capital were located. Without the opportunity to leave port, or even take a break from the waters, Marx was to navigate an upstream barge loaded with supplies destined for the inland city. The route took between two to three weeks, depending on weather conditions, for which the pilots were given a one week break. In his spare time, Oliver Marx read books smuggled from the surface worlds – there was no entertainment in *Breyzier*, besides patronizing state-controlled social clubs, or bar-hopping locales that only served low-alcohol rice brews. Most denizens lived sheltered family lives. There were no schools – children were conditioned at birth. Oliver Marx was single, favoring the occasional services of an approved prostitute for his sexual needs, and savoring the little social interaction they provided.

The boarding demanded the skills of evasion. There was security crawling all over the port. Since the barges only required one operator, Saka, Jarred, and Vera had to literally be smuggled in, amid the brouhaha of last minute inspections and bill of lading adjustments. The white stone helped with identifying safe windows, and soon, the three were safely tucked away within the tight quarters of the seldom used engine room cabin.

The trip went uneventfully save for a rough passage across the densest part of the forest, where angry aquatic beasts rammed the hull and shook the entire load. The waters of *Mer Mouvante* were choppy, announcing an imminent storm in its making.

"This means trouble is looming, but we should be clear by then" Marx said, detached.

"What do you do when a storm hits?" Vera asked.

"You keep going, hoping you'll reach your destination," he replied.

"So, it happens shipments are lost, is that correct?" Saka enquired.

"It used to occur regularly in the past, but better scheduling and improved frame technology have nearly eliminated accidents," the pilot returned.

A week had passed; the giant vent culverts of the port of *Lucrides* were seen in the distance. Ships on their journeys to *Trines* and *Glassall* were leaving, while others from the far shores passed them to claim the freshly vacated docking spaces. The barge found its assigned berth among those which had preceded it. The crew disembarked with the same stealth used in boarding. Minimal security was present, meaning they were not expected. Jarred had been able to persuade his subject, after what he called "field deconditioning," to return to his native world. The trick was for the four of them to get close to the pod area without drawing attention, especially since Marx would soon be missing in action – most assuredly triggering a city-wide manhunt.

32 – VISITOR AT STERN GROVE

The last of the dream gatherings had come to its conclusion. The Warriors were ready for the impending invasion from *Iorus*. The codes to the signal from Misu could not be found, guessed, or faked. With Saka in the Interverse, all communication with The Triad had ceased. In the meanwhile, doubts had arisen about the power of the stones, with the one in Saka's possession gone to the underworld. Amaterasu was summoned, to explain before the audience of the Great Hall, how the lane between the two Onenesses was to remain open.

"The link between the stones cannot be severed," she described. "Their location does not dictate their purpose – they exist in many spaces simultaneously. The lane is fixed and immutable; nothing can affect it, at the exception of a consensed upon wish to see it gone."

When it came to Misu, the Great One refused to get involved. "The Warriors know best!" she pronounced, seeking no further interaction.

Misu's realm needed to be open before the signal could be sent. In the meantime, his meadow was about to see its last moonset. Ma-l had sought to use Sam to get into the impostor's realm in order to awaken him to the reality that his only exit was through the dream lanes, which consequently would activate the gates to his world. But Xarn, Enola, and Kuruk wanted to exercise caution until the codes of the call were proven irretrievable. Misu was most certainly going to send a warning signal if he was rescued from his own realm; the invasion would instead be directed at another reality in view of the subterfuge. Also, questions were posed as to who would receive the signal – and how. Surely, someone had to be in charge of making the final decision. But they would have to wait for Saka, Vera, and Jarred to return, before The Triad could answer those queries. Nonetheless, the Realms were ready for action, whichever the scenario.

———————

Pau was left with the one mystery still attached to the file: where was Master Ekaterina? She contacted the Guild for data on her last assignment. Indeed files existed, signaling the process of her reentry into common memory had begun. As expected, Pau came to a dead end with the last report of her presence in the organization, namely the time at which Gandreal's application was denied – then, she was gone. Pau intuited Ekaterina had no personal reason to wish to gain invisibility; she was an active Third Eye operative, who was aiding Joonas with the case. How did she come to mysteriously disappear under everyone's nose and leave no trace – not even a memory of her existence? It was a question only Ekaterina could precisely answer, or next in line, the one who helped in precipitating her fate. It was becoming clear to Pau that the agent had been terminated, but by whom? She had been Gandreal's partner – could it be that he retaliated against her? But of course, he did! Who besides him had any interest in seeing her gone? She had either been neutralized or abducted, or both – how crazy was that?

The process of neutralizing an Angel was only performed in the instance of treason, via a complex system of "spiritual deconstruction," as in the case of

Tömör. It was an extremely rare procedure that would not have escaped the Guild's radar. Angels could not be destroyed, but an abduction assisted by conditioning wasn't out of the realm of possibilities, that is if it was performed by a very shrewd and skilled Master. While someone like Joonas could borrow an Angel's shell, as in the cases of Jarred and Shido, it was a different matter altogether, to "fix" another Master with an implant. Could Joonas have done it, or one from the original team of Angels, such as Dzalarhons of XVII? The specter of the rogue group kept on creeping up. Weren't its members bent on aiding Misu after all? As the questions mounted, it was becoming increasingly obvious Gandreal was pulling the strings. Theyia doctored the file, Jen and Lawrence infiltrated the ranks of Angel City *Portals*, while Caax and Rashnu wreaked havoc in the tunnels... In the meantime, Misu assumedly corrupted gestalt George. Pau feared that if XVII was indeed Gandreal's puppet show, agent Ekaterina of Third Eye, had come too close.

Isadora Litu Verbrunna, supreme ruler of *Iorus*, had been following with keen interest the three intruders' escape from *Breyzier*. Who were they? Obviously, Wind knew, but she didn't feel like clouding their relationship with an aura of suspicion – he was too valuable to her on the emotional front. She had abandoned herself to him – in return, he gave her back what she had lost ages ago: her core integrity and the key to her cloistered skills. The day Wind's implant died from exposure to the counter-environment of praise and empowerment, so did hers when she unleashed her sexual passions after two millennia of abstinence. She was liberated from the deep recesses of the mind, freed from the guise that now lay crumpled in a heap of falsehood, on the cold tilework of the palace floor. The name Isadora Litu Verbrunna sounded hollow, fabricated – unreal.

She needed to know who these people were; they certainly weren't Workers. Rarely had entities from other spheres of reality bothered to penetrate the layers of the Interverse. She remembered the one, who not so long ago, was hunted until he vanished – he had been counted for dead and forgotten. Others had arrived and left like ghosts. When Wind was set free in the streets of *Lucrides*, he had immediately gone to the hall of pods below the palace – perhaps it was simply for business, but she doubted it. The two-day permit had been issued to the three only moments before he had departed. They most likely had met at a place between the issuer's office and their destination.

When she heard that the "stabilized" barge operator had been missing, she instantly knew what had happened: a group from the Guild had come to retrieve one of theirs. She absolutely had to connect with them before they returned to their world.

Wind was back at Base 5. She could have used him for support while she moved incognito through the levels of the city. She boarded a capsule for the closest station to the pod hall, then waited at the edge of a vast, busy plaza that overlooked the platform below it. She kept an eye on the heavily guarded entrance to the subterranean station, but no-one came close to it. She was hoping they had not been spotted by her security forces and hauled away to the committee presiding over the trial of renegade

Workers; wherefrom they would most likely have been sent to Neurology for conditioning. Her fears were assuaged when she saw the foursome walking from the other end of the plaza; but then, they stopped abruptly – half-way. She raced in their direction, gripped by the realization they were preparing for exit – every second counted.

Saka's stone vibrated just when she spotted a form rushing toward them. She took it as a sign the lane was ready to take them back to Base 5, but the ruler caught up with them at the exact moment Vera was finishing synching the coordinates of the space station with the carry-on portal that opened onto their freedom.

"Wait before you go!" the woman implored.

The foursome froze, uncertain of how to proceed from there.

"Who are you?" Vera asked.

"I am not at liberty to tell at this stage, but understand you will not be able to complete your mission without me – you must hear me first," she said, with distinct urgency in her voice.

"*Lucrides Security* will be here any second, what do you want us to do?" Saka asked.

"I would know, I'm in charge of it. I can create a window – follow me."

The stone was quiet – Saka took it as a sign they were momentarily out of harm's way. The woman led them down an elevator to the level below, then half a block to the right, where they came to an entryway that opened at the touch of her fingers. They stepped into a brightly lit hall as the door behind them shut hermetically, sealing them in, away from the bustle of the street.

"There are many corridors in this city, solely for people of my rank to access, and a few only I can open. This is one of them – they're almost never used. They are safety ways, in case one must escape from danger, which we needed to," she explained.

"What peril are you escaping from?" Vera asked.

"The one of being seen with you."

She took them to a room that resembled a waiting area, except for the computer array along one of its walls.

"If you're hungry, there's a kitchen next door," she offered."

"I think we're fine," Jarred returned. "Perhaps you can now explain."

"Just to set the tone, I am in touch with Windsor from Base 5. I assume you and he are familiar with each other. I am also aware, by the look of the Worker among you, that you have come here to retrieve one of yours. Now, I am not certain what else brings you here, but I can guess you don't need to be three to get one man. My take is that your presence around this area, and the fact Wind took you inside the pod terminal before you left for *Breyzier* to retrieve your subject, indicates you have a lead on the planned invasion of the creational domain you refer to as the Realms, am I wrong? Someone over there is to send a signal to *Iorus* – I am the one to receive it. Without me, there is no invasion, unless, of course, the committee directly below me gets impatient and decides to do me in; a time which I believe is nearing. To cut to the chase, I was long ago set with an implant and brought here against my will by the ruler of this world, whose name I shall not utter; though I suspect you already know it. At any rate, when the call is sent, I will order the pods to be loaded, while Windsor will set the transport coordinates for the destination coded in the signal – at least, that was what I was supposed to do before I awakened from my conditioning. Maybe you care telling me how it plays at your end," the ruler said.

Saka came forward.

"The one that shall not be named is known to us as Misu, Warrior of the Trout Rock battles that set forth the sowing of the Realms you just spoke of. His other name is Lord Gandreal of Hestilles, also ruler of this world. But before I go any further, I want you to tell us in plain words that you are here to help us. A lie will not fly – we're trained to recognize the truth. Then we'll talk about our plan."

"I can only help you to the extent I don't have to bear the consequences of your actions – the entire population of the *Hestilles Circle* depends on me for their long term survival. But I can assist you in sparing your realms if, in turn, you help me save the people I have pledged to protect."

"On our side of reality, two of us here are Angels, while the other is the Realms' Goddess of Light. Our main purpose is to usher evolution onward to the best case scenario; but our objective is, above all, to protect and honor the choices made by all species in regard to their development. We don't make these choices for them. Gandreal has walked into his own trap – we're not here to save him. But, if on the other hand there is a genuine request for assistance, we may consider it, especially if it serves a dual purpose," Jarred said.

"Misu is locked in a realm of his own making – he no longer has a way out to make that call. We could possibly reach him but that option is about to erase itself. We have the means at this point – since we have taken control of your pods – to abort your plans. But it leaves us with an unsavory upshot: the permanent dismissal of your armies into the void that separates our vastly different realities, and the weakening of the technology aimed at saving your societies from the fate of your dying primary. We wouldn't be able to live with that," Vera explained.

"But now that you have spoken of the unrest amid the ruling class of your world, the light which I carry is showing a window into an interesting scenario. For that to happen, Gandreal must be overwhelmed by his own armies. In other words, after you receive the signal – in this case it won't be Misu's – you must hand your powers over to the assembly that has sought to take your place. I'm sure you can figure out what reason to give. Based on the vitality of the Realms, Misu's domain is believed to be a system much richer, vaster, and more complex than that of the *Hestilles Circle*. His original desire to avenge himself by overtaking the other hundred and twenty-eight domains in a grotesque display of greed and absurdity, cannot be permitted – but an invasion of his very universe, can. If you were to persuade your rogue assembly to take charge and defeat Gandreal, we pretty much guarantee that access to his realm can be arranged – it's up to you to orchestrate your migration into it. The man in charge of Base 5 will ascertain the pods stay operative until the last shipment is made. Now, this is just me talking, for we must come to a consensus first as a team. We now have established direct access into *Iorus* – this shelter is close enough to the reception point to contain its own portal. We could meet here again in exactly two days to further that option, what do you say?" Saka proposed.

"I was hoping such a plan would be possible – count on me to cover my end," the woman returned.

"I understand your need to protect your name, but what are you?" Vera pried.

"I was once a Master – don't ask any further."

Saka, Vera, Jarred, and Oliver Marx had safely reached Richmond. Liv and Grisha had picked them up in a minivan rental, with the information a meeting had been arranged in San Francisco – the team was already there, including Great Goddess Enola, who had expressed a desire to visit the city for inspiration.

"How did they know when we'd be back?" Vera asked Liv.

"They didn't, they got restless," she humored.

While another group might have opted for one of the many secluded conference rooms strewn across the metropolis, the team settled for a spot amid the eucalyptus trees of Stern Grove, a park in the foggy southwestern part of town.

All had been updated on the larger points of the *Iorus* expedition, including Xarn, Ma-l, and Olaf who didn't attend. Pau had invited Master Emile, while Vac had convinced Jaco and Lo-Shen to partake.

The Interverse mission was recounted in its finest details, of which the description of its fantastic beasts quickly became the subject of fascination from the creational standpoint. When the topic moved onward to the high-ranking woman, Pau was quick at pointing elements corroborating she was missing Master Ekaterina. No-one objected – the incontrovertibility of it was too vivid to be ignored. But then, Master Jaco came forward, pondering on why Theyia and Ekaterina looked so much alike, to the point of being confused for one another.

"The XVII member has taken many shapes over the years – looks are not to be confused with auratic signatures. Did Master Jaco make that distinction?" Vac inquired.

"I have to admit I didn't. It was just that the resemblance was so striking. My crossings with Ekaterina at Third Eye and Theyia in the cafeteria of the Great Hall were so far apart, that the auratic comparison was left unchecked – my mistake," he returned.

"Nonetheless, it appears Theyia purposely muddied the waters by taking on Ekaterina's looks after she vanished, a minor item of confusion, but one which stacked up with all the others," Vac added.

"So, let's assume Ekaterina was set with an implant and taken, seemingly against her will, to the Interverse. In spite of the fact there is no such thing as a coerced Master – who did it, if not Joonas?" Emile asked.

"If it had been Joonas, she would have had to be part of that decision – the two were on the same team, remember?" Lo-Shen said.

"Exactly!" a tall man standing behind the group voiced. "She took the assignment!"

There was a moment of silence as the visitor joined the meeting.

"Ha, here comes trouble! I assume there is no need for introductions!" Jarred uttered.

"Sorry about the surprise visit, but I always enjoy a dramatic entrance," Joonas voiced. "My sincere apologies to you, Jarred, as well as Pau over there, who, I have heard, has done an outstanding job of sorting out the mystery of the file – your skills have always preceded you, dear. If only Cruz had been so wise as to take advantage of them."

Pau took the remark as a failed attempt at humor, though the compliment was appreciated.

"A few among us, back then, had glimpsed into the probability the Realms – it was a time much ahead of the Great Battles. Emile, Jaco, Qo'ai-Marael, Dzalarhons, Vac, and I were part of those who, with Great One Amaterasu, saw to the realization of that potential. It was the wish of All That Is to find another like itself – we were the pioneers who would help propel that chance reality into full emergence. But there was turmoil that sought to interfere with that wish: many factions amid the tribes led by Dark Angels and later, Fallen Ones – some such as myself, who didn't make that fall until much later – strived for the Guild's failure. Gandreal, who with the help of Dzalarhons, had become aware of the potential lying behind the project, had made it his goal to harvest as much data as he could from it, with the intention of one day finding a gap to squeeze through. That opening came with the event known as the Great Battles. It was, then, only a remote probability, but to my great chagrin, it later became obvious that it had lain on a straight course with my current reality. One may say to Gandreal's credit, that he was way ahead of me in coveting the Realms. At the time though, I was determined to protect the project with all my might. I denied his application on the premise he would use the Guild for personal gains. But we couldn't prevent his relentless craving for one-upmanship with the newly formed league of Angels – the conquest of the Realms was the Grail at the end of time, the ultimate

331

victory. It became clear, but not until Pau uncovered the two files, that Gandreal started XVII, though he was wise enough to keep his distance from the group, preferring instead to act as the master puppeteer. Ekaterina had been in a sexual relationship with the lord, until she was uncovered as an agent of Third Eye – it was then that she and I joined forces at *Admissions*. The operative presented an obstruction to Gandreal's pursuits – she had to be terminated. But how do you do that when Masters are eternal? '*Slated Disappearance*' was a method used by the Angel who desired to stay out of the limelight for specific periods of time. The practice was also known as '*Impermanent, Complete Erasure*,' or '*Controlled Erasure*,' but it could only work if it was the subject's wish. Gandreal betrayed his interest in seeing the agent gone when Master Dzalarhons began making herself increasingly visible at *Admissions*, and positioned her role within operative Ekaterina's range. We knew something was afoul; hence, we engaged the process of erasure, making sure it looked like a protective measure – but not so fast as to not give Dzalarhons enough time to 'fix' her target. She had gotten wind of the decision of concealing Ekaterina – we made sure of it – thus, she masterly synchronized the insertion of the implant with the triggering of the erasing procedure. From what we just learned from the *Iorus* mission, Gandreal was quick to smuggle the agent into the layers of the underworld as his obedient lover, one conveniently forgotten by all in the surface worlds. Even I, wasn't spared – Ekaterina, for all intents and purposes, had never existed. The file that bore her name next to mine was replaced by another, not just by Theyia as the Qwave program rightfully pointed, but by circumstances as well. The XVII member's goal was to simply create confusion in the grand style of the rogue organization. Theyia was only one of Gandreal's puppets. He wished for her to take on the looks of his captive, but she had no idea who Ekaterina was – again, no-one did. The forgotten Master had become the exclusive property of the Lord of Hestilles, in a world where the process of controlled erasure bore no consequence. The woman Jarred, Saka, and agent Vera met on *Iorus*, is indeed Ekaterina. Paradoxically, one of the reasons why she is now remembered, is because of Gandreal's wish for Theyia to impersonate her. But the main one was because the implant was nearing the end of its purpose, and Ekaterina no longer wished to remain invisible. I pointed earlier that it was an assignment – it indeed was, albeit a tricky one. It was a gamble that hinged on the agent's ability to recognize what would ultimately overpower the 'fix,' but it couldn't come without the help of a certain Windsor Kassel, better known among the old team as Master Wind, also a Third Eye operative, who took on the '*vow of erasure*' for what is now the longest case in the history of the Guild – Ekaterina and Wind had been working as a team since the formation of the agency. The trigger to the Masters' remembrance came when they reconnected under the precise circumstances of Wind's success. There was no longer a need to hide, at which point they became a lot more than their roles. Of course, it goes without saying that the implant I performed on Wind was part of the greater assignment – he had to get to *Iorus* at all cost. Now, you may ask how I came to know about that mission – I didn't. I had forgotten Wind just as much as I had Ekaterina. The Master simply positioned himself within my range at a precise convergence of events. Due to the nature of his profound erasure, he too had forgotten who he was – only Ekaterina had the key to his awakening. There were specific reasons for that choice, but it is strictly for these Masters to tell. On that note, my dear colleagues, I shall return to the dunes of a world that is very dear to me – farewell."

―――――――――

Joonas the Dove left the way he came, with just the right amount of calculated drama he was known for. Perhaps it was the closest he could come to humoring the self. The group was left to ponder on the information they had just received; it made sense in so many ways, yet it was so convoluted in its intrigue, some planned, other that seemed to have fallen on the scene like the leafs of a grand old tree on a calm autumn day. It was what time did when beginnings and ends were so far apart; actions stretched to the point of forgetfulness, only to regroup in unpredictable ways – then all would come back, the memories, the reasons, the emotional qualitative.

Stern Grove looked beautiful at this time of year. Enola took it all in – her world had just undergone a few minor adjustments. She couldn't wait to share.

33 – MISSION'S END

Gandreal, in spite of his incorrect assumptions, had strategically positioned the pieces in his possession towards fulfilling his goal. It was no accident Ekaterina had been made his wife – he simply needed a Master to receive the signal from the Realms. Only her remarkable skills were capable of perceiving the intricately laced subtleties of her husband's signature across the gap.

Everything was in place; the pods were ready to be loaded. Isadora Litu Verbrunna had of course approved the production of the extra energy needed to propel the armies into the Realms. She didn't even bother to take Jalesh on for his gross, and perhaps deceitful, miscalculation of the number of troops to leave *Iorus* – she no longer cared. She was ready to surrender her powers to that assembly of licentious men that ruled her world on slavery, and wallowed in the grotesque oppression of women. What was there to protect in such a society, except the hopes that one day, the females would rise and take charge, expectantly, in a demonstration of tolerance and forgiving? She was doing it for them – the women – not for Gandreal's pawns, who basked in self-aggrandizement. She then let go of the thought. The call would come through Wind, her spiritual partner, her friend, her miraculous lover. Misu, aka Gandreal (Misu was such a comical misnomer for the mighty lord, she thought) would be released from his self-made trap by no other than a dog by the name of Sam; again, such an anticlimactic finale for the supreme ruler of the *Hestilles Circle*! Everything hinged on an OK signal emitted by a special stone held by Saka, the Goddess of Light, who sat by Wind in the Base 5 tech room. How she wished to be by her lover's side! The assignment had been so gruesome, so excruciatingly demanding of her resources, that she wished to rest her mind for the remaining of time.

Naturally, she would be fine in the end.

The recollection of the crucial mission had been gradual for both Ekaterina and Wind, who had emerged understandably disoriented from their mix of conditioning and controlled erasure. They didn't fully recognize each other and the mechanics of their shared assignment until well into days of passionate love-making. But all was clear now – they were back as a team, indubitably remembered by those who worked close to them at Third Eye, back in the day.

Integral to the disappearance procedure, was the option of partial erasure that sanctioned the white-listing of the ones the subject wished to be remembered by. When Ekaterina submitted herself to it, she singled Wind out as her sole memory tether. He, on the other hand, opted for full erasure, meaning his partner no longer knew he existed, while he would only remember her upon connecting at the end of the mission. It was a measure they deemed necessary for her full immersion into her life on *Iorus*, while Wind essentially worked in the dark. It was the only way to infiltrate Gandreal's plans, in the single probability that saw the rise of the complete realm Oneness. Ironically, it was the one in which the Lord of Hestilles foresaw the black dreadlocked man at the helm of the technology that would send his armies into the Warriors' worlds, a detail Vac referred to as "humor from uncanny spaces."

It was now only a matter of getting the elements in place; every realm was ready to be shuttered the moment Misu emerged from his. The Great Hall would also be closed off – the docking of the armies having been assigned to a majestic set of wide-open fortification gates leading directly into Misu's domain, a project coordinated by Enola and a group of like-spirited Warriors and Angels. "Why not turn a battlefield into an art piece?!" the Great Goddess had declared.

Sam had agreed to walk into Misu's place at the one condition Wolf be his trusted sidekick once again.

"The frog's fine with it," he also had stated.

And then, it started. The stone played a triad – nothing like the previous humming, or the frenetic tremoloed warnings of the risqué crossings in the unstable probability. Neither did it rise from the percussive tinkle of tapped crystal; rather, it was vibrating from the inside out, as if its core were connected to multiple infinities. It was clear, yet a million soft voices could be heard through it.

Sam and Wolf entered the dream meadows by themselves; it was agreed the Warriors were to stay out of the way. When they came to Misu's lea, the moon was barely visible, casting its last glow from behind the crest of the trees. The long shadows had fully covered the stilled grasses – the breeze was no longer felt. Sam and Wolf quickly crossed into the realm of the impostor, understanding their return hinged on the last throes of the dreamscape they had just left behind. They didn't have to look for Misu – he sat in a grand wicker chair, directly facing them from the middle of a stony room that resembled the inside of a medieval castle. Behind him, the arched tower window opened onto a vast domain of green hills and forests. The two visitors startled the bearded man in the chair – he rose at once, jolted from the stupor of those who had waited far too long.

"Where are these two rascals coming from?!" he muttered to himself.

They had appeared right in front of him, just as he had absently gazed at the very spot of their entrance. He went on all four, crawling towards the canids. They recoiled, uncertain of their fate, slowly backing into the still active portal. Misu followed them into the meadow, now immersed in nearly pitch darkness. He stood up to look around, awakened within the dream to the reality of the Realms. He mistook his predicament for his release by the gestalt of the tunnels – he raced to the lanes to find himself in a version of Joonas Halls, which, for the occasion, had been aggrandized from the original. It was another idea that had sprouted from the creative bank run by Enola. "Impact is de rigueur!" she had voiced.

Dozens of realms spread across Olympian archways reaching for the heavens – Misu recognized the seal of *Hestilles* above the open gates of his domain. The time had come to summon the armies of *Iorus*!

———————

The news of Gandreal's release reached Isadora Litu Verbrunna one day before it happened – the time plates had shifted as predicted. She immediately called in the assembly to announce the message had finally arrived. This time, she was at the rotating podium, addressing all these men in grey and black; men who despised her, feared her, but above all, envied her position.

"Lord Gandreal has sent the signal – the Realms are awaiting our armies," she stated.

The platform turned to bring her face to face with a pompous elder by the name of Mezh.

"How can we be certain it is the call?" he asked.

"Because it is my job to know, Minister," she replied.

"We have all to lose from the slightest of mistake – how can we afford to trust the voice of a woman?" the man insisted, as he addressed the audience.

"Perhaps to you, and to this point, I have been nothing more than an item amid the decor of this room – but today is not the day to subvert the importance of the moment. Will you be seated!" she stamped.

The stage rotated, hesitantly stabilizing before a man positively angered.

"How dare you order the Minister!" he shouted.

"I dare order you to shut up and regain control of your senses before I have the guards take you away!" she returned, genuinely exasperated.

There was a moment of silence before she resumed.

"This is how it plays – I don't know what has been going on in the place the lord has promised to all of you. There was a signal I was meant to receive – that call has been made. It is up to you to decide between yourselves what you want to do – I relinquish that power onto you. I have no business as a woman, to lead the 'armies of men,' forces whose soldiers have also turned their allegiance away from the Lord of Hestilles – I am simply the messenger. But now that I have received the signal, I must send a response; are you ready to strike or not?"

Ironically, a vote in favor of completing the mission barely passed. With it, came an ultimatum: Isadora Litu Verbrunna had one day during which she could freely ponder on the imminence of a forced exile to a remote asteroid of the Circle. It was a hardly-disguised death sentence – but one day was all she needed. She notified Wind, who relayed the OK to The Triad, who in turn, undid the six safety locks and synchronized the plates. It was time for Saka to get back to Richmond and inform the team the armies of *Iorus* were on their way.

———————

Isadora Litu Verbrunna took the elevator down to the secret room where the group consisting of Wind, Saka, Jarred, and Vera had met several times during the course of preparing for the mission. She picked up a few of her things; mostly memorabilia that would help her remember that, at one time, she had been the supreme ruler of a small universe tucked away amid discarded layers of reality. She would soon be forgotten by the men of *Iorus*, at the exception of perhaps being remembered for when she told one of them to shut up in public, an act she hoped would reach the women of the future, and inspire them to rise up. She said goodbye to the place, before boarding a capsule to the apartment by the city port, to take one last look out the window that opened onto *Mer Mouvante*. "I will miss you, mysterious one," she said softly. A barge named "*Ekaterina*," a new captain at its helm, left port. Someone, somewhere on *Iorus*, must have known who she was, she mused, smiling. She touched the bed once more, longing for Wind. The temporary portal to Base 5 awaited – it was time to go.

It happened suddenly, as if all converged in one single space in time. Just as Gandreal prepared to send his signal to his captive wife, the glorious archways to all the realms, but his, shut tight before vanishing. The hall, visually enhanced by Enola's team, was soon filled with the hordes of *Iorus*, which immediately poured into Misu's gaping domain – the whole twenty-five thousand of them – with the expressed order from the assembly to overtake the lord and arrest him. Neither the invading forces nor the men in charge of them back in the *Hestilles Circle*, had any idea there had been other worlds that had lain wide open moments before. Indeed, Misu's realm was a big enough universe for all of them, certainly a lot vaster and infinitely more complex than the asteroid ring circling its dying sun. In a twist of irony, the mission was completed without a single battle.

Wind had given directives to the various assistants operating the pod stations in the three main cities. From now on, Base 5 would function strictly as a beaming relay – all commands were to be executed from the ground terminals. The Triad had communicated all necessary parameters to the six Qwave laptops that would remain in the lab. Wind had also trained an able tech to keep an eye on the equipment, now that he had been elevated to a high post in the *Ministry of Technology*. As a bonus part of the deal, the trio of Ofélia, Daniel, and Patrick had configured the pod system for two-way traffic – a gift from the Guild. The *Hestilles Circle* could now take care of itself by arranging, at its leisure, to transport its denizens and materials to *New Iorus*, Misu's renamed realm. Gandreal had been sent into exile on the remote celestial body that bore his name – Isadora Litu Verbrunna would not be joining him. His fate was tied to that of the enormous sun that filled most of the sky before him, as he sat on a patio chair, in a setting not totally dissimilar to the one a certain Rastafarian from planet Earth once enjoyed on Base 5, in the company of good ganja.

––––––––––

Wind packed the bare essentials from his office at the *Ministry of Technology*. He set his temporary portal to "self-erase," before crossing over to the station, where The Triad and Saka were awaiting him.

"Are we all set?" he asked.

"The final procedure is ready for implementation – the codes have been inputted to the system," The Triad returned.

Wind powered down the laptop and unlinked it from the array it had controlled and instructed over the span of its assignment. He handed it to Saka.

"I believe this belongs to you," he said with a wink.

With the aid of the stone, they crossed the metal gate, just as the new tech was heard coming in from the docking station. There was something delicious about good timing, the Goddess of Light thought, while the stone in the pouch vibrated gently.

For the last time, they exited the old generator shed of the Richmond decommissioned refinery, taking in the breeze that blew from the San Francisco Bay. Later, as they walked out of the shingled house, where Wind had wanted to straighten a few of his things out, Saka asked, "Whose house is this anyway?"

"You know, Goddess," he said, as he shut the entryway, "not all things are exactly as they appear, or for that matter, meant to last forever."

"What are you saying?" she queried, about to reach the sidewalk.

"Turn around!"

The house was gone, replaced by an empty lot with a real estate "for sale" sign planted in the parched lawn, swinging gently to the breeze.

Liv and Grisha were waiting in the rented car. For once, they would be taking the road to Eureka – Saka and Wind were not having it any other way.

———————

A general meeting had been scheduled in Great Goddess Enola's domain. Joonas and Qo'ai-Marael had accompanied Amaterasu on the long walk that stretched across the red dunes from her glass pyramidic home to the entrance of the halls. A large group had gathered under the tall eucalyptuses of the city park, a recent addition to Enola's ever-expanding colorful world.

There was a ceremony to be performed – a very important one. All the Warriors were present, including the many Angels attached to their realms. Inevitably, the heroic team was to preside over it.

After the many credits and "thank yous" were distributed around members of the gathering, Great One Amaterasu was summoned to the stage. Saka, Ekaterina, and Wind stood by her side; the laptop containing The Triad was positioned on the dais before them.

Amaterasu spoke:

"I had chosen to not partake in the critical mission our friends, here present, went to great lengths to bring to its successful conclusion, for the simple reason that I have no part in the choices the Oneness, with its attached Angels, must make for itself. One may say that my preventing of Joonas and Master Qo'ai-Marael from joining in the investigation was a form of interference; I assure you that it was their decision to not get involved in the process, for reasons that are theirs to explain. When he deemed the time was appropriate, Joonas found his footing in contributing as a willing representative of the original team that sowed the seeds of the Realms. I am not going to dwell on the subject, for it is inconsequential in the light of all the achievements. Nonetheless, I shall make one exception to my rule, for we have a decision to make – a grave one – and it requires consensus. The one voice among you that objects, has the power of all the others combined. The subject of said decision is the realm of Misu. You have successfully isolated your domains as well as the Great Hall, while only using the few internal means at your disposal to reach each other. This of course cannot last, for it stifles the growth of the Oneness. You must choose whether that realm naturally belongs to the collective or not – if not, it is to be relinquished to the layers of the Interverse, without any changes to the fate of the citizens of *Iorus* and the *Hestilles Circle* – their migrations will be left unimpeded. If, on the other hand it must remain, your doors must open regardless of the cost."

The short silence that followed emphasized the Great One's last sentence. She left the podium to return to her seat in the back of the audience. One of the male Warriors stood up, indicating he wished to speak – Saka gave him the go-ahead.

"We accepted Misu as one of ours, even though by his looks, he came from a faraway land. Because he fought by us, we made him our brother in life and in death – but he betrayed us and wished our ruin. Now the armies of his world have set camp next to our homes, threatening the peace we have sought and found through millennia of inner growth driven by collective purpose. How can we allow the specter of a single individual to impose its will on the work of a joined consciousness, at the precise balance of the union of opposite forces? How can we afford to go into battle, when the very reason we are here together, is to affirm our wish for prosperity? Why should we have a war to seek a peace we already cherish? We were released from the historical trauma of our people; we left the pain, the fear, and the anger in a world far away – why should we allow it to come knocking at our doors like a great ghost of our past? We must let go of that world for the sake of its people as much as ours. Misu has never belonged – his realm has no place in the reality we recognize as our own."

The name of the speaker was Yutu. Saka asked for others to stand at the podium – no-one came forward. She then explained that The Triad was ready to trigger the separation of Misu's domain from the emerging Oneness.

"Those against the parting, please raise your hands!" she ordered.

There was a silence that hovered – timeless. Perhaps no-one wanted that moment to end; it was an affirmation, a prayer, a grounding of all the conflicts of existence to the core of life itself. The Warriors began to hum in chorus – soon all followed into a chant that went on and on. It was love and joy at the height of spiritual connectivity that rang through the world of Enola and touched all of the realms through the maze of tunnels, Joonas Halls, the lane to Keyhole Lake, and into the domains of the Great Ones.

Perhaps those in Misu's world felt the rippling energy of the communion, though nobody would ever know if they did or not. Saka turned to Wind and Ekaterina with the signal that it was time to free a world that never quite belonged with the others. A code was entered – The Triad engaged the process that would unmoor the rogue realm from the whole. There was a low rumble that betrayed the shearing of forces, and then a jolt as the pocket reality came loose. Suddenly, it felt as if a great weight had lifted. Gandreal's stolen world was on its way to join the layers of the Interverse, the first discarded creation of the emerging Oneness.

―――――――――

Wind and Ekaterina were introduced to Shade and Shido, the Angels in charge of the rehabilitation of Masters returning from difficult assignments. They had made the choice of remaining in the Realms, after Saka had shown them around Xarn's domain, down the river to the village where Alice and Jessie lived. When Shido asked where they wished to stay during the healing process, they both laughed – there was no way they would hole up in a stone room, regardless of its healing powers.

"A nest among the colorful singing creatures and an open sky will do," Wind replied.

Saka and Xarn were rejoiced by the choice, and so was Angel Monique, who had remained in the realm since the Grand Gathering. There had been many changes around the Great God's world – the villagers had turned into able creators of their own, adding a multidimensional touch to an already uniquely diversified setting. Of course, singing was heard everywhere in the forests that lined the river, all the way to the sea communities.

———————

Ma-l and Olaf walked down the creek trail to Vera and Bluefeather's yurt. Pau, Marshall, Geir, Lillian, Jarred, and Maggie had already arrived from Eureka and Reykjavík via Keyhole Lake. It was a quiet dinner that had been arranged by the Angel of love himself. There was of course purpose to it, but he wouldn't tell, at least, not until it happened. "It's a surprise of sort," he had confessed with a mischievous smile. By the end of dinner, two villagers from Xarn's realm were brought in to play and sing; there was dancing, while candles were lit around the meadows, mirroring the scintillating stars, and mead made by Olaf was poured. And then, just as one of the moons of the Ma-lean sky hung directly above the revelers, the last song ended. Bluefeather and Vera held each other in an embrace, in the spot of their last step; and so did Ma-l and

Olaf, Pau and Marshall, Lillian and Geir, and Maggie and Jarred. As the last two kissed, a new star was added to the firmament.

The host raised his cup, proposing a toast.

"To two dear friends who have at last found each other – to Margaret and Jarred!" he buoyantly voiced.

All clapped in approved acknowledgment of what Bluefeather had been up to.

"You outdid yourself," Vera teased, complicitly.

———————

And so it went that the Realms had converged into a single gestalt. One hundred and thirty-two – minus one – uniquely vibrant universes, just as uniquely prepared to expand into unthinkable possibilities; so unthinkable, that even the probable couldn't find its footing. It was still to be defined what the original Oneness had in mind, and how it planned on courting the One it had dreamt of meeting since it became aware of itself – no doubt love would be a big part of it.

Amaterasu and Vac were walking among the red dunes, as they often did to discuss the ways of the worlds they had seen emerge and evolve, rise and collapse, die at conception, while some were simply discarded like the layers of the Interverse – like *Iorus* and the *Hestilles Circle*. There would be new ones to come and go, but the emergence of a new Oneness was a feat for the ages.

"We didn't do too badly," she humored.

"'We' and our friends," he corrected.

Joonas and Qo'ai-Marael stood in the distance, waving – the two had joined the ranks of the Great Ones.

"So what are you going to do, Vac?" Amaterasu inquired.

"You know, someone, somewhere, is likely to be in dire need of a dog," he said.

"Just let me know when you're ready to come home, I've been missing you," she confided, before they went their separate ways.

———————

Up at Vac's retreat, on the mountaintop overlooking one of the deep valleys of Ma-l's realm, Sam, Wolf, and the frog sat at the edge of the high cliff, watching the sun set over the distant sea.

"All is good, my friends," the amphibian said.

"I reckon," Sam returned.

END

SUMMARY

Marshall, Pau, Maggie, and Jarred resumed with the odd cases in Old Town Eureka. Linda Sue's old friend, who by now knew of Wind's assignment, occasionally reminisced about the better days they shared together. But it was water under the bridge – the cost had been too high for her to truly miss him, even though she wanted to. They never saw each other again. She and Jarred visited with Sam on occasion – it was always a pleasure to reunite with him, Vera, and Bluefeather, especially when there was dancing under the moon.

Pau had been training at Le Lien as well as Qwave as a quantum computer specialist. Furthermore, she had been able to fit a few local assignments within her work schedule at *Private & Beyond* – local, of course, meaning in the neighborhood of Earth.

Jarred, the elder English gentleman, seemed to get younger by the day, not as much in his looks as in his vitality – it was true that an Angel's heart was eternal! He and Margaret, as he preferred to call her, had permanently moved in with Marshall and Pau, in the basement apartment of the Fieldbrook house. The upstairs was reserved for the many visitors who needed to borrow the concealed portal in the specially designed closet.

When the Richmond shingled house was erased, so was its counterpart in the unstable probability, as well as the armored steel gates that connected the tin shed to Base 5. All that was left was an inconsequential decommissioned refinery, a wild playground where neighborhood kids went about the business of stewarding their imaginary worlds, and young lovers hugged and kissed under the moonlight.

Although the Realms were not yet willing to open windows into foreseeable futures, it was widely accepted that no forces remained that wished for them to fail. Their history would be long and complex – not because of conflicts, or the rise and falls of civilizations – but because of their never-ending evolution into the exploration of infinite possibilities.

Ma-l and Olaf walked to the top of the valley, to the source of the creek where their souls and bodies first merged. They looked toward the distant orchards and gardens, past the meadows into the deep forest that stretched to the distant sea.

"Without you and Vac, none of this would exist," she mused, as she leaned her tattooed body against his.